The Lost Horseman

by Freida Kilmari

Content Guidance

Violence: This book contains scenes of graphic violence and deals with this both physically and emotionally.

Profanity: This book contains excess profanity from all characters.

Sexual Situations: This book contains explicit sex, including MM, FF, and MMF scenarios.

Dark Themes: This book deals with flashbacks, nightmares, and other PTSD symptoms that some may find uncomfortable. It also tackles gender identity issues.

To everyone who continues to submit to social conformity despite being a square inside society's circle. We'll push through our barriers together.

Chapter One

I stay in the library all night and all of the next day, ignoring everyone's knocks on the door, every annoying mental probe from Nine, and I haven't even bothered with food. I can ask the house for some if needs be, but since I can't die of starvation, I don't really see the fucking point.

A hunter. So my nightmares are real then.

Fuck.

That means . . . All those people . . . I killed them.

That little child who killed himself rather than be dragged to the Supernatural Council; the Vampire I cornered in the ally; the rabbit Shifter I darted six times to keep unconscious. They're all . . . dead.

By my hand.

I don't know how to feel; I don't even know what to say. Fate chose me—a killer—to be the Fifth Horseman of the Apocalypse. It's sick. Disgusting. Almost laughable if the situation wasn't so dire. But above all, it's fucking ludicrous.

How?

How could Fate have chosen me? Me of all people? One of the few responsible for one of the largest turbulent situations in the magical community?

Supernatural hunters are a group of humans working for the Supernatural Council (otherwise known as the SC) to bring in rogue and criminal supernaturals for legal processing. Basically, they're bounty hunters for the magical community. Every one of them is human; every one of them, that is, except me. Apparently, I was some weird Angel-descended Witch wielding death magic. But what the hunters don't know, including me until recently, is that 'legal processing' means execution—or, at least, that's what the head seer of the Witch's Coven said she saw in a vision.

I didn't know they were being executed when I was mortal, before I was chosen by Fate to become the Fifth Horseman of the Apocalypse upon my death, making me immortal (yeah, immortal; crazy, right?). But that didn't make me a good person: I still hurt people. Still mercilessly dragged them to the SC. Still killed that little boy.

His face as blood poured out of his mouth upon swallowing the cyanide pill still haunts my every nightmare—and quite a few daymares, too. His adorable, cute, pale face that'll never know another sunrise.

I take a deep breath and release, freeing the trapped memory alongside it.

I know I need to come out of this library at some point, and many of the team have tried to encourage me with varying tactics: Nine tried encouraging me out with food and the promise of yoga; Connie tried chatting to me for hours on the other side of the door, just talking away about various memories, funny stories, and that one time someone accused her of being a dirty, unmarried twenty-year-old virgin (when she was really 422), so she had a public orgy in the town square and had to be dragged away at the hands of Arrie as they were all kicked out of town for public indecency; Arrie hasn't bothered trying, of course; but Dea's been there, unmoving, not talking—doing nothing, really, just standing there in some kind of presence of comfort.

It's lunchtime two days after the ball, and I'm pacing near the door, waiting to see who'll try next. Honestly, I'm eager to see what Arrie'll do but too scared to ask in case he does nothing.

Am I attention seeking? Hell yes.

There are piles of books everywhere, since I've been spending my time cataloging the library (well, trying to), and I've had a hard time avoiding the stacks, even with my Vampire-nimble feet. I've kicked over so many stacks this morning that my toe now has an actual bruise forming that doesn't seem to go away with its usual gusto. Humph. Instead, it stays there, looking ugly and purple, reminding me of how thirsty I am. I haven't fed in my Vampire form since the morning of the ball, so I've spent most of the time in my male form to avoid the problem, but I'm still more comfortable in my female body, so I torture myself until I can't stand it any longer.

I'm just lifting a stack of non-fiction dragon books and placing them on their new shelf when a familiar sweet smell hits my nostrils that has me dropping the pile on my already-bruised foot and running to the door handle.

Sniffing once more, I detect brownies, lasagna, and . . . blood. Fuck, damn him! Arrie has decided to bake and play on my Vampire weakness on the off-chance I'm in this form.

Maybe he had Nine check?

Nine's ability to read someone's mind usually amuses me to no end, but over the past couple of days, it's been nothing but irritating. The fucker keeps telling ridiculous jokes to make me laugh, trying to encourage me to talk, and randomly dropping in on me whenever he feels like it. So far, I've managed to avoid responding, and I feel pretty damn satisfied about that. Some of his awful dad jokes are hilarious, and they take effort to not laugh at, even in my current mood.

I'm just being stubborn now, and I need to come out, continue training, and help the team try to prevent this war (hopefully). Assuming I even can, given my mortal history.

Ugh.

Don't think about it. Don't think about it.

The door handle is cold under my slender fingers, and as much as I know I need to pull it down and open the closed door, I hesitate.

What if they now hate me? I mean, I would. A killer on the team is just a silly idea. What if I turn out to be some crazy psychopath?

We're all crazy around here, Sweetie. You try living two thousand years and see how sane you are.

I mentally chuckle, and then chastise myself for laughing at Nine's silliness after doing so well avoiding it.

Yes! Score one for Famine.

I pull the handle down with a deep breath and push the door open. I can do this. Any day now courage? I can do this. People always say that if you just act confident it'll naturally imbue you with its gloriousness, like some kind of magical ego bath. But they're wrong. Real insecurity doesn't magically go away just because we're trying to ignore it; it sticks to you like ever-lasting glue you can't seem to burn off.

My bedroom still looks the same. The same burnt-orange

and yellow colors dotting the room, and the same floor-length windows still letting the midday sun trickle through the various shades of green that paint the forest outside in an insulting attempt to retain normalcy while I'm having a breakdown.

I can do this.

I tiptoe out my bedroom door, down the hallway, down the stairs, and creep into the kitchen doorway to a familiar scene: Arrie wearing a fluffy apron while the others sit around the table in their usual spots.

"She's gonna be fine, Nine. Stop worrying." Connie sits drinking a steaming cup of what I assume is peppermint tea while Nine nurses his usual cup of coffee, looking more troubled than I've ever seen him.

"You don't see what's inside her mind, Con. She thinks she's some kind of killer. A murderer." He scowls at Arrie. "And we all know whose fault that is."

"Alright." Dea raises a hand. "Enough with the arguments." Dea looks my way and smiles.

Everyone else follows his line of focus and looks at me with varying smiles: Connie beams at me, Dea gives me a charming smile, Nine tries his best but he's clearly worried, and Arrie gives his usual grunt of a hello but otherwise remains with his back to me as he continues with lunch.

Nine gestures to the chair beside him—my usual place—and I follow his hand and sit down.

I don't know what to say, so I elect to say nothing at all. All I do know is that I need some kind of distraction, so I want to ask about my training from here on out, but every time I open my mouth to speak, no words come out.

Want me to ask for you, Sweetie?

I nod.

"She wants to know about her training from here on out."

Dea looks at me with surprise, and I try for a comforting smile, but it probably looks more like a grimace.

"Well," he begins, "we have no deadline now, so back to normal. Combat with Arrie in the morning, magic with me and Nine in the afternoon, and weapons with Con in the evening."

"Can I add some studying with either you or Nine in there somewhere? I have questions, and I want an actual person to answer them."

Even I'm surprised by my blank voice, by the lack of tone and cadence I'm used to hearing.

"Sure. We can do lessons late morning and over lunch, if you would like?"

I nod.

I don't want to speak more than necessary. I don't know what's wrong with me, but I just feel so broken. So empty. If I thought not having an identity was bad, finding out that my identity is a murderer is worse.

"Lasagna and brownies are done," Arrie calls from behind us as he walks around the table and places both dishes on top. "Here." He shoves a glass of blood in front of me with a silly straw sticking out the top with a genuine smile—albeit a small one.

One sniff and I know it's Arrie's; I can't miss that sweet, woody fragrance if I try. "Thanks."

I take my time drinking it, trying to not let my fangs slip and scare Connie. I don't think my heart could handle that right now. Turns out, I can handle small sips without going full-on Vamp mode, and that actually serves to cheer me up a little.

No one brings up the obvious elephant in the room the

entire time lunch is ongoing, and I'm grateful for it. I don't want to talk, not to anyone—not even to myself. Though I seem to end up doing it a lot anyway.

The need to burn off this inner frustration and anger penetrates my thoughts, but I don't know how. What would I have done in the past? Before I learned who I was? What would I have done when I was mortal?

The image of a gym passes across my mental eyes, and I know the answer: work out.

Okay, that I can do.

Nine mentioned a gym on the other side of the kitchen. Behind me is the kitchen, to the left is the door to the gardens, and to the right is the cinema. So do those double glass doors in front lead to the gym?

Yes. Feel free to use it however you like.

Thank you.

Digging into my brownies, I swallow a heavy sigh. Fuck me, they really are amazing. How does he make these damn things? I mean, hook a sister up with the recipe, damn it!

With two thousand years of practice.

Well, at least one of you has put those years to good use.

Nine scoffs. "You're internally joking now?"

"Might as well make someone laugh." I shrug.

Besides, Nine's smile still makes my insides all gooey, and don't even get me started on Dea's charming grin he probably still practices in the mirror every morning.

Grabbing my plate of brownies, I get up. "I'm going to work out for the rest of the afternoon."

"Hon, wait a minute," Connie says. "Here." She shoves a folder in my hand. At my questioning look, she says, "It's my write-up from the last mission. I was supposed to finish it ages ago, but things got a little crazy. So I finished it up this morning for you."

I nod, still confused, and glance over the few pages of notes within the flimsy file: THE FAE APPEARED FINE, WITH THE USUAL GRIEVANCES OF RULES AND RESTRICTIONS OF THEIR MAGIC USAGE AND DUST SUPPLIES. THE SHIFTERS ARE HAVING SOME PROBLEMS WITH PACKS WARRING OVER POLITICAL ISSUES, SOME ADHERING TO THE SC LAWS AND HUMAN INTERFERENCE AND SOME NOT. BUT THE SHIFTER COUNCIL SEEM ON TOP OF THINGS. I RECEIVED A FULL APOLOGY FOR THE STATE TASHA AND THE HYENA PACK LEFT ME IN AFTER MY LAST VISIT; I HAD INTERRUPTED THEM DURING A PACK RUN AND MEAL. NO ONE HAS SEEN A SEAL, NO ONE SEEMS TO KNOW ABOUT MAGIC, AND ALL IS ITS USUAL ON-THE-EDGE FEEL.

Relief rushes through me. "At least the Fae and Shifters aren't causing problems."

"Indeed," Dea says.

Everyone smiles at me—well, tries to—clearly glad I've progressed past the shutting-myself-in-my-room phase and moved on to the sulking-around-the-house phase. Childish, I know, but I'm, like, two thousand years younger than them, I think I can get away with being a little childish. Maybe. Just a little.

(Hey, I won't tell if you don't.)

Chapter Two

I open the doors to the gym and do a double take. As with everything in this damn house, it's not a gym, it's like ten gyms had a baby and produced the world's most insane fitness arena for gladiators. Everything from cardio machines, to acrobatics areas (including trapeze equipment), to the largest weights area I've ever seen, including some of the heaviest weights I've ever seen, to a jungle gym in the far corner that looks like I can get some serious shifting practice in.

I walk through and notice a sliding door to the right that has a pool beyond. Swimming sounds like a good idea. I slide the door open and inspect what I have to work with. Looks to be about a hundred-meter pool with a diving depth at the far end. Pretty standard. But then I guess pools don't have to be fancy, just functional.

Flick the night switch on the panel to your right.

Err, okay.

The panel to my right is a bit like the one in Connie's room, and after flicking the big red night button, the entire room goes dark for a moment before flittering lights fill every inch of the previously blank ceiling like the night sky. The pool has lights in the bottom that light up a deep lilac color, and a hot tub I didn't notice before bubbles away on the far right.

Fuck damn. This would make one amazing pool party.

Fiddling with the panel, I turn off the night switch and figure everything back to normal, but the aquatic gym is calling my name, and I'll be honest, I'm a little impressed, and for a moment there, I forget all about my mortal life and the horrors I've caused. It's just me and the pool shifting into something that resembles an aquatic jungle gym, with various balls of water hanging suspended in the air to mini pools embedded in raised platforms that dot the airspace of the room.

Wonder who this is for?

The door behind me opens, and the rest of the team stand behind me and gasp.

Connie grabs my shoulder. "What did you do?"

"What?"

Nine steps up next to me. "How did you make it do that?"

"Turned on the aquatic gym setting on the panel thingy." I shrug and gesture to the gray wall panel. "Is this new?"

Nine nods, looking a little speechless.

Dea examines the panel and nods in concentration. "Probably changed when she arrived, or when her Shifter abilities manifested."

I look at him in baffled confusion for a moment before it sinks in—this is where I can train my aquatic Shifter forms. Oh my goddess, I can be a dolphin! I internally clap with excitement before I temper it down in guilt. I don't deserve to be excited while other people have to live in grief because of my actions.

Nine flinches.

Ugh. This is gonna be so hard on him; he has to sit through all of this mental shit with me.

I'm sorry.

Don't be.

I spot some changing rooms in the corner and head on over. I'll have to ask the house for swimwear in both forms, I guess, but it'll be worth it. I end up asking for some kind of modest swimwear in my female form, and it gives me a tank top and shorts (which is better than a skimpy bikini) and then some board shorts. I change into both and step out in my male form, ready to check out my aquatic Shifter abilities.

The team are still standing on the side lines, waiting for me to do something.

I look at them with raised eyebrows.

"Can we watch?" Connie asks on bouncing toes while eying my mostly naked Fae form.

Right, Fae body.

Usually, I would find that funny, maybe even a little hot, but right now I just find it annoying. I don't want any more complications, much less any that would affect the team.

"Sure." I shrug and step into the pool.

I stand in the shallow end for a moment, thinking about what kind of shift I can try. I've never tried a water Shifter before. Picturing a bottle-nosed dolphin in my mind, I force my body into a different form and enter a whole other world of insanity.

Suddenly, my head's underwater, and at first, I panic, but then I remember that dolphins can hold their breath for quite a while, so I take a deep breath from the surface and dive. My tail is powerful, moving me meters in a single flick, and my fins and body allow me to change direction in a flash.

This is pretty cool. Probably not particularly useful on missions, but you never know. Right?

How do dolphins jump?

I engage my body muscles and flick my tail downward, leaping myself out of the water and back in, in what I hope is an awesome-looking dolphin jump.

My ears don't pick up on much below the water other than the gentle rolling of the waves I create, but when I poke my head up out of the water and change back, I hear the team clapping away.

I get out of the water to grab the towel left on the bench for me.

"That was awesome!" Nine runs over, his usual magic-geek self bubbling over the surface of misery I've put us both in recently. "I bet the air bubbles of water are for you to jump in and out of in various aquatic forms, and you can fly between them if you can time your shifts right, and . . ." He trails off.

But I stop listening. I understand the point of the gym, and it's great, but shifting isn't really taking my mind off of anything.

I head over to the panel and switch the pool back to its normal function, change into my female form, which takes an agonizing four minutes of concentration and awkward silence, and head back into the pool.

Lengths.

That's what I need. To feel the burn of a hard day's workout. And I'm going to achieve that through swimming lengths—as many as I can fit in between now and dinner.

I don't bother telling the others to get out, I don't even really acknowledge their presence, I just dive into the deep end and swim.

One.

I could have been normal in my death.

Two.

I could have just died and moved onto wherever the hell the afterlife is.

Three.

I could have not been stuck with these stupid gifts in the first place.

Four.

Why did I join the Hunter Society?

Five.

Why did my parents have to die?

Six.

Why was I alone?

Seven.

Why didn't Mr. Compton take me in instead?

Eight.

Gah! I have so many questions, but I'm really not prepared to find the answers. There's a niggling, however, somewhere in my mind, that in order to understand this war, I'm going to have to find out everything about my life, including the people I left behind.

By the time I've done well over a hundred lengths (and taken many breaks in between), Nine calls for dinner.

My body aches—there are parts of my body that ache that I didn't even know have muscles—but it feels good. So fucking good. And I can't help the smile that creeps across my face as I walk into the kitchen with my wet chlorinated hair, my swimwear still on but covered by a gold-colored slip that falls to my mid-thigh, and my eyes stinging from my stupid decision to swim without goggles for hours.

"You look happier?" Connie is sat in her usual position,

looking me up and down as I sit next to Nine in my not-so-dinner-appropriate outfit.

"Yeah, not bad."

"So, you like swimming, then?" Nine's hand rests on my knee, like usual, but he pulls it back with a smirk. Probably because I'm not clothed like normal.

"Seems so." I grab myself a glass of water and chug it down. "So, what's for dinner?"

"Tacos," Arrie grumbles from the kitchen.

Is he cooking again? Why?

Because he thinks it'll cheer you up.

That's . . . adorable. I'm sure he'll piss me off again before I can thank him, though. He usually does.

Sighing, I grumble under my breath before turning to Connie. "What does weapons training involve?"

"Fighting with weapons." She shrugs and smiles to hide her laugh. "Nah, just training you to fight with all kinds of weapons. I reckon it'll be a challenge to find weapons that'll shift with you, though."

"I'll probably have to have weapons for both forms. Not sure about my Shifter abilities, though." Would my weapons stay on my person when I shift back? My clothes do.

"I'll look into it," Nine says from beside me. "Should be fun."

Arrie places the tacos on the table, and everyone digs in. I'm surprised Dea has stayed silent up until now. He hasn't mentioned plans, what happened at the ball, or anything. Maybe he's trying to be considerate?

Well, that's stupid. I look at Dea to get his attention. "What's next?"

He sighs a lazy smile. "I am not sure, Angel."

"Oh." He doesn't know what to do, either. Maybe it's time

I start making some suggestions, given that this war is mine to solve after all. Somehow. According to some mysterious Fate figure. "I think we need to investigate this rogue Vampire faction, see who they're working for?" I raise my voice into a question so as not to sound pushy or order-y. "They seem hell bent on us, for some reason. And I'd like to deal with them before they become a bigger problem."

Dea nods. "That sounds like a swell idea." He leans back in his chair and goes back to being silent.

Why is he being so weird?

He's letting you lead.

Fucking why? I can barely aim my dick at the toilet bowl most mornings.

He thinks it's the right call to make.

But I don't even know the team all that well, or the world, or fucking anything! I'm clueless.

You won't always be. And you have us.

I take a deep breath and look at the people around me. Nine's right. I might not know everything, but I bet the team's collective knowledge far exceeds anything I could have alone. So even if I did remember every detail of my mortal life, I would still be outmatched in knowledge.

"Okay." I look to Dea. "Shall we leave for Earth next Monday? Give everyone a chance to recover from the ball and for me to get in some kind of weapons training so I don't have to rely on being unarmed."

Dea nods. "Sure. Sounds good."

Chapter Three

<u>Horseman of Magic's Training Schedule:</u>
6am–7am—Morning Yoga
7am–9am—Combat with Arrie
9am–11am—Gym Session
11am–1pm—Lessons with Dea
1pm–5pm—Magic Study with Nine
7pm–10pm—Weapons Training with Connie

The training structure I've found myself in is grueling, and I'm only halfway through day one. I'm not sure I can keep this insanity up. Arrie's combat session went much the same as last time, with us both staying as silent as possible and him teaching me how to block a variety of hand-to-hand attacks, all with varying degrees of strength and technique. My gym session consisted of a mix of cardio and plyometrics and a half hour swim session to cool down.

Now, however, I'm finally sitting in my study, with Dea on a chair beside me that I dragged (begrudgingly) from another section.

"Do you know what you would like to study, Angel?" He places a hand on my knee, stroking his thumb over the soft spot on the inside, and I swear my insides melt.

"I . . . err . . ." Damn. All this does is bring back memories of that stupid kiss. Stupid hot. Stupid hot kiss. Goddess, I could really use more of that in my life.

"Angel?"

"Oh, errm . . ." My face heats a familiar shade of red, and I dart away from his gorgeous galaxy eyes and shift my attention to the suddenly interesting floor. "I wanted to . . ." What did I want to learn about again? Oh, yeah! "I wanted to learn about the SC." I cough my throat clear.

"Ah, I see." He removes his hand from my knee, and I have to swallow the whine of disapproval that threatens to break free from my sealed lips. "Why not ask your Seeing Stone?" He points to the milky-white crystal ball on my desk in front of us.

A Seeing Stone, I learned recently, is a stone that, if you hold and think about your emotions, problems, and/or ask your internal questions, will provide you the answer in book form. Well, mine provides it in book form.

"The Seeing Stone is great, it really is, but I wanted to get some opinionated accounts. You know, from real people who were there."

He nods, shaking a strand of hair away that's fallen into his eye. Goddess, he's beautiful. Like, seriously, insanely stunning. There's not more than an inch of space between us as he sits there in his black jeans and white tee that shows the edges of that delicious golden swirling tattoo inked on his shoulder, chest, and torso, and from here, I can see the ridges of his abs beneath the thin material.

My hand reaches out before I can stop it, and I find myself tracing the edges of that tattoo. I really want to ask what it means, but I know the story is probably a painful one from the dark expression that passes across his face whenever I ask. But I can't stop myself from touching it, tracing its pattern around his shoulder.

Dea watches me with a smug expression, and I gaze at his relaxed eyes in somewhat of a trance until he clears his throat and snaps me out of it. "Angel . . . ?"

"Yeah?" My hand's still resting on his shoulder, but I'm reluctant to remove it.

"About that kiss . . ." He looks away from me, breaking eye contact. "I just wanted to offer my apologies if I was too forward—"

"Stop." I place my finger to his lips. "I . . . liked it."

"Oh," he replies, kissing my fingertip in a gentle breath, "I know." Aaaand there's that famous smugness. Damn him and his confident attitude. It's sexy as hell. "But I know that you would rather wait until you are ready, and I just—"

"Dea, please stop."

He stops talking, thank the goddess.

"I'm not sure what I want. I mean, what I said before still stands, I want a life, a future, a . . . I don't know, life partner? Whatever you'd call it when you're immortal. A family. But I can't stay away from you all forever. Eventually, I . . ."

Eventually I'll what, exactly? Cave and give in? There are plenty of men and women in the world I can casually sleep with that would create far fewer strings.

"Yes?" He opens his mouth and slips my finger inside, gently rolling his tongue along the sensitive tip. "You will what, Angel?"

"I . . . don't know," I whisper between gasps. Just the

thought of other places his tongue could be doing that has me squirming in my seat.

His eyes bore into my soul as he watches me wrestle with my own mind, but in the end, I'm too weak to resist those soft lips of his; I remember their sweetness and their urgency, a hot mix of syrupy heat that buckles my knees and makes my head spin.

Dea leans forward and places a commanding hand on my waist, letting my finger go and inclining his head toward mine.

He's going to kiss me again, isn't he?

"What about Nine?" I mumble before I can stop it. I cringe the moment it comes out. "Sorry."

Dea smiles. "Do not be sorry. I like that you care about him too. But I already told him about our kiss, so there is no need to fret."

I sigh my relief, but before I can rethink my choice, Dea sweeps in and catches my sigh with his lips. His hand travels under my top to stroke gentle circles on the small of my back, the pace of his hand matching the rhythm of his tongue.

As heat pools in my center and I can't help but arch my back against his touch, my body takes over, knowing what it needs and letting nothing stand in its way. I pull away and climb onto his lap, straddling his legs and recapturing that kiss.

Warm hands run up my back, tracing patterns up and down my spine as I run my hands over his chest, tracing my fingers over the delicious ridges of his torso. I inch my hands lower and soon find the waistline of his jeans and underwear. I hesitate. I want this. Fuck, do I want this. My hands fumble with the button, eager to take this further and wrap my hand around his—

His hands catch mine and pull them away. "No, Angel.

Not right now."

Is he being fucking serious?

"Sorry, but I do not want to be a mistake."

I flinch. I didn't even consider that. Would sleeping with Dea right now be a mistake? I sigh. Yeah, fucking probably. I'm not ready. I mean, I'm soooo ready, but I'm still not sure what I want in the long run, and any mistake I make with the team is permanent. And an immortal's permanent is pretty fucking lasting.

"Sorry."

Dea captures my chin in his hand and forces me to look at him. "Stop doing that. Stop being sorry for being yourself." He smiles.

Footsteps echo from behind us as someone coughs. "What kind of lessons are you teaching her, bro?"

I fly off of Dea's lap and back into the chair next to us, my face redder than a tomato.

Niiiiiine. Could've given me a heads up, asshole.

Wouldn't have been half as fun.

Dea and Nine just laugh at my flushed face, but I quickly recover.

"What did you want?"

"Just to see what lessons you were learning today, but I had no idea they would be this exciting. I would have joined earlier." He winks at me and grabs another chair.

"Err, well, I was just asking about the SC before we got . . . distracted."

Nine chuckles. "What would you like to know?"

I look at them both with a serious expression (well, I hope it's serious). "Everything."

Dea clears his throat. "A history lesson, then."

Nine leaves to browse the stacks of books I've spent the

last few days organizing and cataloging (not getting very far), while Dea stands and paces on the other side of my desk.

"A hundred years ago, we helped organize the outing of the supernatural community. As you know, the Witches did not join the other pillar communities in this plight. Nor did a few lesser species."

At my questioning eyebrows, he explains, "Dragons and unicorns, among other things, are still vastly regarded as myth, a few demon creatures we let live after the original war, such as hellhounds and succubae, never came out of the closet, and there are probably lots of hybrid species we know nothing about."

I start taking diligent notes, making a list of things I want to look up, such as demon species and how to recognize them, whether dragons really are extinct, and what the hell succubae are.

But Dea continues with his lecture, and much to my pleasant surprise, he's a natural lecturer. But then, he would be, wouldn't he? His voice is so . . . dreamy.

Focus.

Right.

"When we planned the outing of the supernatural world, we told the human leaders first. This allowed them to conduct counter measures to rebellions, control the media of the mass public, and more importantly, to create the SC."

"So, it really was human created then?"

"Yes." He clears his throat and continues. "The three main pillar communities—Vampires, Shifters, and Fae—negotiated with the human governments to have some say in how the Supernatural Council was run, given that it will be looking after their people."

"Makes sense," I add. "Couldn't have any unfair laws just

because humans didn't understand the culture of the other races."

"Right," Dea adds. "And it was, and still is, run by a council of twelve individuals, three from each race: Vampire, Shifter, Fae, and human."

"No Witches?"

"No. They chose to stay in hiding, and they aren't ever prosecuted by the SC unless it is something extreme and a threat to the general public."

So that's why the Witch Coven aren't worried about the SC intervening in Witch politics. Because they can't.

"Yes." Nine comes back around the corner he went down earlier with a stack of books piled higher than his face. "It would be a violation of the Species Protection Treaty, created at the time of the supernatural outing to protect the integrity and survival of each species."

Dea takes half of the pile from Nine's grasp, and they both place them down on the desk.

"Here," Nine says as his half-pile slams the desk, "start with these."

I grab a couple off the piles and read their titles:

SUPERNATURAL POLICIES AND LAWS

SUPERNATURAL COUNCIL: THE FORMATION

SUPERNATURAL TREATIES AND THEIR PROTECTIONS

"Damn, Nine." I cough at the dust one of the books chucks up as I open the front cover. "This is some reading list."

"I'm sure you can fit it into your schedule, Sweetie."

Yeah, along with dying from sleep deprivation. My muscles twinge at the memory of my schedule, and I stand up to stretch.

"You okay?" Nine walks over and looks at me with a worried expression. "You seem . . . tense?"

"Do I?" I laugh. "I didn't notice."

"Don't be snarky with me just because you chose a stupidly intense schedule."

"Not like I have the time to relax. Might as well train as much as I can." I reach down to touch my toes, and my back pangs. "Ah!" I hiss.

"Stop." Dea steps up with his glowing healing hands at the ready. "You need to slow down. Day one is not even complete yet. You will not be able to keep this up."

I look at them both, their annoyingly worried gazes, Nine biting his lip in concern, and Dea with his glowing hands, ready to heal me.

"Watch me."

I sit back at the desk and ask, "How are the SC run now?" I open the book on supernatural policies and laws and begin flicking through. "Is it still the same kind of council formation?"

Dea and Nine exchange glances and then sigh in unison.

"Technically," Dea starts, "yes. But there is a lot of underhanded playing, tied loyalties, and blackmailing behind the scenes."

I grunt. "Great."

"Well," Nine says, "everyone was present at the ball, so at least no one's been assassinated yet."

"Real helpful." I yawn and look at the time. Fuck. It's already 1:30. "Ready for magic study?"

Nine looks at me and smiles. "Always."

Chapter Four

My training room flashes an ugly shade of heated gray due to the fireplace in the corner flickering against the cracked concrete walls.

"So far"—Nine wraps his arms around me in the otherwise empty room—"we can access all your abilities."

I nod in agreement.

"I think I'll leave your shifting practice to your gym sessions and ask if Arrie and Con'll include it in some of the later physical stuff. That way we can work on everything else."

That's actually a good idea. That way we don't have to work on one of the four sets and can instead focus on the other three.

"I'm also pretty happy with your Vampire abilities, using them to enhance your other powers and be useful in less active scenarios. So, really, I just want to work on your Witch and Fae powers."

Ugh. I groan in frustration. Witch powers means working on unlocking my other elemental abilities, mastering charm magic, and tapping into my seer powers, while Fae magic means learning spells. Honestly, both of those things already hurt my head.

"Hey, quit complaining!" Nine pulls back with a smirk. "This way, you don't have to do anything physically stressful. You can sit down for the whole afternoon."

I raise my eyebrows in disbelief as an overwhelming urge to kiss him confronts me. No moving for the whole afternoon? Bring magic lessons on!

That really all it takes?

Shut up!

"C'mon! C'mon! C'mon!" I yank him into the middle of the room. "I want to try to unlock some more of my elements. I can use air pretty well and am still practicing in what few spare moments I have to use it in unique ways."

Nine chuckles. "Okay, okay."

Nine's Chinese features glow in the firelight, and for a moment there, his brown eyes catch ablaze and glow an intense shade of orange, but it's gone the moment I blink. He really is beautiful in this light.

I watch his cheeks blush. *Thank you.*

Laughing at his formality, I yank his arm once more and sit us both on the concrete floor. "How do I unlock my other abilities?"

He shrugs. "No idea."

Well, great.

"How did you unlock your air one?"

I think about it for a moment and remember how Nine went into my mind and forced me to engage with my magical center. "It was after you went into my mind."

He cringes. "I don't want to do that again."

"Why not?" Is there something wrong with my mind? Is it

a bad place to be?

A hand caresses my upper arm, and I gaze at Nine's grimacing face. "No, not at all. It's just . . . I hate being in people's minds like that. I end up seeing more of them than I would ever like." He looks away and gazes into the fire. "Even with people I care about."

Oh. "Nine, I'm s—"

"Don't do that. My life is nothing to be sorry about." He turns back around and smiles. "Now, how do we unlock those other elements?" He mumbles to himself.

"Out loud, Nine. I want to hear your thoughts."

He stops mumbling and looks at me. "Really?"

"How else can we figure it out together?"

His usually casual smile reaches ear to ear. "I was just thinking that me forcing you to engage with your magic shouldn't have just unlocked a single element. It should have unlocked them all."

"I could just be an air Witch, you know."

He looks at me and blinks in indifference. "Nope. You're designed to engage with the entire magical community: Vampires, Fae, every Shifter . . . and every Witch." He sighs. "You can't just be one type of Witch any less than you can be just one type of Shifter."

I nod. It makes sense. There's so much about my identity that doesn't fit into one pocket of society, from my gender, to my sexuality, to my magic. "Is that how it's meant to be?" I look to the floor. "Fitting in everywhere so that I fit in nowhere."

Nine tilts my head up and meets my eyes in a blazing heat. "I think there's a point to it. I think . . . that maybe you're meant to bring about magical and societal change so that the world remains in peace."

I blink. "That's . . . a tall fucking order."

Nine chuckles and drops my gaze. "I know." He stands. "I have an idea." He walks over to the fireplace and grabs the spade.

"What are you doing?"

"Testing a theory." He opens the glass door to the fireplace and shovels out a piece of lit coal, keeping it carefully on the spade. "I want you to touch it."

But . . . that'll hurt.

"Even if it does hurt, which I don't think it will, Dea can heal you if you don't manage it yourself."

I nod. "What's your theory?"

"I think your first power was air because it was the first thing your magic latched on to. Air is all around us. If we were in a pool at the time, I think it would have been water." He inches closer to where I sit on the floor, the spade hovering at head height.

I know that fire can't hurt me that much, and even if it does, I'll heal in no time, but that doesn't stop my hands from shaking, the sweat from billowing across my forehead, and the ever-quickening breaths my chest heaves over.

It's going to be fine. It's going to be fine.

Goddess, stop being so stupid!

"Go on." Nine pushes the spade to an inch from my nose. "Touch it."

I raise my hand, and Nine pulls the spade back, giving me room to move. Inching my hand closer, the heat bores down between my fingers. My hands get clammy as I flick my fingertip across the flame.

I snatch my hand back, cradling it in my other palm against my chest, but . . . it doesn't hurt. I expected the familiar feel of burning, the sting of bubbling skin, but nothing. I feel nothing.

Nine holds the spade out still, expecting me to try again.

So I do. I edge my finger into the flame all the way until my palm grabs the coal and lifts it off the metal.

Wow. "I'm doing it!" I'm holding fire!

"Well, kinda. You're holding already created fire, but you haven—"

"Shut it, Nine! I'm holding fire." I can't keep the grin off my face. Okay, so I'm not actually creating the flame, and holding a burning coal hasn't magically unlocked my fire powers, but it's a start. And a start I can do.

"There's all kinds of uses for that power alone. You could throw flaming daggers, walk through fire, not be affected by fire magic . . ."

He's right. This can be useful. My powers are growing at such a rate, it's a little unsettling. Do I have any limits? Will I ever stop growing?

Eventually. None of us have gained new powers in centuries.

Oh. Well, that's hopeful, at least.

"Life will be more relaxing one day. Promise." Nine places the coal back into the fireplace and the spade back on the hook on the wall and sits beside me. "You doing okay?" His hand sits on my knee again, and I can't help but be comforted by the familiar gesture, as though his warmth flows into me.

"I don't know." I really don't. There's so much to unload. So much new information I have to unpack.

"You don't have to unpack it all at once."

"But it's not information I can do anything with. It'll just sit there, stewing."

He nods but remains otherwise silent.

"I just wish . . . Gah! I don't even know anymore. I was a murderer, I'm now the Fifth Horseman: I have to deal with all of you, I have to save the world, I have to figure out what's going on in order to save it, and all the while . . . we're just waiting for some war to happen when I would rather prevent it in the first place."

Deep breaths heave my chest as I cling to Nine's hand like it's a life raft in my new crazy world.

"It's okay." He strokes his spare hand up and down my back, and I feel the tears coming before I even have a chance to stop them.

But what am I crying about?

I try to make sense of it, but heaving sobs wrack my brain before I can use even a cell to make a thought.

How could he reject me? The fucking asshole!

Ugh. That's what I'm crying about? But that makes sense. He made the right call.

"Wait a minute, who rejected you?"

I look at Nine through tear-stained eyes. "Dea." Sniffling, I try to pretty up my face and stop looking like an insane victim of heartbreak.

"He did . . . what?" he asks through gritted teeth.

"Please don't be mad at him. It was the right choice."

Nine looks at me questioningly.

"It would have been a mistake to sleep with any of you when I'm still not sure what I want given . . . everything." Given that I can't actually have any of you, I say mentally, fearing the words enough to not say them out loud.

Goddess, I sound pathetic.

Nine chuckles. "You should ask what Dea and I talked about after you made us have that chat."

"Huh?"

"Nope. Not gonna tell you now, Sweetie."

"Nine!" I whine. "Come on!" I swat him on the arm.

He jumps to his feet and holds out his hand.

"Noooo, you promised I could stay sat."

He rolls his eyes and drags the desk chair to where I now sit. "There."

Huffing, I get up with a wince and sit in the chair.

"Let's see if we can replicate that fire with your own." He calls the house for a bucket of water and throws it over the fireplace. "Relight it."

The rest of the four hours I'm stuck in that ever-colder room I spend in magical exhaustion, up to the point where I nearly faint off the chair and Nine forces me to take a break. Still, though, no fire.

Frustration could not have been more evidently plastered across my sweat-sheened face when I sit down to dinner.

Today so far: Arrie's still a god in combat, the SC are assholes (no surprises there), and I'm still a fire-less Witch. If I don't make some kind of progress with Connie this evening, I might just burst.

Arrie is still cooking for me and being . . . nice, and I'm still utterly baffled by his intentions. "So, what you girls working on this evening?" he asks in an attempt to make conversation.

I just look at Connie in bewilderment, as though I can't understand why he's talking to me in the first place.

She, of course, just laughs it off and answers, "See what weapons she likes, introduce her to ones I think she might be able to use, and then spend a few hours putting her on her ass." She shrugs.

Hope she can dodge my knives, 'cos I'm gonna stab her if she doesn't give me a win.

Nine laughs at my inner turmoil, and clearly it's written all over my face because she looks at me with red cheeks and a warm smile.

"No one's good at weaponry straight away. It takes time. Training. Effort."

"I'm sure." My eyes roll of their own volition, and everyone laughs at my own personal world of training pain. "So, err . . ." Breathe, Horseman, breathe. "When was the Hunter Society formed?"

Everyone's heads turn my way, cutlery gently placing themselves down on the table. They all start talking at once, and I can't hear any of them, no matter how much I try to focus on one person's sound.

"Stop worrying and just give me the fucking answer!" I am so done with their tiptoeing around my feelings. I'm a grown-ass woman, I can handle bad news. I'm still here after Mr. Compton's bombshell, aren't I?

Nine's the one who steps up after everyone remains silent for more than a single breath. "About ten years into the supernatural outing and the SC's formation, we had a problem with public supernatural criminals. It was causing bad press for the magical community as a whole, and the SC wanted to change that. So they created the Hunter Society. Humans could take back some semblance of control by bringing in rogue and criminal supes in exchange for money. Not only did it reduce crime, but it helped balance out the new world."

"Thank you."

Chapter Five

Connie meets me in the gym, an assortment of weapons at her feet, as Arrie sits on one of the many weight machines, working away, and I would be lying if I said my eyes don't linger a moment longer than would be polite.

"So, what weapons are you most excited about?" Connie asks, snapping me out of my daydream.

"Errr . . . what weapons are there?"

"Wow. Okay."

She looks far too surprised for my liking, and I suddenly feel seriously underprepared for this session. I should have done some prep.

"Wait, sorry. No. Not what I meant." She shakes her hands. "Just surprised that mortals don't really get weapons these days."

Doesn't really help make me feel better, but I'll take it. Some tension between us will be good for our . . . relationship (goddess, that sounds ridiculous); it'll put some distance between us.

"Well," I say as I peruse the many—did she bring the entire armory?—weapons on offer, "I'm good with knives, so maybe smaller ranges might be good?"

"Good thinking." She picks up a pair of dual blades, shorter in length than most here, but not as short as the various daggers at her feet. "Try these."

I grab the blades from her and hold them by the hilt at my sides. I look at her in question, and she tries hard to suppress a giggle, but clearly, I'm not knowledgeable about all this stuff.

"Okay, widen your stance, like you would when throwing."

I follow her instructions.

"Good. Now hold them out in front you, but ensure your elbows are tucked in, protecting your center." She claps when I have the stance right. "These are dual shamshirs, but they're slightly shorter than what is common to allow for their dual nature. This type of sword isn't usually dualized, but it works well for fast soldiers, and given your Vamp nature, speed is gonna be your friend."

"Especially against her," Arrie grumbles from behind me.

I don't look back; I don't want to be distracted again. Instead, I nod at her. "Now what?"

She grabs a fancy-looking longsword with some Celtic writing on the hilt that glows a faint gold against the bronze wrapping. "We try it out."

Like, right now? Eek. I don't want to fight the Horseman of Conquest ever, much less right now, after a full day of exhausting training.

"Ready yourself. And try to block."

I nod, hands shaking.

"Don't look so terrified, I'm not going to kill you, silly."

"Right."

Connie runs at me with her sword, slashing it in front of

her, aiming for my torso.

I manage to put both swords up in time to block the attack, but they fly out of my hands.

"Grip harder next time."

I pick up my swords, readjusting my stance back to normal. "Right."

She attacks again, this time slower, in a timed attack I manage to predict—somehow. As she brings her sword down on my head, I duck and move out of the way.

"Good." Her arms do some fancy flailing I can't see; they move too fast for me to understand where she's going to strike next.

It works, because the sword nicks my shoulder, and I hiss at the paper-like cut now oozing a thin trickle of blood down my arm.

"Okay." She puts her sword back in its place on a nearby table. "Let's try another weapon."

We spend the next few hours exploring how well I naturally use each weapon, no matter how silly and untrained my form is. A few of them are clunky, difficult to manage, and are a clear no-go for me, so we put those to the side, and we are left with a few options.

"Does it have to be a sword?" I ask.

"Huh?"

"My weapon, does it have to be a sword?"

"Well," she hesitates, "no." She shakes her head. "What were you thinking?"

"No idea. But something less . . . aggressive."

Arrie laughs from behind us, still working out. Probably just trying to watch us and wanting an excuse. "You want something that won't instantly kill someone, don't you?" He walks up behind me and places his hands on my shoulders. I don't respond, not wanting to give my inner thoughts away. "You know," he says, "every weapon is dangerous in the right hands. No matter how sharp its edges might be."

"You can be really wise when you want to be, Arrie."

Connie laughs and steps forward, sandwiching me between the two of them. "Shame he's usually such an ass."

That has us all laughing—even Arrie, who punches her in the arm hard enough for her to have to step back.

They're both standing close enough for me to feel their body warmth, Arrie at my back and Connie at my front. And damn, I don't need this level of sexy from these two (I have enough threesome issues with Nine and Dea).

Heard that.

Ugh, go away.

He mentally chuckles at me, and I sigh.

"You know," Connie says, "you need to slow down."

Arrie grabs my waist from behind in a surprisingly hot grab to press me flush against his front. "She's right." He grumbles something in a language I don't understand, but Connie does, because she blushes.

She steps forward, and I find myself pressed between the two of them in an embrace I did not see coming.

"What is this, see who can make me break first?"

"We did have that bet, yes, but only in a playful way." Connie smiles at me and whispers in my ear, "Though I'm not certain someone hasn't already won."

What? How does she know about earlier?

She blinks at me in surprise. "Wait, what?"

"You were just teasing, weren't you?" I sigh. Damn. I actually wasn't going to tell her about Dea's rejection.

"What happened?" Arrie asks from behind.

"I don't want to talk about it. It . . . didn't go well."

"What. Did. They. Do. Now?" Connie says through gritted teeth.

"Nothing."

Arrie tightens his grip on my waist. "Not leaving until you tell us."

Sighing once more, I grunt. "He said no."

Connie growls. "Which one of those pretty fuckers rejected you after everything you've been through in the last few days?" She looks at me with expectancy.

"Dea."

That answer seems to surprise them both, as they step away from me and glare at each other, clearly having some kind of secret conversation.

"Stop worrying." I start a run on the nearest treadmill. "He was right. It would have been a mistake." Not wanting to cry in front of either of them, I push to a faster pace and run using my Vampire speed for a solid thirty minutes before I stop and turn back around.

They're both nattering away on the floor, waiting for me to come back to the session.

"Okay"—I step up to the weapons—"what's next?"

Connie points to the next few we need to try, and we go at it again; she pushes me to use each one naturally as Arrie makes sarcastic remarks from the side lines. In a way, it's kind of perfect. Almost like home.

The bed that night feels better than it's ever felt. I'm off in mere seconds.

Unfortunately, my mind is not, and clearly, it's not done with these stupid nightmares.

I'm in a room with no windows this time, a concrete room with knives, swords, guns, and all sorts littering the edges and dark corners. I'm in my training room.

"Can't believe I lost that fucking mark," I grumble beneath my breath. Throwing a dagger at the target, I hit dead center and laugh under my breath. "Fucking stupid dog."

A bell sounds in the distance.

Fuck.

It sounds again before I make it to the doorway of the training room. Once outside, I hit a button behind a book on the nearest bookcase and watch as a magical spell activates and a shimmering disguise of wall covers the door.

The bell sounds again, and I realize it's the doorbell.

"Coming!"

Running through the hallway, I answer the door to a pale, smiling face. "Marty! Hey." I move out of the way to let him in.

"Hey, Tay." He smiles at me in a way that's almost charming, but if mortal me realizes that, she doesn't react.

"Want anything to drink?"

"Hilarious, Tay." He flashes his fangs, and I internally panic. I'm not sure whether it's mortal me or dream me that gasps, but it's internal nonetheless.

"Just keeping things light."

So I was friends with a Vampire? Seems unlikely.

"Was just wondering if, maybe, you wanted to grab a coffee this evening?" He fumbles with the collar of his shirt, and I notice his distinct lack of confidence despite seeming familiar with me.

He likes me. He's asking me on a date?

Dream me hesitates, grasping her coffee cup with more force than is necessary. "Err . . . I'm not sure . . ."

"Oh," he says, disappointment filling his features. "That's okay. Maybe next time."

"Yeah, I guess." I don't turn around; I just stand with my back to him like a coward.

Just tell him straight, you asshole! I find myself yelling at . . . myself. (Odd experience.)

"Listen, Taylor. Would you"—he steps up to me and grabs my hips—"like to go out with me properly? You know, one day?"

"I-I-I . . ." I stumble through several reiterations of this sentence starter before I finally turn around and look him in the eyes.

Before I can get out my answer, though, Marty places his lips on mine and kisses me. I gasp into his mouth, and Marty takes his opportunity to deepen his show of affection, and now I find myself making out with someone I'm pretty sure I don't like. No, I'm absolutely sure.

Finally, I peel myself away. "Marty, I'm sorry. But . . . I don't like you in that way."

"But the kiss?"

"You took me by surprise is all. You've never been forward before."

"Thought I'd try a different strategy." He looks to the floor, and I can see the tears rimming his eyes.

Goddess, how horrible could one mortal have been in their life?

"Well," he starts, "I'll just be going. But still friends, right?"

"Always."

My eyes shoot open in the pitch black of my room (I closed the curtains for once), and I try—and fail—to catch my breath.

"What the fuck was that?"

Chapter Six

Nothing quite like throwing up first thing in the morning, and that's how I find myself leaning over the toilet basin at five am the next day. What a way to start a Friday.

Ugh. All that training yesterday really wiped me out, and not to mention the severe lack of sleep all this dreaming and nightmare-ing is causing my already tired body.

Need to be at my morning yoga session in half an hour. Need to get up. Get out. Start my day.

I throw on some clothes after rinsing my mouth out as best I can and head to the garden, where I'm met by a surprisingly peaceful face.

Dea is waiting for me in my *Shinto* shrine, legs crossed and arms resting peacefully on each leg. His glossy black hair falls into his eyes, but he makes no effort to move the stray strands. He looks peaceful.

"Err, Dea?"

"Hmm?" He doesn't open his eyes; instead, he keeps them closed and continues audibly breathing.

"What're you doing?"

"Joining you." He opens his left eye. "Is that okay?"

"Err . . . sure."

I scoot him back slightly so I can have more room, and I begin stretching through my urge to yawn. Goddess, I'm tired. This is going to suck. This whole day is going to suck. Just the thought of Arrie's hand-to-hand combat training in an hour makes me want to crawl back into bed and hide under the duvet until sunset.

Nope, I tell myself, you need to train. You need to be better.

Okay, I can do this.

Stretching into my next pose, Dea interrupts. "About yesterday . . ."

Ugh, that's why he's here. Great. More humiliation.

"I am sorry." He steps up to me and pulls me to standing. "I might not have explained myself well, and now I feel like you might be feeling a little rejected."

He looks shy all of a sudden, and that cute look does nothing to quell the crazy tumbling of my insides; he's so damn gorgeous . . .

"Fucking damn it, Dea! Why are you so fucking hot?"

He blinks and chuckles. "What?"

"I can't ever be mad at you, you're just too attractive. It's annoying as hell." I bunch my fists at my sides. "Nine, too. He gives me that sad puppy-dog look, and I just melt. I swear, he could make me take a literal trip to hell with that look."

Dea's choking with laughter at this point. "I had no idea you were so caught up in us, Angel." He rests a hand on my cheek, and I find myself leaning into his warm touch. "I am not ashamed to admit that I want you. I just want you to be making the right choice."

I nod, swallowing back the tears. "I know. And you're

right." I sigh and hiccup. "I don't know what I want anymore."

"What happened to your plan?"

"What? The seduce-everyone-onto-my-side plan?" I laugh. "It was just a cute fantasy. It's never gonna happen. I don't need my own harem of lovers, Dea." Sighing, I roll my eyes.

He looks at me with a serious expression, all his usual charming smiles and warming eyes vanishing. "To live, to really live, you need to go after what you want and not just suffer with what you need." He brushes the tear that's fallen astray and leans in to kiss my forehead. "If you want us, come and get us."

Stepping back from him, I can't think straight. Is he saying he wants to . . . what? Be one of my lovers? That's . . . crazy. I can't have all of them, can I?

Dea turns to walk back inside, but at the last minute, he stops and turns to face me head on. "For the record, you already have me."

"I . . . I . . ."

Before I can think of anything to say, he fazes back to the house, leaving me standing in the center of the shrine on a misty Friday morning, tears running down my cheeks as a warm sort of nervous relief washes through me.

He . . . wants me? He wants this? All of this? To help me bring the team together and give everyone what they really want?

To give me what I want?

Yoga. C'mon, focus on the schedule. No time to ponder over Dea's declaration of . . . fondness. There're only a few days until our next mission, and I want to be able to actually help this time.

Hopefully, we'll stay together.

Once I'm halfway through my yoga routine, I change into my male form and complete the other half. I'll admit, my male form is much less flexible than my female form; it means I have to dumb down the second half of my routine.

"This is a pile of shit," I mumble to myself as I walk to Arrie's forest clearing.

The sky is cloudy today, and I remember reading that *Sheruta* has a rainy season in between each dry season. Must be coming up to a rainy season.

Arrie's waiting for me in the middle of the clearing and looks at me with surprise. "You gonna train in that form today?"

Oh. I look down at myself and remember that I can't be bothered to change back. "Yeah."

"Why?" He looks genuinely curious, but I can't ignore the accusation in his tone.

Lie: "Need to train both forms at some point. Why not now?" Truth: I'm exhausted and can't be arsed to change back.

Arrie nods and gestures for me to join him in the center. "I'm going to show you how to block better today. Now that I know what kind of stuff you're capable of."

Nodding, I walk on over to him.

He turns me around so that my back is to his front, and it reminds me of the precarious position he and Connie put me in yesterday.

Focus.

Right.

Arrie places his hands on my waist and turns my position so that I'm half side-on, half front-on. "Pull your elbows in, like Con showed you yesterday, and use your fists to protect your middle." He moves my hands into the right places and steps back. "There."

Turning around to my front, Arrie matches my stance. "Block."

And that is how we spend two hours, him trying to punch me, and me trying to block as best I can. Occasionally, he'll adjust my position or alter what I'm trying to do, but mostly, I learn through practice. The more I try to block his attacks, the more I find myself actually doing it.

Arrie isn't a talker, but that's okay because he's a good trainer. I'm actually learning under his instruction, and hopefully, all of this will come in useful on our mission.

Just three days to go. Then, I'll be ready. We'll be ready.

"Enough." Arrie wipes the sweat from his forehead with a towel, then throws it my way. "Breakfast."

I decide breakfast that morning doesn't apply to me. I just grab some buttered toast and run to the gym. Connie tries to protest, but I ignore her.

"She's gonna work herself to death at this rate," she says as I close the door.

"She needs to learn that for herself," Dea adds.

"Oh, don't you start with that wise old shit. You're adding to her problems!"

"Con, could you keep your voice do—" Nine tries to interrupt.

"Stop defending him. If you weren't prepared to actually fuck her, you shouldn't have led her on."

Dea interrupts her ranting. "I will have you know, I fixed that this morning. I apologized and explained myself better."

"Oh my fuck, what did you say to her now? Every time you open your mouth, you confuse her further!" Connie doesn't take any shit from the guys, and now she's extending that protection to me, it seems.

But I can't take any of them getting an ear-full just because of me, so I reopen the door and glare at her. "That's enough, Connie. It's fine. We have more important things to worry about."

She nods but still sits there glaring daggers at Dea, much to my pride. A girl's gotta have some female backup against these gorgeous-as-hell guys. And Connie is some seriously sexy back up.

CHAPTER SEVEN

After a day of training with sore limbs, torn muscles, and magical exhaustion permeating every second of Nine's study session, I can't wait to get into bed and go the fuck to sleep.

I didn't realize training would be this hard. Like, seriously, who the hell decided this is the way to get more badass? Whoever the fuck it was had terrible taste.

I crawled through my earlier gym session, with even the thought of Connie protecting my ridiculously delicate emotions from the guys not helping; my study session with Dea was awkward as hell for us both, his earlier declaration hanging over every second of learned knowledge; and now, with twenty minutes to go, I have still not managed to unlock a single other element.

Blowing out the frustration at my lack of progress in most areas, I ask the house for a glass of water and down it in one. I changed back into my female form earlier, having need of my Witch powers for magic study, but I'm itching to change back. Something about being female just doesn't sit right with me today. I don't even know what it is; it's like an unsettling feeling in the pit of my mind that I'm not who I'm meant to be right now.

"Okay, change back." Nine sighs. "I can't handle your inner frustration any longer, and I hate that I'm making you uncomfortable."

Relief floods through me.

I concentrate and manage to return to my male form in just under three minutes—a new record for me—and have both Nine and me smiling as we walk to dinner.

Today's dinner is pork ramen, and fuck me, it's amazing.

"Sooo . . ." Connie starts, and I can already tell what direction she's planned this conversation to go. "How was your afternoon?" She looks at me, then at Dea, and raises her eyebrows in a not-so-secret question.

Sighing, I answer, "Still a virgin, Connie."

Everyone splutters their food.

Oops, may have forgotten I said that only to Connie on one of our Friday night sleepovers. "You know, immortally speaking. I think."

Dea looks at me in shock while Arrie tries his best not to laugh. But Nine? Well, he just mentally says, *I can help with that,* and winks.

Internally, I sigh.

"You know what, Connie," I say as I turn to her, "let's do something fun tonight. Something without those three." I thumb-gesture to the others and smile.

Everyone pouts, even Arrie looks a little left out, but Connie smiles. "Yes! Training break!"

She loses herself to thought for a moment, and the entire table falls into a strange silence while Connie's internal wheels turn. But it isn't long before she bursts out laughing, and I have to ask her what's so funny.

"Nothing. But I have a great plan for this evening."

Nine looks at her in horror, and suddenly I'm worried. "Con, please don't. I don't think she'll—"

"Nonsense. She's spent enough time *with* you two that it'll be great fun."

"What's going on?" Nerves shoot through my system, and I can't help but be terrified by what the Horseman of Conquest might have me doing this evening.

"It's a surprise," she whispers and stares daggers at Nine.

Nine motions zipping his lips and looks at me with a facial apology. *Sorry. Don't murder me later.*

Err . . . okay.

"Meet me in your room in half an hour." She shoves the last bite of noodles into her mouth and runs off to goddess knows where.

"Okay." I look to Nine, expecting him to spill it. "C'mon, out with it!"

I hear Connie shout from somewhere in the house. "Don't you dare, you pretty little fucker!"

That has me laughing.

"I don't want to ruin the surprise." Nine leans over and whispers, "Just be prepared for anything."

Ugh. I'm not going to like this, am I?

Nine gives me a shrug, as though he doesn't really know if I'll like it or not.

Half an hour later, though, I'm sat on my bed after Connie has just come through the door, but it's what she's wearing that's worth note. A skin-tight, fake leather, strapless dress that barely comes down to her mid-thigh, with her hair loose and falling past her shoulders, landing at the floor in golden strands of beauty I'm still jealous of.

"Damn, Connie, you look . . . err . . . amazing!" I can't help the pooling of heat between my legs and the sudden urge to pick her up and kiss her that flies through my mind.

"Thank you." She turns to me and then looks at my closet. "Your turn."

I'm too busy staring at her to notice what she said, but when I do, my mind stutters. "W-Wait, what?" I rush over to her and grab her hand. "I don't think I can—"

"Nonsense. Male or female?"

I'm not sure which would be appropriate, so I shrug. "Which do you think?" I'm currently still in my male form, but I'll change if she prefers a girly night out. Doesn't really bother me.

"I think you'd feel more comfortable as a female, but honestly, either could work. Your choice."

Okay. If she thinks whatever this is will be better in my female form, then that's what I'll go with. Might as well trust her, 'cos I'm gonna kill her if she's taking me to some weird BDSM club or some shit.

"Okay, female it is. Though, I'm not sure I have something like"—I gesture to her outfit—"that."

She waves her hand at me, as if waving away my concern, and enters my closet. "Can always ask the house for it if you don't like any of my choices."

"Oh," I say, remembering my shopping trip, "Dea did make me pick up a couple of sluttier dresses, just in case they'd come in handy. Maybe one of those?"

Connie looks at me and smiles. "Yas! One hundred percent yes!"

"Over there." I point to the section of the closet I put them away in and grab the three I own. "Here."

Connie snatches them from my hands and runs out of the

closet, holding each one up to the light, assessing them, and placing them against me, until she settles on the one.

The one in question is a thin, strapless piece of material that I seriously hope will stretch when on because as it is now, it won't fit past my ass.

Sighing, I grab it and go back into the closet to change, shifting into my female form in the process. It does feel good to have my boobs back, but something about my tummy feels odd in this form right now. I can't put my finger on it. Oh well, it's just for one night.

Stretching the material (it is indeed stretchy, thank goddess) over my boobs, down my waist, and past my ass is easier than expected, and since it falls just past my ass by a few inches, I can safely assume I'm dressed appropriately for the occasion— given what Connie is wearing. The difference between her dress and mine, however, is that mine is made of something stretchy, and definitely not fake leather; plus, it shows my front tattoo off with its plunging neckline. I match it with some sexy underwear I'm hoping no one will get to see (hey, a girl's gotta feel sexy every now and then), and step out of the closet.

Connie wolf whistles upon my arrival, and I blush hard at the compliment.

She thinks I look good?

"You look amazing, hon. Truly." She comes over and asks me to spin for her, so I do. "Your tattoo is looking awesome, too."

"I know, right?" I beam at her, glad to have some regular, girly moments in my ever-complicated life. "So, can I get a hint?"

She shakes her head.

"Anything?!"

She laughs. "Okay, okay. We're going to a show."

That's it? Why is Nine so worried? I've been to shows before.

She's not telling you the whole truth.

Figures. Of course she would do that. There's gonna be something odd or unusual about this show, isn't there?

Nine doesn't answer. Of course he doesn't. But I take his not answering as a sign that, yes, it probably has something different about it.

But what?

"You hate not knowing, don't you?" Connie looks at me as we descend the stairs.

I nod. "I hate feeling out of the loop."

She laughs. "This is a sucky time in your life for that."

"Tell me about it."

Nine and Dea's wolf whistles reach my ears before we even make the turn on the staircase and come into view. All three guys stand at the bottom of the stairs, just like at the ball, and just like then, they're all staring. But this time, Arrie does not hide his appreciation for how I look. He eyes me head to foot and gives me a flirtatious smirk I haven't seen before.

We've really made progress since we talked during the ball preparations, and so far, we've managed to be friends. I love how caring he really is behind all that grumpiness.

"Damn, Sweetie, Dea was right, that dress is fucking amazing!" He asks me to twirl like Connie did, and I oblige.

Strong hands grab my sides, ones I would recognize anywhere. Dea leans down and whispers, "You look radiant, and a prime article of splendor, Angel."

He twirls me around on his foot and places me gently next to Nine, who grabs me in his usual bear-hug kind of way and squeezes tight. Well, he tries.

Arrie comes up to me next and looks down at me like I'm going to be his next meal, his tongue flicking across his lips and his eyes piercing mine. My heart flutters and skips a beat as I melt into his ice-blue eyes, and a cool smirk flits across his face. "You do look nice, Killer." He leans down and whispers, "Keep it up, and you might melt the rest of my stony exterior."

So he can be flirtatious?

Connie grabs my hand before I can force the big guy into a hug, and she drags me off into the night beyond the open front door. She laughs as we walk down the pathway that heads into town and teases me non-stop the entire way.

"And you thought you couldn't have us all. Look at those three back there. They were practically drooling over you."

"Us," I remind her with a shiver against the cold evening air. "They were drooling over us." I grab her arm and link mine through it. "And I wouldn't have it any other way."

"Really?" She seems uncertain, and I think I might understand the reason why.

"Connie, I don't want you to feel like I'm stealing them away from you. If they're paying you less attention because of me, please just say so. I'll kick their asses. We're a team in this, remember?"

She smiles at that. "It's not that, but thanks for caring. I just . . . I've never been in a relationship with any member of the team before. And what you're doing to the team, to all of us, is feeling more and more like a relationship every day." At my confused face, she explains, "We were just friends with benefits before—maybe a bit more family-like and a few feelings between Dea and Nine—but nothing more."

Ah. "So now I've added feelings and romance into the mix, you're feeling a little uncertain?"

She nods, looking oddly shy for someone of her confidence.

"We're in this together." I squeeze her hand. "All of us."

She nods and speeds up. "C'mon, the show starts soon."

"What show?"

She just laughs and drags us to the center of town in half the time it would usually take. Once there, though, I can see the Witch lights illuminating the streets like Christmas, and the Witch marks on the ground lighting the way around the most populated areas of town.

"Wow! This place looks amazing!"

"I forgot you haven't been here at night yet."

I shake my head but smile at her. When I turn to look at her, however, I'm dazzled by how her eyes now seem to glow a brilliant green-orange in the Witch lights, the nearest one clearly being the effector—it glows bright orange.

"Hon?"

She breaks me out of my reverie, and I find myself blushing. "S-Sorry. What were you saying?"

"We need to go that way." She points down the main street but looks at me with a smile. "You okay?"

I nod, not trusting words to come out okay right now. This is like a . . . date. Like? This is a date, isn't it? I . . . err . . . kinda like it.

"What's going through your mind?"

We walk toward the entrance of a grand building with old-fashioned theater strips around the upper ceiling of the front stoop. In bright lights, the show listing tonight is: FORBIDDEN MAGIC. A dancing man and woman sign flashes next to the words, and my mouth drops open.

We're going to a sexy strip show?

"Hon?"

"Oh." I shake my head, trying to remember what she said. "I was just thinking that this is like a date."

"Well, I hope so, because that's exactly what this is." She rushes us to the queue forming at the ticket booth. Once in line, she turns and asks, "This is okay, right? Not too much?"

I frown at her in confusion for a moment, before I realize she must be talking about the show. "Oh, that. Yeah, this should be fun."

"Sure?"

I lower her head to whisper, "Nothing can be as hot as watching Dea and Nine." I let her back up as we approach the ticket booth.

"Too true." She laughs. "Lucky!"

"You've never watched?"

"No one has. They're really private about their relationship." She shrugs. "We all are, actually."

I stand there, dumbfounded, as I suddenly realize why Dea was shocked Nine invited me to watch that day. They'd never done that before.

I'm gonna kill that nerdy fucker!

"Next!" the young ticketer calls from his old-fashioned booth.

We skip forward, Connie with a cash chip in hand, and pay for two front-row tickets to what promises to be a sexy show.

"So, are the people in the show locals or a group that comes to *Sheruta* every now and then?" I ask as we make our way inside.

"They're locals, but they tour everywhere and are hardly ever in *Sheruta* anymore. They've gained a little fame over the years. You'll see why."

The entire theater is old-fashioned, with large red drapes covering a Victorian-looking stage, upper balconies gilded in golden-looking ornate designs covering its architecture, plush red chairs and sofas dotting everywhere in some semblance of structure, and the ushers dressed in red three-piece suits from a whole different century. It's like I've stepped back in time.

"C'mon." Connie takes hold of my hand and rejects the usher's offer of assistance in finding our seats. "Let's get seated. I don't want you to miss a moment."

I giggle at her and am off, the usual girliness overcoming me like it usually does when I'm alone with Connie.

"Have you seen this show before?" We find our seats pretty easily, given that Connie knows exactly where she's going.

"Yeah. It's one of mine and Nine's favorites. We come and see it together every time they're in-realm." Guilt floods me, and it's clearly written all over my face because she waves away my concerns. "I got Dea to bring him tomorrow. They're here for two nights."

Relief washes over me, feeling slightly better that Nine wouldn't miss the show but still a little guilty because I bet one of the reasons he likes coming is that it gives him some time with Connie without the other guys. It's like a them thing.

"Maybe next time we could go all three of us together?"

Connie smiles. "He'd like that. I'd like that."

"Me too."

The curtains raise, and a steady beat rings out from the soundstrip all around the arena. "And now . . . the night you've all been waiting for. This year's Forbidden Nights show!"

Everyone erupts into a chorus of cheers, whoops, and claps, and I can't help but join in; their joy's infectious, and I can see how much Connie enjoys this, as momentarily she forgets I'm there and rises to her feet to holler along with everybody else.

Yup, I can see Nine here. Clapping along and being his usually excitable self alongside Connie. They would make a cute couple, but I don't think either of them sees each other that way.

The announcer walks on stage, dressed in nothing but a white pair of sweatpants glowing in the club-like lights shining from the ceiling. He clearly works out, and although I can appreciate him, I can't keep my mind from thinking that he has nothing on any of the men back at the house.

Connie clearly sees exactly where my thoughts have gone. "You'll spend your entire immortal life disappointed if you constantly compare every man to the other Horsemen. Trust me." She sighs. "They've been working out for two millennia and have it down to an art."

The show, much to my surprise, is milder than I anticipated. I'm not sure what I expected, but they stay covered (albeit, in a tantalizing way) where it counts. Everything else is on show, though, and nothing is left to the audience's imagination.

Connie spends the entire time drooling over one of the men in particular, who puts on an amazing strip show with full-body paint that glows various colors under the fancy lighting. He's a Fae. She must have a real thing for Fae.

"He's your favorite, huh?"

"Yup! Aaron is my fantasy piece of cream pie," she whispers in my ear at the part of show that's silent.

"He is dreamy."

"So," she starts, "who's your favorite?"

"I'm not sure." I think back to the duo performance at the beginning; they were twins, and they both looked hot as hell, and I'm not ashamed to admit that particular fantasy played on my mind the entire show. "The twins from the beginning."

She looks at me a little shocked, as though she didn't expect that answer. "I think you'll fit in with Nine and Dea brilliantly."

"Why?"

She looks a little shy all of a sudden, something she's been doing all evening. Why is her confidence not its usual self this evening? "Because apparently they threesome well. They know each other really well and can work together without verbal cues given Nine's telepathy."

Right, she's never threesome'd with any of the guys before. Maybe I could persuade her someday?

I give her a questioning look. "How do you know that?"

She points to her ear.

"Right. Hearing." I laugh. "I forget about that a lot."

"I know." She smiles at me suggestively. "It's brilliant."

What has she heard? Goddess, I hope not anything too embarrassing.

She laughs at my spiraling thoughts and puts her hand on my shoulder. "Don't worry. Nothing I won't hear and see for myself eventually." She returns to the show.

I give an exasperated shake of my head and laugh.

By the time the show ends, I've sat through so many naked and topless men dancing to various routines and putting on special performances that I'm well and truly worked up.

Damn, I can see why Connie and Nine like this show.

"Sooo," Connie asks in her usual gossip-y way, "did you like it?"

"Oh my goddess, yes! It was awesome!"

"Hah! And Nine thought it might be a bit much. I knew you were more like me than Dea."

"Not Dea's thing?"

She shrugs. "He's more into private, behind-closed-doors kinda stuff."

"What kinda stuff?" Okay, so I'm fishing. Sue me. I have tempered my curiosity long enough.

"Nope. Nuh-uh." She crosses her arms over her chest. "We are not doing that."

"Doing what?" I feign innocence.

"I'm not telling you what it's like fucking the guys because then a) it'll ruin the surprise, and b) you'll get all jealous and shit."

I stop mid-step, causing her to have to step back to meet me. "I'm not the jealous type. Especially with the team. You could have your own orgy, and I would be content to watch and have fun."

Damn, I cannot believe I just said that out loud, nor how true the words are. What's wrong with me? Fuck, fuck, fuck.

Connie sees my surprised expression and laughs, then hugs me tight. "Don't be horrified, that's kinda hot."

"Really?"

She nods. "Definitely."

We walk back to the house hand-in-hand, chatting endlessly about the show and generally having a fun time, but we're met by three thundering faces upon arrival. We took our time walking home, taking almost a full two hours rather than the usual thirty minutes.

"What time do you call this?" Dea asks as we step into the foyer.

"Err, hi guys, we're home?" I say in a questionable tone. "We're home from the show. Sorry it's dark. We're not children." I list off each item on my mental to-do list and walk past them all to the kitchen.

"You were gone for hours!" Nine whines.

Connie's getting just as irritated by them as me because she snaps, "You've been before! Countless times. You know exactly how long their show lasts. And we took a slow walk home." She sighs. "If you're that jealous, arrange your own dates."

I nod in agreement. "It was fun. Deal with it."

Arrie seems the least jealous of the three (which in itself is a miracle) and leans against the doorway, more at ease now he's seen we're both okay.

I go about making myself my nightly cup of coffee when Dea fusses from behind, checking me over, making sure I'm okay. "Fuck off, Dea! I'm fine."

"Yeah," Connie says from behind, "she was with me for crying out loud. What did you think would happen?"

He shrugs, suddenly looking to the ground in a bright shade of red. "We were just . . . worried. The last time you went anywhere alone with one of us, a rogue group of Vampires attacked."

Connie meets my gaze, and equal looks of guilt snap between us. Shit, of course they're worried. The ball was only a few days ago.

"Sorry," I mumble, "I didn't think about that." I dust myself off and give a twirl. "But I'm fine." I grab Dea's hand and place it on my cheek. "Promise."

He sighs into my touch when I place my hands around his neck, and suddenly the rest of the team's staring doesn't matter. It's just us, and I really want to kiss him, to feel those soft lips against mine—decidedly, I want more than just those lips, but that's probably all the tension from the show.

Before I can decide what to do with that thought, he leans down and places a gentle, chaste kiss to my lips before pulling away.

Smiling, I return to my coffee, stirring in a heap of sugar, and head to bed, trying to ignore the knowing smiles all four pairs of eyes send my way as I walk out of the room.

Halfway up the stairs, Nine interrupts. *You really enjoyed the show?*

Yeah, it was fun. Now, if you don't mind, it's left me needing some time away from all of you. You're all way too hot to be around right now.

He mentally chuckles, and I can picture his head shaking.

Chapter Eight

Saturday and Sunday consist of more training—with a break Saturday night for Nine and Dea's date to the FORBIDDEN NIGHTS show—but it's easier with the lightness of Friday night on my mind. Somehow, having fun makes everything easier.

Should do it more often.

Nine stands opposite me in my training room—topless— the fire glowing against his tanned skin as he tries to show me a way of relaxing my magical center, hoping it'll entice a calm element out of hiding, like water. But so far, all it's doing is distracting me. (I mean, have you tried relaxing when a hot as hell Horseman of the Apocalypse sits opposite you with no top on? If not, then let me tell you, it's distracting as fuck!)

While Nine clearly finds my predicament funny and a great ego boost, he's frustrated with my lack of progress.

"Can you not think of sex for a single minute?"

"Says the not Vampire," I mumble under my breath. "I'd change into my Fae form, but we really wouldn't be able to access my Witch powers that way. Plus, it'd distract everyone else."

Fae forms have evolved to be particularly alluring; since their species almost died out, their magic has evolved and stepped in, making them more appealing to breed with. I still find the entire thing ridiculous, but hey, who am I to argue with magical biology?

I'm starting to think Dea and Nine are right, up keeping a healthy diet of blood while not having sex is difficult. I've read in some of my research that it can send mortal Vampires crazy if it goes on long enough, and there hasn't been a recorded case of anyone lasting longer than a month without starving themselves of blood.

You'll need to feed properly eventually, Sweetie.

I ignore him, trying not to think about it. I'm a Horseman, immortal, and we don't need to eat, meaning I don't need to feed. I'll be fine.

You don't know that.

"Oh my goddess, Nine, shut up!" I take an attempt at a calming breath but exhale in frustration when it doesn't work. "Just leave me alone!"

"You need to feed properly. Eventually, it will leave you too unstable to function."

"This is all your fault to begin with. I should never have started drinking blood, and this would never have happened."

"You know that's not the point," he growls.

"What's going on?" Connie stands in the doorway, clearing having heard our argument and brought Dea along with her—probably for a faster trip.

"Nothing." I growl, forgetting I'm not in my male form with Shifter magic, so it comes out as more of a pathetic mewl. "Study my magic without me."

I hear Nine sigh, but I don't care.

Deep down, I know he's right, but I don't have an answer, so I remain as frustrated as ever. Storming out of the library, I grab my coat—it has started raining as the rain season began—and slam the front door shut behind me.

Cake. Decent cake. That's what I need. Then I'll be right as rain. I internally chuckle at my joke given the season and speed in to town at top Vampire speed, getting there in under a minute.

The café is empty when I arrive, and that's when I realize it's probably close to closing, given that it's four in the afternoon.

"'Ello there." The baker stands at the cash register and waves at me upon entry. "Can I 'elp?"

I walk up, trying to smooth my hair down to resemble some modicum of normality. "Cake. Cake and coffee." I gasp lungfuls of air as I bend over to catch my breath.

The baker laughs. "That bad a day, Miss . . . ?"

I grunt my frustration at my lack of a name. "Don't have a name yet."

He looks at me with sad eyes but nods his understanding.

"And yes, my life has become complicated in the last few weeks. To say the least."

He nods as he gathers a collection of pastries and cakes onto a mini platter. "I can only imagine, Miss. Being the Fifth Horseman and dealing with the upcoming war . . . Must be awful work."

"Ha. That's not even the problem. That I can deal with." Hopefully. "It's . . . never mind." I wave off my words, hoping to get out of talking.

"They can be difficult, can't they?"

I take my cake and sit in a comfy-looking armchair in the corner of the café.

I . . . I don't even know where to start. Nine's right. All I think of recently is sex and war, and it's driving me nuts. I can barely focus on anything, and it's probably my Vampire nature reacting to the blood. Dea did mention Vampires need a healthy lifestyle of both to remain functional, just like Witches need nature. I just didn't think that would apply to me. You know, given that I am immortal.

But it's not like they help. They're all so . . . Argh!

"Wanna talk about it?"

Startled, I look up to see Connie standing above me.

"How did you get here so quickly?"

"Dea gave me a lift."

She points to Dea, who stands outside the café in the rain, and I laugh as how appropriate he looks standing there all sopping wet in his black jeans, black tee, and boots, his face a solemn frown as his lip piercings dull in the rain.

She grabs a chair and sits opposite. "C'mon, spill."

"I'm really not in a gossiping mood."

"Not gossiping this time. Real talk." She looks at me with raised eyebrows.

I sigh. "I couldn't focus in magic study, since Nine was sat there topless like it was fucking nothing. He got frustrated that I couldn't keep my thoughts straight, and it reminded me of what Dea had said about Vampires, blood, and sex."

She seems to piece the puzzle together from there. "It's starting to affect you, huh?"

"I think so."

She grabs my hand and squeezes it. "You know we're not your only options, right? You can sleep with anyone."

I laugh and shake my head. I . . . don't want that. But if it comes down to it, what choice do I have? The guys are being difficult, I don't want to ruin anything between me and Connie, and Arrie . . . I haven't even let myself the luxury of thinking about it.

"I just want . . ."

Connie sits there patiently, not pressing or laughing, actively listening.

"I want it to be special. To mean something." I sigh. "I think it's something I wanted as a mortal, too." I down the rest of my coffee. "I want it to be one of you."

She smiles, a slow blush creeping up her face and neck. "I don't know what to say."

"There is nothing to say. I want something I can't have. Again." I want to wait, to do things right, but unless I can fight this war without feeding my Vampire side, I won't get that choice. "It's fine. I'll deal."

"That's not—"

"It's fine, Connie."

I get up and go to pay, using the payment chip Nine gave me a few days ago. "Thank you," I say to the baker. "Your deserts always cheer me up." I do my best to fake a smile, but it doesn't seem to work.

He gives me a sad smile in return. "One day, you'll have peace, Miss."

"I sure hope so."

Chapter Nine

The next morning, we're all getting ready when Nine knocks on my door, a bag in hand. "Here." He chucks it on to the bed and unzips it.

He pulls out a set of throwing daggers. "They're hollow, so they'll fly better." He then pulls out a chip. "Use this when buying anything on Earth." I nod as he pulls out an old-fashioned mobile phone, but this one looks more modern. "Use this to stay in contact with us over long distances."

I grab it and fumble with various buttons, trying to find which one turns the display on.

"You do know how to use one of those, right?"

I shake my head. "No one uses these anymore. We just use our datachips for communication and a plasmascreen for research."

He grumbles something about kids these days and spends twenty minutes showing me what buttons do what, how to phone people—phone people, like in the movies!—and how to use all its basic functions.

He goes to leave, but I grab his hand and pull him back. "Nine, I . . ."

He holds out his hand, but something about the look on his face tells me he really is hurt. "It's fine."

I shake my head. "No, it's not. I shouldn't have snapped at you. You were just trying to help." I've already decided how I'm going to make it up to him, so I yank him into my arms and hug him as tightly as possible without causing him too much harm.

I try to hide my thoughts, and hopefully I succeed because he seems surprised when I pull his face to mine and press my lips to his.

Kiss me. Please.

He melts under me, his shoulders loosening and his hands beginning to wander up my back and into my hair. As our tongues slide together and I sigh into the relief of finally being with Nine.

Breaking away, he gasps. "Sweetie, why?"

Because I like you.

But . . . I thought, Dea—

I do like Dea—he's alluring in a way I haven't seen in anyone else—but you're the most amazingly caring person I've ever met. Watching you be your amazing self and not kissing you has been like walking through a desert with no water.

I grab him by his shirt, yank him the rest of the way toward me, and tumble us both onto the bed.

What are you doing?

Enjoying you.

His smile beneath my lips holds the promise of long summer nights spent under the stars, the guarantee I'll always be taken care of by this man, the security of knowing he will never hurt me. I can't help but smile back.

Always.

I would be lying if I said I didn't want you, but I want it to be right. The moment, the time, us . . . I want it to be . . .

Loving?

I cringe at his use of the L-word but sigh my acquiescence. Yes.

Let me help you.

He climbs from underneath me and rolls us so that he's on top, his arms resting on the pillows beneath me. One arm lifts, and he shifts his weight onto the one elbow as he moves his hand down my body, grazing gentle thumbs over the thin material of my t-shirt and bra.

I gasp into his mouth, and he groans in response.

I've always wanted to know what you sound like for myself.

As his hand travels lower, brushing over the hem of my shirt and reaching the skin beneath, I lift my hips to meet his and feel his hardened cock beneath his jeans rub against my clit.

Not holding back, I groan into his embrace.

"Nine, I . . . I . . ."

"Yes?" He trails a gentle finger along the rim of my trousers.

I can't handle his teasing anymore and buck my hips to gain some kind of friction—anything. I need him. "Please . . . Help me." At the thought of his cock in my hand, the familiar ache of my gums signaling the descending of my fangs overtakes my body.

He chuckles. "You shouldn't have left it this long, Sweetie."

He's right.

His hand delves deeper, underneath the material of my pants and panties, and trails two teasing fingers along my clit, making me gasp.

Kiss me.

He places rough lips against mine and trails needy kisses along my jaw, all the way down my neck, before coming back up and licking my fangs.

Need pulses all the way from my fangs to my clit, and I give an involuntary thrust of my hips as I hold in a light moan of pleasure. Fuck, those are sensitive.

Don't hold back.

The echoing sounds of footsteps outside of my bedroom door meets my ears, and I grumble.

"I . . . err . . ." I'm honestly caught between some sense of modesty and the insatiable need coursing through me. I want him—need him. But I don't want to be caught naked by the others if we continue.

Let them catch us. They all want to fuck you anyway.

At that, Nine moves his fingers in slow circles, massaging my clit, and I swear I can hear the blood rushing through the artery in his neck.

"Dea," I hear Connie warn from outside the door, "I don't think that's a good ide—"

Just as Nine presses harder, easing another moan from my lips, Dea bursts through the door and stands frozen at the sight of us tangled up in each other on the bed.

My moaning echoes through the silence, and heat flushes my already red features.

Connie and Arrie stand behind him, both looking awkward.

"We were . . . looking for you both."

I jump up from underneath him and readjust my clothes. "Knock next time!"

"Bro, seriously?" Nine looks just as pissed. Even his lack of fangs doesn't take away from the menace on his face. "I was helping her!"

Helping? He was only doing that to . . . help me?

Nine sighs. "No, obviously not. That's not what I meant."

I growl under my breath and storm into the bathroom to straighten up.

Nine sighs as I shut the door. "Seriously? Now she's mad at me again?"

"Then don't say stupid shit!" Connie yells at him.

As I pull my panties down, I totally understand why I'm having tummy cramps. Period. Ugh, great. I don't even have anything here to help. No tampons. Nothing.

That's why I'm preferring my male form right now. No cramps, less hormones, etc. Wait a minute . . .

Concentrating for a few minutes, I shift into my male form and the cramps are gone. Like magic. I laugh at myself. I'm still frustrated but not nearly as hormonally charged. And bonus, no cramps, blood, or other period nonsense.

I come out of the bathroom to everyone's surprised faces, but they quickly shrug and roll with it.

Only Nine laughs, knowing the truth behind my choice. *Connie is going to be so pissed.*

Why?

After two thousand years of periods, she's fed up of them, and you just come along and manage to avoid them.

Oh. She's gonna kill me, isn't she?

Nah. She's totally falling for you. She wouldn't lay a finger on you. Well, she might if you ask her nicely.

We all head to the Earth portal packed and ready to kick some Vampire ass. I'm going to make them pay for what they did to Nine. The portal in question is just as shit as last time; and just like last time, I nearly hurl my guts up upon arrival.

"You have a weak stomach in both forms," Nine points out

in his usual nerd tone.

"Gee, thanks for that assessment." I bend over my chair, trying not to cover the pretty foliage covering the floor in vomit.

Dea hands me another gingersnap, and I thank him. Aren't anti-sickness spells a thing nowadays? And if not, then why the hell not?

If I'm going to have two sexes, can I at least not puke my guts up in one of them? Ugh. For fuck's sake.

After having stood up with the help of Connie and Nine and devouring my gingersnap, we head outside, where I'm reminded of one of the greater things in my immortal life. The cars!

Fuck yes, I forgot about those.

"Shotgun!" I start humming some song from one of my playlists before I add, "I don't care who I'm riding with."

You should ride with Arrie. He's a great driver.

"Nine says I should ride with you," I say as I walk on up to Arrie to where he stands beside the beautiful black Aperta 9000X.

Arrie looks at me with a scowl—oh, how I've missed those scowls—and crosses his arms over his chest.

"Oh c'mon, big guy." I laugh. "It'll be fun!"

He smirks and gives in, looking at Connie with an apology.

"It's okay," she says through a chuckle of her own. "I'll ride with Nine."

And so, I get into the passenger seat of Arrie's car while the others get into theirs, and off we go, racing down the highway at ungodly speeds, a giant smile on my face.

"You really like cars, don't you?" Arrie manually changes gears, his shirt sleeve rolled up to his elbow as he shifts the stick. "You never smile like you are now."

I blush. Did he just compliment me? "Arrie . . . can I ask you something?"

"Sure."

"Why are you being so nice to me?"

He quickly looks my way with raised eyebrows, then turns his attention back to the road we're going down at over three hundred mph. Sighing, he answers, "I had a change of heart, I guess."

"Was it because you heard of my fantasy plan?"

"W-What?"

Aha! Got him. "Nine mentioned it's the kind of relationship you wanted with the team back in the early days . . ."

He groans, and if he weren't driving, he probably would have placed a frustrated hand through his long white hair. "He shouldn't have told you that."

"Sorry, but I know lots of things about the team." I wink at him. "If you wanted to get your own back, now's the time."

He smiles but shakes his head. "It's okay. Maybe one day." I can see the wheels turning in that pretty head of his and wonder what his plan is. "You're an amazing person, Taylor."

I flinch at the use of my mortal name, and I can feel the pinpricks of tears edging my vision as I remember all that name symbolizes—all the death, the lies, and the destruction.

"You manage to get along with all four of us because you fit perfectly in this team. It's like you were made for us."

That has my wheels turning. "You think Fate intended it to be that way?"

He shrugs. "Dunno. Never really been a big believer in Fate. Not like the others. Maybe?"

Goddess, watching this guy drive is making my cock hard, and the faint echo of Nine's fingers running over my skin ignites the memory of where that would have gone.

"I'm gonna kill Dea later. The fucking wet drip," I mumble under my breath.

Apparently loud enough for Arrie to hear, as he looks over to the very noticeable bulge in my pants and laugh.

"Con mentioned you were starting to have problems . . . ?"

He's fishing, and I'm not even mad. I just nod. "All the blood is making my female form insane. But in this form, I feel fine, if a little flushed at the memory of Nine."

"We're pretty open people, you can just chat to us about it, you know."

"We're not the chatting type, Arrie. I think this is the longest conversation I've ever had with you."

He laughs at that, and it sends those familiar bubbles of happiness through me. "Driving makes me a little more . . . me, I guess." He shrugs.

"Well, I like you." I backtrack. "This you." Sighing, I give up.

Foot, meet mouth.

But Arrie isn't laughing, he's . . . blushing? "That is why I like you."

"Why, because I actually like you?"

That doesn't make sense.

"Because you cared enough to look beneath the surface in the first place."

We turn off at the same junction as last time, heading toward that familiar quaint cottage in the familiarly quaint town. With the stupid leylines.

"Ugh, who the fuck designed these lines?"

"I know." Arrie growls, the deep rumble echoing through the tense air, and I can feel my cock throb in response.

That's . . . unexpected. Wonder what kind of things this guy can do while driving? Damn. Should have asked earlier.

He could probably fuck you and drive at the same time. He's got serious driving skills.

Damn. I have a new appreciation for those skilled hands that're parking us just outside the Colorado safe house. And driving while having sex? Something I really want to try in the future.

Not like I can die, right?

You're gonna be a handful, aren't you?

Chapter Ten

"So," Connie asks once we've all sat down and ordered take out, "what's the plan?"

She directs the question to Dea, but he looks at me expectantly. He wants me to plan this? I don't think that's such a good idea.

"I, err . . ." I cough to clear my throat. "We find the rogue Vampires, fight to the top, and interrogate him?" I shrug my shoulders.

Dea sighs. "Okay, so strategy might need to be included in our lessons." He stands and hands out the same equipment as last time: teleportation crystal, stungun, and a regular pistol. "We will hunt down the rogues, get them to take us to see their leader, or whoever, and then we will chat with him. Or her."

But I want to fight them . . . Oh well, guess there are more important things to worry about. Like who's controlling the rogues, who they're partnered with, and are they working for the SC?

My muscles ache from all the training, and the thought of sleeping on this sofa has me swallowing a low growl.

I'll sleep with Dea. You can have my room.

Thank you.

After endless chatter, me staying mostly out of it, and a few yawns, Nine's had enough. "Of to bed with you." He yanks me off the sofa and scoots me out the door.

"I'm not a child!"

"Then stop acting like one. Go to bed when you're tired!" He shoves me up the stairs and leads me to his bedroom. "It's this one." He points to the first door on the left.

"Thanks," I mumble through a yawn.

"Go to bed, Sweetie." He wraps an arm around my waist and pulls me in for a hug. "We'll regroup in the morning."

I nod and leave to go to bed, but he pulls me back last minute. He grabs my shirt collar, yanks me forward, and pins me to the nearest wall. When his lips meet mine, I'm transported back to my bedroom at the house, his hands running all over me, and the amazing orgasm he would have given me . . .

I can finish what I started, if you'd like?

My cock throbs at his words, and he damn well knows it, as he rubs his hand over the tip through my pants, causing me to let out a groan.

Even your male form is affected by your Vampire needs. Fucking you is going to be my life's greatest pleasure. However, I'm going to wait.

A groan of protest slips through my lips, making him chuckle.

Sorry. But what you said earlier about wanting it to mean something? I . . . I'm going to make it mean everything.

He pulls away, running one last stroke down my stiff erection, sending an impulsive shiver up my spine, and goes back downstairs.

I, on the other hand, go to bed.

The next morning, we all head to New Orleans—have to start somewhere, and New Orleans is Vampire central. On the plane, which is even more annoying now the entire team are here and I have more than just Dea's mindless chatter to contend with, I start to formulate some kind of plan.

It'll be a good idea to at least ask the Vampire Royal Council what they know, therefore working with them and keeping good ties, and at the same time they might genuinely be able to help. They seem to listen to Dea, so maybe sending him might be a good plan. I want to find that young Vampire Prince and grill him about the end of my mortality; plus, he's the one who started everything with the Vampires and the SC to begin with, so he might be a good person to chat with.

But what to do with Nine, Connie, and Arrie?

What are the main objectives?

1. To find the group of rogue Vampires who attacked us at the ball.

2. To speak to their leader (with Dea's help).

3. To learn who they work for and/or with.

But how does one achieve that?

By causing a scene.

Seems I'm going to be particularly useful on this mission after all.

When we land an hour later, I've finalized my plan before the wheels touch the tarmac.

"Dea?" I look his way, waking him up from whatever thought trance he's in. "Where are we staying?"

He grimaces, but Connie steps in. "Nope. We are staying in a proper hotel. Not some cheap, rundown motel." She sighs and looks at me. "Unless our plan requires us to be covert?"

She has such hope in her eyes that even if I did need us to stay hidden, I'm not sure I could have stood my ground.

"No," I say, smiling at her.

"Thank fuck." She grabs my hand. "In that case, I have a great idea." She drags me along and hails a cab from outside the airport once we've grabbed our luggage.

The cab ride's tricky, since Dea can't go visible yet and there aren't enough seats. I make him sit on Nine's lap, much to Nine's annoyance, since Dea keeps purposefully wiggling around, giving Nine a very obvious hard-on that everyone who isn't us can see.

Connie and I find the whole ordeal hilarious, hiding our snickering behind coughs and hiccups the entire journey.

It's upon arrival, though, that I have to really cough at my choked surprise. "We're staying here?"

Connie nods while Dea groans.

Here—the hotel in question—is not what I expected, even given Connie's more flamboyant nature. The *Lucifer's Devil* hotel is well-known throughout the world as one of the more openly-minded hotels. Okay, so real talk: it has a Vampire live feeding menu, a menu with your personal choice of on-staff hookers, and various sex-themed rooms.

"We're really staying here?"

"Con, are you serious?" Nine steps up beside me. "What if that's not what Sweetie wanted? Did you even think to ask?"

Connie stops in her tracks, her smile falling into a frown. "Oh, well, no . . . I didn't. I just assumed you might find it fun?" I don't think she meant it as a question, but it came out as one.

I shrug and walk on in.

Nine? Own rooms or are we sharing? Tell me what to do

so I can walk up to the desk all confident and swagger-like. C'mon, help a guy-girl out.

He chuckles and says, *Own rooms.*

I walk up to a posh-looking lady with blonde hair, red-polished nails, and a lip-line to die for. Like, seriously, I would die for those fucking lips.

"Hello," she says with a sickeningly sweet smile. "What can I do for you?" She looks up from her plasmascreen and notices me, eye fucking my entire body from where she sits behind the desk.

Ugh. Stupid Fae form.

"Five rooms please. All on the same floor, as close together as possible."

Dea makes himself visible and places a card on the desktop—it's gold and has the logo for the SC on it, which I guess gets us into more places than I can manage on my own.

She coughs to cover her surprise and looks in the system. After a few seconds, she smiles at me and hands me five separate keys. "They're the only rooms available that are all next to each other. Any preferences on who goes where?"

I shake my head.

"Very well. I'll book you all in now. Names?"

We all give fake names, and she gives us each a random key, mine with a dangling handcuff keyring. Using keys is a bit old-fashioned nowadays, but I guess it adds to the general feel of the place. The black-and-red décor theming this hotel definitely gives the devil's vibe, and it gets me thinking if this at all offends Nine and Arrie, given their demon-descended powers.

Nah. We got over that a long time ago.

Oh. Well, I guess you would learn to move past things when you're that old.

I'm not that old, he jokes.

I don't give him a response, just in case he's age sensitive—but the very thought has me holding in a laugh so hard I end up snorting and making Nine laugh harder. An immortal who's age sensitive? Ha!

Arrie grabs our wrists and drags us, I assume, to our rooms. Dea looks at us with a scowl and mumbles something about stupid children while Connie just smiles at me in a way that suggests she might find me and Nine adorable.

We all head up to the top floor, where there are five rooms in this wing of the hotel. How convenient. I find my room, which is sandwiched between Connie's and Nine's (not a bad sandwich if you ask me), and enter, dragging my bag behind me.

My bag tumbles to the floor with a thump upon entering, however, as surprise shocks my system. I didn't know they made hotel rooms like this!

The whole room is black and pink, with the wall behind the biggest bed I've ever seen striped in a hot pink, matte-black combo that has me jealous I don't have the personality for a room like this back at the house. The bed is the black cashmere kind with silver jewels studded along at various intervals and has attached metal bed poles on the ends of the headboard. I can take a pretty good guess what those are used for.

The room is bigger than any kind of bedroom I've ever seen (including Connie's, and that's saying something); it has a sunken hot tub in the glossy back floor opposite the bed with pink rose petals scattered around the rim. The room has a loving, feminine, light BDSM vibe going on that I actually rather like. If I were in a romantic relationship, this would be kinda cool, but I'm not, so it just kinda sucks.

I empty the contents of my bag onto the bed and start carefully putting away my clothes, shoes, weapons, and assortment of things. Although I'm in my male form, I really need to go and buy some lady things, just in case my Witch or Vampire powers are needed.

Nine?

Yeah.

Just popping to a shop quickly, then I'll be back and want to run through my plan with everyone.

Okay.

There, I've let the overprotective men of the team know where I'm going; now, I just have to find a shop and be back before anyone freaks out.

The shop I find myself in is one of those massive grocery stores, with the plasmascreen shelves where you can scan each item that you require using your datachip, or a chip card in my case, as you shop, and then you go to the collection point, grab your items, pay your total, and leave.

I head down the sanitary products aisle in search of tampons and eventually find what I'm looking for. A few women surround me, looking at other related products, and I don't get it at first—why they're giving me strange looks—but then it hits me. I'm in my male form.

Shit. Is it weird buying tampons as a man? Should I be doing this in my female form? I consider switching, but that's gonna freak them out even more. Goddess damn it.

I scan my chip card over the nearest tampon screen a few times and rush down the aisle, heading toward the collection point.

The collection point is run by a lanky Fae woman with scraped-back red hair and freckles that would have been cute a hundred years ago. Her scowl before I even get to the desk is enough to make me want to turn around and go back to the hotel empty-handed. Is she going to be weird about it too?

"Please scan your chip," she says in that sullen voice everyone gets after working in retail for too long.

I scan my card.

She briefly frowns at the plasmascreen in front of her before masking it and continuing with her usual frown. "Your products are at door three, sir." She gestures to the numbered door behind her.

I walk up, scan my chip card again to pay, and rush out of there like the devil is on my tail.

Turns out, no one freaks out about my absence because Nine lets them all know where I've gone, and by the time I come back, they're waiting for me in my room on a set of comfy black and pink sofas in the corner by the bed.

I shove my shopping bag in the bathroom and join them. Connie looks kind of tired, and I wonder when the last time she got some sleep was.

She's been freaking out over the mission.

Right. Vampires. Well, I'm going to help with that.

"What's the easiest way to find a group of murdering a-holes that probably don't want to be found by their council?"

Dea smiles at me but stays silent while the others look at me in befuddlement.

"You draw them out." I grab Connie's hand. "Wanna help me punch some Vampires in the face?"

She shoots up straight with a wide grin. "Oh my fuck, yes!"

"Thought so."

Arrie chuckles and Dea smiles appreciatively.

"Dea," I say, "I think you should go to the council to ask for information. And take Arrie with you because he'll be useless for the other part of the plan."

"Yes, Angel."

"Connie and Nine, we're going to stage a coop."

Everyone smiles, and I can't help it, I beam with pride. I've come up with a plan everyone agrees with. "You know this could put us in danger of exposure, though, right?" You know, just in case that's a big deal to them.

Dea is the one who answers. "We are not going to be able to hide forever now the community is out and on the warpath."

Thank goddess he sees reason.

Arrie speaks up, because of course he would be the Debby downer on all this great planning. "Do we really want our first public appearance to be an anti-Vampire fight?"

Grrrr! (Pretty sure I do that out loud, too. Oops.) Why is he always fucking right when he complains? We need to draw them out somehow, and clearly, they're all for Vampire freedom and against the SC's controlling BS.

"What if the Vampires we fought knew what was going on? Like, volunteers?" Nine raises his brows in that sexy, nerdy way of his, and I melt.

Seriously, does this guy just ooze sexy nerd? Is he the reason it's a thing? 'Cos I could get behind that. OMG. What if he wears glasses?

Nine just looks at me with a smirk, blushes, and shakes his head. *Focus.*

Right. Back to planning.

Dea's speaking. "We do not know any Vampires who could help—outside of the council."

An idea sparks, and I shoot to my feet, accidentally scaring the shit out everyone. Oops.

"I know a Vampire who owes me a favor." I look to Dea, hoping he'll get my meaning.

"No, absolutely not." He stands to join me. "That could be

dangerous! He is the reason you were killed in the first place."

Connie gasps. "I'm with Dea. We shouldn't use that contact."

I wave them both off, going ahead with my plan anyway. Who the hell do they think they are, my keepers? I'm a grown-ass adult. An immortal adult. What the fuck could happen?

Chapter Eleven

"Oh, c'mon . . . please!" I place my hands together and beg the Vampire Prince in front of me to help.

I find him at the last place we saw him—partying, feeding, fucking . . . generally living it up.

"Nope. Nuh-uh. Not happening, little hunter." He crosses his arms where he lies on the couch—stark naked with two women curled up on either side. "I'm not doing that. That's insane."

I blanch. "I am not a hunter anymore."

"Riiiight, sorry." He shrugs. "Little Horseman?"

I growl, frustrated this is the place I have to be—in my female form of all things. Turns out, he doesn't recognize me in my male form, so here I am, standing in a Vampire den (with no help from the others, I might add), hungry, horny, and on my period.

Turns out, things can go pretty badly.

"Can we talk somewhere else?" I mumble, knowing he can hear me. I seriously can't take the crazy directions my thoughts have gone in while in this room. The things my Vampire side wants to do to those women . . .

He creases his brows and sighs. "Fine." He shoos the girls away, downs the last sip of blood left in his glass, and gets dressed. "Where to?" He turns to face me.

"Follow."

I Vampire speed out of there, waiting to see if he can follow me at this speed—he can—and continue all the way to our hotel.

"You're staying here?" He looks at the hotel in front of us with an amused smirk.

"We're all staying here, yeah." I shrug, and we head on in. "Listen," I say once we reach the elevator, "please behave yourself. They are not your biggest fans."

He flinches ever so slightly, but it's enough for me to notice.

"Scared, little prince?"

"Of the Four Horsemen of the Apocalypse? Yeah. Yes, I fucking am."

"I won't let them kill you, don't worry." I clap him on the back.

The ping of the elevator signals we're on the top floor, and I gesture for him to follow me to my room.

Here's to hoping no one's doing anything sexy in there. It might just pop the last lid on my mental pot of crazy right now. Seriously, how long can one stay permanently turned up to eleven?

Luckily for me the room is empty.

"Sit," I say as I stroll to the lounge area. "You don't mind if I change form, do you?"

He sighs once more. "What do you have against being a Vampire?"

"What?"

"It's obvious you're not feeding properly. What's the problem?"

"That is none of your business." I huff and fold my arms.

"C'mon"—he smiles—"just tell me. I have a little experience when it comes to being a Vampire, little Horseman." He flashes his fangs and laughs.

He isn't going to let this go, is he?

"It's not the feeding that's the issue. I feed at least once a day, sometimes twice, and carry extras everywhere I go."

He smiles in approval.

"I don't need to feed, I only do so because it helps keep me healthy."

"Then, what's the problem? Why do you look like you're starving yourself . . . ?" He trails off, realization hitting him like a storm. "You're not having sex, are you?"

I shake my head, blood rushing to my cheeks. Goddess, kill me now. Please, I can't sit through this conversation.

He doesn't laugh; he doesn't even smile. "It's not funny or embarrassing." His voice has turned stern, and he looks . . . disappointed. "When a Vampire doesn't feed and mate, or keep up a healthy lifestyle of both, it can kill them. It's how our biology works, just like how Witches need the outdoors to settle their magic." He sighs and sends an order of blood through the e-ordering system. "You can't die, so all it'll do is send you crazy, and that's how you'll stay."

"I know!" I snap. Taking a deep breath, I try again. "I know."

"You going to tell me why you're so adverse to something so goddamn normal?"

"I'm not adverse! I'm just . . . waiting."

"On what?" He leans forward and smirks. "It's not hard. Rod A goes into slot B."

"I know how sex works!"

"Clearly." His sarcasm knows no bounds. He grabs my hand and yanks it toward him. "If you want, I can help?"

The suggestion in his tone does not go unnoticed, and even though I'm not particularly attracted to this guy, the thought of feeding and having sex at the same time still sends a thrill through me. But . . . I'm waiting.

What am I waiting on again?

The pounding in my head matches the blood rushing through my body, making it hard to think.

Why does it matter?

All rational thought flies out the window, and I find myself leaning into the Vampire Prince. "Lucien . . . I . . ."

No. I shake the haze from my head. This isn't what I want. I want the team, my home, my family. I want to wait and finally find my place. I want to be with the ones I love.

I pull away. "I can't. Sorry. You wouldn't understand." I sit back down and focus on shifting while he complains in his usual drama-queen tone.

As the magic tingling sensation washes over me, I force the urge to vomit down and refocus on the task at hand. "We've gotten off topic."

He leans back, but as he does, the doorbell rings. Yup, this hotel has doorbells for each room. "Ah," he says through an exhale, "dinner's arrived."

I roll my eyes and sit back.

Nine, get the team in here please. I'm having issues with my guest.

What guest? Where did you go? You said you were going for a walk?

Ugh, just get your ass in here.

He siphons the other Horsemen, and they all run, but not before he takes a long look through my memories and grumbles the entire time. Until he gets to the part where I nearly kiss Prince Lucien, and then he just remains silent.

Shit, did I piss him off? Does he hate me now? What if I messed everything up?

Stop being stupid. I was just surprised that you actually admitted your feelings to yourself rather than burying them. And you've never called the house home before. It caught me off guard.

Oh . . .

Connie, Nine, and Dea barrel through the closed door, weapons ready, after Lucien sits back down, and they all stop dead upon noticing my guest.

"What were you thinking?" Arrie growls.

"Woah," I say, getting up and walking over to him, "calm down, big guy. I'm doing my job."

"No," Dea interrupts, "you were being reckless."

Says the Horseman of Death with his whole I-do-not-fear-death bullshit.

I roll my eyes at him and gesture for us all to sit. "C'mon, we need to persuade him to help us. He won't budge." I growl under my breath at him. "It's starting to piss me off."

I'm seriously tempted to just go all bear on him and growl in his face, but I manage to restrain myself from threatening the little Vampire Prince.

Little?

I shrug. He calls me little Horseman. Who knows, maybe he's small.

That has Nine laughing. *You should have found out.*

I . . . err . . . didn't want to.

I know. I'm just messing.

Oh.

Back to the task at hand. "I swear I'll bite your ears off if you don't at least listen to me—to us." I add a bit of a growl to the end of my sentence, hoping it'll add to the effect. I really don't want to have to put anything of his into my mouth, even in animal form.

"Okay, okay." He raises his hands in social submission and smiles. "What kind of a stupid plan did you have in mind?"

Well"—I step forward—"we want to draw out the rogues. By doing so, we'll hopefully be taken to wherever they're based and get to speak to whoever their leader is. But we need to gain their attention first. They're not going to just attack us again after losing so spectacularly last time."

Nine steps in, all charming smiles and blinking innocence. "We want to stage a fake fight: Horsemen vs Vampires."

"Ah, so that's where I come in. You need Vampires willing to 'go down' at the hands of the Horsemen?"

"That's about it, yeah." I shrug.

"Sorry, can't help you."

Arrie growls behind me.

Lucien stiffens ever so slightly. Smart man.

"Why not?" Arrie asks as he sits beside me on the couch.

"Because I'd need to explain who you are, and even then, people wouldn't believe me." He raises his eyebrows. "You guys are a myth. The only reason I know about you is because I'm on the Vampire Royal Council."

"Yeah," I say, "about that . . ."

He raises one eyebrow at me.

"We're not staying in hiding throughout this war. We won't be able to. Might as well start coming out of the closet sooner or later."

Lucien blanches. "Really? You're all on board with this?"

Everyone shuffles their feet.

Clearly, they don't like it, but honestly, I'm past caring. It doesn't matter. We can't win a public war against magic while remaining hidden. It isn't fair to the humans we're asking to put their trust in us. They have a right know what's out there.

"When everyone figures out who I am, do you think they'll like me?" I ask. "Do you think they'll like a previous supe hunter hunting her own kind being the one to bring about peace?"

Arrie visibly tenses beside me while Nine places a hand on my shoulder—which does not go unnoticed by Lucien, who smirks at the gesture.

"Because they won't. We need to come out to the public eventually, and we need to do so in a way that is beneficial to the balance of power."

That was pretty well spoken, Sweetie.

Thanks. Channeling my inner Dea.

Lucien opens his mouth to say something but closes it again, as though reconsidering. "Okay." He shrugs. "How long do I have?"

Dea answers this time. "As long as you need, Prince Lucien. But try not to make us wait too long. We do not like being stuck on Earth longer than necessary."

He nods and gets up to leave. Just before he turns to walk out the door, he smiles at me. "Just so you know, that offer's still on the table. If you're too scared to deal with"—he gestures to the team—"that."

I wave him out and rake a hand through my hair. "Well, he's a handful," I mumble to myself.

"Your choice of contact, hon." Connie just has to pick that moment to turn into Arrie, doesn't she?

"I know." I look at her and smile, hoping to be as dazzling as Dea, but I probably still have a few hundred years to go before mastering that look.

She blushes nonetheless, and I'm thankful I don't look like

an idiot.

Can't we all stay together this evening, just for one night?

But even I know that's asking too much of them. I just want to feel less . . . alone. Just for a few hours. One night with no nightmares, no concerns, surrounded by . . . family.

Nine looks at me and nods, a smile forming on his face. *You just have to ask.*

It doesn't matter. I'm just being stupid. "I'm going to bed. It's been a long day, and I'm tired."

No one speaks for a moment, but Dea and Connie smile while they all have an internal conversation with Nine.

I can't be arsed with it all, so I go into the bathroom to get ready for bed. Ten minutes later, two sets of teeth all sparkly clean, two bodies freshly showered, and guy-me dressed in nothing but a pair of sleep pants—hey, it's not every day I can sleep half naked and not have to worry about flashing my boobs everywhere (#maleperks)—I step out of the luxurious bathroom and freeze in the doorway.

Nine, Connie, Arrie, and Dea are all in my huge bed, all wearing pajamas (and the sight of Arrie in pajamas is enough to have me stifling a laugh), with a clear and defined space for me between Nine and Connie in the center.

Are they serious? They want to keep me company just because I feel lonely?

"Yes," Nine says. "Now come to bed." He pats the empty space beside him, and Connie smiles.

Connie looks tired, and I'm glad she's choosing to get some rest before the mission—she looks like she needs it, which is saying a lot for her (she always looks pristinely beautiful, even when injured).

I smile as I climb into bed, Nine lifting the covers and Connie snuggling into the crook of my shoulder once I've gotten comfy. Arrie snuggles into her back beside her—the big guy looking almost cute as he wraps an arm around her waist—while Nine entwines his hand in mine as we lie side by side. Dea lies on his left with a peaceful smile on his half-asleep face.

This is nice. Warm. Surprisingly attractive. And it feels like . . . home.

Chapter Twelve

We spend three days in the city of New Orleans, waiting for Lucien to get back with some more info for us. We party, hang out and watch movies in my suite, go shopping, and just generally act like tourists. Dea is his usual quiet self, but even he enjoys the shopping trip he's visible for. Today though, I've had enough of waiting and send Dea and Arrie to the Council, where they're planning on extracting information at any cost (hence Arrie tagging along). We need to know who these Vampires are; they're the only lead to the oncoming war we have, other than tabloid nonsense and the Witches being . . . well, Witches.

That just leaves me, Nine, and Connie to find Lucien and see if he has an update. Fuck this no datachip bullshit and relying on mobile devices—no one uses those anymore. When we come out of the supernatural closet, we're getting datachips. That way, I could be calling Lucien right now. The fuckwit.

"What we gonna do today?" Connie asks as she steps out

of my bathroom in a towel, exposing her upper thigh.

All of them have slept in the same bed with me every night, and I would be lying if I said it wasn't the best feeling in the world. None of us are having sex or doing anything remotely sexy, but it warms my heart to know they're doing it just for me.

I get the feeling they wouldn't usually sleep all together like that.

You'd be right. But everyone is enjoying it more than they're letting on.

That is an interesting tidbit.

"I'm not sure. I wanted to track down Lucien to see how he's doing." I shrug. "What would you like to do?"

"I really wanna go dancing with you in your female form." She shrugs. "But I totally get why you don't want to do that right now."

Is female me still on her period? I change and go into the bathroom to find out. It's only been four days, but between the lack of blood and the calming of the insanity in my head, it's safe to assume that I can remain in this form if I want.

There's still the whole crazy Vampire no-sex issue to work with, but that's much calmer off my period. Okay, I can do this. I can do this for Connie.

I step out of the bathroom dressed in the last thing I wore in my female form—combat gear from when I planned to go on this Earth mission—and jump out of the doorway. "Let's do this!"

Connie smiles, then falters. "You sure?" She walks up to me. "I mean, your male form is seriously hot, but there's something about you like this that I just like. But I don't wanna be the reason you spend the day all crazy."

"It's okay. I'm good."

She raises an eyebrow in question, as if doubting me. The

bitch. But I can't stay mad at that pretty face. Grrr. I swear, they all have me wrapped around their little fingers. I can never stay mad at any of them. Well, maybe except Arrie.

"I'm good. Seriously. No period, so less crazy Vampire me."

She scowls. "That is so fucking shit!" I step back as she clenches her fists. "You get to just magically avoid your periods for the rest of time while I'm stuck with them?" She laughs in that crazy way of hers, and I get really worried for my pretty face for a second. "How is that fair! What did I ever do to Fate to deserve this bullshit?"

I rest a hand on her shoulder. "Sorry?"

She takes a calming breath and looks me in the eyes. "It's okay. Just a little . . . annoying."

"Hey, I get it. Two thousand years of periods must be seriously sucky."

"You have no idea." She rolls her eyes and turns away to get changed.

I rummage through my wardrobe to find something more appropriate to wear and settle on a simple look of black ripped jeans, sparkly pink knee-high boots, my punked-out denim jacket (pink sequins and skulls included) and a black tee. Oh, and don't forget the black choker (what even is an outfit without one?).

Okay, so maybe it isn't a simple look, but I swear that's what I was going for to begin with.

Scout's honor.

Okay, so I wasn't a girl scout, either. But, hey, a girl can only go so long without pink sequins in her life—trust me— and this is a pink sequin kind of day.

"You girls done?" Nine asks, exasperated from watching our antics and having to turn around from us getting changed.

"Yeah!" we both say in unison and giggle like a couple of teenagers about to go out drinking for the first time.

So far, the partying hasn't really interested me that much. Maybe it just isn't my thing? It all seems so . . . over the top. Like each club is trying too hard to be something they aren't.

Goddess, I sound so old.

Ha! Good one.

Oh, right. Partying with two-thousand-year-old beings; I am not the old one in the room.

It's two in the afternoon, Dea and Arrie left three hours ago, and none of us have heard from them, so we have time to kill. If Connie wants to party, then I guess we're partying.

Weirdly, I feel more comfortable partying in my female form. Wonder why?

I shrug my shoulders, grab my handbag (also black with pink sequins), shove my stuff in, grab my room key, and shove everyone out of the door. "Let's go!" I wrap my arms through Nine's and Connie's and drag us all outside.

It's on them from here; I'm not exactly filled with a map of the area, nor do I know where all the best afternoon bars and clubs are, so I let them guide me.

Nine seems to have some kind of idea, so he drags us girls behind him with fervor, past blocks, streets of tourist insanity, and onto a quieter back alley path that leads to a wide street with low-key parties, no through traffic, and a wonderful-smelling food place on the corner that I nearly drag us into before Nine promises some place better.

On the corner end of that street sits a wonderful-looking, café-style eatery with an attached bar: DISASTER CAFÉ. Apparently named after their famous Disaster Vodka Shake—drunken shenanigans are likely to ensue. (Please look away now if you do not wish to be embarrassed alongside me.)

"C'mon!" Nine grabs our hands as we look at each other and shrug. Seems Connie hasn't been here before either. "This'll be hilarious!"

What's he up to?

You said you wanted to live life a bit? Get drunk and stumble home. Well, their Disaster Shakes are a good way to go! C'mon, live a little with me . . .

Well, when he puts it like that . . . Why not?

When we get into the café and sit down on the food side, me being starving (as usual) and Nine wanting me to try one of their Death-Defying Donuts, I instantly take a liking to the place. It's cozy, but at the same time it has a unique, dancing kind of atmosphere.

Nine smiles at me once he's ordered us three donuts, clearly enjoying my approval of his choice. It's so easy to please him—I love it!

The donuts are as big as my face! Oh, and dripping in chocolate. Two donuts later (I go back for seconds, they're fucking great, don't judge me), Connie is ready to party, so we head to the other half of the floor where they have a mild club atmosphere going on, complete with small dancefloor, a couple of pool tables in the back, and some tables dotted around.

A few people are here but not many. That being said, it's only five in the afternoon.

"Okay," Nine says, "I'll get the drinks, you two go off and . . . do whatever it is girls do on nights out." He winks and heads toward the bar.

Connie grabs my wrist and heads over to a pool table. These are a little old-fashioned nowadays but really add to the cultural, cozy vibe this place has going on.

"Wanna play?"

She gives me such a sweet smile, I can't say no. Despite having no memory of this game or any real experience. Here's to hoping my Vampire nature might help. Or I could cheat using air magic. (Shhh, don't snitch on me.)

"Sure." I grab one of the digital cues and act as though I know what I'm doing, but I think Connie sees right through that, as she laughs and rolls her eyes at me.

"Need me to explain the rules?" She doesn't even wait for me to put on a fake load of confidence and shrug off her suggestion. "Yeah, whatever. Here it goes."

She goes on to explain the basic rules, and I think I kinda get it: just shoot my color balls into the pockets using the cue's aiming feature and don't pot the white or black. Got it.

Halfway into the first game—I'm losing, by the way—Nine comes back with our drinks: one Disaster Shake for each of us. Connie downs half before her next go while I try to compete and fail miserably, spluttering half the foam all over Nine's shirt.

He just laughs it off and whacks me on the back, trying to get me to stop choking. "Easy there. Drink slowly." He eyes Connie with a scowl. "Don't challenge her. Milkshake's hard to chug, you know."

She shrugs. "Age has its perks." And downs the other half.

Damn it, I'm not going down like this. I take a deep breath and chug the entire two-liter vodka milkshake in one, hoping my immortal system will save me from getting too drunk too soon.

Neither, I think to myself, am I losing this game. I bring my attention back to the pool table and pot a ball by coaxing it into the hole using a little bit of air manipulation.

"Oh, so we're allowed to use magic, are we?"

Nine watches and laughs. "You shouldn't have done that.

She has magically perfect aim, remember?"

Ah fuck. I forgot about that.

"She's won hundreds of thousands of piles of gold over the years hustling poor folks at pool, darts. Anything with an aim." He shakes his head. "Fun while it lasted, but it usually got us thrown out of town."

"Hey, it ain't my fault they can't keep up."

She was seriously high maintenance back in the day, wasn't she?

You have no idea. She was such a fucking handful. Mellowed out since men and women have become equal, though.

Damn. Would have been fun to see.

You might get lucky.

Connie goes ahead and pots every ball of her color in under a minute, and I sulk on the nearest chair.

"That's not fair! I was just using a little magic!" Part of me wants to go all out and stomp my feet, but I manage to restrain myself. One point to adult me.

Nine wraps an arm around my shoulders. "Told you so." He pulls me into a hug and runs his hands up my back, dipping his fingers under the edge of my vest tee.

Connie walks over and coughs, interrupting the moment. "May I?"

Nine lets go of me, and Connie moves in, placing a hand to either side of my face and tilting it up. "Let me make it up to you." Her voice is huskier than usual, and I recognize the movement of her head and the half-lidded haze of her eyes. She's about to kiss me.

Closing the distance, I grab her lips with mine and make out with the sexiest woman on the planet in a bar half-full of people.

Nine stands next to us and furiously blushes.

But she isn't done. She's not letting me go. Not this time. Especially not after seeing how far Nine and I got before we left for Earth—at least, I suspect that's the direction her thoughts have gone.

She grazes her tongue along my bottom lip, and my lips part on instinct. She uses the opportunity to slip her tongue in my mouth and tangle it with mine, deepening the kiss. Her hand leaves my cheek and brushes the edges of my vest and bra, teasing the sensitive skin there and flaring a heat I've been ignoring into a blaze of passion that has me running my own hands under her top and creeping under the edge of her bra.

I can feel my panties getting wetter by the second, and the only thing that stops me from taking things further is Nine's mental reminder that we are in a public place and lots of people are staring at the two hot women making out in the corner.

Before I can pull away, however, Connie dips a finger into my bra and brushes it over my nipple. I groan into her mouth and feel her satisfactory smile press across her lips.

"Connie . . . not here." I pull away and look around, noticing Nine smirking at us as he casually watches the show, along with a lot of other people who've started to file in for the evening.

She just smiles and plays it off, but I know she wants to go further with me, and I would be lying if I say I don't find her struggle to hold back hot as fuck. This woman is going to be the death of me. When I get her home to *Sheruta,* I am going to spend a very pleasant afternoon with her sprawled on the bed, discovering exactly what she's imagining right now.

Nine blushes at the direction my, probably very loud, thoughts have taken, but I just re-challenge her to another game of pool.

"Another drink, ladies?"

We both nod, and he goes off in search of more alcohol. He's right, it does wear off quickly for us; I'm already feeling less light-headed.

I lean forward and whisper, "Don't worry, I'll give you everything your little heart desires when we get home," into Connie's ear.

Watching her blush as she fumbles with setting up the pool table is an absolute delight. For all her confidence, I sometimes forget that she's as nervous as I am about taking this further. At least with me she is.

I wonder . . .

"Connie?" I walk over to her so we can have a more private conversation. "I have a question, though it's a little . . . personal?"

"Well, it is a Friday." She laughs. "Ask away!"

"Have you had relationships with women before? I mean, I get the entire team is more fluid than other people, but . . . I was just curious . . ."

She sighs, as though expecting my question. "I've had a few threesomes with women before, when trying to please the guy or whatever." She groans. "But I've never had sex with just another woman." She tries to shrug off her blushing, but I can tell this is actually a semi-serious topic for her. "You're the first woman I've ever really been attracted to, I guess."

Really? "I just assumed you'd done it all."

"Oh, don't misunderstand, I've done a lot with other women over the years during group sex, but that's not a frequent thing for me. Nor is it something I've really wanted to do. Until now." She raises my hand it to her lips. "I really want to explore things with you. It'll be new for us both, which I know is something you'll look forward to."

She's inexperienced in this area, too. Well, kind of. As inexperienced as you can be after two thousand years. She's right, that does make me smile.

Nine comes back with two more shakes each and a series of shots. We down them all, play a hilariously drunken game of pool where we both lose miserably while Nine distracts us, and then we start dancing.

Nine takes over DJing from the guy after he refuses to play anything recent, and once that happens, everyone in the bar area, and a few from the café, too, dance with us.

By the time ten pm comes around, we've each drunk over a dozen of those Disaster Shakes, more shots than I know how to count, and I can't keep from stumbling around the dancefloor like an idiot.

"Okkkaay," Nine says, "I think I should get you two home." He seems pretty sober, which is a total bore.

"Nooooooo," I scream a little too loudly. "More dancing . . ."

He chuckles. "One more song. Then we're off. We have work to do tomorrow."

"We do?" I'm struggling to think straight.

"Uh-huh, but don't worry about that just now." He kisses my forehead. "Keep having fun."

He lines up another song and joins us on the dancefloor, and I soon find myself dancing between them, Connie in front and Nine behind. And I would be lying if I say I don't find this hot as fuck. This would be a legendary way to lose my immortal v-card, and the more I think about it, the better an idea it becomes.

Not while drunk. I'm not fucking either of you until you're sober. And before you even think about it, neither will Arrie or Dea.

Boooo! Buzzkill.

He drags us off the dancefloor at the end of the song (well, as much as Famine can drag Conquest and Magic anywhere—which is to say, barely anywhere). He sighs and mumbles, "Fine."

Three songs later, Dea and Arrie arrive, and we're finally being dragged out of the cool shake club and down the winding cobble-stoned paths toward our hotel.

Connie and I sing and dance down every street, getting strange looks from all three sober men behind us as they each find our antics hilarious as we trip over every possible thing in our way. (No, I didn't trip, the floor rose up to say hello.)

Connie grabs my hand and drags me along, both of us singing that nursery rhyme about the spider's water spout and the ring of roses. Or is it the one with the sheep? I dunno, I think I get confused and sing a mixture of both.

"Just call me the nursery rhyme rapper and bow down to my glory! Mwuhahahaha!"

Nine bursts out laughing while Connie tries to pull me into the nearest club to dance some more.

"Nope." Arrie grabs us both by the waist and throws each of us over his shoulders, Connie on his left and me on his right. "Let's get you to bed."

"Yessss! Take me to bed. Grooooup orgy time!"

Dea and Nine give each other a look that clearly means something, but I have no idea what, while Connie just laughs and agrees, and Arrie mumbles something in a foreign language.

"Stop mumbling prof-f-fanities under your breath, big guy."

"I wasn't," he whispers. "I was saying how much of a great idea that would be if you both weren't flat-out drunk."

"Yes, three votes for the orgy. I win. I win. I win."

Everyone's cringing at my stupid antics, but I'm having the time of my life.

That is until Arrie drops us both off at our hotel rooms and I have to run to the bathroom to throw up all of the evening's happiness.

Ugh. More vomiting. Yay.

Chapter Thirteen

The pounding of my head wakes me up with a groan of complaint to an empty bed; everyone must have slept in their own rooms last night. Makes sense, since I was pretty drunk.

Memories of my stupid antics—losing epically to Connie at pool and dancing like a weirdo—flash through my mind. And did Connie and me . . . ? Yup, we made out and had some less-than-innocent fun in public. Great.

On the plus side, it was a fun night.

My stomach turns upside down and I sprint to the bathroom before I vomit all over the floor.

Horsemen get hangovers? How is that even fair?

Because we're still human (kind of).

Ugh. Fuck off, Nine. You're making my headache worse.

Tough, because we have a meeting this morning with your little Vampire Prince.

Really?

Uh-huh. Come to breakfast in Dea's room, and we'll all chat.

Be right there.

There's only one way I'm getting through my work day and dealing with Lucien: cheating. I focus for a few minutes and change forms, stepping out of my bathroom as a male like some kind of weird sex-quick-change magic act.

Sigh.

I get dressed, genuinely dressing down this time in jeans and a plain, white tee, and head to Dea's room. His door is glossy black and seems to fit him perfectly, and upon entry, I realize I may have the better room.

The entire suite is a glossy black-and-white monochrome with pictures of less-than-child-friendly women dotted around. It has a sexy, black, boudoir feel. But when I notice Dea laying on his four-poster bed with black satin linen, I notice that he fits right in with the décor, as though the room were made for his emo-style, and his style alone.

This room is smaller but has a seriously awesome built-into-the-floor lounge area with strip lights and a cinema-style screen on one end.

"Damn. These rooms are awesome."

"That, Sweetie," Nine says from behind me in the doorway, "is cheating." He grabs my hand and drags me to the lounge area, where Dea joins us. "When Connie gets here, she's gonna take one look at you and punch you in the face. She's spent the past two hours throwing up in her bathroom."

I chuckle and laugh him off, but true to his word, Connie plods in half an hour later and looks around the room for me with a smile. That smile falters, however, when she notices I'm in my male form.

She storms over and stands in front of me, arms on her hips. "What the fuck is this?" She gestures to me.

I shrug. "You'd do it if you could."

"Fuck you!" She sits on the couch opposite us, glaring

daggers my way until Arrie walks in and laughs at her obvious problem with me.

"Damn, Killer, you wind her up better than anyone with that trick."

Trick? Is he being serious right now? "My sex changing ability is not a trick!" I mean, how dare he? As though I'm some weird magician with some basic magic tricks? As though this doesn't make my life one giant comedy?

I shift back into my female form instantaneously, form a clenched fist, and punch him in the face, sending him flying backward into the couch with a surprised look on his face.

Nausea overtakes me from all the jostling around, and I have to run to Dea's bathroom. But upon exiting, I feel better, and I manage to stay in my female form without coloring the black-and-white décor in vomit.

Everyone stares at me with smiles on their faces when I sit back down, taking my place next to Nine. When no one says anything and they all continue to stare, I begin to wonder if I have some vomit left on my face.

"What?"

Nine chuckles. "You just changed instantly."

Thinking back to Arrie's now-black eye, I smile. "I did, didn't I?" Ha! Take that, Fate. The Horseman of Magic is growing up.

Arrie grumbles in the corner next to Connie.

I give him the stink eye. "My sex changing ability is as much a trick as your battlemode focus."

He flinches, sensing where my agitation has come from, but he doesn't say anything, choosing to remain sat there with his eyes avoiding mine at every turn.

Ugh. (Told you my good relationship with Arrie wouldn't last.) Well, I'll work on it later. Right now, a pretty little

Vampire Prince is knocking on the door.

"Come in." I don't raise my voice, knowing he'll hear me and equally knowing the door has been left ajar in preparation for his arrival.

Little Prince Lucien waltzes into the room and sits opposite Connie and Arrie, smiling a flirtatious smirk Connie's way. If I were in my male form, my Shifter side would likely have growled at him, but as I am in my female form, I settle on glaring at him in the most menacing way possible.

He can stop flirting with my girl . . . friend. Friend who is a girl? My bestie?

Lucien takes one look at my descended fangs and smiles, backing off, hands raised in surrender.

"What have you got for us, little Vampire Prince?"

He raises an eyebrow at my nickname but smiles and crosses his arms over his chest. "A team of twenty Vamps willing to be beaten up by you four in exchange for payment."

Payment? Seriously?

Just agree.

"Very well. How much?"

He laughs. "You misunderstand me. They want to be the first civilians to see your powers for themselves."

I stiffen. I'm not sure that is such a good idea. What if they use it against us?

Don't panic. We'll only show them a bit of our powers.

I nod at Lucien, who smiles and holds his hand out to seal the deal. I shake it, disgruntled I have to be a show monkey. Again.

"And," he says, "you'd do well to show them what you showed us, otherwise the discrepancy could cause an issue. No?"

"Yep. Already on it." I sigh and stand. "When would they

like this payment. In advance, I assume?"

"Nice assumption."

A knock at the door interrupts our conversation. "Breakfast, as requested."

Oh, right.

I answer the door and dismiss the teenage waitress, wheeling the silver tray in myself. I place it just above the lounge area and sit back down.

"Breakfast, Lucien?"

He frowns. "No. But thank you. I have someone more appetizing in mind." He strolls toward the door. "This evening in council room 3B. Be there." He leaves, creating a breeze that billows his long white hair behind him with his dramatic exit.

He really is a show pony, isn't he?

I sigh, honestly not comfortable with the direction this agreement has taken. Something about showing off our powers doesn't sit well with me. But we need to get their attention—we need to get to the top.

I need to get to the person sitting at the top.

Nine grabs my arm with a worried gaze. "What aren't you saying?"

I shrug. "I don't know what you're talking about." I yank my arm back with a little too much force and grab a sweet-smelling pastry on my way out.

What I really need is blood, but the thought of asking more from them right now makes me nauseous. I could order from the hotel menu, but my one experience with human blood was . . . less than satisfying.

Ugh. I can feel the crazy lust permeating my mind, my body, every cell on fire like it is trying to force me to turn around and drag one of the team back to my room with me.

I ignore it and open the door Lucien closed, aiming to drag my Vampire ass right out of that room whether I like it or not. But something stops me, something sweet, honey-like, with the faint aroma of smoky lavender hidden beneath the tresses of the metallic tangs permeating every breath.

Blood. Dea's blood.

I turn around, run to him faster than the others can blink, and sink my fangs into the part of his neck he made bleed for me.

He staggers a step backward, but I catch him with one arm as he lets out an audible moan of pleasure as I suck a little harder.

I know where everyone in the room is: Nine still by the breakfast tray, watching with intent, his ever-annoying presence in mind ready to intervene if need be; Arrie staring daggers in my back with his usual glaring hatred whenever I feed from someone other than him; and Connie who . . .

I gasp my surprise at where Connie is in the room. She usually turns away, scared of my glowing eyes and blood-red fangs, but she creeps closer today, peering around the corner of my back I purposefully put between me and her.

What does she want?

To watch.

Ah, she wants to confront her fears. Give me just a moment—one last lick of the spilled drops—and I turn around to face her.

She gasps at my face, her hands trembling as she balls them into fists while frustration crosses her scrunched-up face. I make no move to hide my eyes or fangs, not bothering to concentrate on tempering it all down. At some point, she needs to move past this. We need to move past this.

I don't really think today is that day, but if she wants to try,

I'm not going to deny her.

My body doesn't move. I stay stock still, like a feather caught between two different breezes, not really sure which way to go: to back off or get closer.

Everything in the room freezes, everyone holding their breath—even Arrie remains silent, not a single hard line on his face as he looks on with curiosity.

Connie takes a single step toward me, making an effort to close the distance separating us despite every instinct screaming at her to run. "I . . . Can I . . . ?" She raises her hand toward me, wanting something, but I'm not sure what.

What does she want?

To touch your fangs.

I give her a solemn nod, prepared for the sensual response of having them touched this time, prepared not to react, lest I frighten her away. This is progress. (I hope.)

She closes the distance in a single deep breath and lowers her hand to my face, tracing the lines of my glowing eyes down my cheeks and across my lips.

Fuck, it really does heighten everything being in this state. I can feel every ridge of her thumb as she brushes it over my bottom lip a second time, and it takes every ounce of strength to swallow the gasp of pleasure that rolls up my throat.

I don't know if I can hold back when she reaches higher and touches my fangs. Don't know if I can not react. Would that frighten her? I feel as though any sound I make might terrify her, even otherwise pleasurable ones. She's like a deer caught in headlights, stark and terrified of every movement I make.

Slowly, ever so slowly, I raise my hand—palm up and non-threatening.

She flinches at first, but then she relaxes when she realizes

I'm just as terrified of this moment and am trying not to scare her away. Eventually, she wraps her fingers through mine, and I sigh in relief as I smile and she smiles back.

Progress. Fuck yes, Fate! Take that, you crazy bitch.

She brings her other hand up and raises it questionably to my mouth, as though asking my permission. I nod, and she goes for it, stroking a single light finger down my fangs.

I can't hold back the moan that escapes my lips, but it thankfully doesn't scare her, just gives her a playful smile as the guys laugh.

Fucking assholes.

"I didn't know that felt good," she whispers. "Sorry." But by the look of the smile plastered across her face, she isn't sorry in the slightest. I'm right, because she uses her other hand to stroke them both at the same time, and fuck me, I don't want her to stop.

Just like last time, it's like my fangs are directly linked to my clit, and I can feel every wave of pleasure pulsate through me, every throb of need that has me arching into her.

Connie giggles and grabs my waist, holding me tight, and I can't help the slight rocking of my hips as I look for any kind of friction. She delivers. She drops one hand to the button of my shorts and undoes them before slipping a single finger below the waistband of my panties. That one finger is enough to have me moaning all over again as she continues stroking my fangs in tune with the gentle circling motion she strokes along my clit.

Fuck, I can't breathe. Every part of me is on fire, as though she's lit my skin with a torch and never intends to douse me in the cooling aftereffects of water.

I want to say something—anything. But I don't know what. Words fail me.

Connie gives a final giggle in that girly way of hers that is so defiant of her kickass powers and general badassery and pulls both hands away. She lifts her finger to her tongue and licks it dry, drawing groans from all the guys, even Arrie, and turns away with renewed confidence as she skips out of the room.

Fuck. Shit.

What am I supposed to do with that?

There is only one thing my body does do, and that is buckle and slide to the ground, needing something solid to ground me.

That woman is such a tease. She is going to be the death of me. If she wasn't terrified of my Vampire nature, I would have pinned her to Dea's bed and taken everything I wanted. But . . . no.

That isn't me.

"Angel?" Dea's voice penetrates the fog in my mind, and I look up to see all three guys sitting on the floor around me with worried expressions.

Nine, is Connie okay?

Yeah, just a little shaken at her own confidence. She just needs a moment.

I nod.

Dea and Arrie continue looking at me with worry, until Arrie asks, "Is there anything we can do to help?"

Nine and Dea laugh, knowing full well there are lots of things they could do to ease the molten puddle of need Connie has left me in. But I'm so shocked by Connie and reeling from her interactions that I don't think I could do anything right now.

I shake my head and focus on changing back into my male form, hoping it'll take the edge off. It only takes around ten seconds this time, but I'm not in the right mind to enjoy my success.

I lift my downcast head and run my eyes across all the guys' faces and down their more-than-pleasing bodies. Seems I am not the only one enjoying Connie's show, as I can see three very prominent erections bulging three very tight-fitting pairs of jeans.

I had to persuade Dea to leave you both alone. Nine chuckles out loud, making me laugh. *He wanted to jump into the fray and fuck you both into oblivion.*

CHAPTER FOURTEEN

"So, we're agreed?" Nine asks for what feels like the hundredth time.

"Yes," I growl. "I'll do the same demonstration from the ball, Connie will show her archery skills, Arrie his strength, Dea his Angel of Death form, and you your telepathy." I sigh.

He's been so worried about all of this, as we all have, but Nine's consistent pestering is getting on my last nerve.

"Are you sure this a—?"

I growl at him, edging my voice toward a roar, and cut off his question.

"You had that coming," Arrie says on a chuckle.

Sorry.

I shake my head. "Just stop being so pestering about it. I'm aware this is a shitty idea. But what other choice do we have? We need to come out of the closet sooner or later. When doesn't really matter." I shrug.

"I agree," Arrie rumbles.

I cannot believe the person on my side in all of this is

Arrie. He's seemed a little off with me ever since I fed from Dea this morning, but he isn't being openly hostile, so I can comfortably respond with, "See, even Arrie doesn't seem worried."

Arrie raises his eyebrows at me. "I do not worry about most things, Killer."

I laugh. "We both know your moodiness comes from worrying. Don't worry, I won't spoil your precious bad boy attitude." I slap his arm and walk ahead of the group slightly, wanting to get a glimpse of the Vampire Council building we'll be entering soon to be a group of show monkeys.

Arrie grumbles something in a foreign language behind me, but I shrug it off. Well, I try to.

For once, though, I'm curious.

Nine, what did he say?

He remains silent.

Nine?

Nope. Not getting involved in this.

N'awww, c'mon. Please, help a guy-girl out?

He sighs. *It's always something dirty or offensive. Do you really want to know?*

Yeah.

Fine. He said he'd like to slap your pretty ass into next week.

That is not what he said!

I wouldn't lie about something I didn't even want to translate in the first place.

I suddenly have the urge to slap Arrie on the arm again just to see how far he would go. But I shake that crazy thought from my head. I know he doesn't hold back during sex, Connie eluded as much, but with her refusing to tell me anything about the guys in the bedroom, I don't have much more to go on.

I suddenly find myself wondering what each would be like in the bedroom, and I find myself in a rather compromisingly tied-up position on Arrie's bed in a fantasy I would very much like to try one day.

Please stop.

I look over to Nine, who's trying to discreetly rearrange himself, and I laugh harder than I have in a while.

"Sorry." I pat him on the back, rubbing the tears from my eyes. "Didn't meant to turn you on, too."

He blushes at me. "Kinda hard not to be around you." He smiles, trying to be charming, but he just looks like he finds the whole situation awkward.

Dea looks at me with a raised eyebrow, and I nearly melt on the spot. "What were you thinking, Angel?"

I just wink and shrug. "Guess you'll just have to use your imagination."

Dea pouts and looks to Nine, who shakes his head. "No way. I'm not translating that fantasy to anyone. Sweetie can imagine whatever she wants between Arrie and her female self." He shrugs, suddenly gaining confidence in his ability to manipulate the team around his little finger.

"You little shit!"

He runs forward, and I go to chase after him, knowing I'll catch up to him with ease, but Arrie grabs me by my waist and holds me back.

"What were you thinking?"

He doesn't seem put off by my male form; in fact, the entire team seems to find my sex changing ability less than weird. Accepting, even.

I shake my head. Not the time to get lost in my non-identity issues.

"Don't lose confidence now, Killer," he whispers in my ear.

"I want to know."

Shaking my head again, I look to Connie for a rescue, but she laughs and walks beside Nine. Traitor. What happened to girls always stick together?

Dea follows, leaving Arrie and me alone in a less-than-innocent embrace with my ass pressed against his groin.

He growls softly in my ear, and I shiver, my animal side calling to his gruffness. He nips my ear, sending more pleasant shivers down my body, and now I'm the one sporting a hard-on in public. Great.

"Tell me."

"I had Nine translate what you said." I can't look him in the eye as he stiffens. "Not that I know if he gave me a true translation, of course. But it had me wondering what it would be like. You know . . . with you?"

Arrie chuckles, his chest rising and falling with the delicious sound. "What did you imagine?" He lets me go but walks by my side as we chat a few feet behind the others.

"Err . . ."

"Come on, don't go shy on me now, Killer. I'm just curious. Promise."

Goddess, that nickname melts me every time it escapes those bright red lips.

"I thought about being tied to your bed and left at your mercy."

He licks his lips, my eyes tracing every swift movement of that tongue as he leans in to whisper, "If that's what you want, all you have to do is ask."

I shake my head. "I don't think taking you"—I gesture to his giant of a body—"as my first time is wise." I mean, the guy is huge. Not just he-works-out-a-lot huge, but Horseman of War massive. Like, I wouldn't want to be anywhere near him when he's really angry. Pretty sure I wouldn't live through the endeavor.

Arrie chuckles again, that sweet, melodious sound caressing my ears. "All right. Once you've deflowered that precious little body of yours with someone less . . . me, we'll come back to this discussion."

"We will?"

He nods.

Taking a deep breath, I ask my next question, the one that's been playing on my mind for the last few minutes. "So, does that just go for my female form?" The words rush out in a mumble before I can stop them, and I can't help the red blush that creeps over my neck and face, making my ears hot with embarrassment.

Arrie looks at me with a serious expression before leaning back and whispering, "I guess you'll just have to wait and find out.".

It never even occurred to me that I could sleep with Arrie in this form; I always just assumed sex in my male form would be with the other three, but I'm trying to learn not to be so presumptuous when it comes to them. They're a surprising bunch of people.

"There it is!" Connie yells, her voice traveling to my ears without much resistance.

I have good hearing in both forms, though my Vampire hearing is the better of the two.

The council building looms in front of us in all its modern-day glory and un-Vampire-ness. Like, seriously, it isn't at all what you'd expect a Vampire Council building to be. It has bright open windows, a white-and-gray-slated design, and plasmascreens built into the sides displaying all kinds of graphics. No castles. No dark, dingy corridors, no loud wailing or pitchy screams that'll keep you up at night.

(I know, I was disappointed too.)

"Can we just go inside?" I ask the rest of the team.

Dea makes himself visible, and the guards suddenly notice our presence and step aside, allowing us entry.

"I'll take that as a yes."

We enter through the glass double doors and walk right on up to the receptionist.

"Excuse me?" I say, getting her attention.

She lifts her hand and looks me over, leaving her red-eyed gaze on my torso a few seconds longer than what I'd consider comfortable. "Can I help you?" She practically purrs at me, making me internally grumble.

"Yes. We have an appointment with Prince Lucien in council room 3B."

She recoils, and I don't have the damnedest why. "Oh, you're that appointment. I . . . err . . ."

Sighing, I lean in and smile. "If you could just point us in the right direction, I'm sure we can make our own way there and be of less inconvenience to you, ma'am."

She giggles at my use of ma'am, waving her hand to cover her blushed cheeks. She really isn't all that special; or at least, I don't think so. She has manicured hands with long, pointed black nails, badly dyed hair, and far too much makeup. But she points us toward the elevators anyway. "It's on the basement floor, sir." She winks.

I turn around and walk away, waving her goodbye with a small thank you as I roll my eyes. "I'm ashamed to be female right now," I mutter under my breath.

The others find it hilarious, especially Dea, who prods and pokes fun at me the entire trip downstairs—with Nine's help, of course.

Upon exiting the elevator, Dea says, "Is that how you lured all of your hits in when you were a hunter, by flirting them into a corner and then, bam! Taser them?"

That is it. His jabbing has finally crossed the line. Before the doors fully close, I grab him by the scruff and shove him back inside, closing the doors and sending him back upstairs.

"I cannot believe Arrie is not my biggest problem today." I turn to Nine. "What has gotten into you two?"

He shrugs and continues walking down the corridor we've found ourselves in. It is, contrary to the rest of the building, a little rundown; the walls are less pristine, with flaking paint here and there, and the whole hallway smells of a musty kind of rust I have no intention of smelling again.

Connie walks on ahead, muttering, "3B . . . 3B . . . 3B." Until she stops outside of a metal door and shouts, "Found it!"

I wince. They can hear everything through that door, as I can hear everything beyond it. Muffled conversations, a few laughs, and Lucien's voice silencing them all flutters through the doorway cracks.

I hold my hand up to stop the team as Dea rushes toward us. Shushing them, I ask Nine, Anyone have any questions, concerns, or problems? There're twenty-one Vampires through that door, all of whom sound as though they don't believe we exist.

After a couple of seconds, Connie comes up to me and wraps her arms around me, hugging me tight.

I hug her back, knowing how hard this must be on her. "You'll be okay," I whisper so low I know only she can hear it.

She nods.

Nope. Everything's fine.

I step forward to open the door.

CHAPTER FIFTEEN

What greets me beyond the door is not what I expected; twenty Vampires stand around Prince Lucien, none of whom I recognize, except one.

Mr. Nice Vampire from the club walks forward with a quizzical expression, clearly not recognizing me in my male form, and smiles. "Welcome."

Essh, he is nice. I should probably change and inform him who I am.

Why ruin the surprise?

You are evil, Nine.

But he's right, it will be fun to see his face. Bonus, he isn't the grumpy or angry type, so hopefully he won't try to punch me in the face for tricking him.

Dea turns himself visible and smiles that charming smile. "Thank you for hearing us out and for agreeing to help should you like what you see."

Prince Lucien steps in front of everyone as Mr. Nice Vampire steps back into the ranks. "Well, well, well, little

Horseman"—he turns to face me—"you showed up."

"Of course. A deal's a deal, little prince."

"That it is." The smile vanishes from his face as he turns around to the group. "These are the Five Horsemen of the Apocalypse. I'll let them demonstrate their own powers. Step back in line against the wall." He steps back, too, but remains a little forward, introducing us one by one. "Horseman of War."

Arrie steps forward, pinches his thumb and middle finger together, and flicks the wall no one is leaning against. It cracks from floor the ceiling, leaving dust flying around the room.

Everyone murmurs, but from what I can hear, they aren't all that convinced, so I step up to Arrie and whisper, "Punch me."

He blanches. "I don't want to do that."

"Just do it. And make it a good one."

He sighs and nods. He lifts his arm up with a clenched fist and throws a right hook to my face, sending me through three walls as the entire team wince and rush to my rescue.

Every bone in my back hurts, but I wait patiently for my body to heal. Crack after crack, my back rights itself, and I manage to get to my feet without crumpling back to the ground.

Dea rushes over and looks at me with love in his galaxy eyes. "Are you okay, Angel?" His eyes flash gold for a moment before he reaches over to touch my arm, his hands glowing a bright green, and smiles. "You healed okay."

I nod. "Let's get the rest of this over with. Next time, someone else can be the assistant." I rub soothing circles around my lower back but join everyone in the other room.

Most of them are talking, but one conversation stands out. "Only Princess Alberta could throw someone that hard, and no one has lived to talk about it. Not even a Vampire."

Interesting piece of information. Wonder who Princess Alberta is?

"Next," Prince Lucien says, "the Horseman of Famine."

Nine steps forward and looks to the audience. *I'll need a volunteer.*

By the shocked looks on everyone's faces, he sent that to everyone in the room. Vampires included.

Mr. Nice Vampire steps up, cautious after Arrie's display of brute strength. "I'll help."

"This won't be pleasant," Nine says. "But it won't hurt."

Mr. Nice Vampire balls his hands into fists in an attempt to control his nervous shaking.

Cute.

Nine focuses on the man stood in front of him, hand raised in concentration. "Jump."

He jumps, eyes going wide.

"Stick your tongue out."

He sticks his tongue out, much to the hilarity of everyone around us.

But we stay silent, knowing how much Nine hates using his powers like this. He defends himself and the team, but without permission, he wouldn't enter someone's mind like this—not even ours.

"Pinch yourself."

He pinches himself lightly on the arm.

Nine releases his mental command. "I can use it to make someone do anything, even kill themselves."

I wince. Really?

Yes.

The solemnness of his voice takes me by surprise. He really doesn't like what he can do, does he?

Nine steps back in line.

It takes Prince Lucien a moment to announce Connie as he processes Nine's statement. "Horseman of Conquest."

Connie jumps forward, lightening the mood. "I can shoot any target I can see, no matter the distance." She takes the bow off her back and shoots a couple of arrows between people's heads.

They shout in shock but aren't impressed.

Well, they're about to be.

Arrie lifts Connie above his head and throws her into the air. She shoots an arrow mid-spin into the ceiling above her with ease, not even breaking a sweat, then she lands and splits the arrow with another shot with her eyes closed.

That has everyone murmuring their surprise.

"I can also hear, taste, smell, and see better than any species on the planet and never run out of energy in battle."

We weren't going to announce all of our powers, Connie, I complain in my head.

She didn't want to have secrets with the world. If we come out of the closet, she wanted it to be honestly.

Damn. Self-righteous bit—

"Horseman of Death."

The team take a step back as Dea steps forward. He changes into his Angel of Death form instantly—much to my awe. He is beautiful. His golden skin shows off his tattoo—which I think is odd he has in both forms—and his black-feathered wings reach wall to wall in this empty, cellar-like space.

"This is my Angel of Death form." He voice is like silk, drawing a lot of the Vampires forward in a trance-like state.

I can feel my mind turn to mush, and I just know I would do anything he asked in that moment. My feet try to move, but Arrie grabs my arm and Connie grabs the other, a smile on her face.

I briefly hear her say, "I didn't know that would affect her."

Arrie grumbles his agreement, but I don't care. I just want to go to Dea, to run my hands over that beautiful golden body.

Dea turns around in shock as he looks at me, ignoring the Vampires now on their knees (a few are still standing unaffected), and walks toward me. He places a hand on my cheek, relieving the ache in my chest at not being able to touch him. Like the world was all topsy turvy but is now the right way up, the blood rushing back to the rest of my body, and my lungs finally inhaling that sweet, sweet oxygen.

He turns back into his normal self.

Relief floods through me, like a tidal wave of tension has finally ebbed, but my shore has been left ever changed.

What was that?

"It controls the dead," Dea says.

So that's why it affected me? Because I'm technically dead?

No, otherwise it would affect the rest of us, too. You had a different reaction to him. One I don't understand. We'll think about it later.

Dea turns back around. "I can also heal almost any wound or injury, persuade your soul to have different desires and grievances, and can open and close the gate of the dead at will."

Also being honest. Interesting. It seems only Arrie and Nine have been semi-dishonest with their powers. But everyone gets a choice; it's their existence, after all.

I, on the other hand, do not get that choice. I step forward at Lucien's command: "Horseman of Magic."

"I'm new. Arrived a few months ago. These guys"—I point to the team behind me—"are two thousand years old. But I'm barely even a year old in my immortal life. You're all here today because of me."

They look at me with confused expressions.

"Horsemen are only born when there is a need for us. The Four Horsemen fought the ancient war, ending most of Demon- and Angel-kind and lifting the gate to the afterlife, allowing magical souls to pass through. But now, we're fighting a different war, one that hasn't fully started yet." I cough to clear my throat. "The war against magic."

Everyone gasps. Questions fill the room, and most of them are the same kind of questions I had when I first woke up in the house.

"I have the powers of each pillar community: Fae and Shifter in this form." I lift various Vampires and swing them around the room gently, then place them on the floor. I then shift into my panther form, bear, swallow, eagle, cricket, house cat, wolf . . .

They get the picture.

Turning back into my male form, it's time to shock the hell out of Mr. Nice Vampire who has so far leaned against the wall and watched with vague curiosity.

I blink and change. "But in this form, I can use Vampire and Witch powers."

Mr. Nice Vampire gasps. "You? You're . . . ?"

"Uh-huh. Sorry for the deception." I shrug and step up to him. "And thank you for being so nice. Balancing all these powers isn't easy."

He chuckles. "You're welcome." He has another question on his mind but is too afraid to ask or is too embarrassed. It's written all over his face.

I leave it be for now, choosing to turn back to the audience. I leave my fangs come out and hope that's enough. A mini-tornado rips through the room moments later, sending everyone flying and making me laugh. Goddess, it's good to be stronger than everyone in the room at something. For once.

Alright, asshole.

Shut up. You'd be just as happy as me right now if you could be this awesome.

You are awesome.

I blush, letting my air magic slip and allowing everyone to right themselves.

"That about covers it." I momentarily consider being honest like Dea and Connie and telling them about my Angel-descended Witch powers, but it's pointless because I have no control over them and can't be of use that way anyway.

"So," I ask, "will you help us?"

Everyone steps forward and, one by one, gets down on one knee. Eventually, Prince Lucien and Mr. Nice Vampire join them. "Always, Horsemen."

I turn back to the team, who look at me and smile. We did it.

Now to stage a coup.

Chapter Sixteen

Back at the hotel, we all crash on the couches in Dea's room and exhale our sigh of relief together.

"We . . . did it."

Dea smiles at me. "We did indeed, Angel." He scoots closer and wraps me in his arms, pulling me into a hug as we lie on his couch.

I breathe in his smoky lavender scent and curl up on his chest. Nine joins us by resting on my stomach between my legs, while Arrie and Connie lie behind us. We stay like that all afternoon, watching movies and eating junk food.

So far this has been a much better mission than the last, but I get the feeling the hard part is still to come. The coup is set for tonight, then we'll hopefully be taken by the rogue Vampires and I can murder their leader's fucking ass.

Flashes of Nine's lifeless, bleeding body cross my mind, and I bristle.

I won't let them get away with that.

My fangs slip in my anger, and I have to control my

breathing for a couple of minutes to calm down. Not to mention the slight breeze I'm causing. I hope no one notices.

Well, no one but Nine because he knows everything about me.

Everything you know about you. And only because you think so loudly.

Right.

Arrie, however, interrupts the blissful afternoon in the only way Arrie can. "We should talk about what happened this morning."

Nooooo. "Or we could not." I don't want to talk about why I'm so physically attracted to Dea, almost magically, in his Angel of Death form. It's . . . embarrassing.

Connie laughs. "C'mon, it can't be that bad?"

Nine snorts. "She was magically drawn to his essence and wanted to lick every part of his body. Not touching him physically hurt."

Dea gasps. "Really?"

I just keep my head on my chest and nod. I can't look anyone in the eye right now. Goddess, it's so embarrassing. Why? Why is it always me?

"It really is, isn't it?" Nine asks.

I just whine.

"So," Arrie asks, and I internally shudder, "what was it?"

Nine shrugs. "No idea."

Everyone looks at him in disbelief.

"What?" he asks. "I don't know everything. I've never come across anything like that before."

"But . . ." Arrie trails off.

I'm pretty sure I have some vague idea, but I'm uncertain. "I think it's my Angel magic calling to his." I sigh. "I just don't know why it only works with Dea and not Connie."

"Because my magic doesn't work the same way, hon.

Although it is Angel magic, I don't transform into a literal Angel."

Ah. "Makes sense."

"And that theory works with how your mind was at the time. You weren't in control. Connie and Arrie had to hold you back, and I'm pretty sure if Dea was naked they wouldn't have managed that." Nine laughs, and I throw him an irritated scowl. "Sorry. Sorry."

"Can we see it again?" Connie asks. "Just to make sure. And this time, we don't have to hold you back or anything."

"See where it goes," Nine finishes. "I agree. It would be useful."

I don't want to become some mindless magical slave to Dea's Angel form.

Dea must have sensed my hesitation because he grabs my chin and lifts me to eye level. "Do not worry, Angel, I will not let anything happen against your freewill."

I nod. "Okay." I trust him.

He stands and pulls me to my feet. "Here it goes." He closes his eyes and transforms, his wings reaching the floor in a wide arc of beautiful darkness.

Does this have to be in my female form? I mean, why can't my Angel powers be in my non-Vampire form. This is gonna be a bitch.

I look up at Dea, now even taller than before, and am struck with the same sense of mind-melting awe as before. His golden skin shines brightly in the afternoon sun, and his wings look like I could soar on them for hours.

Damn, this man is beautiful.

His tattoo swirls over his chest, which always seems to shift with him topless, and I can't resist reaching out and touching it.

He lets me, thank goddess, because my mind and chest hurt not touching him. I follow his tattoo down his shoulder and onto the ridged lines of his abs, following it through to the edges, where I run my hands along the boned ridges of his wings.

Dea groans and leans into my touch.

He likes it. Maybe it's like my fangs. Speaking of fangs, they slipped out at some point during this experiment.

His wings encompass me as he yanks me into his arms.

He's so warm, so comfortable, so . . . him. The lavender scent I always associate with him envelops every sense, and I can't help but take a deep breath as he leans down and places a gentle kiss to my lips.

A caress of his lips against mine, like a gentle brush of *I love you* that scorches its way into my heart. He sighs into me, then presses his body against mine and forces his tongue into my mouth, causing me to moan at the sensation of his mouth on mine in this form and all the various areas of his lips and tongue grazing my fangs.

I can vaguely hear the rest of the team shouting in the background, but I ignore it in favor of tasting more of the man who has his wings wrapped around my torso.

"Bro," Nine says as he intrudes past Dea's wings and into our space, "change back. She doesn't want this. Neither do you. Please. We'll have her together one day, or you can have her alone, but when you're both yourself."

Dea snaps out of our trance and stumbles backward as Nine catches me and steadies me on my feet. His wings vanish, and with it, the foggy haze I've found my mind in.

"Fuck," Dea swears. "That was . . . intense."

"I need some time in Sweetie's library to confirm, but I think I have the answer."

We look at him expectantly, but he remains tight-lipped. "Later." He waves off our concern. "Not an immediate concern, and I don't want to worry you both without getting all the facts for your no doubt endless list of questions."

I nod, understanding his reasoning, but the lack of immediate answers bothers Dea, as he begins to protest.

Nine cuts him off with a quick kiss, though, and then blushes when he realizes the entire team are watching. "Trust me."

Connie smiles at them with relief while Arrie stands with his arms across his chest, like usual, but there's a hint of a smile underneath that resting scowl face.

Dea sighs. "Very well."

The next thing on our dossier is the coup, and I can tell we're all a little nervous about it. Fake fighting Vampires is gonna suck, especially with Arrie not really being able to hold back and Connie not wanting to.

"Errr . . . Arrie?"

He turns toward me with a smile, and I cringe. He isn't going to like this conversation. He frowns and sighs. "What is it?"

"Ummmm . . . Are you able to hold back in a fight, or should I bench you?" I wince, knowing it's a sensitive subject.

His brows furrow for a moment as the room holds its breath. "I'll stay on the side lines as back up but hop in last minute so I'm with you when we're caught."

"Thank you." I can't help it, between Dea's Angel issue and everyone being so nice to me since the whole 'I was a murderer' thing, I need to comfort him. I run right up to him and throw my arms around his neck—having to jump to reach that high.

He chuckles and holds me in place, and we sort of hug. I

think.

I'm hugging the Horseman of War. Goddess, that's a strange thought. But it feels so . . . nice. He's strong—stronger than anyone I've ever met—and it makes me feel safe. Protected. More so than with the others, since I'm stronger than them in my female form.

He nuzzles my neck and breathes me in as I do the same. He smells of that familiar metallic twang mixed with the scent of the pine forest outside the house. It smells like home.

I eventually release him and jump back to the floor. Turning around, everyone is smiling at us, even Dea, who has been frowning since the whole incident a few minutes ago.

"What?"

They say nothing, but Nine goes ahead and answers, *We rarely see him like this. It's . . . beautiful.*

Oh. "Ready for the coup, then?"

Everyone grimaces but nods.

"Remember, we need to hold back and not seriously hurt anyone, but it does need to look realistic."

"Yes ma'am," they all say in unison, causing me to grin.

Chapter Seventeen

The coup is to take place on a busy tourist street with lots of attention, so the rogue Vampires will hopefully notice in time to step in once they realize it's us causing the problem.

Rule number one: do not attack or harm innocent bystanders.

Rule number two: do not kill the volunteers.

Rule number three: be as disruptive and annoying as possible.

Arrie would have been great at this had his mind not been so focused on battle that he accidentally loses control every now and then. Not that I could say much when it came to control. We should be able to make do with us four, especially with Connie and her hatred of Vampires.

The 'enemy' Vampires are walking the street as innocent civilians, and we're all stood on the corner looking as menacing as possible in all-black hoodies and combat boots.

Guess it's up to me to make the first move. I see one of the volunteers and Vampire speed up to him, throwing a light punch. "Bloodsucking a-hole!"

There, that should start everything up beautifully.

He fights back, struggling to get a good grip on my arms as I flail in his hands, pretending to struggle. Truthfully, he's weak as fuck, but I don't want to make the poor guy feel bad.

His brown hair and mundane features wash into my vision as I punch him in the stomach, causing him to bowl over. "Where are they?"

"Where are who?" he yells back.

"Your little friends, the rogue Vampires that tried to murder me!"

He slides to his knees and begs for his life. "Please . . . please, I know nothing."

"Pfft." I wave an arm and send him sprawling to the floor. I watch until I'm sure he's okay before moving onto my next 'victim.'

Nine's interrogating another Vampire while Connie is spending a fair deal of her time punching another in the face.

Tourists have started videoing with various plasmascreens, and I'm sure it's everywhere by now. The whole street has erupted into terror and screaming, with humans and other innocents running away.

We could catch them if we want, but that isn't the point.

I run up to Mr. Nice Vampire and swing at him.

He smiles and blocks my punch, sending him flying backward. "Why, hello there. Can I help you?"

Seriously? He's playing nice even now?

"Tell me where they are?"

He scowls and screams, "Never!"

Sprinting at full Vampire speed, he rushes me, taking me by surprise and throwing me off balance. "Ha, caught you by surprise, newbie."

He punches me in the stomach, and I double over in pain for a moment before pulling my air magic back and flinging it at him, sending him flying a few feet away from me.

I transform into my male form and then into a lion before roaring down the street at him. Everyone stops screaming and turns my way; even Nine, Connie, and Dea have turned around to see the commotion with amused yet surprised looks on their faces. Connie, of course, is sporting a proud mama-hen look, clearly delighted at my show of violence.

I run at Mr. Nice Vampire as he looks at me in terror—real, edging terror—and pin him to the tarmac as I roar in his face. Transforming back into a man, I yell, "Where are they?"

You are surprisingly good at this whole bad guy thing.

Thanks. I think.

"I-I-I . . . I don't know. I swear." He sounds genuinely terrified, and for a moment I think he's being real with me and I feel bad, until he uses that to his advantage and throws me off, sending me flying through the air.

"Fucking friendly asshole," I mutter as I land in a heap on top of a magicar, groaning at the pain spiraling through my back and ass.

That's going to be a bitch to heal later.

I really hope they're coming soon, as I have figured out this evening that I dislike being the bad guy more than I do reliving my nightmares of actually being the bad guy.

Fuck it all to hell. Time to kick it up a notch.

I lift my female self into the air, hair splaying backward in an attempt to look as cool as possible, and use air manipulation to stretch my voice along the entire street.

"Where are the rogue Vampires?" I demand of everyone in the nearby vicinity. "We'll keep killing your kind until you come here and pay for your mistakes!"

I pull a car up to my level and smash it in the general vicinity of one of the volunteers but nudge him out of the way just in time to save his life.

He gives me a grateful smile before schooling his features and running to help a 'fallen' Vampire to safety.

Just at the end of the street, I see a flock of Vampires marching our way through a thick shroud of fog, and my breath hitches. Finally. I was wondering how much more public chaos I was going to have to cause before they decided to actually show up.

"Enough!" a voice I barely hear above the carnage shouts down the street. "They're innocent Vampires. Leave them be, you monsters!"

I fly toward them and go to attack, Nine, Connie, Dea, and Arrie following suit. I swing a punch at the leader as I descend toward the ground faster than I knew I could fly, but he ducks out of the way, causing my fist to land in a crater hole I punch into the tarmac.

We're gonna have to pay public damages, aren't we?

Don't worry about that.

Right. They have lots of money.

Focus.

"So," the man at the front of the army of Vampires says, "you've finally decided to fight back. Show the world what you really are." He raises his hand to the army and closes his fist.

Everyone descends on us, penning us into a circular army of Vampires, each one with their fangs out, eyes glowing red, and a menacing scowl on their faces.

I grab hold of Connie's hand and rub soothing circles in the center of her palm before I drop the knife I've drawn from my collection on the floor and get to my knees.

No point in fighting if we're going to be captured anyway. "Take us to your leader."

The man laughs. "You don't want that, monster." His sickening smile mars his otherwise handsome blond features.

I shiver. "Take us to your leader."

He sighs. "Well, you're in luck, because we have orders to bring you straight to him."

Thank fuck. For a minute there I was worried this plan had been for nothing and they were going to kill us on the spot. Not that that would work, of course, but it would certainly ruin the whole 'get to the top' part of the plan. Luckily for us, villainous leaders are predictable.

They strip us of all our weapons—much to Connie's annoyance—and stuff us in the back of a van in magicuffs. This time, however, I'm prepared for not being able to get out of them and don't even bother trying.

"Well," Connie says, "this fucking sucks."

I grumble under my breath, suppressing the growl that threatens to erupt from my open mouth. "Yes, I know. Don't worry about it."

Our weapons are in a locked storage chest beside us, tantalizingly out of reach.

Dea huddles in the corner, his visibility wearing off now he's in the cuffs; Nine sits next to me, his shoulder pressing up against mine; while Arrie sits next to Connie, trying to provide some modicum of comfort despite the fact we're trapped in a van by Vampires with no magic or weapons.

Yup, this part of the plan sucks, but at least it's expected. We won't be stuck like this for long. I hope. At least I had the decent decision to change into my male form before they put us in handcuffs, so I don't starve into insanity in the process; goddess only knows how that would have gone down.

Nine squirms uncomfortably beside me. "I fucking hate these cuffs. It's like being blind."

Right, he wouldn't be able to use telepathy like this, since it's a form of magic. Wow, that would suck. I shimmy around on the spot a bit before grabbing his hand with mine and squeezing. "It won't be for long."

"I know." He sighs. "It's just like having my main way of communication and seeing taken away. I hate it." I can hear the tears he's holding back; this really bothers him.

I shouldn't have put him through this.

"I don't need to read your mind to hear that, Sweetie. Stop being silly. This isn't your fault. It was the right plan to make."

"He's right," Connie says through a sigh. "I mean, I hate this plan, but we need to see who's at the top."

"They can hear everything," I say. "You know that, right?"

They all nod.

"As if they didn't know we had some sort of plan." Arrie scoffs.

It takes over two hours to get to wherever their headquarters are, and by the time we get there, I seriously have to pee. They yank us out of the van, and I squirm. "I gotta pee!"

Nine chuckles while Arrie sighs.

The Vampires just scowl at me and roll their eyes. "No."

I growl under my breath at the pair of them. "I. Need. To. Pee." When they look at me with disdain, I sigh. "Look, I really gotta pee, I can't be arsed to punch you in the face—which I couldn't do anyway given these." I wave the cuffs and jangle them in front of me. "And my plan won't work if I fight now. So please let me fucking pee."

They give each other a silent shrug and drag me through a door down the alley the others all stand in, waiting. Through the metal door, I find myself in a bathroom. A public bathroom. The guy who dragged me in here doesn't make a move to leave.

"You're gonna watch me pee?"

He shrugs.

"For fuck's sake."

There are two other guys at the urinals, and I look at me and shudder. Shit. I wish I could speak to Nine right now. Isn't there a bunch of rules about peeing in a men's room? I'm gonna fuck this up, aren't I?

Luckily they cuffed my hands at the front; this way, I can undo the zipper of my jeans and actually pee without sending piss everywhere.

Walking up to the nearest free urinal, next to the guy with the blond hair, I unzip my pants and pee. Ugh, and I thought peeing as a guy was hard when I wasn't handcuffed. (Let me tell you, it's not fun.)

The blond-haired guy looks at me funny with a heavy amount of side eye, but I have no idea what's wrong.

"What is your problem, dude?"

He coughs his surprise, rushes to finish up, and runs away to the sink.

Did I say something wrong?

The Vampire guard snickers at me, and the two men run out of there like I'd served them my shit on a stick at a hotdog bar. Seriously? I'm just trying to pee.

Once I zip back up and turn around, the guy stares at me with slight disgust. "What? I seriously needed to fucking pee!"

He shakes his head and drags me back outside to the team, who wait patiently for us to return.

"Peeing as a man while handcuffed . . . Not fun."

Nine laughs, but Arrie just grumbles something I actually can't hear for a change. Thought I would be relieved about that, but I find myself feeling out of the loop, instead, and desperately wanting to know what he said.

Our two escorts lead us down the alley and out the other side to stand before a large derelict building. It has at least four stories and looks like it could all come crumbling down at any moment. My thoughts are clearly written all over my face because the escort standing next to me laughs.

Huh?

They push us toward the half-broken door with pieces of splintered wood jagging out at odd angles. But the moment I step onto the broken pathway that leads to the front door, the light shimmers and everything changes. The once derelict building shines a brilliant white and pale blue—an office building with heavily shaded windows.

A Vampire building. A seriously expensive, well-funded Vampire building.

Everyone stands aghast at the sight of the building and the surprise of the whatever-the-hell magic conceals its real appearance.

"C'mon," one of the guards says. "She's waiting."

So the leader is a woman? Interesting. Wonder if it's anyone we know?

They lead us through doors, corridors, and hallways that all looked hauntingly like the ones of the official Vampire Council building; seems they want to create a new government, if this imitation is anything to go by.

Up ahead is a small office door—no grandiose framing or other over-the-top frills, just a simple door—leading to a simple room. But the person standing in front of the desk in that room is far from simple. Her every facial move is calculated, from the vague twitch of her eyebrow feigning surprise at seeing us, to the gentle smile feigning delight at having to deal with us.

"Horsemen." She gestures to the seats lined in a row on the far wall a few feet from the desk. "Please, sit."

Chapter Eighteen

We all sit without fuss. It isn't as though she's really more powerful than us, so the whole sitting versus standing power play isn't going to work here.

She doesn't look at Dea, so he probably can't be seen right now, but she looks at the rest of us and frowns at the cuffs. "Remove those. They won't be necessary."

The guards who escorted us here unlock the cuffs with a spellbead of some kind (would be good to have one of those on hand in future) and when he undoes Nine's, I hear him release a gratifying breath.

I grab his hand and smile. "Better?"

He nods, then returns to his stoic, not-caring-about-this-bullshit expression he was sporting before.

Right. Stoic. Play the long game.

Is she really their leader? That's the first question I need answered.

Dea knows her.

I glance Dea's way. He knows her? How?

Nine stays silent, and I just look at him and know instantly how he knows her.

He's slept with her, hasn't he?

Nine nods.

Great. Just what we fucking need. Tell Dea I won't hesitate to remove her head from her shoulders if she pisses me off. I don't care where his dick's been.

I change into my female form and step in front of the woman trying to look as scary as possible. It isn't working.

If she's responsible for this Vampire group's actions, she's the one I need to have a little chat with. The team aren't going to like this, so I keep them in their seats using an intense increase in air pressure so they can't move.

Refocusing on the annoying-as-fuck piece of Vampire shit in front of me, I tighten my fist.

She starts choking as the air surrounding her disappears. Her hands grasp at her neck, trying desperately to stop what probably feels like being strangled.

Good. Let her suffer a few seconds longer.

I unball my fists as she inhales large gulps of air, swallowing them down with eager abandon. "So, tell me, who are you working for?" Because she has to be working for someone; Vampires don't take war-level grudges against the Four Horsemen without a serious grievance, and since no one has pissed off anyone that much, I'm guessing they're working for or with someone.

"No . . . one." She coughs as she leans against the wood of her desk. "We work . . . alone." Her voice croaks and cracks the more she tries to talk.

The more her denials are voiced, the more pissed off I become. I would ask Nine to look, but I don't want him to feel any more uncomfortable today. That isn't fair.

"Nope." I shake my head. "Not the right answer." I remove her air supply once more, thinking about nothing but Nine's bleeding body on the floor of the garden, Dea's face when he realized Nine was seriously injured . . . "You wouldn't know enough about us if you weren't working for or with someone."

Her lips turn blue. Lucky she's a born Vampire, or this would be harder. And messier. Born Vampires are born, live, and die. Turned Vampires, however, really are undead—though, the magic that keeps them undead dies eventually. We got lucky, or I would be totally ruining these clothes.

"Stop." It's Nine's voice. I can hear them all pleading, but I don't care. We need answers, and this is the best way to get them.

I let her breathe once more and catch her by the arm before she collapses to the floor. "Gonna tell me what I want to know?" I sigh. "Not a fan of torture, would rather you just tell me."

"You're crazy," she says. "Get off of me!"

"Yeah, probably. Immortality'll do that to you." I pick her up by the scruff of her perfectly-placed shirt and deposit her scrambling body on the desk chair.

Her surprised face and uncomfortable posture gives me a revelation: she doesn't sit there often. Sighing, I wipe a hand over my face. "Who's the real leader?"

She blinks at me and smiles. "You're as good as they say." She stands up. "But I can't answer that."

I release the team behind me, but they don't move. Only Arrie comes to stand next to me, placing a hand on my shoulder. "What now?"

I look up at him and nod, hoping he will understand my meaning.

He grimaces slightly but understands, because he grabs her

body and throws it through the nearest wall. It isn't enough to kill her, but it is enough to shock her into a new sense of talkative, as she realizes we are all a little crazy.

It's a good act, but I don't know how long I can keep playing the bad guy before my moral compass spins in the right direction. I need answers, and I need them now.

There is one thing Vampires don't like, and that's more powerful Vampires. I don't want to scare Connie, but answers are more important.

I sprint at the female Vampire with full fangs, red eyes, and hopefully looking a tad scary. Scratching a gash on the side of her neck, I let the trickle of blood wash over my finger before raising my hand and licking it off.

"No, please!" she whimpers. "I can't tell you anything. He'll kill me."

"He?"

She nods. Her shirt slipped in the fall, and I notice finger marks surrounding her neck. Ones not created by me given the width of the fingers compared to my tiny ones.

I trace the bruises with a finger and ease up on the whole scary interrogation thing. "Who did this to you?"

Tears spill down the side of her face, and that's it, all my fake, mean-faced bullshit crumples to the ground.

Sighing, I help her to her feet and offer a small sip of my blood to help her heal. Least I could do. "Take it. It'll heal you in no time. I think."

She raises an eyebrow and licks it off my finger.

I watch, astonished for a moment, as her cuts, scrapes, and bruises vanish, her pale Vampire complexion returning to its normal color.

"C'mon." I grab her hand and guide her to the desk chair she was not so comfortably sat in earlier. It's designed for

146

someone taller than her, by the looks of it. "You know," I say, "we could always bring you back to *Sheruta* with us."

We can do that, right Nine?

Yes.

"Listen, we need to know who the leader is so we know who he's working with. We can't prevent or stop this war without the right info."

She nods. "I know. I just . . ."

"Look, I know you're scared, but this isn't about you. The world is in danger if we let war run rampant through the streets. Thousands of innocents of every species known to man—and probably some unknown—will get injured in the crossfire. Not to mention what this'll do to the humans. I don't want that. Do you?"

"So, you're not crazy?"

"I'll do whatever it takes."

She looks to where Dea sits, not quite meeting his eyes. "It's him. He's leading this."

Dea stands and pales, going visible so she can see him.

Her eyes meet his with affection, and I recoil in annoyance, spending a split-second of my time reconsidering the decision to let her live.

Relax. You know Dea's obsessed with you.

Nine's right. I really need to relax. I'm not a jealous person, so where is this coming from?

Focusing on the task at hand, or trying to, I turn to our new informant and ask, "Who is he?"

"My husband. Prince Phillipe."

Well, shit. The future Vampire King is working against the SC and has some serious beef with us. Just fucking great.

Chapter Nineteen

"Now what?" I ask Dea. "This was not what I imagined when I planned this fucking trip."

"What did you imagine, exactly?" He looks straight at me with exasperation, then steps toward the perfect-looking Vampire and wraps an arm around her shoulder. "Come on. Let's get you sat down."

"This isn't going to end well," Connie mumbles.

I shoot her a please-shut-up look and stare daggers at Dea. "I imagined being able to end the existence of whoever's plan it was that nearly got Nine killed." You know, figuratively speaking, since he would just come back from whatever death he would have suffered.

Dea turns my way with a shocked expression—his arm still wrapped around that Vampire's shoulder that I can't seem to stop staring at.

"What? Were you expecting some kind of nice Horseman of Magic with aims of peace and dropping candy off to poor children's houses?" I shift into my male form and growl. "I'm only one person!"

I can feel the anger well beneath the surface, ready to explode. I'm not feeding properly, Vampires and Shifters are known to be territorial over their loved ones, and he's intentionally making my life harder!

My body flits back to my female self of its own accord, causing everyone in the room to step back with a gasp.

I mean, could he be any more inconsiderate right now? I'm sure if I wasn't so strung out, come off my period not two days ago, and starving, I wouldn't be having a problem, but clearly I am, and I really wanted to rip her throat out because of it. I can see her main artery pumping away underneath that delicious skin of hers. I could easily peel that pretty, delicate skin off of that pretty, delicate neck.

Dea steps back from the Vampire whose name I still haven't bothered to get with raised hands. "Easy there, Angel. Calm down."

What's going on? Why do I feel really hot all of a sudden? "What's happening to me?" Sweat beads down my forehead in washes of desert-inducing sweat.

The Vampire on the chair looks horrified, and I turn to see the rest of the team with similar expressions, though admittedly less shocked.

Nine steps forward, though he still doesn't come near me. "You're on fire."

Wait, what? I look down at my body and scream.

Flames engulf my entire being from head to toe. My instinct is to try to bat the flames out—somehow put the fire out—but I'm not in any pain, I can just feel the intensity of the heat with every breath and every slight movement.

Err . . . Calm, Magic, calm. Remain calm. You can think your way out of this. The others can't help without getting burned, so it's up to you. Triggers? Jealousy. Definitely jealousy. Maybe anger. How to turn those emotions off?

Ha! That's like asking me not to want brownies. Or at least, it feels that pointless.

Come on, Magic, you're not the jealous type. You barely reacted to Dea and Nine's flirting on the last mission; and he's not even flirting. This is just some kind of heightened Vampiric response because of my lack of a sex life.

Dea steps forward, but I hold up a hand. "Please don't open your mouth and make things worse. Just . . . gimme a minute."

He nods.

He loves you. I know it's early days, I know we have all of eternity, but he thinks about you differently to anyone else. Even me.

That . . . He . . . What?

I've rendered you speechless. Who knew that was possible?

I smile amidst the tears leaking from my eyes and look back down at my body. No fire. But I can feel the simmering of heat just below the surface, ready to burst the moment someone pisses me off.

Male form. Male form. Male form.

I feel the switch come over me, and before I know it, we're safe from me bringing the building down to a pile of ashes.

Deep breaths—and promptly avoiding Dea's eyes—has me walking over to the Vampire. "My name's Magic." I help her to her feet and grasp her hands. "If you need anything at all, come and find me. The moment you change your mind and want somewhere safe, a real life, call me."

I ask Nine to pass on some kind of contact information to the poor Vampire bride and walk out of the room, practically running out of the building. My skin itches in a way I can't explain, like it's crawling with a deep sense of uncomfortableness; I need to be outside right now, some place where I can't hurt anyone.

Shift. I need to shift. The moment I get outside, I shift into the first instinctive animal I can think of and pace outside the building while waiting for the others to join me.

What's wrong with me? Why have I gone from semi-innocent and wanting to wait and be myself to this sex-obsessed, jealous girlfriend? That's not me. At least, I don't want it to be. I just want to go home. I want to go back to my library, back to family dinners, back to watching Arrie get annoyed every time I feed from someone else.

Normality.

The others stalk toward me with serious faces. They all stand around me, stopping me from pacing and caging me in place.

Connie crouches down to my level and runs a hand through the fur on my head, eliciting a purr from me. "You okay, hon?"

I nod my panther head and stalk off in some other direction, hoping to grab a cab so we can get back to the hotel. I shift into a small tabby housecat the moment Connie hails a cab from the nearest busy road, allowing me to rest in her lap as she strokes comforting hands down my back and scratches between my ears.

I won't lie, that feels like a brilliant massage, only better. I purr the entire way back, content in my own little cat universe as I ignore all my problems and the pending doom of the upcoming war.

Connie carries me back to my room in the hotel, where we have to sneak around to avoid all the stares and whispers from everyone who saw us attack Vampires earlier this evening.

"Are you going to shift back?" Dea asks as we all sit on my

bed in silence. "Because we need to make plans."

Internally sighing, I shift into my male form and then female form. "I'm done with plans. You make them." I walk into the bathroom and run a bath, adding in generous amounts of bubble baths, salts, and other smelly, relaxing liquids I don't recognize.

I can hear them all chatting in the bedroom but decide to ignore them in favor of sinking into the best moment I've had all fucking day.

Sweetie?

I sigh. Yes.

Dea's worried you're mad at him.

I'm not.

I know.

Tell him to come in but with his eyes closed.

Nine chuckles, and two minutes later, Dea walks in with his eyes closed, taking small but measured steps into the bathroom.

"Give me a minute." I yank the curtain across the bath and lay back down. "There you go." He can see my silhouette but nothing else. That'll do.

Dea remains silent for a few minutes, and I worry he might bail and run away. "I am sorry, Angel."

I sigh. Again. "Don't be. I'm not mad at you. You helped an innocent woman into a chair." I grumble some non-words and start again. "I don't know what's wrong with me. I'm not usually a jealous person."

"I know." Dea sits on the floor by the bath, his back to the tub. "I cannot change the past. She was so miserable, I just wanted to show her what it should be like. Just for a night."

"Stop." I sniff, trying to hold back the tears. "You don't need a reason or an excuse. You could sleep with whomever you wanted. It doesn't matter to me." I creep my wet hand around the curtain and rest it on his shoulder. "I care about what you do now."

I can feel his shoulders rise a little at that, and he turns to grab my hand and place a gentle kiss on the palm. "Do not be too angry at yourself, Angel. Your powers are new, as is this . . . link between our Angel powers. It will take time to figure out."

I nod, hoping he can see.

"We'll be waiting in bed for you."

The sleeping arrangements are a little different this time, with Dea and Arrie on either side of me and Connie and Nine on the outside. Dea's gentle charm to Arrie's gruff warmth is a perfect combination of . . . contentment.

One day, you'll be brave enough to say it. One day, you'll be ours as much as we've become yours.

Chapter Twenty

A loud knocking disturbs the five of us early the next morning, merely four hours after we all fell asleep. Grumbling, I get up to answer the door.

"Huh?" I ask as I open the door to a servant holding out a letter. An actual letter. On paper! I don't think I've ever received one.

Grabbing it, I sprint back into the room to find everyone awake and sitting up in bed, a space still left for me to re-join them.

"What is it?" Dea asks.

"A letter . . . I think."

"You think?"

"Well," I say, as I sit back down between Arrie and Dea, "I've never received one before."

Dea chuckles as Arrie rests a hand on my shoulder. "I do not feel this is going to be a good first." Dea grabs the letter from my hand and frowns. "It is from the Fae Council."

"How do you know?"

Connie leans over Nine and points to the fancy symbol on the front. "That's their emblem."

Ah, so the Fae want us for something. I groan. "What now?" I rub my eyes to try and wake up, but nothing I do makes a difference.

"Here," Arrie says as he holds out his wrist but keeps his eyes on the letter.

I take his hand in mine and rub circles over his knuckles, making the big guy shiver. Breakfast time. The moment my fangs slip and I bite down on Arrie's wrist, he stifles a moan—well, he tries.

I haven't fed from him directly before. His woody, metallic scent trickles down my throat as I suck harder.

"Fuck, that's . . ."

"Intense," Dea finishes for him. "More so than other Vampires."

That vaguely registers in the back of my mind as I focus on the task at hand and not getting lost in the moment, accidentally draining the Horseman of War dry.

I lean over his body slightly and can feel his erection pressing into my thigh that rests between his legs. Resisting the urge to reach down his pajama pants and help myself takes an impressive amount of effort in my current state; one I am rather proud of.

Dea comes up behind me and trails lavender-scented kisses down the nape of my neck, forcing my body to arch into his, and I'm lost in the sensations for a moment before snapping back to reality.

I unlatch from Arrie and look up at him, giving what I hope is a thankful smile, but realize I am probably covered in blood. "Thanks."

He looks at me with a glaze over his eyes as he runs a hand

down my side and settles it on my waist. "You're welcome." Shaking his head, he tries to readjust himself, but it's pretty pointless in those loose sweatpants.

I realize in that moment that they would have let me continue if I wanted. That this is something they're prepared for. Goddess, that actually scares me a bit.

We've talked about it.

Really?

"Yes," he says out loud. "When we saw the direction this was going to go back at the beginning, we talked about all of this. Don't worry." He winks and grabs the letter from Dea's hand. "Now," he says, "about this." He waves the letter and opens it. Quickly scanning the words, he chucks it onto the bed with a groan and glares at Connie. "Why did you have to make that agreement?"

Understanding dawns on her face as she blushes and whispers, "Sorry."

"Huh?"

Nine grabs my hand. "We have to dance with the Fae Court. It was the bargain Connie made for answers in the last mission. They saw the fight online and know we're on Earth."

I sigh. "Better get going then." I have no idea what dancing with the Fae means, but since I'm part Fae, I gather it won't be as hard on me as the others.

"We should definitely tell her," I hear Connie say.

"Yeah, but Con, she's gonna freak." Nine's ever-annoying words of wisdom.

"What lollipop of sucky shit do I have to deal with now?" I throw on some clothes, not bothering with a shower if we're going to spend the next ten-plus hours on an airplane.

Dea winces. "Dancing with the Fae is dangerous for humans. They become entranced and dance until they die. It is an extreme event. One you will not like."

"You don't know that." But by the looks on everyone's faces, I get the feeling I really won't like it. "Okay. Can we just get this over with?"

Arrie stands. "I have a question for the Fae Court anyway." At everyone's confused faces, he explains, "Who among them are working for Prince Phillipe?"

"Right," Nine says, "they had to have some Fae magic to create that illusion spell to hide the building." He looks at Arrie in surprise. "Nicely deduced."

Arrie grumbles something in another language, and for once, it's aimed at Nine; that fact alone has me smiling.

I can do this, right? Dance with the Fae, not die, tell the truth while avoiding the juicy bits to a court famous for its flaunting of the laws surrounding lower paranormal lifeforms. The Fae are in charge of the world's dust supply, and rumor has it they cage pixies in giant farms and bleed them dry until they eventually die.

Yeah, Dea's right, I'm not going to like these people.

Everyone is dressed and ready to go in little over an hour, but it's me who seems to think of the politics in our decision. "Can one just pop in on the Vampire Council? Is that, like, a thing?"

Dea looks at me with furrowed eyebrows. "No. Why?"

"Because I think updating them on the fact we really weren't attacking their Vampires is a good move."

"If it's just an update you want, we can screen-message them." Nine's busy repacking the clothes in the small suitcase he dragged in not twenty minutes ago.

"We can do what to them?"

He lifts his head to smile at me. "Right. You were unconscious still when they brought it out."

Arrie gruffs as Connie mumbles, "Here we go."

Nine abandons his clothes folding—which shocks me enough into a standstill—and stalks toward me. "I invented a type of video message you can use via a telepathic spell the Fae helped me utilize. It was released a few months ago."

"Video messaging? But that's so . . . 2000s."

He laughs. "Yes, but this is more like a holographic video than a recorded image." He grabs my hand and sits me on the bed. "Here, I'll show you." Nine rummages around in his bag and pulls out a small black disk that he sits on the floor.

Okaaaay. I am officially weirded out.

He pushes a button on the side and says, "Vampire Royal Council." The machine sparks to life in a series of blue flashes and beeps like straight out of a science-fiction movie.

"It uses telepathic linking magic to connect two separate devices, similar to how our magiphones work, but this device scans the people and sends a holographic image instead of a video."

The device glows a deep green for a moment before it announces, "Vampire Royal Council member, Prince Lucien."

"Ah! Little Horseman."

I hear the little prince's voice crystal-clear through the device's speaker strip running around the outside. Or, at least, I assume it's a speaker strip.

The green glow beams toward the ceiling as a faintly-glowing image of Prince Lucien appears, looking like he's standing on the device.

"Wow!" I jump to my feet and walk around it, but the image stays the same. "This thing is awesome, Nine."

"Stop stroking your boyfriend's ego and say what it is you want."

My . . . boyfriend? Shaking my head, I reply, "Just wanted to make sure the Council were aware of our plan and they don't want us dead."

"Updated them for you this morning, little Horseman. No need to worry."

"And, err . . . who was present for this update?"

Prince Lucien blinks. "The entire Council, other than my father, he was busy. Why?"

"Nothing you need concern yourself with. Thank you for your co-operation, Prince Lucien." I bow lightly and look to Nine. Turn it off.

He flicks a button on the side, and the image goes dead, the lights dimming as the device shuts down.

I sigh. "To the Fae Court, then."

Chapter Twenty-One

New Orleans to Paris is the longest piece-of-shit flight I have ever been on (that I can remember, of course). Feet firmly on solid ground and my stomach back where it should be, I can finally breathe easy.

"Nine, when we get home, please remind me to help you invent easier, cheaper, Earth-to-Earth teleportation crystals. I'm sure I could do it with my Fae magic."

"Noted." He wraps an arm around my shoulder and directs us to the nearest cab outside the airport. At least, that's where I think he's taking us, but just as we get to the cab station, we keep on going until we stop in front of a limo.

An actual limo!

"We're getting in that?"

Connie smiles. "We are."

"Unlike the Vampire Council, who are terrified of us," Dea starts, "the Fae like to flaunt their excessive wealth and power to intimidate us."

I laugh. "Hilarious."

"We think so, too."

We all fit inside the limo with room to spare—much to Nine's delight after the last cab fiasco—and Connie decides that the offered champagne is the best way to start this trip.

"Gonna drink with me?" She offers me a glass.

I look at the glass with some trepidation. I don't trust the Fae, especially not with the possibility that they could be working with the rogue Vamps. What if they've poisoned it with something like Silver Leaf Vain?

You're too paranoid. Just drink the champagne.

I change into my male form and grab the offered glass. Waving a hand over the rim, I check to see if there are any spells or enchantments present. I might not be able to do anything to get rid of them, but detecting magic is as easy as breathing.

Clean. To my untrained magic hands, anyway.

I take a careful sip, not really confident in my abilities to detect Fae magic, even in this form, and sigh with contentment as I lean back and relax.

"You really thought they might poison us?"

I shrug. "Don't know what to think right now. Just making sure none of us have to expel poison in the middle of the Fae Court." I raise my eyebrows to her in challenge. "You're welcome."

Nine laughs. "Sweetie does have a point."

Dea and Arrie nod, but Connie just frowns.

I want to say not all of us are obsessed with the Fae, but given how little I know of Connie's background, it could be insensitive.

That gives me an idea. "What's the craziest thing you've ever done?" I direct the question at everybody, hoping they catch on.

Nine does, obviously, and answers, "This should be good."

Connie laughs, but Dea and Arrie grumble, as though sharing their massive amount of past is a chore, rather than a good way to get to know each other better.

"Oh, err . . . don't worry about it." It's not that important. I don't want to inconvenience them or make them uncomfortable. I change back into my female form and huddle over my plasmascreen to read a new book: mystery thriller this time. (I know, I'm shocked too.)

Dea gets up and sits beside me, placing a hand on my arm. "Sorry, I did not mean to upset you."

I shrug, wanting nothing more than to sink into my book and forget things for a few hours. I'll work on getting to know them better later. For now, life is too . . . Horseman of Magic-y. And everything little thing is bothering me, but I'm trying hard not to snap.

Instead of interrupting me, however, Dea merely lifts me into his lap and wraps an arm around me while I read. I won't lie, I melt a bit on the inside. Okay, a lot—my insides are a puddle of molten feelings right now. He can be so sweet when he wants to be.

Ugh. No. Still mad.

Arrie joins us—not wanting Dea to take the apologetic spotlight, I assume—and lifts my feet onto his lap, sending gentle strokes up and down my legs.

The book is good, or would have been if I could get past page five; being in Dea's and Arrie's laps is more than a little distracting. But mostly it's just comforting. They run hands over the small of my back, my shoulders, and my thighs, soothing any wayward thoughts that they don't really care, or that it's too soon to care in the first place.

They avoid any too-sensitive places, thank the goddess

because I don't think my Vampire-self could take that right now, but everyone is seemingly comfortable with each other, despite group intimacy not having been a thing with them in the past.

"Err . . ." I start as I put the plasmascreen down. "I . . . umm . . ."

"Just ask," Nine says in his no-nonsense, factual attitude.

"How are you all so comfortable with"—I gesture to Dea and Arrie—"this?" I can barely contain the blush that creeps over my face and neck. "It's just so . . . unusual, and you're all so comfortable with it. I thought this take a miracle to acheive."

Dea sighs behind me while Arrie tenses—something about his reaction bothers me. I grab his hand from my thigh and stroke comforting circles over his palm.

Arrie sighs this time and opens his mouth to speak. "I think we're all at different places with this, and for different reasons." He looks at Dea with a questioning look, and he nods.

"We are all okay with it but for different reasons." Dea points to himself. "I like that I could be in a relationship with you both." He gestures to both myself and Nine.

"And I, Sweetie"—Nine grabs my hand—"like the freeing nature in the way you think about it. I would be free to explore any relationship with any of you. I like that level of family between us, and you make it complete."

Connie goes next. "I've never wanted this before. Not with any of you." She looks to the floor. "But I like you, even . . ." She shakes her head, her blonde hair spilling out of its bun slightly. "Never mind." She walks over, hunches to avoid the roof of the limo, and grabs my hand as she sits on her knees. "I like you, and I would never restrict you. Besides, what if one day I didn't want to be restricted with any of the guys?"

"You'd be free, of course."

She nods and smiles.

I look to Arrie, but he shakes his head and sits up, getting out from under my legs and returning to his original seat. He's hiding something, and one day, he'll be comfortable enough to share. But until then, I'll smile at him and do my best to be a good friend.

I hope.

None of us deserve someone as naturally loving as you.

Where are these compliments coming from?

I just . . . Sighing, he says, *it doesn't matter. We'll talk about it when we get home. Besides, I've got a surprise in the works for you.*

"Ohhh, a surprise? Really?" I bounce on the spot, my spirits lifting almost instantly. Okay, so call me basic, but it's been a tough few months, and a girl can only have so many love interests without wanting to be spoiled every now and then. (You would if you could.)

He nods. "You'll just have to wait and see."

The others look at Nine and smile, catching onto something I'm missing, but I don't mind; they know me well enough by now that I'm sure I'll love anything Nine surprises me with.

We ride the rest of way in moderate silence, the occasional question from me breaking the tension; seems everyone is worried about this visit to the Fae Court.

"But I'll be fine in my Fae form, right? I mean, what harm could they really do to me?"

Nine nods. "You'll be fine. We're not worried about that."

Huh?

He sighs and says, "You're just not going to like the Fae Court. But it'll be easier to show you rather than explain. Just promise not the murder the Fae Queen, alright?"

Connie chimes in. "Yeah, don't go all crazy on her. They're a very particular type of people. We can work with them, we just need to be a little open minded."

That sounds ominous at best.

Another hour in the limo, drinking a second glass of champagne and finally getting past the fifth page of my new book, we're finally ready to get out of the moving vehicle.

Goddess, I hate all modes of transportation that don't involve my feet on solid ground and my stomach where it fucking should be.

Upon exiting the limo, I come to a halt—my thoughts, actions, reactions, and feet all coming to an abrupt standstill.

This is the Fae Court?

It's . . . beautiful. Old-fashioned. Rustic. Peaceful.

We're pulled onto the sidewalk of a wide, cobble-stoned street with red, gray, and white-bricked buildings surrounding every inch of our view of the city. There are no magically-enhanced displays, no modern magitech, and no cars. It's so . . . dated. But in a way that makes me release a sigh of contentment.

We're in a courtyard, and every building is like it's stepped out of the twentieth century; it's like stepping into one of my textbooks. Like I've gone back in time and can't quite catch my breath at the tranquility of the past.

"Is all of Paris like this?"

Connie shakes her head and grabs my hand. "No, just the Fae Court. They prefer limited technology. They're old-fashioned like that."

One day I want to see the rest of Paris. The city of love, of beauty, of upstanding technological advancement. It would be . . .

"Breathtaking," Nine finishes for me. "Paris is breathtaking."

I look at him with a smile as the limo drives away. "Maybe we could go see it one day?"

Dea steps up to us and wraps an arm around each of our waists. "Maybe we might all have time to go together after this."

He looks at me, and I understand: this is him making good on his promise to show me the world, the reasons to live, the benefits to being immortal.

"I'd like that."

Connie joins us and stands in front of me, grabbing my hand. "Me too."

Arrie doesn't say anything. He's lost in thought, it seems, as he looks into the distance without really looking at anything in particular, a hazy gaze covering his eyes.

I wonder what he's thinking about?

The past.

I flinch. I never really considered that their past might be as sucky as mine. Goddess, how selfish of me. I should make more of an effort to ensure they're doing okay.

Arrie still gazes into the distance, so I run up to him and wrap my arms around his neck, simply hanging there until he looks at me. As his gaze turns to mine, the look of solemn hurt forms tears in my eyes. So I do the only thing I know to do in that instance, I wrap my legs around his waist and my arms around his neck while my head buries into his hair.

I don't talk, I don't use words, I don't try to eke out a conversation I know he doesn't want, I simply hug him, trying to show him that I'll always be here. And eventually, he wraps his arms around my body and buries his own head in my neck, breathing me in.

"Thank you."

I can hear the tears in his voice, and I really want to know what kind of pain is in his past that makes him suffer like this, even after two thousand years. Maybe I can help?

"I'll always be here," I whisper into his hair.

I climb down the big guy's body and grab his hand. "C'mon, let's go deal with this stupid Fae Court and then go see Paris."

He walks beside me, not letting go of my hand.

I need to change into my male form while here ideally, but holding his hand feels too good, and I don't want him to let go.

Arrie leans in and whispers, "You should change form while here."

I nod and try to pull my hand away, but he keeps hold of it firmly. A few quick blinks and I'm in my male form, my hand actually large enough to not be engulfed by his. But still, he keeps holding my hand.

I look at him in confusion, but he smiles dazzlingly. "You're still you. I'm not too stubborn that I won't hold a man's hand." He rolls his eyes and moves us forward.

The others surround us with smiles that reach ear to ear while Nine mentally says, *Thank you.*

I don't think I've done anything of note, but appreciation is a girl's—guy's?—best friend. Damn it, I really need a neutral pronoun for my self-absorbed internal ramblings.

We walk down a stone corridor that has wide, empty arches looking out into the center of the courtyard where a grand statue of an old Fae Queen stands.

"That's the first Fae Queen, Titania, and inside the other courtyard is the first Fae King, Oberon." Nine sighs. "They were king and queen of the summer court, the first court of the Fae. Now they're all a single court, united a long time ago, but once upon a time, they were all separated. It was Oberon and Titania that brought the courts together and created the Fae we know today."

I nod, thankful for the info.

"She's beautiful."

Nine chuckles. "That she was."

"This was in your lifetime?" I ask in surprise, my eyebrows raising in shock.

He nods. "I wrote the entire thing down once in a lore book; I'll lend it to you when we get home."

"Oh, yay!" I almost clap my hands but refrain.

Connie groans. "Could you two stop geeking out every two seconds." But she has a smile on her face that lets me know she's joking.

"Puuuhhlease, if I were geeking out over you, you'd love it."

She winks. "Yeah, but instead you're geeking out over some long-dead beautiful Fae Queen." She pouts.

"Don't worry. You're way more beautiful."

She blushes, and Arrie laughs. "That you are, Con." He squeezes my hand slightly, and I squeeze back, letting him know that I don't mind. She is beautiful. I would be more pissed at him if he didn't think so.

We walk through all kinds of ancient stone corridors: some with armored statues, some covered in vines and roses and other flowers I have no idea how to identify, some with nothing more than grand-framed paintings of lewd and beautiful images. The entire place is breathtaking.

It extends into the buildings surrounding that courtyard and beyond. Nine tells me that most of the Fae live in relative seclusion, other than the ones who prefer the outside world; in that sense, they're similar to the Witches.

That's why you see more Vampires and Shifters in the world.

We reach a set of golden-brown doors with intricate roses worked into the wood, twirling into one another like lovers under the moonlight. I pause to admire the handicraft. "Whoever made those doors is talented."

Arrie, who is still holding my hand, huffs and hides a chuckle.

"Who made them?"

He shrugs but looks to Nine, laughs and shakes his head. "Arrie did."

I turn to Arrie with shock and admiration to watch him blush.

He shrugs. "I loved the original Fae Court. The one created by Titania and Oberon. It meant something. It was my gift to them."

So Arrie likes the Fae Court, too.

It's changed over the years, especially since the outing.

Ah, so they used to like it.

The doors open, and Arrie tightens his grip on my hand. I squeeze it, telling him I'm okay, but I get the feeling he keeps hold of me for more than just comfort. The fucker is keeping me on a leash, and I growl at the prospect of even needing one. I'm a free, independent woman——man——dammit!

The hall beyond is more eloquent than anything I've laid eyes on, including our house. The ceiling is so high I can barely make out the intricate design work painted onto it——but I manage with the help of my Shifter eyes——and the buttresses and arches trailing down to the stone columns covered in rose vines stand out with their stone artwork of more lewd images.

The whole room screams 'look at me' in the most attractive way. Even I can appreciate the time and effort that must have gone into the making of this room, especially before magical technology.

"Before technology altogether, actually."

"Really?" I ask Nine.

He nods.

"Damn."

A gilded throne sits on a singular dais at the end of the room, trailing roses in every color imaginable drape in waterfall designs behind, and sitting on that throne is a lady I can only assume is the Fae Queen. Her beauty exceeds anyone's I've ever seen—other than Connie's. She has pointed ears, just like me, glowing green eyes, and white hair that lands in a heap on the floor. Her smile is warm but obviously fake. These people can't lie, but they can act however they want. Luckily, my Fae form is not restricted in the same way.

Still shouldn't lie here. It's seen as disrespectful.

Noted.

"Ah, the Horsemen of the Apocalypse. It is good to see you once again." She smiles at everyone, including Arrie, which is unusual, but stops when she sees me. "And the new Horseman. It is a pleasure to finally meet you."

Her voice is melodic, and I can tell she uses it to charm most of her subjects, or at least foreign diplomats. Probably both. She raises herself from the throne and floats down the dais' stone steps to meet us in the center of the room.

"Horseman of Magic, charmed." She holds out her hand, but I'm not sure what's expected of me.

Kiss it.

Ugh. Fine. I grab her hand and raise it gently to my lips, much to the surprised smile of the queen.

"My, it is a pleasure." She smiles at me. "Someone of Fae heritage is always welcome in my court."

I bow my head slightly. "Thank you."

"Queen Darianne," Connie starts as she steps forward, "it

is a pleasure to be welcomed once more into your court. We are most looking forward to your party this evening."

Queen Darianne sits back on her throne and waves Connie's compliment away. "Dancing with the Fae is a grand gesture, but one you have all received before." She pauses to look at me. "Well, everyone but our new guest, of course." She laughs, and her pleasant tones dance across my ears. "I assume you will be wanting to take part in the festivities on offer this evening, too?" She raises her eyebrows.

What is she talking about? Goddess, why do the team never give me a heads up?

All members of the team tense, but it's Arrie who steps up, a smile on his face as fake as the pleasantries on offer by our fancy-looking queen here. "Actually, Your Majesty, we will be retiring after the party. We are rather busy of late."

Her scowl darkens the room. "My court does rather enjoy your presence at the festivities. You are all much practiced in the arts of lust and love."

Oh, those kinds of festivities. Nine, you guys can participate if you'd like.

He shakes his head slightly—enough for me to notice—and returns his attention to the queen.

We all stand in solemn unity on the matter, and the queen sighs. "Very well. If that's all, you can be seen to your rooms." She dismisses us with a wave of her hand, and we follow a servant out of the room.

The servant is a small, wispy type of girl with the same pointed ears as all Fae, but her skin tone has a subtle green tint to it, and I wonder why that is. I've only ever seen pale, white-skinned Fae. Do they have different skin colors to match what would have been their old season court?

Yes. Green is the old summer court. Pale-skinned Fae would have belonged to either the winter or autumn courts, while the blue-skinned Fae would have belonged to the spring court.

She guides us down singular corridors and multiple hallways, all made of stone, and all as beautiful as the rest of the court. "There are five rooms prepared for you down there and to the left. We have taken the liberty of—"

Nine interrupts. "We'll just be needing a singular room for our stay. Which one has the biggest bed?"

The Fae girl blushes and says, "The first one." She smiles at me and says, "We have taken the liberty of acquiring fresh blood for our new Horseman. I'll have it stocked in the room you choose."

I bow my head and walk past her toward the corridor she referred to. Five doors lie alongside the roses and tulips brushing the walls and ceilings, each one wooden with the same kind of decoration as the main door to the throne but not quite as elegant.

"Not your work, I assume, Arrie?"

He shakes his head. "How can you tell?"

"It's not nearly as beautiful." I enter the first room on the left and stop to take a breath at the beauty of the room. "Will we always be staying in beautiful places?"

"When we can, Angel."

The bed is the biggest I've ever seen, and that has to be a coincidence. We'll all fit, assuming that was what Nine had in mind when he requested a single room.

"It was." He smiles at me.

I just blush. "I . . . I'm sorry."

He frowns. "Why?"

"Because you're all going to so much effort just for me."

He walks up to me and wraps me in a hug. "It's not just for you. Everyone in this room prefers sleeping this way. It was one of your better ideas. But even if it were just for you, it would be worth it."

I blush once more and feel weirdly uncomfortable with all of this in my male form. Bushing as a man isn't normal, is it? I mean, I never catch any of the other guys doing it. Maybe I should just change into my female form for a while.

"No." Nine steps up to me once more and wraps another arm around my waist. "Don't do that. Just be you."

"But—"

He silences me with a finger to my lips and whispers, "Your sex does not define who you are. It is merely an aspect of your biology, of the way you work. You can be whomever you choose to be."

He's right. Fuck whoever thought being a single sex was a good idea. I get the best of both worlds this way, and I am going to damn well use that to my advantage, starting with Nine.

He raises his eyebrows at me, but I silence whatever remark he was about to make with a kiss. I grab his shirt in both hands and yank him flush against me, his body flat against the panes of my torso.

Groaning into my mouth, he runs his hands up the ridges of my body and around to the small of my back, hooking a thumb under the waistband of my jeans and underwear.

Before I can progress things any further, a knock at the door interrupts us. It's my turn to groan, and I pull away to answer the door. "What?"

The young girl from before flinches. "I'm so sorry for disturbing you, Mr . . . Mrs." She flushes. "I'm so sorry." She bows. "Please forgive me."

I sigh. "It's okay. Just call me Magic."

She nods. "Magic, I have been informed to supply you

with garments for this evening's festivities." She bows her head as she thrusts her hands forward, and out of nowhere, a large pile of clothing forms on her hands.

"Thank you." I grab the clothes from her petite hands. "Is there anything else?"

"No, Magic. I will leave you in peace."

"Thank you."

I bow back to her, and she smiles, hiding a laugh. Seems she isn't used to respect from people above her.

She closes the door as I turn around, and the others all look at me with gentle smiles. It's Connie who says something, though, as she walks up to me and wraps her arms around my shoulders. "It's so nice to see you be . . . you."

"Huh?"

She laughs. "It's just beautiful to watch the person you're becoming, and to have a hand in that."

The others nod.

She brushes a kiss across my lips and walks away to finish unpacking, which they all started to do while I made out with Nine.

Goddess, they are all so okay with this. I don't get it. I thought it would take longer for them to adjust, but here I am, romantically engaged with them all to some degree or another, and they're just acting like it's a normal average Tuesday.

Nine and Connie are locked in an intense internal conversation, with Connie shaking her head in disgust at something Nine is saying. "C'mon," he says out loud, "it'll be a good test, and I'm sure Sweetie will be fine with it."

I think I know what they're talking about. "Connie?" She looks my way. "It's fine. If Nine needs this as proof that I'm seriously okay with all of this"—I gesture to me and the team—"then go ahead."

She raises her eyebrows but nods.

I'll be honest, I want to watch. I want to see them all together as much as I want to be with them all together; just the thought has my cock twitching in pleasure.

Nine laughs but shakes his head and walks slowly up to Connie, who wraps an arm around his neck and leans in, lightly placing a kiss to his jaw. Nine angles himself so she can get better access to his neck, and she continues trailing kisses along his jaw until she meets his lips.

Dea and Arrie join me, both with an arm wrapping around my waist, all three of us leaning against the wall, enjoying the show. Dea leans down to my ear and whispers, "Someone's enjoying the show."

I look down to see my cock straining against my jeans and blush. For fuck's sake. "Sorry."

"Don't be," Arrie says, "you're in good company."

I look down at both the guys standing beside me and see them having the same issue.

Nine runs his hands under Connie's top, grazing the edges of her bra with his thumbs, and she moans into his mouth. Fuck, just the sound of her moaning has me hardening further. I wish I could be in my female form without going all Vamp-crazy right now because this would be easier to deal with.

"Nine," Connie gasps as he grazes her nipples, "just how far were you planning on taking this?"

"I've already got my answers. I'm just enjoying myself."

She giggles and runs her hands down his chest, but eventually she pulls away and looks at me. She flicks her eyes from my crotch to my heated face and smiles.

Arrie and Dea inch their hands closer to the rim of my jeans, but I pull away before they can do anything.

"Four cold showers it is," Arrie grumbles, and we all laugh.

Chapter Twenty-Two

The garments, it seems, barely cover anything. In my male form, all it does is drape down my chest, leaving not much to the imagination, and then hangs from the waist and glides along the floor, a slit going up the side for leg exposure. Nine helps me use a magical body hair remover potion to look all sleek and shiny, but thank the goddess I don't have to shave, because apparently facial hair isn't a thing for the Fae.

Lucky me.

In my female form, however, I wear what I can only describe as a belly-dancing outfit. You know, one of those things with layers of cloth that shows your legs with sexy splits and your belly with a sexy crop top that pushes my boobs up to maximum effect. If it wasn't so bright and colorful—and totally barf-worthy—I would have liked how it makes my curves flaunt a little. But it's bright and colorful and therefore yuck.

I step out of our bathroom in my female form, wearing the barf-outfit, and my displeasure is clearly written all over my face because Connie smirks and Arrie laughs. This is one of those occasions where Arrie's beautiful laughter is not worth the trouble it took to get him to laugh in the first place.

"Stop laughing, asshole. This isn't funny." I cross my arms over my chest. "I look like someone's seamstress threw up on me."

Nine comes to stand beside me, barely containing his laughter. "Well, what about your male form?"

I change, and everyone stands still, mouths agape.

"Damn, that's . . ." Connie seems at a loss for words.

"Hot," Nine answers for her.

Dea steps up off the bed and says, "Insatiable."

Arrie grunts but gives me a smile.

Seems they all like it. "It really looks that good?" I twirl around in front of a huge mirror beside a vanity, trying to see everything about this look.

"Hon, you look fuckable. Like, seriously fuckable."

Nine and Dea agree with confirming nods and stand either side of me, both in their own barf-clothes, but I have to admit, it looks good on them.

Nine? Guy question.

Go for it.

How the fuck do you hide an erection in this thing? It's just so . . . flowy.

You don't. The Fae are . . . highly sexual.

"Ugh. Great." Is there a magical species that's not sexual?

Witches. Shifters are a little more enclosed depending on the individual species.

Connie looks at me in confusion, but I wave her unasked question away.

I turn to face Arrie and really look at him for the first time in this stupid get up. The soft material hangs off him in waves of bright colors that contrast his skin, and his hair is pinned back into a low bun so I can see his edgy jawline and cheekbones more prominently. His entire top is empty of clothes, and my mouth momentarily waters at the sight of all that muscle. He . . . he looks . . . damn! Like, seriously, hot damn. It looks good on him.

"Just noticing, are we?" Dea chuckles from behind me, wrapping his arms around my waist. "Looks good, right?"

"Yeah, Arrie, you look . . . good in this stupid get up."

"Thank you." He's still a little off from earlier, and I'm worried tonight might be a bit much for him, but he smiles at me nonetheless.

You should stay with him this evening.

Good idea.

We're escorted to a ballroom just south of the throne room, and upon entering, I have to admit that I kinda like this party. Okay, so everyone is involved in flirting, playing, or fucking of some kind, some hidden in the shadows at the edges of the room, some on display, some on various couches and chairs dotted around the space, but it's mutual, consenting, and kind of beautiful. Towering flower cascades are dotted every few feet, circling a large, empty area of floor space—a dancefloor, I presume—and there is a champagne fountain, naked waiters with small canapes walking around, and lots of non-Fae supes, even some humans.

What are humans doing in the Fae Court?

"They're used as dancing partners," Nine leans in and whispers.

"But you said—"

"Yes, I did."

"Oh." I grab Arrie's hand, hoping he'll steady the growing rise of unease in my belly. "I can do this," I mutter to myself.

Connie leans in from behind me. "Yes, you can. Just ignore the bad and focus on being a Fae."

I can do that. I hope.

Just as we enter the party, the lights dim and the queen strolls into the center of that empty space. "Now that our guests are all here, let's begin."

Stringed music plays, and some tall, muscly Fae steps up to the queen and grabs her hand. They start twirling around the dancefloor in no particular pattern or form, and I realize that I will have to dance.

Shit. I'm fucking terrible. And I'm in my male form. I can't lead, I don't even know what I'm doing.

Arrie leans down to whisper. "Don't worry, sexuality isn't a thing here, either. Come on." He pulls me by the hand I'm holding onto the dancefloor. "Just relax." He pulls me flat against him, resting one hand in mine and the other on my waist.

I take a deep breath and follow him around the dancefloor, trying to keep my eyes on his so as not to freak out about everyone staring at us.

"Just focus on me, we're doing fine."

I nod.

Soon the other Horsemen are all on the dancefloor, Connie dances with Dea while Nine dances with a pretty green Fae girl, twirling her around and making her laugh.

"Arrie," I start, not sure whether now is really the time, "I know you don't want to talk about it, but I'm here."

He darts his eyes away from mine.

"Hey." I grab his chin and force him to look at me. "It's not the end of the world. You don't have to be a part of us, you know. If you don't want to." I sigh, hoping he'll get my meaning. "I still wouldn't stop you from being with the team."

He blinks, catching onto my meaning. "It's not that." He sighs and brings us to a standstill. "Sorry, no, I do want this. It's just . . ." He looks away from me and blinks tears from his eyes. "I'm the only one of us who had a family before we died and were chosen. The others? They all lost people, but I had a wife and children. It's hard to do this again."

I stiffen. "Really?"

He nods.

He had a family? Children? A wife?

"What was she like?" I smile, genuinely curious.

He has this wispy smile on his face that lights him up in the most gorgeous way. The reality of his situation is starting to sink in, though, and I can't help the growing pity on my face. He had a family, one he could have very well returned to via the Earth portal, but he held back. Couldn't have been an easy transition.

"She was beautiful. Stubborn, like you." He laughs. "I couldn't get her to do anything I wanted. It was most frustrating." He starts dancing again, dragging me around the dancefloor after him.

I don't have my Vampire speed and precision in this form so step on his toes a few times, but I hope it goes mostly unnoticed by anyone else.

"She was an amazing mother, but she was a warrior, too. Much better than human-me."

That surprises me. "Is that why you mostly keep your interactions within the team?"

He shrugs and nods. "Partly. It's also 'cos holding back is hard for my magical abilities, so Con just makes that easier, I guess. Believe me, you wouldn't be celibate for two thousand years, either."

"Not judging." I laugh at his embarrassed face. "Just

curious."

He nods and returns to focusing on the dance.

I catch Connie staring at me from across the dancefloor a few times, breaking her visual contact with Dea momentarily to flash appreciation my way; at least, that's what I think that expression is. Hard to tell while being whisked around the dancefloor by the Horseman of War.

He's good at dancing. Like, really good. We waltz, swing, and leap through the people with no care for anyone else around us. Over the past few weeks, Arrie has become a . . . friend, and I can't wait to explore what that means.

Arrie looks down at me as he slows our movements, boring holes through my soul with those ice-blue eyes of his, and I nearly melt. He's so beautiful, it hurts. Now would be a great time to kiss him, but I'm still in my male form. Quickly changing, and internally grumbling about the shitty female outfits for this dance, I wrap both hands around his neck (while standing on my toes to reach him) and meet his gaze.

He sighs and leans down, inches from my face, inches from closing the final bit of distance between us and finally becoming something more than friends. Completing the final piece of my familial puzzle.

The moment his lips connect with mine, I internally exhale a metaphorical breath I didn't realize I've been holding. He really is perfect. His lips brush mine in gentle waves of affection, like the sea caressing the sand amidst a storm, and calm envelops me.

He lifts me into his arms, and I wrap my legs around his waist as my arms entwine around the back of his neck.

I pull away to take a breath. "Arrie, I—

He silences me with eager lips—all pretense of gentleness gone in the blink of an eye—as a small growl vibrates his throat, awakening that pesky lust-starved part of my Vampire brain.

I meet his kiss with equal fervor, biting his lower lip so he'll open and entangle our tongues in equal amounts of passion. He doesn't hold back this time and crushes my lips against his, his fingers digging into my hips where he holds me up.

Pulling away slightly, he puts me on my feet with a smile. I notice the other Horsemen are not still dancing and look a little out of breath—everyone except Connie, of course, who just stands on the side lines watching us with a smile.

How long have we been dancing for?

About an hour.

An hour? But I don't feel exhausted.

Arrie is starting to tire with all the Fae magic draining us. Though, you aren't affected by it.

Okay. Time to drag Arrie off the dancefloor.

We meet up with the others, all smiles and no judgment. "So," I ask, "they extract the energy of those dancing to fuel what, exactly?"

"You felt that, huh?" Nine wraps an arm around my waist while Arrie holds onto my hand. I nod. "It's like a drug. An ancient spell. They use the energy stored later to create an atmospheric drug. Plus, it's a pretty traditional part of Fae culture."

Makes sense. "But what kind of drug?"

He shares a look with Dea, who shrugs and answers for him. "They harvest the energy of those around them to create a drug that stimulates a sexual high."

"Sexual?"

Nine nods. "See the queen dancing in the center?"

I look at her.

"She's fueling the entire thing, having all of the energy

flow through her and into the vent below her small dancing circle."

I bristle. They're harvesting magic, sometimes at the cost of human lives, so they can get high? My gums tingle, and I cover my mouth, taking calming breaths.

Male form, Magic. Male form.

In a quick, imaginary poof of fancy magic and an intense bout of nausea, I return to my male form. I shrug to the team. "Best not to be angry in that form right now."

Nine nods, but Dea snickers. At my questioning eyebrow, he says, "I would pay good money to see you rip out the queen's throat."

"Dea," Connie warns and points to her ears. "They're not deaf."

I shrug. "They're not going to care what we think of them." They clearly think enough of themselves. But what Dea said gave me an idea.

In my male form, I'm taller than Nine and the others, except Arrie, who towers over everyone, so I lean down to whisper in Nine's ear. "I think I have a plan."

He throws me a questioning look, but I don't bother explaining. I can't do anything until we're home anyway. And away from prying ears.

Connie pulls me toward her and embraces me; the randomness of the act takes my breath away a little, and I pull away, hoping to take a look at her face. But Dea swings me around in his arms and pulls me into him.

What are they up to?

"You're not going to be able to do that all night," Arrie grumbles.

"Do. What?" I huff and yank myself out of Dea's grip.

"Distract you every time a human dies or faints or

something else tragic happens."

I growl at Dea and Connie, who both back off.

"I am more than capable of not getting involved." They both raise their eyebrows. "In this form." I gesture to my male self.

My female form is a little more irrational right now; though, it has nothing to do with my sex and everything to do with my lack of proper feeding.

I want to see, to make sure I really can handle this, but I don't want to look overeager.

Nine saves me from my predicament by grabbing my hand and pulling me onto the dancefloor. "There's one behind me."

I briefly gaze over his shoulder and watch in horror as a human falls to their knees and is scooped up by a Fae guard, one of many dotted around the perimeter. Is she going to be okay? I shift to my female form and hone my hearing in on the body, listening for a heartbeat.

Nothing.

She's dead. The blood quickly running from her cheeks as her arm dangles from her Fae coffin's hold.

Dea and Connie were right, I can't handle this. She died for nothing!

Deep breaths. Male form.

I shift back—reluctantly—and take a deep breath. I can do this. Just stay dancing with Nine.

I'll keep you distracted.

I look back to his face as I rip my gaze away from the Fae guard's retreating back and notice Nine's playful smirk.

What do you have in mind?

Sooooo, you and Arrie?

Ugh. He's going to girl-talk me into distraction.

Arrie and I are . . . more than friends?

I can see that, he says through an audible laugh.

Well, I'm just trying to see where I am with you all, and it's difficult given that I have two sexes, four species, and a huge destiny that sucks donkey balls.

You're doing great. Promise.

He waltzes us around the dancefloor, me taking some lead every now and then, wherever I'm comfortable enough.

I was thinking of distracting you with this.

He sends me a mental image of a very naked Arrie on his back lying on a low-lying bed. The viewpoint is Nine's, obviously, since this is most likely a memory, and I watch as what looks and feels like my hand shoots out and caresses Arrie's cheek.

His stubble grazes my hand, and it sends shivers down my spine.

Nine, stop. I don't want a hard-on in the Fae Court.

Too late.

I groan but watch the scene play out before me as I let Nine guide me around the dancefloor. I probably look ridiculous right about now, but oh well. Nine's mental abilities are rather fun.

Nine's hand moves down Arrie's chiseled frame, smoothing over creamy skin, and wraps around his cock. Its silky smooth skin slips beneath my—Nine's—hand, and I groan as Arrie groans under Nine's tight grip, but Nine just grips harder until Arrie grabs his hand and guides it down in one smooth motion.

Memory Nine gasps, clearly turned on and hard, and one look down his body tells me that is very much the case. "Dude, are you sure?"

Arrie leans his head back and groans. "Yes. Fucking do it, Famine."

Nine nods and bends over, ready to swallow Arrie's cock. He takes a breath and wraps his lips around the tip, and the salty, perfect taste hits my tongue like a firecracker, causing both me and Arrie to groan once more. Nine smiles and lowers his mouth as far as he can, his hand covering the rest.

Arrie's hips buck underneath Nine's moving head, and Nine's hand works in tandem with the rhythm Arrie sets.

I can feel my own cock pulsing with need in time to Nine's hand. "Fuck." This is different than watching, this is like I'm experiencing it with Nine—through Nine.

Nine sucks a little harder as they move a little faster, both moaning in pleasure.

I look up in the memory to watch Arrie's face as his brow furrows and his eyes close. His hand grabs the back of Nine's hair tight, and the sting sends a lightning bolt through me, but that doesn't deter Nine, it just spurs him on.

"Come here," Arrie mumbles, pleasure taking hold of his every syllable. He reaches his hand out beside him. "Let me help."

Nine swivels around and allows Arrie to grab his cock, and I can feel the punishing grip of his massive hand stroking Nine's cock—my cock—and I buckle. Nine pauses a moment when Arrie brushes a finger over the tip, causing him to move his hips gently and me to groan.

As they both continue sucking and using their hands to please each other, me feeling everything, they speed up, the crescendo building, their moans growing louder, and my own dick begs for release.

"Nine . . ." I gasp.

Change.

I do as he asks and change into my female form just as I watch—and feel—Arrie thrust his hips frantically.

"Nine," Arrie groans, "I'm going to . . ."

His sentence ends on a moan as Nine sucks harder.

Arrie's release explodes into Nine's mouth, and Nine follows soon after while swallowing. It hits the back of my throat (Nine's throat), and I swallow his scent, his essence, and the sight and feel pushes me over the edge, my own orgasm ripping through me. I collapse into Nine's waiting arms, burying my head into his chest to at least attempt to muffle my own scream.

I stand back up, the memory having left my mind, and heave air into my lungs. "Why would you . . . ?"

Thought it would be fun. Didn't realize it would be that fun, though.

He escorts me off the dancefloor into Connie's waiting arms.

Oh goddess, Connie probably saw and heard the entire thing. My face burns red as she wraps her arm around my waist and pulls me into a hug.

I don't want to come back up and face Nine and Arrie, but I have to at some point. First, I pull away and change into my male form; I really don't want to be dealing with this horseshit of a party in my female form. I'm too easily agitated. And that mind-blowing orgasm left me a little hungry, too.

"So," Connie says, "have fun?" She grabs me a glass of something pink, fizzing, and tasting of raspberries.

"Uh . . . yeah."

Nine laughs out loud. "Better than Arrie's dance?"

I raise an eyebrow at him. "Not going to let you guys be in competition, especially considering none of the rest of them can do that." I cross my arms over my chest.

"Do what?" Arrie asks. "I'm confused."

Oh my goddess, I don't have the straight face to answer him. Luckily, I don't have to because he goes bright red the moment I open my mouth.

Yeah, I told him for you. You're welcome.

I throw Nine a grateful smile and just avoid Arrie's eyes.

Dea laughs from behind me, and I spin to see him watching our exchange with mild humor in his eyes. "Seems you are enjoying this party more than I anticipated, Angel."

"Well, it's hard not to with this lot." I thumb the team and walk into his arms.

He wraps me tight in his arms and whispers, "I know. I was watching."

I blush but keep my head resting on top of his. "Oh."

"Do not do that. It was . . . seductive watching you. What memory did Nine show you?"

"He didn't say?"

Dea shakes his head, and I turn around to find Arrie shaking his, too.

"I can not say, if you'd prefer."

Arrie just sighs. "He put her in Nine's shoes on that night in Japan a few hundred years into our immortal life."

Dea coughs. "Oh, that." He leans up and whispers into my ear, "Well, that is good to know."

I shiver at the feel of his warm breath on my ear and his hand moving slowly to the rim of my flowing skirt.

"You're all impossible." I move away and stand on my own for a minute, catching my breath. Are they always going to be this . . . persuasive?

Probably. Nine shrugs.

Arrie is still blushing—which is weird in itself—Connie is laughing, Nine just stands there looking innocent, and Dea has his arm around Nine's shoulders.

You ever get those moments when you step outside of your own little bubble of reality and realize how blessed you are to have such amazing people in your life? Well, this is one of those moments. It's like watching them in slow motion, and I'm able to take each and every ounce of the moment in, etching it to memory. It's then, however, that I realize I might totally be in love with them all.

Nine smiles at me and blinks hard, trying to hide the tear that threatens to escape.

The rest of the party passes by in much the same fashion, with me trying to ignore the ugly, evil parts and enjoy some relatively good downtime with the team. They each take turns dancing with me in either form, but we mostly keep me in my male form; not only because I'm a Fae in that form, but because I'm less likely to explode in anger when a human drops dead.

Is it wrong of me to enjoy this? I don't enjoy the things around me, but we rarely get to spend time together, and this entire mission has included lots of bonding.

The queen interrupts my inner ramblings with a halt to the music and an announcement. Seems we're here for more than just a dance. "My people, and the people of other species present tonight, it has been an honor to have you all in my court for another wonderful evening. But now the dancing part of the night must come to an end and the entertainment come to fruition. Everyone is invited to the after party, of course, where we will share our spoils and come together, no matter the species."

She grabs an old-fashioned piece of paper wrapped in a bow off a silver tray dangling in mid-air beside her and reads from it.

"But now we have an announcement to make. We, the Fae Court, have teamed up with the future Vampire Royal Council to create a new world of supernatural order. A new leadership. And a new force where the Supernatural Council will have no jurisdiction."

The crowd cheers, especially the Vampires and Fae, but turning my head to the team, we all stand with our mouths open.

"Well," I start, "that answers your question, Arrie."

The queen continues, of course, and then addresses us directly. "We understand that this goes against the wishes the Four Horsemen of the Apocalypse, who have always worked hard to keep the peace. But your war is over now, Horsemen, and it is time we learned to govern ourselves."

I clench my fist and watch as Connie does the same, but it's Dea who steps forward and gives a nod.

"Please, my fellow people, enjoy the rest of the festivities."

"C'mon," Nine says as he drags us all off to the side, "we need to leave."

"Agreed," Dea says. "The new Vampire Royal Council do not like us and have tried to kill us on multiple occasions. This is not the safest place for us right now."

Arrie grumbles something under his breath. "Hopefully they'll just let us leave and be done with it."

Connie remains silent but eventually speaks up as we enter our room. "I liked the Fae. I can't believe they'd do this."

"Like them?" I gasp. "They're murderers for pleasure. No better than Vampires who kill for blood."

She flinches but doesn't respond.

The Fae Court might look beautiful on the outside, but it's rotten at the core.

Chapter Twenty-Three

We pack quickly, all of us throwing things into our bags, even Nine, and run out the door and down the corridor. Everyone is armed, me with the throwing daggers Nine gifted me before we left, Connie with her bow and arrow, Arrie with a massive sword hanging from his belt, Dea with a pair of dual black daggers, and Nine with a series of magiguns.

Dea leads us out of a maze of silent corridors and up into the main entryway. We pass no one, there are no sounds coming from any of the closed or open doors we pass, and even the servants are mysteriously absent. Just as we are about to exit the building, and I'm about to jump for joy at our easy exit, an army of Fae surround us, magiguns and swords drawn.

"They're going to have the same technology as the rogue Vamps, most likely, so . . . yeah. Sorry guys." Nine steps back, not really sure how to help beyond basic fighting. They're likely using Silver Leaf Vain to block his telepathy and mental abilities—just like last time. But hopefully, not like last time,

Nine won't nearly die (you know, 'die').

Arrie draws his sword. "Go."

"Nope." I draw a couple of daggers, ready to throw them.

Arrie places a hand on my shoulder. "Go."

Dea, Nine, and Connie join us, weapons at the ready, supporting my decision to stay and get us all out.

Connie drags me back so I have a better vantage point, both of us having long-range weapons, while Arrie directs himself, Nine, and Dea around the room using his strategy ability.

Clangs of swords, bangs of guns, and the sizzle of magic erupts around us. Dea moves faster than I can see but is invisible to the Fae so manages to get a few on their knees before the fight really begins.

"Back up the guys, I'm gonna shoot some of their long-range defenses down," Connie orders me.

"Right!"

She runs off to the sides and shoots arrow after arrow into the back of the head of every archer and long-range spellcaster around the perimeter of the room. Most are in the air, using air magic to keep themselves above the fight.

I change into my female form and wave a hand at Connie, lifting her into the air on a small board of compressed wind I hope she can quickly learn how to use. I designed it like an airborne hover-board, so hopefully it shouldn't be too hard.

Meanwhile, Nine is struggling against four Fae with longswords, so I throw a couple of daggers and hit two in the eyes, reducing his opponent count.

Thanks.

"Argh!" Dea flies into a wall, having been hit by a flying lightning spell.

Shit.

I fly a dagger toward who I think the spellcaster is, but I have to dodge an oncoming fire arrow in the process and miss.

"Killer, help Con!" Arrie shouts as he rushes to Dea's side.

I look up and see Connie hanging from a buttress and give her a lift to the ground.

"Thanks!" she shouts.

I don't answer as three Fae rush at me. I shift form and then again into a bear, roaring them to an abrupt halt.

My feet thunder forward as I swipe. Swipe again.

They all duck and dodge with ease.

This form is too slow. I shift into a panther and sprint at them, taking one head off with a powerful swipe.

I pant, already getting out of breath with the force of all this shifting.

Some spell hits me in the back mid-shift, and I tumble to the ground with a whine. Three thunks follow me to the stone floor, and I look up to find three Fae with familiar arrows in their backs.

Connie.

I jump to my feet and change form again, feeling my energy reserves faltering with every change, and look around to see where I might be most helpful.

Connie is caught between a group of five Fae, all with shorter weapons, and is doing her best to outmaneuver them, but she didn't come with short-range weapons and is relying on just a dagger.

I have to help her.

I grab my last dagger from my thigh and throw it, shifting the air to make it hit the one about to slice her face in two. It pierces his shoulder. He cries out as I force the air around it to push deeper until it flies out the back of his body.

Connie turns to me and smiles, pride smothering her

features. But the other Fae seize the moment and grab her arms, yanking her to the floor.

"Connie!"

I sprint forward in a burst of Vampire speed but am not quick enough. They have her in magicuffs before I can rip their heads off.

Four more Fae rush out of the corridor beside us and step in front of Connie. "Stand down, Magic."

"No." I create two small balls of air in each palm, hoping they'll be enough.

The sounds of fighting can still be heard behind me, but all I'm focusing on is the one in front. The sight of Connie on her knees struggling against two Fae pushing all their strength onto her magic-less body makes my blood boil.

"Let her go." I don't yell, I just force the words through gritted teeth, trying my hardest to hold on to my anger and not let it fluster my decisions.

The Fae laugh and pull Connie to her feet.

She grunts, and a trail of blood trickles down the pale skin of her neck and adds to the mess of colors painted onto those hideous clothes.

Every Fae draws their sword at me, but the sound of Nine and Dea screaming behind me has me turning around.

I stop dead. One of the Fae has managed to sneak up on Arrie and put some magicuffs on him, rendering him useless.

Shit.

That's it for me. I flip the lid on my anger, my crazy Vampire lust making me frustrated that I've been holding back, and my hunger for not having fed yet today. It seeps into every movement as I rush to sink my teeth into three Fae, one after the other, freeing Arrie's immediate vicinity.

I yank Dea off the ground, throwing him and Nine toward

Arrie so I can better protect them all in one place.

Heads fly off bodies, ears rip from heads, and bones snap and pop as I tear limbs from joints. Blood coats every inch of my skin, but eventually an army of dead bodies lies before me. Despite all the blood I've drunk while ripping throats with my teeth, I'm still hungry.

Seems I need the team's blood specifically.

I turn to make sure everyone is okay but only find Arrie, Dea, and Nine huddling on the floor, looking at me with a mix of fear and amazement on their faces.

I probably look like a monster.

"Where's Connie?"

They shake their heads.

"Why didn't you help?" I roar.

None of them speak, but Nine says, *We're all in cuffs.*

I turn around and look at their hands. They're all indeed in magicuffs.

Ripping them off one by one, I yank them all to their feet and drag them to the front door. "We need to find her."

Arrie nods. "Why did they take her?"

Dea shrugs, but Nine shivers. "You don't think it was him, do you?"

Dea and Arrie go stiff, but I just sigh in frustration. "Someone's going to have to fill me in, but for now, we need to leave."

Dea leads the way, yanking out one of those holographic phone devices Nine invented. "I will get us a jet."

Nine yanks us all down the courtyard and to a back alley. "You can't walk around like that. You'll likely be arrested."

I look down at myself. Most of the blood is on my torso, but even my legs look tortured. I turn to Arrie. "Shirt."

He sighs but throws it my way.

Yanking these stupid clothes off, I strip in the middle of an alleyway in Paris in the middle of the night. None of the guys look my way, but I can see them all hiding pained smirks.

"Now isn't the time," I snap.

"She'll be fine," Arrie says.

"I'm not worried about her life."

He flinches.

But it's true. She'll live. Of course she will. Her seal is back at the house. But will she be okay? She's been through something truly horrific with the Vampires, and I fear that whatever it is has come back to haunt her.

I look down at myself and sigh. I need a shower. It isn't great, but it'll have to do. Arrie's shirt falls to my knees, so at least I'm covered. For now, I'll stay in my male form, but at least I can change without looking like a horror movie.

Dea walks up to us and says, "Let's go." He throws Nine over his shoulder. "We need to run."

He gives me a pointed look, and I shift back into my female form, grab Arrie and cradle-carried him as I run after Dea, who fazes through the streets of Paris faster than I can run. He slows for me, but it isn't much use; I'm exhausted, hungry, and have depleted most of my magic reserves.

"Okay." Dea stops. "Arrie, come here."

Arrie steps up to him as Dea draws one of his daggers and cuts Arrie's wrist open. I watch as the blood drips onto the paving stones beneath us, spilling all of the glorious life onto the dead concrete. No one is around, and my control isn't solid right now, so I yank his wrist and drink. I don't stop, not even when Nine asks if I'm okay, and certainly not when I know I should. His blood is my only focus, my singular drive, as though without it I'm nothing spinning into a void of empty pointlessness.

I'll carry Arrie to the jet, and he can recover there. Right now, Connie needs me. I'm too focused on her to feel the full effects of feeding, but a distant throb pulses low in my body, one I'll have to deal with later, I guess.

Arrie slumps on my shoulder, and I steady him as I pull away. "Okay." I pick him back up and turn to Dea. "Lead on."

Dea fazes at top speed, and this time, I'm able to keep up with him. We speed through street after street, down alleys and past midnight drunken assholes, and on toward a small country estate whose name I don't recognize.

MORT MONTANTE.

Chapter Twenty-Four

"Where are we?" I ask Nine and Dea, who open the gates and walk on through.

Arrie is still passed out in my arms, so I carry him for the time being until we can get him to a bed.

"We, Angel, are at our Paris safe house."

Nine looks over his shoulder at me and Arrie and smiles. "Top level security in this one, so we came here instead of our townhouse."

"I will continue getting us a jet for tomorrow. We should rest."

"Rest?" My hands tighten around Arrie's body as I my blood pumps faster at the ridiculous suggestion. "Connie needs us. We can't rest now!"

"Shhhh," Nine says. "I know. But we can't help if we're tired and drained." He looks to Arrie. "And he needs to rest for a couple hours."

I flush. That was my fault. If I didn't need their blood in particular, this wouldn't have been a problem. "Why is that?"

"Why is what?"

So he doesn't always pay attention to my thoughts.

"I drown it out when you're angry or upset."

I wince but quickly get back to the question at hand. "Why do I specifically need blood from you four?"

"Probably due to the level of power you get from it. The blood is fueling a Horseman, after all. Vampires gain power from blood, not just sustenance. They cannot use their speed or strength if they have not fed."

Dea opens the grand double doors, and we all enter into the main entrance foyer.

"Other people's blood has no effect on you other than basic sustenance because it doesn't hold enough power."

I huff. Talk about a pile of Vampire shit. What happens if I need blood and they aren't around?

Nine goes to say something, but I cut him off. "Not now." He nods. "Just show me where I can sleep."

Dea smiles at Arrie's limp form in my arms. "We can sleep in the larger bedroom upstairs."

"We?" I can't stop the gentle smile that curls my lips. "Like, all of us?" I just assumed that would stop the moment our bubble was popped.

"If that is what you want, Angel."

"It is."

The bedroom is two floors up, and the stairs are stone concrete like the Fae Court—and huge. I'm not having problems carrying Arrie other than the fact that he's huge and bulky to hold, but if I were human, these steps would be a pain.

"That's the point," Nine says. "Not many people could reach us, other than Vampires."

"And they are unlikely to attack us here in Paris and risk

pissing off the Fae." He takes a deep breath. "Well, usually."

Right. Their alliance. Vampires and the Fae, both working toward a world they can be themselves in without SC restrictions. That places the SC as their main enemy. Right?

"We need to talk to the SC." I turn to Dea. "How do we do that?"

He grumbles. "I will arrange a meeting if I can. But they are not fond of all meeting in the same place."

"Then tell them war is on their doorstep." I yank Arrie and me up the last step. "That should get them moving their asses."

Dea leads us through a huge door and into a room with a bed bigger than I've ever seen. Seriously, it could fit five Arries. Which, I guess, is the point.

"Whose room is this?"

Nine shrugs. "No one's. Was just here for guests."

With a bed that huge?

Vampires and Fae tend to live in groups rather than monogamous pairs.

Oh. Well, I guess that makes sense.

I don't bother with pleasantries, I just dump Arrie onto the bed and throw the covers over him, then take off my bra underneath Arrie's shirt I'm still in and get in next to him. Anything else can wait until morning.

"Well?" I ask Nine and Dea, who are looking at me in amusement.

Dea strips, and I can't help but stare, but my usual fun reaction is marred by the possibility of where Connie will be sleeping tonight. He grabs some spare clothes out of the bags he was carrying and throws on a pair of sweatpants and comes to bed.

Nine does the same, sleeping on Dea's other side.

Curling into Arrie, sleep takes hold quicker than I realize it could, but before I drift into unconsciousness, I hear Dea and Nine kiss each other goodnight and smile. Just a little.

They're perfect for each other. I'm glad I could bring them together.

Some big, muscly, grumbling thing awakes me hours later, and I open my eyes to find Arrie chatting to the guys.

"She's going to be fine, Arrie," Nine says. "Con's strong."

"They've probably taken her to that piece of Vampire scum. I should have killed him decades ago."

"You cannot murder everyone that wrongs one of us." Dea sighs. "We are better than that."

I move my head to speak. "Not all of us care to be better."

Arrie squeezes my shoulder and lets me go. "You're awake?"

"Yup."

I shoot up and hop out of bed. Or, I tried to, but Arrie grabs my thighs just as I'm climbing over him. "You're still tired, Killer."

"Hmmm, tired. What a revelation. Wonder what bad things Connie is feeling right about now?" I shoot him a death-by-Magic stare and watch him flinch.

He lets go of me, and I climb out of bed. "Clothes," I mumble to myself.

"In the bags over there." Nine points to the pile of bags in the corner.

I mumble some semblance of a thank you and go in search of clothes.

"You know," I hear Arrie say, "I could get used to seeing you in my shirt."

I'd totally forgotten I was wearing it. Looking down, I also remember it's all I'm wearing. Heat creeps up my face as I bend over to grab more clothes, hoping I'll find something at least clean, and equally hoping my ass will stay covered given the lack of panties.

I turn back around and am about to ask where the bathroom is before I bump right into Dea. "You have no need to be embarrassed about anything with us, Angel." He grabs my cheek and brushes the tear threatening to break free. "It is rather alluring watching you walk around a bedroom in nothing but Arrie's t-shirt." He looks me up and down, checking me out, and I fight hard not to blush.

Arrie and Nine join him, ganging up on me on either side, a wall to my back, so that I'm now trapped between three very hot guys, and my mind is doing all kinds of things to my body.

Arrie grabs the collar of the shirt and yanks me toward him with a growl. Pressing up against his body, I can feel just how good he thinks I look before he leans down and captures my mouth in a heated kiss that has me moaning the moment he parts my lips with a forceful lap of his tongue.

I pull back to take a breath, but Arrie just stands there with a smile on his face. "Good morning."

"Oh, right. Good morning." I turn and see the other two watching us. "Good morning."

Dea smiles, Nine smirks, and I nearly lose my virginal shit and pull them all back into bed. But it wouldn't be right, not without Connie home safe and with us.

"I want to rescue Connie," I whisper.

Dea pulls a hand through my messy bed hair and whispers, "I know. And we will."

I nod. "Then I want to shower." I shoot raised eyebrows at Nine, who points to a door on the left I didn't notice before.

"Thank you."

I shower, brush my teeth with one of the numerous unopened brushes on the side, and get dressed. Black sweatpants and a white t-shirt: nothing fancy, just simple clothes I can move in. Then I switch forms and do it all again in my male form. What to wear, though? Guess the same. Right? Sweatpants and a plain t-shirt.

Upon stepping out of the bathroom, hands in the middle of tying my hair back, all three guys stare at me as though I pissed in their morning coffee.

"What?" I mumble beyond the hair elastic hanging from my teeth.

"The clothes . . . They're not very you, Sweetie."

I shrug. "T-shirt's from my guy wardrobe, and the sweatpants are something I would usually wear to bed." The plain white t-shirt in question hangs from my frame, so I tie it into a knot at the front, having it clinched at the waist and therefore out of the way. "Happier?"

Dea nods. "Much."

I roll my eyes. "You don't see me critiquing your choice of clothing."

"And what would be wrong with what I am wearing, Angel?"

I look him up and down—past his fitted white-and-black jacket, hover on his studded cross earrings and then again on his snake bites, and fly past those ripped skinny jeans that make his ass look fantastic—and mumble, "Absolutely fucking nothing."

He looks smug and goes back to grabbing a few things from his bag before entering the bathroom.

The other two are in equal states of undress, so I lay on the bed and watch as Nine pulls a shirt over his head and Arrie wiggles into sweatpants (still shirtless, and still looking like a god).

"Having a good time there, Killer?" He winks at me, and I melt, my mouth opening and closing multiple times before it gets itself under control.

"Yes." I cough to clear my throat. "You're all looking gorgeous. Carry on." I gesture for him to continue with a smirk of my own, and he just laughs as he yanks a t-shirt over his head. Similar to me, he's going for comfortable and practical. Probably because, like me, his magic is active, and we'll likely have to fight and move in whatever we wear today.

"So," I ask the moment Dea steps out of the bathroom with his hair all brushed and gelled into place, "where is Connie, d'you reckon?"

Dea shares an ominous look with Arrie, and I sigh.

"I get it." They all look at me. "I don't need the details, but I'm not going in blind just to protect her secrets. She wouldn't want that. So tell me who you think has her, who we're likely up against, and where she probably is."

Nine nods. "You're right." He sits down next to me on the bed and pulls me into a hug. "Given that they took only her, and they're working with Vampires, we're pretty sure The Diamond has her. He's a Vampire who controls all the black-market blood supplies, and recently, we also reckon he's the reason for the increase in black-market Fae magic supplies."

I wince. "The increase in pixie dust. You reckon that's 'cos of him?"

He nods. "Last we heard, his base is in a remote part of the Andes Mountains. Not sure where, though."

Dea sits on my other side and places a hand on my shoulder.

"Well, is there any country the mountains go through that has a special connection to Vampire blood or pixie dust?"

They all shake their head. "Okay, so we get a plane and fly over. My Vampire vision should be able to see down to the ground if I try hard enough, assuming there's no clouds in my way or some shit."

Dea smiles. "Good plan."

"That jet?"

He nods. "Got one while you were in the shower, Angel. Coming to get us in one hour."

"From here?"

He smiles. "We have a landing strip through the forest behind us. And a helipad in the garden." He shrugs.

Of course they do. "Do all of your houses have insane levels of shit?"

He smiles. "Just the ones Nine's in charge of."

I look at everyone confused for a moment, but they all just laugh.

Nine answers. "There's a lot of safe houses. So we divide them between us. So long as I'm having a good day, I can make money and resources increase just by being near them." He laughs at my mouth hanging open. "Famine, remember?"

"Riiiight." I shake my head. "But if you're having a bad day?"

Dea laughs. "Then we let him nowhere near our finances."

Arrie laughs alongside him, and I can't fight the giggle that escapes my mouth at the sight and sound of Arrie laughing. It really is melodious and surprising. I don't think I'll ever get tired of making and hearing him laugh.

Nine coughs, and I realize I've been staring at Arrie like a freak while the room filled with silence. "Errrr, sorry." I shake my head.

"What were you thinking, Killer?"

"It was nothing sexual. Not this time, at least." They all

laugh. "I really like it when you laugh."

I just said that out loud, didn't I? Ohhhh, no. No. Nope. I did not just tell the Horseman of War that I like his laugh. Gah! What is wrong with me?!

"Stop freaking out." Nine snaps me out of my thoughts and brings me back to the present. "You're fine."

I look at him with raised eyebrows.

"Promise."

Arrie looks at me and blushes. "It's . . . err . . . fine." He shrugs. "Just not used to it."

I place my hands around his waist. "Well, get used to it. Because you are adorable."

He laughs and I melt—again. What are these guys doing to me?

"Only someone as crazy as you would find the Horseman of War adorable, Killer."

I shrug. "Then everyone else is blind."

"Come." Dea walks to the door with a smile on his face. "It will take twenty minutes to get to the landing strip, and I want something to eat first."

"Ugh, nope. Not eating if we're flying. Not unless you want me to blow chunks all over you."

Nine laughs. "Yeah, maybe not for you."

Arrie wraps an arm around my shoulders. "We'll get you something when we land."

I miss his cooking. Nothing is as good as Arrie's food. Nothing.

"Don't you have one of your restaurants in Argentina, Arrie?" Nine asks. "We should land there and get her something to eat."

"Restaurants?" I look to Arrie.

He grumbles and shoots Nine a 'shut the fuck up' look

before turning to me. "Yeah." He scratches the back of his head. "Opened an entire line of them back in the 1980s, and they've just kinda stuck around."

"Which chain? What's the name? What do they serve? Tell me everything!"

Arrie chuckles and grabs my hand. "Kappi Matur. It's Icelandic for Warrior Food." When I look at him with a questioning gaze, he explains, "Icelandic is the closest thing we have to the Old Norse language—my native tongue."

"Why not just stick to using Old Norse?"

He shrugs. "Felt more appropriate if someone other than us four knew what it meant."

We sit down to breakfast, where I eat nothing, and leave via the grand backdoor into the overgrown gardens. "So, Nine, isn't this your job?" I gesture to the uncared-for garden around us. It's a couple of acres, and honestly, a costly job for very little outcome, but teasing him makes me smile. He just looks at me with a mimicking death stare, and I laugh. "We'll work on that death stare when we get home."

Dea stops dead, and I walk right into the back of him. "Hey! Watch it."

"You called it home?" he asks.

"Err, what?"

"*Sheruta.* You just called it home."

Arrie and Nine are smiling at us, but eventually, Dea turns around, and Arrie lets go of my hand so he can scoop me up into a massive hug.

"Is it really home to you?" he asks as he squeezes me tight—not really causing me any pain, but bless, he tries.

I nod. "Of course. All of you are there." I sigh as I take in his lavender scent, nestling my nose into the crook of his neck. "Besides, who the heck would give up that house?"

Nine laughs. "She is magnificent."

"She?"

He shrugs. "Just feels . . . right."

Dea puts me back on my feet and continues walking, him on my right, Arrie on my left, both holding my hand as we walk.

Seems I didn't have to fight very hard for my little harem fantasy after all.

Don't speak too soon. We haven't talked about it yet.

I look at him. You don't want to?

I didn't say that. I'm just saying it's not all tied off with a pretty ribbon until we all chat.

He's right. He's always fucking right. I swear, being surrounded by two-thousand-year-old assholes twenty-four seven gets old.

I heard that.

I shake my head at him. "Nope. You didn't."

Connie, I tell myself. Stop flirting and save Connie. Then you can flirt with them all in sexy bikinis the next hot season in *Sheruta*.

"So, where's this airstrip?"

"Center of the forest," Nine answers. "It's about two miles that way." He points in front of us, right toward the dense tree and foliage in the distance.

Gah, I could just sprint there in, like, ten seconds, but I have to be social and walk with these goons. I bet Dea has the same problem.

We walk through the forest, ducking under branches and hopping over roots, and I have to admit, it's a beautiful place. The light filters through the trees at just the right angle this time of morning, and it lights the fall leaves up like a cinnamon-roasted latte; divine, tasty, and made of the only real goddess we should worship. Coffee.

Yup, nature is like coffee. Kind of smells similar, too, when you take in all the scents through a Vampire's nose. Strong, slightly bitter, smooth, but mostly just relaxing.

I hear Nine chuckle at nothing beside Dea and can only assume he is listening to my nature-coffee comparison.

"Your mind is the best place to be, I swear." He grabs Dea's hand and walks a little faster. "C'mon, we can't be late."

Another plane, another flight, another piece-of-shit few hours in the air. I consider seeing if I can fly myself that far, but considering the vast expanse of ocean beneath us for most of the trip, I decide not to. You know, wouldn't want to drown. That would be an awful afternoon if I couldn't die.

The pilot is an odd man, someone who looks as though they shouldn't be flying an airplane, let alone carrying out a rescue mission. "So," he says, "where we off to, Death?"

"He knows who we are?"

"Not until recently," Nine adds.

"Everyone knows who you all are, now. Though, no one really knows you, darlin'." He looks to me with a smile plastered onto his rough, bearded face. "No one really understands you."

I roll my eyes. "Join the club."

The airplane in question is a small, sleek-looking black jet with room for ten passengers at full capacity. It's posh but practical, with white leather seats in a fancy wooden interior, magitech screens glowing all over the place, and every seat has a cup holder.

"Can I get coffee?"

Dea rolls his eyes. "How addicted to coffee are you, Angel?"

"Ah yes, as opposed to my less murderous addictions, I guess coffee really is the devil." I point a glare at him, and he shrinks into his seat.

"There's a coffee machine over there." Nine points to a tea and coffee station just in front of the front two seats. "It's basic but decent."

I hop to my feet to grab a cup before take-off.

I read two small books between Paris and Argentina; oh, and I finish that gruesome mystery. Her lover kills him! What a shocker. I internally roll my eyes and read the last few lines of my newest romance.

"Sweetie, we're about to land."

I just nod.

Dea laughs at me. "Does she ever not read on a flight?"

"She gets travel sick in both forms, so it distracts her."

Dea smiles at me, which I only just about catch above the screen, but my Vampire eyes seem to have the ability to zoom in on my peripheral vision and bring it into focus without losing sight of my normal circumference of sight.

That could be useful.

"I can zoom in on my peripheral vision without losing my central line of sight," I shout to Nine.

"Really? That's quite cool."

"Ohmigod, I could totally pull off one of those super sexy ninja moves where the person throwing the dagger doesn't realize the cool, hot-as-fuck superwoman character can actually see with her back turned, and then bam! She catches the knife mid-air." I internally high-five myself but remember why we're on a private jet in the first place.

Connie.

Not a time to be smiling.

The guys all smile at my stupid antics—like usual—and even Arrie cracks a smile in his usual stone-wall façade.

The plane starts its descent just after we all buckle ourselves back in, and I try hard not to throw up on these lovely cream-white leather seats while my stomach tries to persuade me otherwise.

I just about make it as the wheels touch the ground, but I have to run out of the plane (whose door mechanism is like a thief's worst nightmare, by the way—totally unnecessary) to throw up nothing but gross yellowish-green bile that has me wishing I'd eaten breakfast to at least have something to throw up.

I am seriously sick of being sick.

"Here." Nine hands me a gingersnap. "Started packing them when I realized this was going to be a continuous issue."

"Thanks," I say as I take slow nibbles.

"That's really some travel sickness, Killer."

I death-glare him. I wish he would pick me up and carry me to wherever the hell we are going because just walking is making my tummy tumble.

He sighs and wraps an arm around my waist. "If you want help, just ask."

"Traitor," I whisper to Nine.

He shrugs, not really caring.

"Would you like me to carry you?" Arrie asks.

I look to the ground, embarrassment flushing my features, and nod. "Please."

Goddess, I sound so pathetic, but seriously, travel sickness sucks eggs. Ugh, eggs. That thought alone nearly has me vomiting again, but I manage to hold back as Arrie sweeps me into his arms, bridal style.

"Anti-sickness charm. Add that to my list."

Nine smiles. "Added." He taps his head and smiles brightly at the sight of me in Arrie's arms, probably finding us adorable. *It's kinda hot, too.*

Nine! Now is not the time to wake up the crazy Vampire side.

Right. Sorry.

I promptly ignore all the crazy, sexy thoughts Nine's words elicit in my mind, which in turn has me noticing just how close to Arrie's jugular my mouth is, and instead focus on the current disaster.

Connie. Need to find Connie.

Chapter Twenty-Five

"So, where are we going?"

Dea turns around to us and smiles. "To dinner. Well"—he looks at his watch—"lunch-dinner."

"Good." I am kinda hungry. "But I want to take off again to find Connie asap."

Arrie grumbles, "So do we."

I flinch. Right. They care, too. I run a calming hand along Arrie's shoulder and whisper, "We'll get her back. And we can kill that son of a bitch together."

Arrie grins from ear to ear, a menacing look that makes me shake a little in his arms. He laughs at my reaction and whispers, "Don't worry, I won't touch you." He pauses and looks down at me with a wink. "Unless you ask nicely."

I can once again feel my cheeks heating. Damn it. Are these guys trying to make me lose my immortal virginity in the most public of places? Because I really want them all right about now.

Maybe back on the plane would be a good place to—

"We're here," Nine announces over the top of my internal

chatter. Maybe a little too loudly, because Dea and Arrie look at him like he's crazy.

"Thank you." I climb out of Arrie's arms.

Here is a high-class restaurant with a red-and-black interior that speaks volumes about the type of people who usually eat here: rich people. People who could afford to eat at a place with windows for walls, who never have to worry about when their next meal will be or if they'll continue to have a roof over their heads tomorrow; people who usually look down on the rest of the world with their immortal stupidity.

Arrie coughs loudly behind me. "Shall we?"

That is when I realize this is Arrie's restaurant. Shit. So glad he isn't the one who can read my mind. That would have been aaaawkward.

Nine ushers us inside, and Dea turns visible so he can eat in public.

"Don't worry about that, dude," Arrie says in Dea's direction. "I called ahead. We're eating in one of the empty VIP rooms."

Dea exhales loud enough for us to all be thankful he isn't too uncomfortable and turns back to his usual self.

When we reach the front desk, where we're met by a handsome waiter whose name I can barely pronounce with swept-back hair and tattoos on both arms, I take a second glance around and feel even guiltier. It seems to be full of regular people; not rich but not poor, either. So just a regular restaurant, then, but with a very five-star feel.

Arrie likes to have his recipes actually eaten.

I roll my eyes to hide the embarrassed flush that has settled on my face red enough to let everyone around us know how flustered I am behind the social mask.

The restaurant itself has black circular tables, encouraging families to talk, eat, and chat with everyone, with a few two-person circular tables lining the large window wall on the right by the entrance. The plates fly around the room on a type of invisible air conveyor system, latticing the entire roof of the room in various plates, glasses, and cutlery. Fae air magic.

Waiters and waitresses sit people to tables, take orders, and then send them to the kitchen via their plasmascreens; all the while, you can see the cooks making the food in the far corner, all dancing along to the music playing over the soundstrip.

It's all very . . . fancy.

"Killer?" Arrie walks up next to me and stares at me with a questioning gaze.

"Sorry, huh?"

He smiles. "I said are you coming?"

"Oh, yeah."

He gestures to a deep-red velvet curtain in the far back, and we both step beyond into a corridor of other heavy curtains, some closed, some held back by thick black ties, and Arrie leads us into a closed one at the end. A massive circular table is beyond, surrounded by high-end décor and a few waiters waiting for us to get settled. Dea and Nine sit at one end, both having made room for us either side of them.

Nine pats the spot next to him while looking at me. *Sit next to me?*

I scoot across the long seat bed circling the table until I reach the place his hand rested. He places a plasmascreen in my hands, one with the menu on, and I scroll through until I pick three courses: sushi for starters, pasta al pomodoro for mains, and chocolate mountain lava cake for dessert (because who the fuck wouldn't order that from the menu?).

"So," Dea says, "what is the plan from here?" He looks to me, and I gulp.

None of my damned plans ever work, but here's to one last try. "We're eating, then we're getting back on that jet and finding Connie. We're going to break in, break her out, and then go the fuck home."

Arrie smiles his approval.

"How do you plan to break in, Sweetie?"

"I'm gonna wing it." I wink. "I could plan all day long for that, but I don't even know what a base in the Andes Mountains could possibly look like, so we might as well just be cautious and play it by ear. Carefully." I look to Arrie as I say that last word, knowing he'll lose his shit the moment he sees Connie in whatever awful condition she is likely in right now.

He raises his hands in surrender. "All right. All right."

"I mean it. I'm not losing any of the rest of you just because you've decided to be an idiot. I'm also not saving anyone else if they get caught because of their own stupid choices." I look to everyone. "Am I clear?"

They all nod, and I get immense satisfaction from being the one whose orders are being unquestioned. Mwuhahaha. We could make a leader out of me yet.

You've already gotten us wrapped around your finger, Sweetie.

With that, we finish our food—which is all fucking delicious—and head back to the jet.

"So," I start as I buckle myself in, "we're flying over the Andes to see if I can spot anything that looks suspicious?"

Dea nods. "You should be able to zoom in with Vampire sight."

While the take-off procedures are ongoing, I practice using my Vampire sight. I've used it a few times, but nothing on this scale. The coffee station comes in and out of focus as I concentrate, and if I try hard enough, I can zoom in on the buildings and people milling around outside the plane.

But looking a few hundred feet out of the plane and down a mountainside? That is a tall order. I don't know if I can do this.

Arrie sits beside me, probably sensing my torrid emotions from the other side of the plane, and brings my hand to his lips, placing a delicate, soft kiss to my knuckles; it's so soft, in fact, that it takes me off guard, and I find myself melting into the warmth of his lips and the cool ice of his blue eyes. "You've got this, Killer."

His rugged voice meets my ears, and I snap out of the reverie.

I nod, a little shaky but determined. "I know."

He remains beside me, his hand in mine, the entire flight. Once in the air, however, we all unbuckle and stand by the big window on the right; I'm in front, using my enhanced sight to try to see anything below us.

It takes about half an hour to hit the mountain range, and once we do, I get myself comfortable on the floor as the guys supply me with various cups of coffee—Arrie even spikes his with a bit of blood.

We fly in a zigzag fashion around the mountain range from south to north, and I spend hour after hour looking for something—anything—that will lead us to Connie. I can zoom all the way down to the ground if I have a good supply of blood on hand (which Arrie is happy to supply), and I find myself looking at what is probably a very beautiful landscape, with all kinds of animals roaming, natural wonders beaming, and nature at its best, but I can't get the image of Connie being tortured out of my head so don't really take much pleasure in the task at hand.

"I can't spot anything!" I slam my hand down on the jet's red carpeted floor. "There must be something . . ." My voice breaks at the edges. I don't want to leave her there a moment longer than necessary.

Someone rubs a hand on my shoulder while someone else, probably Nine, places a hand on my knee. "We will find her, Angel."

Taking a deep breath, I get back to searching what seems to be an endless supply of mountains. Rock . . . more rock. And even more rocks. It's all I can see for miles. By the time another hour has sped by, we're a quarter way through the mountain range and are just about to enter the Bolivia-Chile air space.

"Nothing in Argentina, and so far, nothing in Chile."

"Noted," Nine says and probably notes it down. "Bolivia, Peru, Ecuador, Colombia, and Venezuela left to go."

I sigh. "Does someone have some sugar or something?" I roll my eyes. I am going to need as much sugary goodness as possible to get through this. My eyes are itchy and sore, and I can feel fatigue starting to set in. Zooming in this far with my enhanced sight is as straining as using my Witch powers, it would seem, and it's beginning to make me shake and feel queasy (though there is no telling if that is the crazy movements of this jet).

A donut appears in my lap. "Thanks," I mumble around a mouthful of sugary sweet goodness that has me moaning. It's like I can feel the food fueling my magic reserves.

"Here," Arrie grumbles. He bites his wrist the moment I finish my donut and offers it under my nose.

I shake my head. He goes to complain, but I hold up a hand. "Not a stubbornness thing. I need you conscious. I know it's been you feeding me this entire time." I meet his eyes for a brief second before peeling them away and readjusting my focus to the mountains below. "If I need blood, it'll be from the others."

He groans and wipes a hand down his face, but he sits beside me in resolute comfort nonetheless.

Nine's bleeding wrist is the next underneath my nose, and I briefly take a moment to wonder. I've never had Nine's blood before. Dea's tastes just like he smells: lavender and smoke. Arrie's taste just like he smells: forest and fresh laundry. Nine doesn't really have a scent, not like the others, but that doesn't mean his blood won't have a particular taste.

The plane slows down to a crawl as I take a break and focus on Nine's bleeding wrist. Blood trickles down the side of his arm, and his fingers twitch on his other hand, as though he wants to pull his own arm away.

I look to him. Are you sure?

I was going to force your head forward not bring my arm away. Yes.

Okay.

I allow my fangs to descend and run my tongue along the trickling line of blood before sinking them in.

Nine gasps and moans beneath me, his hips thrusting upward desperately while Arrie and Dea aren't stupid enough to come close to a feeding Vampire who is also tired and sex deprived. Smart men.

"Damn," Nine says on another gasp.

I look up with a smile—which probably looks menacing and insane—but he just looks at me with wide eyes that briefly shine with a promising amber glow for a moment before he blinks, and they turn back to their normal brown color.

It turns his magic on.

Yes. It's . . . fuck. I can't even explain it.

I know.

No wonder you're going insane. This is how you feel every time you feed?

I think so. Never been on the receiving end.

I take another mouthful, then detach from Nine's wrist and return to the window with a swipe of my mouth on my jacket sleeve.

Dea places a comforting hand on Nine's shoulder while Arrie sits back down beside me, but not before throwing a jerked smile Nine's way.

Men.

"You can all chat about sex later. Connie." I don't even need to attach a sentence to the end of that—they know what I mean.

Arrie rests an arm around my shoulders and pulls me into him. "You're doing great," he whispers into my ear. "But it's fun to see Nine come undone." He winks.

That has my head reeling with sexy possibilities, but I shake them clear and focus back on the task at hand. Connie. Mountains. Enhanced vision.

Chapter Twenty-Six

I spend hours kneeling by that window, gazing out at nothing but mountains and regretting even bothering to help the guys instead of Connie. I mean, they were three, she was alone. What kind of stupid idiot makes that decision? Every minute that ticks by has my emotions reeling further and further out of control. Pretty sure my fangs haven't retracted at all in the last half hour.

She could be screaming out in agony right now, and I'm not there to help. I'm just sitting here doing nothing! Every second of conversation without her frustratingly sexy sass is agony, every lack of a sex-related response to every stupid scenario we find ourselves in is like a breath of ice, and every interaction with the guys I have without her reminds me of how important just her existing in my life is. She completes us. She might not be a guy, and maybe that makes everything between us stranger than what most other women would be comfortable with, but without her, this relationship between us all will never be the same.

I have to find her.

Jumping to my feet, I grab each guy by the arm and drag them to me. I grab my empty coffee cup from the floor and hold it out to them. "Blood please. Mixed, from all of you."

Nine looks at me with a quizzical expression, but I just shrug. "Trying out a theory and seriously hoping it works."

He nods and bleeds first, filling the cup a third of the way. Dea goes next. And then Arrie. Soon, the cup is full of all three of my . . . team's blood, and the smell is a heady mixture that almost scents like home.

I grab the cup from Arrie and sniff with caution. My lips edge over the rim of the cup, and as the first drop hits my tongue, my fangs extend and I down the entire thing in a few gulps. It's . . . intense. Usually, I can feel the blood filling an internal need, but this is like the blood is filling almost every need.

Complete. That's how I feel. Well, almost. Something is missing . . . Connie. Her blood would complete this. Wonder what that would be like? Eh, now's not the time to wonder.

I sit back down by the long window and zoom in. "Wow." I can see every detail of every crevice, crack, and inch of the mountain range beneath us. "It's like I have telescopic vision."

Nine chuckles behind me. "Well, you just got a power-up from three of the most powerful supes on the planet. What did you expect?"

Arrie grumbles, "Do not use your powers right now in this plane."

I chuckle. "I don't like flying, either. Remember?"

Turning back to the task at hand, I have no problem seeing, and it doesn't seem to upset my eyes or magic supply. This is awesome.

"We're heading into Ecuadorian airspace," Nine kindly

informs me.

"Noted." I keep my eyes peeled, hoping this might be the place.

A few minutes later, something in the air around us shimmers, like someone has turned on a switch in the energy surrounding the plane.

"What's that?"

"Huh?" Nine asks.

"The air . . . it shimmered." I take a deep breath and zoom my vision in, but nothing. It doesn't look any different than the other countries' section of the mountain range. "It's a Fae spell," I realize. "Like the one on the Rogue Vampire Council building."

"Where?"

I look around us, peering through as many windows as possible, and change into my male form. I can feel the magical pressure of the spell. "Everywhere."

Nine looks to Dea. "They can't do a spell that powerful without some serious magical supply."

"Let's worry about that later," I offer. "I need to get out of this plane. Now."

I run into the captain's cabin and shout, "Can I jump out at this height?"

He nods. "Parachutes are in the back cabin."

"Thanks!" I run back out of there.

Nine follows me. "What are you doing?"

"Disabling the spell."

"You don't know how to do that!"

I reach the back cabin and look through boxes and shelves before I find the parachutes. "I can feel the magic, the intricacies of the spellwork at hand. I should be able to pull at a crucial point of the spell and watch it all crumble."

"That's just theoretical!"

I turn around to face him. "Theories are what my life is currently based on, Nine. I have to do something."

He sighs and grabs the parachute next to me. "Then I'm coming with."

"We're all going!" I shout loud enough for Dea and Arrie to hear. "Worst comes to the worst, I'll change form and fly us all to the ground. We'll be fine."

The other guys run into the cabin and grab a parachute each as Nine nods at me.

"You're going to hate this, Killer." Arrie smirks at me.

He doesn't need to tell me that. Just the thought of hurtling to the ground at goddess knows what speed after jumping out of a plane has my stomach in knots.

I can do this.

And I will do it without puking everywhere.

C'mon, Horseman of Magic, time to woman up . . . or man up . . . or WoMan up. Yup, going with that. You can do this, I keep chanting to myself.

"Okay," Nine says, "the back of this plane opens and we're gonna jump out. You got that?"

I nod.

"I will signal when we're low enough to pull the parachutes. They're air assisted, so we should be able to guide them where we want to go."

"Okay." I try my best to ignore my stomach's somersaults and all the dangers I am about to put us all in.

Don't worry, if you do this and we all get out 'alive,' I'll make sure to reward you handsomely.

Reward me? I look up and see him winking at me. Oh, that kind of reward. I just smile like an idiot and blush, fully aware the other guys are watching me blush at nothing, probably figuring it's something Nine said.

"Okay," Dea says, "open the hatch, Fawn!"

A whirring sound fills the air around us, and I can feel some kind of spell opening the back hatch of the plane wide enough for us to jump out.

Fuck me, this is insane.

I am sooooo going to die today.

Arrie runs first, headlong into the air, and jumps as far away from the plane as possible. Dea goes second, following the same strategy as Arrie. Which leaves me and Nine, and there is no way I am jumping last.

Go. Nine pushes me forward, and I run full-sprint into mid-air with a scream, and whomph . . . I jump out of a fucking plane.

The air rushes past my ears at such speed, I can't hear anything around me—not even the guys signaling me to form a circle with them. But their hand gestures are enough for me to get the message, and soon I am holding hands with Arrie and Dea, who still have one hand left spare each—for Nine, I presume.

Yup.

Nine hurtles in front of us and grabs Dea and Arrie's hands, completing our little circle.

Time to disable that spell.

Now? In the air!?

Before we land into unknown chaos would be lovely, Sweetie.

Oh, right. Don't want to land into trouble we can't see. That wouldn't be a good plan. Time to learn on the job.

Again.

I let go of the guys' hands, and they shimmy me into the center of the circle—where I can work while they protect me from any unknown threats. Something tells me I'll need some concentration for this.

Closing my eyes, I reach out to the spell with my Fae magic, sensing its form, shape, and how it was created. It seems to be coming from a powerful energy source that is constantly fueling it—day and night—which makes me think it might be an object. No person can sustain a spell this complex over this large an area indefinitely.

I can see the spellwork in my mind as I trace my magic over it: the patterns, words, and ingredients that make up the building blocks of the magic at work. Hopefully, if I can find a way of removing some of those blocks, it'll all come crashing down.

I can't get rid of any incantations because that would require knowledge of reverse cantations, and I don't know any yet, so it'll have to be based on either the ingredients used or the patterns created. Ingredients will take too long, and I'd need to pray and hope we find the right ones upon landing; and besides, that wouldn't fix this damn issue before we land.

Patterns then.

It's intricate, like the caster (or casters) weaved together a giant circle surrounding the entire Ecuadorian Andes mountain range. Well, it's more of an oval. Kind of. It stretches the length of the entire country from north to south along the mountain range and is some of the most complex spells I have ever seen before.

This is going to suck.

Parachutes!

I pull the lever without really thinking, my mind still trying to find a way to change the spellwork to our advantage. Maybe there is a way I can write us into the spell, so we can see beyond the glamour designed to keep us out. Speaking of which, how did they even manage that? That would take something more powerful than the Four (Five) Horsemen.

Not the time. Spellwork. Focus, Magic.

There's a section of the spell, repeated at each compass point, designed to keep us out—specifically—so we could fly through the air space and never notice. Seems they underestimated my ability to sense Fae magic.

I mean, hello, Horseman of Magic . . . Does that mean nothing to some people?

Okay, Nine, I'm going to redesign the spell in four places, and each one is going to take me around ten minutes. How long till we hit the ground?

He flinches. *About ten minutes with these parachutes. They're designed to make us descend a little faster.*

I sigh. Well, disabling that air spell would make good practice, I guess. I reach out with my magic, testing my own chute's spell first. It seems to be a simple Fae spell to displace the air around us and only uses a small circle pattern. I fling my own magical energy at it and rub some of the pattern away, rewiring it to a halt.

My parachute slows down, and I descend with the wind rather than with magic. Perfect.

I quickly do the guys' and ask for a new time analysis.

Don't really know. Maybe thirty minutes.

Still not perfect, but at least it buys us some time. I'll have to do the last one on the ground.

Using my hands as guides, I start on the nearest compass point—south—and get to work. I throw my magic left, right, and center, disabling pattern points, rubbing out sections of runes, and generally trying to rewrite it all to fit us into the spell. Once I am satisfied, I move on to the next one. Each takes about eight minutes—which I am pretty proud of— and after each one, I whoop and yell as I manage to beat my previous record. The more I practice, the easier it gets.

I have just finished the northern part of the pattern when I look down and realize I am a few feet off the ground. Damn. So much for getting it all done in time.

I brace my legs in front of me for the landing, hoping I don't break anything in this form because healing will take longer than in my female form, and I have to rush this last eastern pattern point.

My ass hits the ground with a thud as I drag along the dirt, my parachute ripping on the mountain edges around me.

The guys are just behind me, all coming down a few meters away. I unclip myself and run over to Arrie, who wraps me in a warm hug before I clamber out of his arms.

"I still need to disable the eastern point. Cover me."

He draws his weapons and turns his back to me.

I stand behind him, my back up against the mountain edge as Dea and Nine come to help, effectively forming an arc around me as I close my eyes and get to work.

"Fae incoming," I hear Nine say from what sounds like far away, but opening my eyes, he's right in front of me. "About a dozen."

Arrie steps forward. "Stay there."

Nine and Dea confirm his instructions and form a tighter arc around me.

"Hurry up!" Dea shouts at me over his shoulder.

Following his instructions and trying to ignore how dangerous fighting alone will be, I start rewiring the eastern point of the spell.

Goddess, I hope this fucking works. If it doesn't, and I get it wrong, I'm going to have to start all over again, and that will mean everyone being in danger.

Five minutes in, and Arrie is still fighting in the distance, with Nine helping from the side lines by trying to use his mind control magic on anyone not under the influence of Silver Leaf Vain.

It is kind of working, and I am nearly done.

But even when I am done, the most that will happen is we will see our surroundings properly, probably showing us more enemies we'll have to fight.

"Dea?"

"Yes?"

"If this works, I am about to raise the barrier for us. What do we do now?"

"We fight, but knowing our true surroundings."

Right. We could literally be anywhere right now, and we wouldn't know. I don't bother taking down the entire spell; there is no time for that (and I wasn't sure I could), so the rest of the world won't be able to see the truth, but we will. And right now, that is all that matters.

I move one last rune around, changing its meaning, and bingo! I open my eyes and watch as the shimmer around us folds and vanishes. What was once natural, open mountains, shifts and changes into a more manmade path that forks, potentially taking us to Connie. Or perhaps away from her.

Arrie is fighting the last three Fae standing; the others lie dead at his feet, blood pooling around them and sinking into the dirt-filled path. Arrie turns and looks at me with a smile, clearly proud of my progress. "Well done, Killer," he whispers, my Shifter hearing just picking up on it.

I shift into a panther and leap into the air, tackling one of the Fae to the ground and ripping his head from his shoulders in one swift movement.

Arrie swings his sword one last time, skewering it through the two remaining Fae in one move. "There." He sighs.

Nine walks up. "Five minutes? Dude, you're lacking."

Arrie punches him in the arm. "I'm tired."

Dea laughs. "As are we all." He gestures to the two paths before us. "This is like some kind of fabled nonsense. Which path do we take?"

Still in panther form, I sniff the air in both directions but don't scent Connie in either.

"She wasn't brought in this way," Nine translates for me. "Sweetie can't scent her."

Dea looks at me. "Try your Vampire sense."

Right. I'm all hyped up from the mixed blood.

I shift back into my male form, then into my female one, and immediately take a step back and wince. All the surrounding scents and sights are playing havoc on my mind. Too bright. Too many scents. Too much . . . everything.

I wince and cower to the ground but continue sniffing nonetheless. Eventually, I pick up on a faint scent of Connie coming from the north. "She's north," I whisper.

Dea nods and goes to lift me up, but I shift back into my male form with a relieved sigh. "This way." I point to the pathway that leads toward the northern point of the spell (the only way un-navigational me can sense any kind of compass point).

With no more Fae around, we relax slightly. I will likely pick up on anything close by, with Nine picking up on anything within a ten-mile radius, so we all walk down the path a little—away from the blood and dead bodies—and relax into a heap on the floor.

"That was . . . fucking intense." I hold my head in my hands.

Dea sighs. "That it was, Angel. But you did brilliantly."

"Yes, you did," Arrie grumbles. He sounds tired, and I

wonder how much sleep he's gotten over the last few days. Between being drained dry by me, fighting with his battlemode focus, and running around with the rest of us, he probably hasn't had time to rest properly.

"Rest a little," I say to everyone. "We need to be in full strength for traveling and fighting later."

"I agree." Dea nods. "We should rest. Connie cannot be saved if we do not have the energy or magic supply to do so."

Arrie thumps his head to the ground, falling asleep almost instantly, while Nine and I slump against the nearest rock and close our eyes.

"I will take first watch," Dea says.

"Wake me for the second," Nine mumbles as he falls asleep, but Dea just sighs at him and smiles.

Chapter Twenty-Seven

The sun is beginning to set when we all start heading north. I try suggesting Dea and I carry us all north because it would be faster, but everyone wants to conserve energy.

"So," I start, "what do we know about this organization?"

Nine grabs my hand as we walk. "They're in charge of the legal and illegal blood supply for all Vampires across the globe. They work for the SC, but they also undermine them whenever they can. And since Fae are here, and there has been an increase in pixie dust distribution, we're pretty sure they're also helping with that global stream, too."

"Great," I mutter. "And how are we going to get Connie free from an organization like that?" I sigh. "They must be huge!"

Dea nods from in front of us, where he walks solo—Arrie is bringing up the rear. "They are. Their leader, Sanio Bontanos, is a right mumbling cove."

"A . . . what?"

Nine interrupts. "It means a deceitful and unpleasant

person."

"How many people work for him?" I ask. "Will it be a hundred or an army? How many will be here at the base? How big is the base?" I resist the urge to stomp my foot like an impetuous child and instead growl out, "Info!"

Arrie catches up to us and wraps an arm around my shoulders. "We don't have all of that information, Killer. He's an ass, but he's kept to himself up until now. The blood supply was going well, and everyone knew the illegal supply was happening, so we just let it slide."

Makes sense, I guess. Why fix something that ain't broke?

"Nothing to do but follow Connie's scent for now." But I swear, I am going to bring her home the moment I damn find her, no matter how many heads I have to roll to make that happen. I pick up the pace a little and catch up with Dea, who shifts beside me and grabs my hand.

"Are you doing okay, Angel?"

I nod, not really knowing what else to say. "For now."

The road north is long, winding, and tiresome; even for my Vampire-level stamina, the entire trip is tough. It takes us three days to trek through the mountains enough for Connie's scent to get stronger, and we spend the entire time dodging groups of Fae, skirting well away from any Vampires at night, and not one of us has had a decent night's sleep since the battle at the Fae Court. We are tired, exhausted, and hungry. But mostly, we're all pissed off.

The guys all takes turns babysitting my high-strung emotional state, and it's starting to take its toll on them. I can tell by the exasperated looks they try to hide whenever they think I'm not looking. I appreciate the effort, but I think it's best they just leave me alone to sulk and growl in my own ball of stewing nonsense.

I just want Connie back, and then to go home to my books, my comfy (so very fucking comfy) bed, and Arrie's homemade brownies. I didn't realize basics are so luxurious—or that brownies count as basics—but boy doesn't this shitty trip prove me wrong.

Halt, Nine calls out to us all. *We're heading toward a large group of Fae and Vampires.*

Okay, we're probably at some sort of gate. Nine? Feed me into the other guy's heads.

Done.

I'm going to fly up and see if I get a better vantage point. Dea, sneak around as much as you can, try to gain some credible info. Nine, try to poke around in their heads. See what we're up against. Arrie, find somewhere we can make camp.

They all agree, echoing a chorused *yes* into my mind that leaves a ringing bell effect in my ears, as though they all just shouted loud enough to partly deafen me.

Shaking my head, I start climbing the nearest mountain ledge in my female form—promptly ignoring the overload of sensations whirring my senses—and use my flying ability to climb and glide up the side with ease. I don't want to shoot straight up into the air, in fear of being shot out of the sky or spotted, but I can climb in among the mountains, using them and the clouds as cover while I try to get a better look at whatever is in front of us.

Maybe I can see the base from here.

I never thought I'd say this, but climbing the mountain's edge is easy. With the use of air magic, it's . . . a breeze (get it?). Laughing at my own internal dad joke, I focus on the task at hand. It takes me all of fifteen minutes to reach some kind of high up ledge long enough crouch on and high enough to see a few miles into the distance, and with my Vampire sight, I can zoom in all the way to anywhere I can see.

Handy.

Mountains surround us. No surprises there. But in front of us, around the path and a couple miles west, stands a giant metal gate in the middle of a wasteland; it honestly looks like something straight out of a medieval fantasy movie, and I'm caught halfway between an impressive snort and rolling my eyes. Of course this Sanio Bontanos guy has a gate like that. Seems Connie's enemy has a god complex—an evil one. But whatever, I think as I shrug my shoulders.

The gate is armed by rampart crossbows, ballistae, well over a hundred archers, and various Fae dotted around the upper gate's ledge. And that doesn't account for the army behind the gate.

This is gonna be a pain.

Nine? Tell me you were serious about needing an army to take you guys down?

No answer. Great.

Slowly, I ease my way back down the mountain's edge and land firmly on a spot of soft grass. Now I need to find Arrie. Taking a big sniff, I seek out his scent. The effect of the mixed blood is starting to wear off, because I can actually look into the sky without wincing into a ball of pain.

I follow the scent that leads me to a cave large enough to make a mini home in. "Arrie?"

"Over here." A light flickers around the corner, and I walk over. He's started a fire, grabbed some logs, and unpacked our meager supplies. "That expression does not give me hope of good news."

I shift my feet. "I think we should wait until the others are back."

He pats the spot next to him, his arm raised in question. He wants to cuddle?

I hesitate slightly, my foot not quite hitting the ground as I pause.

"Unless you'd rather not," he says, and I don't miss the disappointment in his tone.

Damn it. I can't upset him like that. I scoot over to him and plant my ass next to his. "I'm just not used to you being so . . . cuddly."

He chuckles, and damn if that doesn't do crazy things to my insides. "I want this to work." His voice is barely above a whisper, but I catch the hesitation in his tone.

"You don't have to try so hard, Arrie. I like you for you."

He leans down and places a gentle kiss to my temple. "I will always try for you."

I shiver at the warmth of his breath. "I . . ." I don't know what to say to that. It's far too close to a declaration of love for my personal level of comfort, and I don't think I'm ready for that. "Thank you, but just be yourself. Please."

His smiles ever so slightly. "Okay."

I turn around and wrap my arms around his shoulder, only just managing to do so, and kiss him. Not hard or urgent like last time, but soft and gentle, with enough need to let him know that he matters, that I'm telling the truth.

But Arrie has other ideas. He grabs me by the waist and hauls me onto his lap without breaking the kiss, and suddenly I find myself straddling his lap as his hands wander up the edges of my top.

I break the kiss to gasp at air and watch him smile at me.

"We can stop," he whispers.

I shake my head, afraid that if I stop us now, it'll ruin the moment.

"It's just . . . Connie . . ."

He puts a finger to my lips. "She's going to be fine. We can't do anything more without a plan, and that requires waiting for Dea and Nine." He takes a deep breath. "She wouldn't want you being miserable and upset for days. Especially when we are going to rescue her either way."

He's right. I can't just fall into a stupor every time one of the team is hurt. We are all immortal; it's not like her life is in any danger. "I just don't want her to hate me."

"Oh, Killer." Arrie places both hands on either side of my face, forcing my gaze to his. "There's nothing you could ever do to make Con hate you. She's totally in love with you."

I flinch but smile. "In . . . love?"

His face turns a deep shade of red. "We all are."

"B-b-but . . . it's still really early, and—"

"We know. We have all the time in the world to make cheesy declarations and be honest." He rolls his eyes. "There's no need to freak out over normal evolving emotions. Just enjoy your new immortal life." He leans in and places a needy kiss to my lips, parting them with a forceful sweep of his tongue. "Besides," he says between breaths, "you wanted romance."

I smile. He's right, I did. It means something to me that they're willing to be slow, go on dates and do silly, non-sexual things before we all get too entangled, and do everything at my pace.

I kiss him back, hard, pushing us both off the log we were sat on and onto the floor, where I straddle his waist and pin his hands by his head.

He groans into my mouth as I shift my hips to meet his rapidly hardening cock, and his tongue moves more fervently, his hips shifting to grind into me. He grinds against me, his control slipping as he struggles against my hold.

I laugh under my breath, but it strangles into a moan against his decadent lips, my lust-crazed mind coming back into the driver's seat.

Someone new enters the cave and coughs. "Can't leave you two alone for two minutes."

I break away from Arrie's mouth and growl in the direction of Nine. Way to ruin the moment.

Not sorry. I have plans, and he's ruining them.

I get up off of Arrie, holding out my hand to offer him some help off the dirty cave floor I pushed him onto. But he doesn't take it and instead glares daggers at Nine.

Nine shrugs at him and sits down. "Stop ruining my plans."

Arrie huffs. He stomps out of the cave and into the rain, leaving me alone with Nine and a crazy libido.

Damn it.

I concentrate for a moment and change forms, exhaling a sweet sigh of relief at the immediate change in bodily functions. The need is still there, but without my Vampire senses, it's dulled.

"So," I say as I sit next to Nine, "what are these so-called plans of yours?"

Nine chuckles. "Nope. Not telling." *You'll just have to wait and see. I've told the rest of the team already.*

I'm the last one to know?! I internally growl at him, hoping it translates.

I wanted you to have something to look forward to. He crawls over the log and sits behind me, placing me between his legs. His hand travels over my shoulder, tracing the outside of my ear and down my neck and stopping to stroke my collar bone. He dips his head low to whisper, "You'll like it. Promise," in my ear.

I shiver.

Dea fazes in and sits beside Nine, placing a hand on my shoulder. "Everything okay, Angel?"

I clear my throat. "Yes," I squeak.

Nine chokes on a laugh, and Dea smirks while shaking his head. "Cannot leave you two alone for two minutes."

A laugh bubbles out of me before I can stop it. I am beginning to think it might just be me that can't be left alone with any of the team for two minutes.

"Where is Arrie?"

Nine groans. "He went off in a strop."

Dea raises his eyebrow in question.

"Nine interrupted us," I explain, hoping he'll get my drift.

"Ah, I see." He turns toward the fire and smiles. "He will come around."

"I hope so." I rest my head on my knees as Nine wraps his arms around my torso.

Half an hour later, and just as my stomach starts to complain it's hungry, Arrie stomps back into the cave carrying an alpaca carcass on his shoulders.

I have to resist the urge to vomit.

It's no different than the meat on your plate every evening.

It's not that. And it truly isn't. Something about my Shifter senses goes into overdrive; it feels wrong. Seeing its blood dripping onto the cave floor like it's nothing . . . Like its life means nothing.

I can't hold it in anymore and run off to vomit in the corner.

"Change form, Angel."

At this point, I'm used to changing on command and just decide to follow his instructions rather than argue about being bossed around. When my female senses are back in control, everything flattens out. My nausea vanishes.

"That's . . . weird."

Nine looks at me with recognition in his eyes. "Some Shifters are sensitive to seeing dead animals. Kind of like seeing dead kin." He rubs soothing circles on my back. "Most of the Shifter world are vegetarian."

Arrie mumbles something in what I am starting to recognize as his native language and begins laying out the carcass to gut. And although it is kinda gross, it isn't sending me into a weird vomiting state of depression, so I just turn my head and watch the flames flicker against the cave wall.

"They have an army behind their gate." I break the silence. "At least a thousand soldiers. Vampire and Fae."

Arrie curses, and I turn around to see he nicked his thumb, but the blood has no effect while mixed with the alpaca's scent.

"Be careful," I huff.

Arrie laughs while Nine and Dea stifle giggles, and I realize I have just told the Horseman of War to be careful.

"Sorry." I shake my head.

Nine breaks the following silence. "No Silver Leaf Vain in the regular troops. But should probably expect some in the higher-ups."

I nod. "Archers, ballistae, and crossbows . . . The place is like a fortress. Not to mention the strategic pockets of Fae dotted along the outer gate walls."

"They will have spelled traps everywhere." Dea sighs. "It will be like dodging a minefield. They have probably also noticed your interference with the cloaking spell by now." He places some more wood on the fire, causing it to snap and crackle. "The troops are loyal. We will not sway them. They agree with the cause of destroying the control the SC has over the magical community."

"Ugh." I sigh. "I don't even know what to do about that.

They're right, the SC does have too much control. There's no balance."

Nine looks at me with surprise. "Explain."

"Well, if the SC control everything and the individual councils have no legal room to move, what do you expect? Them to just roll over and ignore how they've ruled their people for centuries?" I cough, clearing my throat, and Nine taps me on the back. Stupid smoke is hurting my Vampire senses. "But the councils can't just run in, weapons drawn, and hurt innocents in their plight."

I sink to the cave floor. "Can I not just take the entire system down and start from scratch?" I laughed.

Nine, ever the voice of literalism, says, "Sorry, but probably not."

"Rhetorical question."

"Right, sorry."

Dea grabs my hand. "I did not find anything of interest. Just a normal army guarding a gate."

"Right." None of that helps. It all just reaffirms what I already know: we have no hope of winning.

"We could win," Nine says, "no army could truly defeat us if we were going all out, but it would be a waste of energy. We should find a better way in."

All out? What, have they been holding back this entire time? 'Cos I won't lie, that shit ain't cool. But alas, my sexy nerd is right. We need a better way in.

"I could fly us in. Clouds would provide some coverage if we didn't freeze that high up." I shrug.

"We would need to know where Con is being held for that plan."

"We just need to get behind the gate, Dea. And either me or Nine getting a good grasp of where to head." I smile, a plan coming to mind. "Ohmigoddess, it's time to be ninjas!" I laugh. "Connie is going to be so proud of this plan."

Nine laughs and rolls his eyes at the image of me and the guys dressed in black trying to blend in. "We'll just steal some army uniforms, Sweetie."

Right, of course. That makes sense. But I can't hide my disappointment at not being able to wear any ninja clothing.

Damn it.

I will get my ninja fantasy!

"All right, get some sleep. We'll go when it's dark. More cover that way. At least from the Fae." Vampires can see just as well in the dark.

Chapter Twenty-Eight

It's midnight exactly, and we're all crouched just outside of the cave we made camp in. All of us are armed to the teeth, and I have so many sets of knives strapped to my body that I might as well be a walking kitchen appliance. The set Nine gave me before we left *Sheruta* are strapped to my thigh, but I'm only going to use them in tricky situations, since they fly faster and more accurately than my regular ones.

I'll get him to make me some more when we get home.

"Okay," I start, "I'm going to fly everyone over the gate under the cover of the clouds. I've never flown this many people before, so . . . err . . . sorry if I drop you all a hundred feet on your heads?"

Nine chuckles but rests a reassuring hand on my shoulder. "You'll be fine, Sweetie."

Dea and Arrie nod when I look at them, and that's all the reassurance I need.

"Brace yourselves."

I raise my hands in the air like some kind of weird magician (hey, it looks cool and helps me focus) and we all lift into the air. I test everyone's balance; everyone has a different airflow and current around them because everyone is a different shape, size, and weight. Arrie takes three times the amount of air displacement than Nine, for example, and is harder to maneuver around. Eventually, after fiddling and nearly dropping Arrie on his head (oops, but I did warn them), I get the hang of managing this much air.

"I'm going to fly us up and over the gate, and then I'm going to drop us somewhere less crowded as close to Connie as I can get. I can't keep this up forever, it's difficult to manage, so I can't have us fighting in the air."

Dea nods. "That is okay, Angel. Just get us there as silently and as close to Con as possible."

Everyone nods their affirmative, and off we go. I take us up beside the mountain's edge to provide some cover, just in case any of the enemy are looking up. We aren't exactly inconspicuous.

Once we reach the top, I drop us on the ground to catch my breath and practice trying to wrap the clouds around us by using the air.

This would be so much easier with my water element unlocked! I internally grouch to myself as I let the clouds slip the moment they reach us, and I watch in frustration as they float away like the shitty pieces of water vapor they are.

"Fucking clouds."

Taking a deep breath, I focus on just moving the cloud itself, rather than trying to float it this way. Luckily, clouds aren't too scarce this high up. The guys are all in various states of shivering, and I could have created a fire for them, but I'm worried we'll be seen, so they'll just have to be cold for a while until I figure this out. Not like they can die from hypothermia anyway.

"C'mon, c'mon . . ." I beg the cloud in front of me, trying to persuade it to move.

I'm hoping the presence of air in the cloud might make it easier for me to move the water, therefore moving the entire thing.

"C'mon, c'mon . . ." I gradually move my hands closer, the cloud following inch by inch. "You can do it, cloudy cloud, come here."

I can hear Nine trying hard not to snicker at me treating the cloud like a cute puppy, but I don't care. Anything to get this fucking thing to bloody move. I can bring down a building with fire, kill dozens of Fae in a fit of Vampire rage, but I can't move a fucking cloud?

Eventually, I have it surrounding us, and moving it while I am inside seems to be easier than dragging it from afar. "Okay, huddle up!"

The guys rush to my side, careful not to displace the cloud too much in their hurrying.

"And up we go."

Since we are inside the cloud (clouds are soaking wet and freezing cold, I might add, so don't try this at home) we can see out of it, so I only hope no one can see in.

We rise as fast as we can without garnering too much attention from the army below us. Nine keeps an eye on their minds (all one thousand of them at once, which I hasten to add is the most impressive thing I've ever seen) to make sure.

"If this is what you find most impressive about me, Sweetie, then I have not been flirting hard enough."

Dea and Arrie chuckle.

"You're looking into the minds of a thousand Vampires and Fae all at once? That's just . . . insane."

He blushes as much as his skin will let him at this cold height.

"Don't distract him," Arrie grumbles.

"Right." I look away and watch in my peripheral as Nine goes back to the task at hand.

"I don't want to take us much higher, lest we freeze and I have to manipulate fire in a controlled enough way to defrost out frozen bodies without getting seen."

Dea points down and to the north. "Okay, then head us in that direction." He sighs. "It seems to be where the rest of the army is."

"Sure, let's just walk right up to an army and say hi." I laugh at my joke, but Dea frowns at me. "All right, all right." I throw us in that direction slowly.

Ten minutes later, when we're all a little warmer from being at a lower altitude, Nine winces.

"You okay?" Dea asks.

He winces again, and I stop us. "What's wrong?"

"Nothing. Just a headache."

Arrie grumbles and Dea sighs. "Nine gets headaches from overuse. We have been up here for an hour already, and he has spent the entire time flitting through a thousand of minds."

"We're nearly ready to land, just hang on."

I speed us up as much as I can, frustration easing out of its familiar hole in the pit of my mind where I tried to bury it with the lid glued in place. Looks like I need to invest in some stronger mental glue. A growl escapes my lips, which causes Dea and Arrie to flinch.

"Just give me a minute." I take a few deep breaths and descend us. "Keep an eye out for a good place to land without being seen."

Sniffing the air, I search for Connie's scent. I can't really get anything this far up, but I keep trying.

"Here." Dea holds out his wrist.

I need everyone fighting fit for this, so I hesitate.

"I will be fine, Angel."

I sink my fangs in and take a little while Arrie has to place a hand over Dea's mouth to keep him quiet. (I'd be lying if I said it isn't the hottest thing about this new existence.)

After just a couple of mouthfuls, I start to smell Connie's scent in the air and stop. "Got it." Looking down, I notice Dea is hard, and I am damn curious what my bite feels like, but I'll never fucking know.

It's more potent than a normal Vampire bite.

But the human in the club wasn't affected?

It might just be a Horseman thing. I don't really know.

Hmmm. Something to think about later. Right now, I fly us as fast as I can toward Connie's scent. A few minutes later, I've found a good place to drop us down: a small pass between two mountains.

Using the cover of the clouds, then the mountains' edges, I dump us on the ground in an exhausted huff. "Did it." Mini celebration for me.

Honestly, that was exhausting, but at least now I only have to focus on ninjaing around while tracking Connie's scent. Hopefully, it won't come to an all-out war. I am trying to keep the peace, not purposefully break it.

Connie's scent heads west, so that's where we go. "Can you not extend your invisibility into a charm or spellbead of some kind, Dea?"

"It's super hard to do, actually," Nine chimes in. "I can place it into a spellbead, but it only lasts around twenty to thirty minutes."

"So that's what my mother used on me?"

Dea nods.

Is now the time to ask? Oh, to hell with it. "Dea, how did you know my mother?"

He flinches. "I really do not think this is the time for that question, Angel—"

"Just answer her. It's not a bad answer, bro."

"Very well." Dea takes a deep breath. "I knew all of the Angel-descended Witches. We all did. They were powerful, so we wanted to stay friends in case we needed them. Mostly, they stayed out of everyone's way and off the radar." He falls back to grab my hand. "Your mother and father were the last ones left. I only really knew them as acquaintances. They did not know what I was, of course, but they knew me as Derek."

I snort in laughter at the chosen name.

"Do not judge me. It is hard coming up with a name on the spot. I gave them a few spellbeads, just in case."

"It was just coincidence," I mutter to myself.

"A fucking huge one," Arrie grumbles just loud enough for me to hear.

For once, we're on the same page; that is a stupidly huge coincidence, and I am starting to not believe in them. Maybe Fate designs it that way.

But that poses the question of whether Fate really exists, and I'm not sure I believe in that level of magic. After all, magic is just science we don't understand yet. Not some mystical force of nature no one can quantify.

We exit the pass to a worn path, and Nine holds up his hand. "Soldiers, a few hundred meters that way." He points left. "Heading this way."

His telepathy has a wider range than my Vampire hearing, so he's on lookout (hearout?) duty, but my sense of smell is the best on the team, so tracking Connie is down to me.

"She's to the right."

Nine nods. "We're going to steal their uniforms and head right."

Arrie steps forward and draws his longsword, a hardness setting to his features I haven't seen before. He's being serious this time. He'll do anything to get Connie back. Just like me.

I step up next to him and draw a few knives as my fangs descend. I nod when he looks to me. "Stay here," I order the other two. "We'll be right back."

We run—well, he runs, I jog—and before long, we see five soldiers walking down the path. Other than those five, it's silent. We need to do this quickly and silently, so it doesn't raise any alarm.

"I can probably take two before they realize what's going on, then maybe throw some daggers on the way to take out a third."

"I'll handle the other two."

I sprint at full Vampire speed toward the group, who don't see me coming, and rip out two throats before anyone even breathes; two daggers later, four Vampires are on the floor before the one Fae in the group has any time to react.

He goes to scream, opening his mouth in terror, when Arrie jumps from his spot a few meters away and moves his sword in one giant swing. The Fae's head comes clean off and tumbles to the ground beside my feet, blood spurting out of the man's body like a fountain until it slows to a dribble down the side of his neck.

"What happened to leaving me two, Killer?"

"Got a little carried away, sorry." I shrug and realize I probably look a little crazy with all the blood over my mouth.

I go to wipe it away, but Arrie grabs my arm and yanks me to him. He spins me around into his arms and presses a kiss to my mouth. I flinch and pull away. "Doesn't that bother you?"

He laughs. "If blood bothered me, I probably wouldn't be a very good Horseman of War. Besides, it's not like it can kill me." He looks me in the eyes and winks.

He actually winked.

I'm going to melt. I'm going to die right here while my body is on fire from the heat caused by this man. I wrap my arms around his shoulders and kiss him back. Hard this time.

He groans and presses his body flush against mine.

A coughing in the background has us pulling apart. "Now is not the time," Dea says while placing Nine on his feet after fazing them here. "We need to wear these clothes to blend in better."

"Right. I really would rather not start a war. Already have one to deal with."

"Soooo . . . who's gonna . . . ?" Nine gestures to the bodies with a cringe that matches Dea's.

"Seriously? How many dead bodies have you guys seen in the last two thousand years?"

They both shrug.

My sigh matches Arrie's, and we get to work stripping the soldiers of their uniforms. I just pray that something here will actually fit Arrie.

"Ugh, I'm gonna have to change twice, aren't I?"

I tell you, this sex changing business makes my life stupid hard. Like, who the fuck has time to get dressed twice every morning? Not me, that's for sure.

By the time I've taken all of the clothes off three of the five soldiers, Arrie has managed the same with the other two, and we lay everything out.

"Arrie, you take the largest stuff."

He nods and grumbles, "You should take the smallest."

I nod and grab it, then leave Nine and Dea to sort through the other three. Luckily, their uniforms aren't difficult, and I manage to get dressed without needing to ask for assistance.

"Here." Dea hands me the last uniform. "You should put this on in your other form."

"Right." I sigh and roll my eyes.

You'd think being naked in front of these guys would be an issue, but it isn't. Firstly, I have nothing to be embarrassed about, and they'll all see me naked eventually anyway, but it is also really not the time. Weirdly, though, I do have an issue showing them my penis, and I catch myself thinking this is a strange thing to be worried about for someone who primarily identifies as a woman and seems to have no issue showing them my boobs.

I turn around and get changed with my back to them—much to Nine's amusement.

We walk up the worn path toward Connie's scent, and I just hope we find where they're keeping her before nightfall, because otherwise we'll have to hide out in enemy territory overnight. Nope, not happening. We'll have to work through the night.

"I'm going to use the crystals to take us home the moment we find her. That way, we won't have to fight our way back." I look to Nine, hoping it's a good idea. "We just have to get to her."

He nods and smiles.

"Good plan, Angel."

Yay me!

Chapter Twenty-Nine

Three hours later, and we still haven't seen anyone else on our travels through enemy territory. It's all seeming a little too easy. Part of me is waiting to be ambushed by a thousand Vampires and find out just how painful this immortality shit is.

We're all chatting harmlessly, but keeping our voices to hushed whispers considering the good hearing of our enemy, when Nine holds up his hand.

"Hush."

We left the bodies hidden in a small crevice in the side of the mountain, but I get the feeling that won't last forever once the Vampires scent the blood, so despite our camouflage, we are all wary of bumping into others.

We kinda stand out.

"Another five-person group."

I sniff the air and catch on to the familiar scent of Vampires and Fae. "Three Fae and two Vampires."

Dea steps forward. "We will take care of this." He looks

back and gives me a smug smile. "Stay here."

Arrie laughs, but I stamp my foot like the petty child I am. "Doesn't feel good when someone else does it."

Arrie wraps an arm around my shoulders. "We should move to the edge of the mountain. Stay out of sight."

I follow him to the edge. There aren't many hiding places at this point of the path, and we have to strain hard to fit into a small crack in the stone.

Arrie wraps an arm around my waist.

I suck in a breath at being this close to the Horseman of War. This close, I can feel *everything*, and it makes me tense.

He chuckles, clearly sensing my dilemma. "Sorry, Killer," he whispers in my ear. "We can move soon."

I just grumble, "*Kutabare*," and shift against him. If I'm going to 'suffer,' so is he. Mwuhahaha!

He groans behind me as I arch my ass back into his groin after standing on my tiptoes. "Stop that." His voice is strained, and I love that I have that effect on him.

"Why?" I place a hand behind me and go straight to the buckle on his pants. "Scared?"

"Of letting the entire army know where we are by fucking you senseless? Yes. Very much so." I sigh and move my hand away, but he grabs it and yanks it to his mouth. "Later. When we're home."

My head nods of its own accord, and I am getting slightly fed up with how pliant I'm becoming with these stupid Horsemen (and women, because let's not forget how wrapped around Connie's finger I've become).

I swivel around as best as I can and look Arrie in the eyes. "You are not the boss of me. In this instance, you are right, but goddess damn it, none of you are escaping me when we get back." I have to whisper, but I hope my whisper shouting works to get my point across.

He grabs both arms by their wrists and pins me to the rock wall. "Who said you were in charge, Killer?"

Goddess, my entire body melts and arches into his—much to his amusement—and if he wants me to be submissive, I know he'll have no trouble persuading me. Instead of an answer, however, I just let out a pathetic mewling sound and internally beg him to do something—anything—to help rid me of this need driving me insane.

I drop my hands to my sides when he lets me go and walks out of the crevice. I take a moment to breathe, but then I follow and see why he left: Dea and Nine are back, watching us from afar, and Nine has the world's largest smirk on his face.

"We dispatched them," Dea announces with a smile at my flushed face. "Time to keep going."

"I want to run there." They look at me like I'm crazy, but I shake my head. "We're taking too long. None of us want to be here when night falls and the rest of the Vampires that are too sensitive to sunlight to wander the day come out and say hi and scent that blood. Plus, I don't think anyone can see us run, anyway."

Dea sighs but nods reluctantly. "Very well. You carry Arrie, I will take Nine."

Arrie grunts his dislike at being carried by me (someone half his fucking height), but he walks over nonetheless.

I sweep him into my arms bridal style, and he wraps two arms around my neck; the entire thing looks hilarious, and I have to stifle many, many giggles to keep him from punching me in the face.

Once Dea has Nine on his back, we both take off as fast as we can, making much better progress than earlier. I'm all for slow and steady and careful, but it'll all be for nothing if we're caught here at night now.

The only thing that matters now is Connie.

About an hour later, Nine tells us all to stop, and we hole up in a small cave Dea spotted nearby. "Okay," Nine says, "there's an entrance to the mountains just around the corner and about a hundred soldiers posted outside."

I sniff the air. "All Fae."

Dea grimaces. "That means heavy spellwork."

"There's a heavy spell going on inside somewhere, I can sense it," I inform them. "Also, Connie's scent is much stronger here."

"We're close," Arrie says in surprise.

"No one expected us to get past that gate," I say. "Hence the lack of patrols on the main path."

"That ends here," Dea says. "From here, we are going to have to fight to get inside."

He looks to Arrie, who grumbles but smiles. "At least we're killing assholes this time."

I am not going to point out that they're only doing their job for a cause they believe in, because that would make him feel bad, and we really need his magic right now.

Drawing my daggers and letting my fangs descend, I prepare alongside everyone else. Dea has his dual blades, Arrie his longsword, and Nine his magiguns and dual daggers.

Time to fuck some shit up.

We run around the corner and immediately stop dead in our tracks at what the entrance looks like: a massive spell circle.

Damn it. I'm going to have to break that to get in.

And surrounding that spell circle is at least a hundred Fae warriors.

"Fuck," I mumble under my breath. I turn to the guys. "I'll disable the spell; you guys take the army."

They run ahead while I hang back and change into my male form. I still have a bunch of knives on me, just not my special ones, but I mostly rely on my magic and shifting powers in this form anyway.

Nine and Arrie are back to back in the center of a circle of enemies while Dea whizzes around the group and thins the numbers from the outside. Nine's abilities are working well, so he's managing to join the fight properly.

Might need him to train without his mental abilities when we get home, and see if we can't stretch them further.

The sounds of battle rage on around me while I stand in horror and watch. We've killed people before, sure, but only ever small groups or individuals, and those at the Fae Court were only a couple of dozen. This . . . this is different. They're dropping like flies, a body count piling up in a ring of death.

Movies don't do enough justice to the sounds of people screaming, of bones snapping; to the smell of death, blood, and piss that permeates the air; and the sight of everyone around you dying and the light leaving their eyes. It's harrowing. As though it'll be the last thing you ever see in this world.

How do people live like this?

I don't move, I just stand there, my mouth hanging open and my ears ringing from the clash of swords and the sounds of exploding spells.

Snap out of it! Yes, it's horrible, but Connie needs you. None of us can break through that spell circle.

I shake my head out of the dark hole it's creeped into and raise my arms to try to feel out the spell. Luckily, it's not nearly as complicated as the concealment spell. It's simply there to keep anyone out in the event no one is guarding the door or the army are defeated. It's made purely of runes, so all I have to do is magically rub them out.

Three, two, one . . .

And the spell is down.

Once the spell releases with an almost silent pop of air pressure, the guys look my way and smile.

I run to them and leap over the army in my panther shift, joining Nine and Arrie in the center.

Back in my female form, I arm myself with the knives and aid the effort.

"No point. We're just wasting time. We can outrun them," Nine says.

He's right. "Get Dea in here."

I watch Dea struggle to break through the mass of bodies attacking us, so I airlift him to us and place him gently on the ground.

He looks at me with a questioning eyebrow.

"We're gonna run. They won't be able to keep up."

"Right." He grabs Nine by the scruff and shoves him over his shoulder as I grab Arrie and throw him over mine. "Now!"

We run full-sprint, knocking over dozens of Fae, and I blow the rest out of our way.

The cave tunnel is dark, dank, and smells of rotting mushrooms. I nearly vomit, my Vampire senses taking the brunt of the vile onslaught, but I can't change forms because I need to run Arrie and me to Connie.

We pass plenty of Vampires on the way, but none of them can keep up with us at this speed. Pretty sure we have a full army chasing after us like some weird cartoon scene, but oh well, it's working.

We'll have to stop at some point to get Connie out.

I smell the air and adjust our speed to slow down. She's

close. Like, a few hundred meters at most.

"Stop!"

Dea and I come to an abrupt halt at my order, and I place Arrie on the ground as Dea does the same for Nine.

"She's close."

Arrie perks up at that and moves forward.

Just around the dark corner no one but myself can see is a hollowed-out cavern a few meters across. It forms a square with a lab table in the middle with all kinds of torture instruments laid out in a surface nearby. The smell of piss, shit, and sweat permeates the air, burning death and decay permanently into my nostrils, but I don't care. Connie is in there somewhere.

I shiver. "What the . . . ?" I don't need to voice my question because the guys all take one look at that table and stand still in horror.

"Really?" Dea asks. "He did not stop with his experiments after we rescued her last time?"

Last time? This . . . this is what happened before?

At the sides of the room stand multiple prison cells, and I sprint around the room and tear each one off its hinges. Whoever is being kept in here is now free; I don't care who it might be. No one deserves this.

A meek voice in the back of one cell in particular has me rushing forward, barreling past pixies, Witches, and all manner of creatures.

"Connie?"

"Ma . . . gic."

She lies in a heap in the corner, barely a reflection of the person she once was. Her skin is gray, her hair is covered in so much grime it's turned a dark shade of brown, and there are bite marks that haven't healed all over her.

I have to keep my fangs from slipping in anger, and instead change into my male form when approaching. "It's me." I raise my hand slowly, asking permission to touch.

She nods her head with a smile, barely a whisper of happiness, and I crouch and grab her hand.

"We're gonna get you out of here. Take you home."

She shakes her head. "No."

"Connie, you can't stay here." I don't understand.

She points behind me, and I turn around to find the guys in a heaped pile on the lab table, all in those stupid magicuffs, and all screaming through their gags.

I must have been so focused on Connie that I didn't hear their struggle.

Standing at the head of that table is a man I instantly know not to fuck with. He has a scar the length of his face, eyes a piercing bright red color, and is almost as stocky as Arrie. His buzz-cut does nothing to ease the edge of menace in his eyes. "You must be the Horseman of Magic. You've done quite a number on my army."

I stand to attention and block Connie from view. No way am I letting her go again. "You must be the piece of shit I've heard so much about." I grin at him, trying to make it as menacing as possible, but next to this guy, I probably look like the Easter bunny.

I don't care how mean and villain-like this piece of shit looks in the dim light of this cave-hole, I am going to enjoy tearing him apart.

Boss fight, bitches!

"I'd love to see you in action. Come on at me." He doesn't move to defend himself, nor does he look even an ounce afraid.

"They trained me." I point to the pile of men on the lab

table. "And you're not scared at all?" Sue me, I'm curious. But I also want to get him talking. He looks like the monologue type, and I am going to use every advantage I have; this is the real world, after all, not some video game with dumb rules.

He laughs, and the maniacal that rises and echoes around the cavern makes me shiver. I try to tamper that shit down, but I can't help the small shaking to my hands that escapes my control. The bastard notices, of course. "Scared, Horseman?"

I shrug and move forward, worried about leaving Connie behind me but not really having much of a choice. If we want to leave, we have to get past the dungeon boss first.

I'm in my male form, and I know that one of the first things I need to do is test this guy out. How strong is he? How fast is he? Does he have any magical abilities? To do that, I'll need to be in my female form.

Okay, I can do this. Breathe, Magic, breathe.

If I strategically use my magic, I can take this guy easy.

Flipping into my female form, I charge him faster than I can blink.

He flies across the room in utter silence.

No screaming. No maniacal laughing. Nothing.

It's more horrifying than the sounds of battle from earlier, if I'm honest.

He crumples a few feet into the wall but gets to his feet and walks out with a confident swagger, as though I didn't just use supernatural-level strength to throw him *into a wall.*

Freak.

"Hmmm, Conquest was right. You *are* strong. Perhaps, when properly fed and trained, stronger than my old friend, War, over there." He smiles at Arrie, and I nearly throw up.

Please tell me they weren't actually friends?

I don't bother waiting for an answer, since Nine can't give

one anyway, and I fling my air magic at him, hoping to do the same thing as before but in a different way.

It works, though not as effectively.

He flies to the ground in a skidding halt. This time, he jumps to his feet with renewed vigor. "Your air magic isn't as strong as your Vampire strength. I see."

Is he observing me?

Shit. I don't want to give this guy all the knowledge in the world about my powers. That would be stupid. But I guess it won't matter because he won't live through the day to do anything useful with the knowledge gained.

I hurl a fireball at him, taking a few extra seconds than before given my lack of practice with the volatile element.

"Not as well practiced?"

I growl. Nothing slips past him.

Use your brain, Magic. Think.

Aha!

I twist an air current in a continuous circle to create a mini-tornado (don't want to bring the mountain down), and ad fire to the mix. Double usage!

Take that, asshole.

I throw it at him full-force, holding nothing back.

This time he grunts and has to suppress the squeal of fear that escapes his lips; but nothing gets past my Vampire hearing at this close a range. I hear it. And it is all I need.

Fueled by the image of Connie weak and fragile, and the guys in a pile completely useless with their cuffs on, I sprint through the fire tornado and leap onto his writhing body.

"You," I grit through a heavy breath, "are going to regret the day you ever decided to deal with me." I punch him in the face harder than I've ever punched Arrie in training, and the satisfying clunk of his cheek bone breaking under my knuckles draws a smile from my pained expression.

The man beneath laughs as he takes a few quick breaths. "You're doing so well, Magic. You are a force to be reckoned with, for sure." He throws me off his body with a flick of his arm. "But you haven't bested me yet."

I let the fire tornado diminish and watch what he's about to do. My hands instinctively protect my middle, and I internally thank Arrie and Connie for all the repetitive drilling of basic fighting stances over the past month.

His fangs descend, and he walks up to me with a calm demeanor and a placid expression on his face. He's trying to exude calm and collected, but I can see through it. He's worried. You can see it in the occasional twitch of his fingers and the widening of his eyes with every step he takes.

Fear races through him.

He looks me straight in the eyes and flicks a finger.

I wait for something to happen—anything. But nothing does. The room remains silent except the guys' breathing over their gags and Connie's pained mewling in the background, and I remain conscious and in control.

"What?" he asks, looking baffled. "Why isn't it affecting you?"

I look at him confused, baffled. Whatever power he has, it isn't working on me. That's the best news I've had all fucking day. I smile, making sure to show my fangs, and leap at him.

We fly to the ground in a crash as I push his body into the dirt about an inch, creating a villain-sized hole in the ground.

Punch left. Punch right. Uppercut. And he is out like a light. Unconscious.

I run to the guys, uncuff them, and yank their gags out. "What was his magic supposed to do?" I ask Nine.

"Control your body."

I shiver. "That's . . . awful."

"It works on the rest of us." Nine looks to the ground and then up at Connie with tears in his eyes.

Shit. Connie.

I rush to her aid and help her up, simultaneously ripping off her magicuffs.

She heaves a sigh of relief as magic flies through her again uninhibited. But her wounds don't heal instantly like they usually do, and it causes my brow to crease in worry.

It'll take time. Dea can help.

I scoop her into my arms and watch in tearful joy as she loops hers around my neck with what little strength she has. "Let's go home." I place a kiss to her forehead and walk out of the cell to the guys.

"What now?" Arrie asks, looking frustrated and on edge.

I don't blame him. I'd be just as pissed if I was left out of the fight.

I hand Connie to him while I look around the other cells and think about what to do. In the other cells are various creatures that have been experimented on: pixies, fairies, Witches, Shifters, humans . . . You name it, this sick creep has it. We can't take them all back with us, but we can't leave them here. The army'll be coming any minute. Goddess knows what they'll do to them when they find their leader unconscious.

Speaking of whom. He lies on the floor still breathing, and I want to put a swift end to that. "Best way to kill a Vampire, guys?"

"Decapitation," Arrie responds on autopilot as he tries to be gentle with Connie's body.

I grab Arrie's sword and swing it above my head, ready to swing down and—

"Wait!" Nine runs up to me and grabs my free hand. "Are you sure you want to do this?"

I don't bother answering him. I swing the sword down and take off the bastard's head without a second's hesitation. "Yes."

Nine shudders and Dea grimaces.

"I'm not some innocent, lollipop-sucking child. I'm the Horseman of Magic, and this guy is fucking up my destiny." I shrug at their looks of exasperation. "Deal with it."

For good measure, I set his body and head alight, hoping to get rid of the evidence before anyone enters and notices. It'll give us a few days at least before people start to worry.

That just leaves the other cells. "Break everyone's cuffs off. Check to see who's still alive."

Dea, Nine, and I go to work, systematically ripping off cuffs and asking for names. Most of the people here are female, I notice, and all look a little like Connie; or, at least, would have if they weren't looking so grim and damaged.

"Nine?" He looks my way as he helps an elderly lady out of one of the cells. "Were you serious when you said you'd need an army to defeat you all?"

He looks to Arrie with a questioning grin, and they both turn to look at me with matching nods.

"Then I want you three to stay behind and get these people to safety. Get them on whatever transportation you can to their nearest council or whatever. Get them home."

I grimace as I give the order, because I don't want to leave the guys behind, but Connie is in no condition to help fight, and she needs to get home to rest and recover.

I guess I could stay and help, and someone else could take Connie? But I'd rather not—

"No," Nine answers. "You take Connie home. We'll handle

this."

I look at him with doubt, and he feigns insult.

"I just . . . don't want to lose any of you again." I look to the floor in a whisper of fear, hoping no one really sees it, but who am I kidding, I'm practically opening up my friggin' heart right now.

All three of them walk up to me and smile.

Dea places a hand on my arm. "We are going to be fine, Angel. We have nothing to worry about now. We can just kill the army and leave."

I nod, but I'm still worried about them. I know they can't die, but still . . . They can get injured, or be tortured, and what if I'm not there to—?

"Hey"—Nine cups my cheek with his hand—"stop that. Dea's right. We've been doing this a lot longer than you. We'll dispatch the enemy and get these people home. It's the right call."

Looking around at the half-dead people, I know he's right. I can't be selfish and leave these people here. "Okay." I sniff to clear the tears threatening to spill over my tentative barrier. "Then use the teleportation crystals and come straight home."

"Yes, boss," Arrie says, and I laugh for the first time in days.

I yank the crystal out of my pocket and look at it in question. "How do I use this thing again?"

Dea answers, "Smash it on the ground and think of home." He rolls his eyes. "You'll need Connie's, too. They only take one person each."

I nod and search Connie's person for hers but can't find it.

"On . . . the . . . table," she whispers just loud enough for me to hear.

I walk over to the lab table with gritted teeth. Honestly,

I've tried to ignore it until now, but all the blood on the various instruments and vials and bottles of goddess knows what makes my stomach boil and vomit rise to the back of my throat. But sitting on the corner of the table is a purple glowing crystal that matches the one in my hand. Seems Mr. Freak-a-zoid didn't have a need for it.

Thank fuck.

Arrie hands Connie to me, and I smash the two crystals on the ground and think of Connie's bedroom, the way the afternoon light plays well with the crystal chandelier.

The familiar rushing sensation of teleportation overcomes me, and I might have vomited somewhere in the ether of wherever. If it lands on anybody in the process, I'm not even the least bit sorry.

This shit is an awful way of traveling.

Chapter Thirty

We land in an unceremonious on a heap on Connie's bedroom floor, Connie's landing having been softened by landing on me. But fuck if I don't want to throw up again. I gently nudge her off me and run to the bathroom.

Goddess, Connie needs me and I'm stuck with my head down a toilet bowl. Great friend I am. Okay, Magic, calm down. The more you think about it, the worse it'll be.

Five minutes later, I walk out of the bathroom to find Connie unconscious on the floor. I sprint to her side and check her pulse on reflex. Yeah, I know, it's stupid considering we can't die, but it's concerning how little she's healing: her bite wounds are still fresh and bleeding, and the bruises all over her are an ugly shade of purple.

"Connie?" I rub her cheek before scooping her into my arms and laying her on the bed. "You're home now. Safe." A kiss to the cheek has her stirring a smile.

"Ma . . . gic?" Her eyelids struggle to stay open. "I'm . . . sorry."

"Shhhh," I whisper. "I'm right here." I blink away the tears and take a deep breath. "Everything's going to be okay."

I need to heal her wounds before doing anything, so I get to work taking her clothes off and seeing just how bad they are. She has bite marks all over her, some in various states of healing while others are fresh as daisies; I have to suppress the growl that escapes my lips lest I scare her.

Okay. So I don't have Dea here to heal her (goddess I hope the guys are okay), which means I have to do it some other way. Vampire blood has healing properties, right? I mean, mine would. Right?

It's the only plan I have.

Sitting myself underneath her head, which I lay in my lap, I make sure her eyes are closed before ripping my own wrist open in a hiss of pain with my fangs. "Here." I force my wrist to her mouth. "Drink."

Connie tries to fight my arm away, but I hold her down. "Please." My voice trembles in a desperate plea. I don't want to force her, but I will. I can't keep my hands from shaking as I hold my wrist firmly to her mouth.

She goes slack in my arms, and I watch as her throat bobs up and down with the gentle swallows of blood.

Please work. Please work. Please work.

I have to break open my skin a couple more times before I start seeing any results, but eventually, her bite marks start closing over and scabbing. A sigh of relief hisses out of my lips.

"Thank the goddess."

Okay, now I can work on everything else.

I have already torn her clothes off, so now I want to give her a bath and clean her up a bit. She'll appreciate that. Throwing a blanket over her body, I go to run her a bath.

Her bathroom is just as huge as mine, but her bath is smaller, though still inlaid into the floor. Crystals matching her chandelier surround hers, though, and I wonder if they mean anything to her.

Once full and appropriately bubbly, I carry her into the bathroom and lower her into the water. She's half-conscious, as she'll smile and sigh and whimper every now and then, but she's mostly out of it. I scrub her body, going gentle over all of her wounds, which makes it a slow process, but I eventually have all of the blood, dirt, and goddess knows what off of her body so her skin glows its normal beauty, if slightly pallid in complexion.

Next is her hair. I ask the house for a jug to help me pour the water and get to work washing the blood and dirt out of her hair. Everything below the waist is pretty matted, and I can't detangle the strands.

"Shit. I'm going to have to cut them, aren't I?" She's going to murder me when she wakes up.

Fuck. Fuck. Fuck. Well, there's nothing to it.

I grab a pair of scissors from her vanity and get to work. Her once floor-length hair ends up falling to the middle of her back, and I cringe with each snip of the scissors, but I hope waking up to her usual appearance will help her mental recovery. Hopefully, this doesn't put all of that at risk.

"Okay, Connie," I say once I get onto using her special mango-scented conditioner, "please don't murder me, but I had to cut your hair. I'll try and create a growing charm for you before you wake up."

That'll soften the blow a bit. You know, hopefully. And, hopefully, I'll escape that day with my own hair intact.

Once done, I towel dry her and her new hair and then carry her to bed, snuggling her in three duvets once she starts shivering.

A kiss to her forehead and I am out of the door to my own shower.

She'll be all right, I keep telling myself. She will be just fine.

I check on her every hour, like clockwork, and every time I go to see her, she stirs a little and smiles at me before drifting back off to sleep. I know I have to get her to eat something at some point, but I don't know what or how. She hasn't been conscious longer than two minutes at a time, so how I am supposed to get her to eat something?

Maybe some soup would be all right? Or a smoothie? That way she can have a little every time she wakes up. Yup. I'm going to make her a smoothie, some cookies, and anything else that's easy to eat in under a minute. Hopefully she'll be strong enough to keep it all down.

Best not make too much.

I navigate the kitchen with a little clumsiness and realize that I seriously need to stop relying on Arrie and the house for my meals. I don't even know where the blender is, for goddess sake.

I use as much good stuff from the fridge as possible: apples, kale, pears, kiwis—all the healthy stuff I know Connie likes— blend it all together, add some water, and get the tray ready to take up to her room, complete with cookies and mini pastries (okay, so I ask the house for that last item).

Her door creaks open, and her body shifts as her eyes blink in the dwindling daylight. We've been back for six hours, and I still haven't heard from the guys. I'm getting worried. I assume Nine'll send me some kind of message to update me, and the fact that he hasn't only tells me one thing: they're still fighting.

"Hey, Connie . . ." I keep my voice low and happy, trying

to encourage her to wake up in a good mood—goddess knows she deserves it.

"Mmmmm . . ." Her eyes are open, and she turns her head to look at me with a smile. "Hi," she whispers, her voice raspy and distant.

"Hey." I walk over and place the tray on the nightstand. "I made you a smoothie and grabbed some cookies and pastries. Try to eat something every time you wake up, okay?"

She goes to sit up but winces.

I rush to her side and lift her into a sitting position, then take a seat on the stool next to the pillow. I push the silly straw her way, and she smiles.

"Tha . . . nk you."

Light from the floor-length window filters through, and I can't help but feel a melancholic happiness—a slightly broken peace. I've gotten her home safe, and she's on the mend, but the guys aren't back yet. I know it'll be a few days, but I still miss them.

Damn. When did I go from wanting to be part of a family with this team to actually having them and missing them? Goddess, my life is crazy.

"It's . . . Friday," I hear Connie croak. "C'mon, spill." Her voice is barely a whisper, but she knows that's all she needs with my Vampire hearing.

I laugh at her. She's right, it's Friday, and I have so much to gossip about. "But . . ."

She shakes her head as she continues to sip her smoothie. "I'll be fine." Her eyes distance themselves as she says it, and I get the feeling she won't be fine at all, not on the inside.

But I indulge her. "Well, you were there for most of it. You saw me kissing Arrie, you probably heard me . . . you know, when I was dancing with Nine in the Fae Court." I wince as I remember the rest of that night, but I shake my head to clear the memories. "After you were taken, we raced to the Paris safe house, the Mort Montante."

She raises her eyebrows in surprise.

"We slept in the guest room with the big bed." Her face blushes at my comment, but she smiles. "No, nothing happened. I'd drained Arrie to have enough magic to Vampire speed all the way there, so he was unconscious, and I was kinda . . . out of it."

"You were worried about me." Her voice is getting stronger now that she has something in her system and some water to parch her dry throat. It's so beautiful to hear, like fresh lilies after a rainstorm.

"The next day we flew on a private jet to the Andes." I smile. It was a nice jet. "Oh, but we did stop at one of Arrie's restaurants."

She laughs, and I join her. "He's fucking brilliant in the kitchen, truly."

"That he is." I smiled wistfully. "He's been . . . different since the moment in the Fae Court."

"Different how?" She's moved on to the pastries and cookies, and I can't help but smile at my genius idea of nibble food.

"He's been nice. Flirty. Kind." I sigh. "It's disconcerting. I asked him about it when we landed in Ecuador, and he said he was worried about messing things up. So I told him to stop being so stupid and to just be himself."

"C'mon . . ." she whines. "The good stuff." She waggles her eyebrows, and I know what she wants.

"I've still not slept with any of them."

She complains and pouts.

"We've been a little busy saving you."

She sighs and lays back down, clearly done with the conversation if I don't have any juicy gossip.

"But . . ."

Her ears perk up, and her eyes snap open.

"Arrie and I did have a few hot make-out sessions along the way to your rescue." I fake-fan myself. "Got a liiiitle carried away there."

Her eyes beg me for more details.

"It was just a kiss."

"Arrie doesn't just kiss." She spears me with her green gaze. "Spill."

"Nine and Dea had gone on ahead to take down a patrol after Arrie and I had taken down the previous one and stole their uniforms. So we hid in a crevice in the mountain, and there was not much room in that slither of space, let me you tell you." I could feel myself getting carried away. "He pinned me to the wall and, fuck, it was insanely hot."

I blush furiously as I realize how much detail I just gave away. Thank goddess I chose to tell her that story and not the one of us making out covered in enemy blood. That would be hard to explain.

Connie coughs to get my attention, and I realize I've slipped away from the conversation. "If you need some alone time, I'm going back to sleep."

Chapter Thirty-One

Four days since I transported Connie and myself back to *Sheruta*, and the guys still haven't returned. Nine sent me one of those holomessage thingies on the second day, saying that they had defeated the army and were transporting everyone to their nearest council or home. But that doesn't stop me worrying about them.

Connie is making great progress, though, and is up and about like her usual self. She thinks I'm not watching, but occasionally she gazes off into the distance with a fearful frown in her brow, and it's during those times that I'm reminded just how fragile we Horsemen can be; we're still alive, after all.

We aren't just Horsemen of the Apocalypse.

We are people, too.

Connie has spent most of the time in the gym and outside, trying to regain her strength, while I've spent most of my time training with her in the evenings, practicing my newfound fire magic (outdoors), and studying in the library. We've fallen into a routine since we've been back, with me making breakfast and lunch and Connie making dinner at the same three times every day. We could have asked the house, but I want the practice and Connie wants to have something to do. I suspect to take her mind off of the torture she must have endured.

On the morning of the fourth day, she clears her throat at the breakfast table and asks, "Did you kill him?"

"Huh?" I swallow my mouthful of French toast. "Who?"

"Sanio. Did you kill him?"

I blanch at the name, not realizing they were on a first name basis, and nod. "Decapitation, then burning."

She nods slowly, visibly digesting the information. "I see." She gets up and goes into the garden, leaving half a plate of French toast behind.

I can't help my curiosity from wandering. How did she know Sanio Bontanos? Why was he so obsessed with her?

I can't help it, I follow her outside. Even if she doesn't want to talk about it, making sure she's okay is paramount; the rest of the team aren't here right now, so that duty is mine. It'll always be mine.

The previous mini rain season came to an end while we were on Earth, and the sun is back out in all its glory, beaming waves of heat onto my bare back and stomach (I'm wearing a bikini and shorts today).

"Hey, Connie! Wait up." I jog after her and go to walk by her side. Her cheeks are stained with tears. "Wanna talk about it?"

She takes a deep breath and lets it out through a strained jaw. "Maybe . . . I dunno."

I've never seen her like this, withdrawn and folded in on herself, and it scares me. Will she be okay? I loop my arm through hers and guide her around my favorite spots in the garden.

"You don't have to talk. We can just walk."

We walk along the edge of the rainbow forest, through a few pixie gardens and past a fairy's nest I'm still wary of, until we reach the *Shinto* shrine I usually do my morning yoga in.

"This," I say, "is my favorite place in the entire garden." We climb the hill slowly, me helping her up when her knees start to shake. "You can see everything from up here."

She breathes a sigh of relief when we sit on the grass outside one of the arches. Her hair shines like the sun in this light, and the usual golden glow of her skin, though dimmed slightly from recent events, has started to peek through the dull pallor of pasty white it's been over the last few days.

"About fifty years ago, not long after the magical community came out of the closet, I had a boyfriend."

I raise my eyebrows in question.

"I know. I know. We've all dallied in relationships in the past, but they're always fleeting, and we know that, so we just don't do it often." She smiles at me. "Well, I guess that's all different now."

Blushing, I lower my head to the floor, but Connie grabs my chin and forces me to look at her. "I like it."

"I . . . Err . . ."

I don't know what to say.

"I like what you're doing to this team. You're bringing us together, circling us around you so you can better lead us in the future." Her cheeks swell into peaks of pride. "We want you. All of us."

I still don't know what to say. "Thank you."

"Anyway, his name was Anthony. He was . . . very caring." I watch her vision go off into the distance again, and I wonder what memory she's reliving. "He once told me that it didn't matter who I was—despite never being told the truth—that he knew I was someone important but didn't want to pry."

"You never told him you were a Horseman?"

She shakes her head. "It just . . . didn't feel like the right time." She sighs. "I should have. If I did, it might have saved his life." Her eyes meet mine again, and I see the tears glistening in front of those bright green eyes before they escape. "If he knew what I was, he might have asked for my help, and I might have been able to save him."

"You can't know that—"

"Please don't." She shakes her head. "He wasn't anyone more special than anyone else I'd dallied with in the past. It gets a bit lonely, immortality, so sometimes I liked to seek something semi-permanent."

She looks like she doesn't want to tell me any of this, so I place a hand on her knee like Nine always does to me, to let her know that her past boyfriends aren't anything to be ashamed of.

"But he was abducted by a blood trafficker one night on the way home from a gig." She waves my curiosity away with a flick of her hand. "He was a small-time musician."

Nodding, I wrap an arm around her shoulders and squeeze gently.

"Anthony was allowed a single phone call to say goodbye, but he tried to use it to call for help, and rather than call me, he called his brother—a police officer—who died trying to save him." She shudders. "I ran after his trail, but by the time I'd tracked him down in the Andes Mountains, it was too late."

Her tears are flowing openly by this point, but I just let them fall. If she needs to be sad for a while, then I'll sit with her while she cries.

"I was foolish. I should have turned back and asked the guys for help, but I didn't. I wanted to free him like one of those superheroes from the movies and watch his awe and fascination as I dramatically revealed who I was . . ."

"So you broke in?" I ask.

She nods, her eyes far away, her tears still falling. "Killed half an army before I was finally captured. Magicuffs weren't a thing back then, so it was harder to capture us."

So magicuffs are a recent thing? Interesting.

I store that away to unpack later.

"But they did capture me." She shudders. "Took the guys four-and-a-half years to find and rescue me, but by that time, the damage had been done."

"Four-and-a-half years?" That's . . . fucking nuts. "What did he do to you?"

"He experimented on me, quickly coming to the realization that I was unique and didn't fit into any known species. He tortured me for information on the Horsemen for years. Eventually, I'm ashamed to say I cracked." Her voice breaks at the end. "He used Vampire venom to force an addiction, using a mixture of pain, horror, and pleasure to confuse my senses. It's an effective form of torture."

Decapitation was waaay too easy an out for that cunt. I should have left him writhing in pain. I have to resist the urge to growl with my fangs as they descend. Luckily, I hide that fact from Connie by burying my head in my knees.

"When the guys rescued me, it took months, years, before I left the house."

"That's why you're scared of Vampires," I realize, my voice still muffled from where it lies buried.

Connie lifts my head into her hands and stares intently at my fangs and red eyes.

"Sorry." I try to pull away and give her the privacy she needs.

"It's okay. You don't scare me, Magic."

Fuck, I love the way she says my name, and the fact that she isn't scared of me nearly makes me kiss her, but I resist. That might be too soon given the reliving she's undergone recently.

But Connie has other ideas.

"Can I kiss you?" she asks.

At my nod, she grazes her lips against mine, trembling her pain across my broken smile, her smooth lips across my fangs.

Pleasure shoots through me, even at the softest of touches, and I stifle a whimper. This is about her, not me.

Her face scrunches, a moan slipping free from her mask, and she plummets her mouth against mine, crushing my fangs, and forcing us to the grass. She forces her tongue past my lips and tangles ours in a dance of sorrow and ecstasy.

With pain and passion all intermingled, I can taste her grief on my lips from the tears that continue to flow freely down her cheeks, and I can feel the fear racing through her erratic heartbeat as she presses herself up against me. I grab her waist in a desperate grip, doing anything to hold on as she throws wave after wave of life at me. The good and the bad. The memories and the dreams. Everything that makes her alive. Everything that makes her . . . her.

Goddess, does this woman know how to kiss. They all do, but Connie's are the best. (Shhhh, don't tell the others.)

Far too soon, however, she pulls away. At my moan of complaint, she laughs. "Nine wants to be the first."

"First . . . ?" Oh. Realization dawns on me. "Why the fuck does he get to decide?"

It should be my choice. No one elses.

"That's what I said, but he made a sound argument."

"He did?"

"Sex with Nine is different than with anyone else. He knows exactly what the other person needs or wants at any given moment." She looks at me. "He's the perfect choice. Trust me."

Oh. I suddenly understand. And I do trust her.

I'm going to lose my immortal virginity to the Horseman of Famine.

Chapter Thirty-Two

That evening, after a beef pot roast, we train in the gym together; more weapons. Cue eye roll. I am legit terrible with fucking weapons.

Connie stands back watching my stances and movement with the twenty-fifth sword/dagger/knife combination we've tried to date. Nothing seems to work.

"Oh my fuck, of course!" Connie yells from nowhere and runs out of the gym like her ass is on fire.

Least she's gotten her spark back.

I continue with the drills she set me—no way am I disobeying her—and twenty minutes later, she runs back in with a stick of carved wood nearly the length of her body in hand.

She holds it out to me. "It's a bo staff."

"A what?" I ask, baffled.

"A bo staff. Originated in Okinawa, Japan in the . . . fifteenth century—I think." She moves her hand along the carved light wood with grace. "It's not as deadly as other, bladed weapons and should work well with your elemental magic with a few protection charms ingrained into the wood."

Realization dawns on me. "You mean, I could use this to assist my air and fire magic? Like a goddamn wizard in the movies?" I can't help but bounce on my feet a little.

"Pretty much."

"Ohmigoddess, this is awesome." I twirl it around in my hands using my air magic, trying out a few basic magic-staff movements. I might have fumbled a little, but I'm doing much better with this than anything else we've tried so far.

"This one is a little too big for your height, and they're usually created personally for the wielder, and you'll need some fire protection magic on the wood, so we'll have to get you one made, but . . . you can practice with this one, if you like?"

I hesitate. "Whose is it?"

She sighs. "Nine's."

I get the feeling there's a story there, but I don't pry. There is always a story with this lot.

"He won't mind. Not for you, anyway."

She grabs the nearest sword, one she isn't massively familiar with, and lowers into her usual protective stance. "Ready?"

I stand a little higher than usual, ensuring all of my enhanced knives are attached to my thigh, and smile. "Bring it on, Conquest."

She smiles that delicious grin of hers that makes her cheeks rise and her dimples deepen before attacking first. Her arm comes in for a jab.

I reflect it with an air-enhanced swipe of my staff. "Damn. This thing is cool."

Her laugh brightens the room, and I find myself distracted momentarily by the smirk on her face. She's planning something, isn't she? Of course she is. The bitch.

I smile as though oblivious, but when she twirls and tries to attack from the right while feigning left, I block with a flick of my wrist, extending the staff outward as though my arm were four-foot long.

"Nice," she says with surprise.

"This staff is easy to use with my magic."

She grins and goes for another attack, which I go to block, but I get there a little too late. "Just think what you could do with it when you unlock your earth magic."

Right, because it's made of wood. "Ohmigoddess, I could extend it, mold it, shape it . . ."

I get distracted by the possibilities, and Connie throws the sword to the floor and leaps at me, arms outstretched. I catch her, and she wraps her legs around my waist.

"This," she says as she kisses me, "is what I've been missing in my life." She showers my face with small kisses that tickle, and I have to fight to get her off of me.

"Stop," I say through a laugh. "I'm . . . going to . . . pee myself."

I push her off and look up, finally able to move my neck, and gasp as Nine, Dea, and Arrie stand in the doorway, looking a little worse for wear, but all are safe.

"Guys!" I run to Dea and jump at him, just like Connie did to me, and he catches me mid-air and twirls me around.

I feel like a princess for a moment, and I won't lie, it feels amazing. Every one of the guys embraces me and lays a small kiss to my lips, and Connie just hangs back and watches us with a smile on her face.

"You're back!"

"We are, Angel. That we are."

"Well," Nine says through a smile, "as great as kissing you

is, I'm going to shower. It's been days since I've had a shower."

I wave them all off as they go to their own rooms to shower and rest. Goddess knows they need it. Maybe I can make them all some late-night dinner and bring it to their rooms? Yes, that'll be good.

Or is that too clingy? Too much? Not enough? What if I get their favorite food wrong?

"Stop," Connie says from right beside me. "Whatever spiral your mind has entered, stop." She hugs me. "What you thinkin'?"

I blush. "That I could make them some food before they fall asleep. They're probably hungry."

Starving.

I laugh, and Connie looks at me quizzically. "Nine's hungry."

My favorite food is pizza.

"Pizza for Nine." I think for a moment. "What about Dea and Arrie?" I look to Connie for help.

She looks at me and smiles. "You asking me for advice about how to woo the guys through food?"

Thinking about it for a minute, I nod. "Yes, yes I am. Now woman up and help me." I widen my eyes as much as possible and stick my bottom lip out (yes, I am pleading with the Horseman of Conquest, and yes, I'm also quite shocked at how my life has turned out).

"How can I say no to that?" She sighs. "Arrie doesn't have a favorite food, he just likes variety. Dea likes cheese a lot."

"Fancy cheese pizza, a mixed pizza, and spicy meat pizza. Got it."

She looks at me with a chuckle.

"What?" I sigh. "I only have until they finish showering."

I pick my plasmascreen up from the kitchen table where I

left it earlier during dinner and look up fancy pizza recipes. After a couple of minutes, I find a nice-looking one on ciabatta rounds.

"Fancy mini pizzas!"

I ask the house for all the ingredients we don't have and get to work. In twenty minutes, I have three trays of various pizzas, OJ, and coffee/tea.

Connie sits back and watches me work, finding my antics hilarious, and probably checking to make sure I don't burn the house down. Which is fair. Last time I was in here doing anything difficult I nearly burned toast.

"I'll be back," I say to her.

But she shakes her head and says, "Chill with them. I'm going to play some games and head to bed."

She seems solemn, and I wonder if maybe dividing my time between them isn't such a great idea right now.

She needs me.

"You sure? We could play together?"

She frowns at me and turns away, storming off down to the cinema room.

What is that all about?

The trays of food are steaming heat into the otherwise cold kitchen, and I honestly don't have time to go after her. I'll pop down and see her after I make sure the guys are okay.

Yup. That's a good plan.

Right?

I carry the trays on top of one another using air magic and try my best not to trip up the stairs at the same time.

We're all in Dea's room.

Right.

I get to the top of the stairs and don't know which way to turn. It's then I realize that I don't know where Dea's room is.

I'll come get you.

Two minutes later, Nine bumbles down the corridor I explored my very first day out of bed. It's down the other side of the staircase, rather than the left I'd usually take to get to my, Nine, and Connie's room. This corridor eventually leads to Arrie's room, but along the way we enter a small door I haven't thought to check in. It's just a foot taller than Nine and solid black with those large fancy hinges you see in movies based in medieval times.

It's so . . . Death.

That thought has both me and Nine chuckling as we enter the room. The room is . . . not what I expected. It's an odd mix between medieval, gothic Victorian grandeur, and modern-day technological.

I expected the black chandelier and the four-poster bed that has black netting draping down each side, but I didn't expect the workbench in the back that looks like a potion master threw up all over it; nor did I expect the small, hole-in-the-wall feel the room gives me.

Dea clears his throat, and I realize I've been staring at the room while the guys stare at me. "Sorry," I mumble.

"Never been in here before, Killer?" Arrie's tone is slightly suggestive, but he also looks curious.

"No. I've seen everyone else's but not Dea's."

Dea looks at his feet, and if it were possible, he probably would have blushed.

"What's the matter?" I ask as I give each guy their tray of mini pizzas.

"Errr . . ." Dea rubs the back of his neck with his hand in that sexy way all three of these guys do, and I have to focus to stay on track. "It is just . . . the room is always a little surprising to people. It is not what people expect when they look at me."

I sit down next to him on the bed and smile. "It's perfect." It really is. Dea is a down-to-earth kind of guy, and this really reflects that. Sure, he's vain when it comes to how he looks, but he's practical and realistic.

He pulls me into a hug.

"You made pizza?" Arrie asks. Surprise etches at his voice, and I wince.

"I tried." I look to the floor. "The last time I cooked anything I nearly burned toast, so . . . I won't be offended if you ask the house for a decent replacement."

Nine chuckles and looks at me with a strange expression I haven't seen before. It almost looks like . . . love.

No. Nope. Definitely not.

I shoot up from Dea's bed and say, "Err . . . So, goodnight. See you all tomorrow." I rush out of the room.

But Nine grabs my wrist just as I rush out of the doorway and drags me back in. "You're not doing that."

"Doing what?"

"Running away the moment someone cares."

"I don't . . ." I don't know.

Nine turns me around and pulls me into a hug.

"Sorry," I mumble, "it's been a tough few days."

Arrie pipes up at that and asks, "How's she doing?" through a mumble of mini pizza.

I shake my head and let Nine lead me into a chair that he sits on first so I'm sitting on his lap. He wraps his arms around my waist and takes a deep breath.

"She was doing great until . . ." They look at me expectantly. "Until she asked if we killed him. Obviously, I told her the truth."

Nine flinches beneath me. "Well," he says, "she would

have found out eventually." He rubs circles along my back. "You haven't done anything wrong."

"That's not the point."

"No, it is not," Dea says. "The point Angel is trying to make is that Connie is unhappy, and she does not know how to fix it."

"Time," Arrie grumbles. "Give her time."

I think about Anthony and how if Connie didn't give him some time, he'd probably still be around today and old enough to have gray hair and grandchildren.

"She told you?" Nine asks incredulously.

"Right after I told her we killed him." Looking around, we all wear matching expressions of concern. "She'll be fine," I say, more to myself than anyone else. She has to be.

Nine reaches for my shoulders and rubs them, placing gentle pressure in all the right places, and I nearly moan—I just manage to hold back before I take this rather sweet moment in a whole other direction.

"You need to stop worrying about everything all at once."

Dea nods. "Take things one issue at a time. Connie will be fine." Dea comes over after finishing off his last mini pizza (he ate them all, woo!) and wraps his arms around my waist as he entangles them in Nine's. (Two-way cuddles are great, by the way—in case you needed to know.)

"These weren't half bad, Killer." Arrie smiles at me. "We can make a chef of you yet."

"Really? You like them?" I shoot out of my seat and run over to Arrie. "They were . . . nice?"

He laughs. "Yes." He stands and wraps me in his arms. "Now stop making me all gushy and start being annoying again. It's much easier to deal with."

Now it's my turn to laugh. I tickle him and, just when I

have him writhing on the floor, I kick him in the ass. "Good enough?"

He growls, so I take that as a yes and leave to head to bed. I'll check on Connie in the morning.

Chapter Thirty-Three

"What now?" I ask over breakfast the next morning. "We've lost the entire Fae Court and half the Vampire population. We officially have an enemy."

"We do not have anything, Angel. Humans have an enemy, and it is our job to ensure balance is kept."

Connie's been quiet all morning, but she chooses that moment to participate in the conversation. "They're trying to replicate Horseman blood."

The room falls cold and silent as everyone digests her bombshell, but it seems I'm the only one who doesn't understand the implications, because Nine looks up at me and says, "When a Vampire feeds off of someone more powerful, their magic gets a big boost. The more powerful the donor, the more magic they get." His eyes plead with me to make the connection.

"So when they feed off of a Horseman . . ."

"They're never more powerful," Connie finishes for him. "They'd be unstoppable with a Horseman-fueled Vampire army."

"But they can't even synthesize human blood," Nine says with a frown. "What makes them think they can synthesize Horseman blood?"

Connie's eyes fall to the floor as her hands start shaking.

"What is it?" I ask as I grab her hand in mine.

"They were experimenting with using magical properties of different species' blood to try to recreate Horseman blood, but to do that they had to extract a lot of blood from me."

"That's why you were so weak . . ." I realize.

She nods, still avoiding our gazes.

"Just how much blood did they take from you, Connie?" Dea comes over to rest a hand on her shoulder.

She flinches at his touch, and he pulls his hand away. "Enough to fuel an army for a few days."

Nine's jaw drops. "They know that we heal quickly?" She nods. "So they used your ability to quickly replenish your blood supply to bleed you dry."

It wasn't a question, but she nods anyway.

Arrie grumbles something in his native language, and for once, I'm not curious as to what it means because I whisper my own expletive in Japanese at the same time.

"*Kuto*."

I stand and place my dish in the dishwasher. "We need to alert the Vampire Royal Council. Bring them here." I direct that at Dea, who nods and clears his own dishes before walking off to follow my orders.

"Nine?"

He looks at me in question.

"Meet me in the library, and bring your genius mind with you."

He follows Dea out the kitchen.

"Arrie?"

"Yes, Killer?"

"I need to know where the Shifters and Witches stand with this new development." I turn to Connie. "Feel up to going with him?"

She nods and smiles. I thought having something to do might help. Something far away from Vampires.

"Right, wait until tomorrow. I might have something to help."

I really, really, really want to work on some teleportation crystals that'll work backwards, and take us from *Sheruta* to anywhere on Earth. That way, mission times will be shorter, we can portal straight to councils, and I won't have to deal with the portal-vomiting situation.

Racing to the library, I find Nine in the stacks, pulling various books on Fae magic, charms, and teleportation. He's heard my idea.

Yup.

"Good. I'm going to start researching by using the Seer Stone."

Okay.

The Seer Stone has trouble answering my questions:

1. How do I create a teleportation crystal?
2. Teleportation Fae magic
3. Can you mix Witch charm magic with Fae spell magic?

It doesn't even give me an answer to that last one. I guess they wouldn't usually try. Goddess, what I wouldn't give for a Witch-Fae hybrid. Ha! If only that were biologically possible.

"Okay," Nine says from behind a shelf to my left. "I've got some good resources on creating teleportation crystals so you can see the theory behind it for yourself, though I'll teach you how to make them anyway." He pops around the corner and smiles from behind a stack of books that reaches his chin. "I've also got resources on charm magic, and thought if we looked at the basic building blocks of both Witch and Fae magic, we might be able to find a way to combine them."

"Sounds like a plan."

He places the books down on the desk with a thud, and we get to work. Nine has a penchant for remembering details while I like to take notes and flip back through when necessary; I find more links that way. But there is one thing we share: we both leave books open on various pages, spine up, so we can come back to them later. The floor is littered in various books, papers, and objects, all in complete disarray to anyone not included in our system, which we started piling onto after the desk creaked with the ninety-second book I placed on it.

We've been at it for ten hours, and dark has finally descended. No one has bothered us, so we assume they are all okay, but I'm getting hungry and frustrated with our lack of progress.

"There must be something somewhere!" I growl, mirroring the growl of my stomach. "We can easily create transportation crystals that use a mental-magic link to take us anywhere on *Sheruta*, so why can't we just reverse the spell?"

Nine runs a hand through his hair. "Because that would require reversing an ingredient there is no cure for. Not one person in history has ever managed to reverse the side effects of the gugi plant."

"I know, I know." The question is rhetorical.

Nine huffs at me, and I can tell we are seconds away from having an argument over something stupid. We need a break.

"Dinner!" a familiar gruff voice rings out from behind us. Arrie stands there with a tray in each hand.

It smells like . . . ramen!

"Fuck, yes," I mumble and run over to him, dodging various stacks of books along the way. "Thank you." I place a quick peck to his cheek and take the tray to a relatively clear spot a few meters from the desk.

Nine follows me, and we both sit in exhausted silence as we eat our ramen and drink our smoothies. Goddess, I've never been so thankful for food before.

Arrie stands there and stares at our mess in astonishment. "What are you trying to do?"

"Create a teleportation crystal that can get us from *Sheruta* to anywhere we want on Earth."

His eyebrows shoot to his hairline. "You can do that?"

Nine and I look at him and shake our heads. "We've come up with most of the theory, but we've been stuck for the last four hours on how to reverse the effects of the gugi plant used to stabilize the Fae magic's direction."

"Why would that need reversing? Surely you can just use it the other way around?" He sits down where I've just been and starts rummaging through my pile of useless papers.

"Could you . . . not?" I whisper, afraid he'll mess with my system.

"He can't mess with your system," Nine says, "he's literally a strategist."

Arrie nods. "I can see what strategy you've used and am only picking things out of your discard pile."

"I didn't realize that applied to non-battle scenarios," I say, and then wince. "Sorry."

Arrie shakes his head. "I don't use it outside of the battlefield often, I just didn't want you mad at me for ruining your strategy."

"Good shout," Nine says.

I punch him in the arm. "I'm not that scary."

They both look at me like I kicked a pigeon—dumbfounded—and laugh.

"We both know you would have punched him in the face if he ruined that system of yours, Sweetie." Nine's red hair dances in the light as he continues laughing.

"Would not."

Arrie comes over and sits on my other side. "Yeah, you would have, Killer. But that's okay." He wraps an arm around me. "Think I can handle a little temper tantrum."

Nine scoffs. "None of us can handle yours, and it's going to be the same with her. She's stronger than any of us. And when we've trained her up properly, she'll beat us all in a fight, one versus four."

Arrie slumps his shoulders and agrees.

"I don't think that's—"

"He's right."

But . . . that could be dangerous, couldn't it? One bad day and I could bring down a fucking country. I don't want that kind of power or responsibility. I just want some ice cream, some more of Arrie's cooking, a good book, and some great sex. Is that too much to ask for?

"Stop spiraling!" Nine shouts. "It's fine." He grabs my hand. "You're not alone."

Arrie grabs my other hand. "He's right."

"You say that a lot."

Arrie shrugs. "He's right a lot."

Nine chuckles and lightly taps Arrie on the arm in that way guys do to show affection that I'm not sure I'll ever get used to.

I'm a hugger, what can I say.

"Ugh. Guy nonsense."

"You know," Nine says, "you're a guy, too."

I groan. "Don't remind me."

"Does that . . ." Arrie begins and pauses, looking for the right words, "bother you?"

"What? Suddenly growing a dick every time I want to use my other magics?"

He grimaces while hiding a laugh but nods.

"Yes."

"I thought you'd come to terms with that, Sweetie?" I get up to leave the conversation, but both Nine and Arrie grab a wrist each and hold me back. "Nope. Nuh-uh. You're going to talk about it so that you don't freak out and melt down about it three days from now after your mind has overthought it."

Gah! This fucking shitty asshole.

"I'll have you know," he begins, and I can tell by the smirk on his face that he's about to say something inappropriate. "I have a fantastic asshole."

Arrie tries hard to hold in the laugh but is unsuccessful, and he barrels over in a fit of giggles I didn't realize he had in him. Goddess, that laugh melts me every time. I hoard every little chuckle, every snort that slips his defenses, but this, this is just gorgeousness on a silver platter.

You have a real thing for his laugh, don't you?

I don't give a shit how insane it is, it's the most beautiful laugh I've ever fucking heard, and the fact he doesn't laugh a lot just makes hearing it all the sweeter. Quit judging me!

He holds his hands up and backs away. "No judgment." He runs a hand through that gorgeous red hair. "But seriously, what's so wrong with having two sexes?"

"Seriously?" I give them both an incredulous look. "How many things are wrong with being a guy? How many times have you been looked at funny when you smile at a child in the street? How often have women crossed the sidewalk to avoid you for just being a guy?"

They both look to the floor.

"Now times that by two, because I also have all of the sexist issues of being a woman, and you might start to see the problem!"

Arrie huffs and continues sifting through my piles, careful to put them back in the same order and place he found them.

"You get both the good sides, though, too. Like, you get to be the only person on the planet who knows if childbirth or being kicked in the balls hurts more." Nine smiles handsomely and angles his face toward the light the moment he notices me staring.

He's such an egomaniac.

Yeah, but you love me really.

That I do.

He freezes. I freeze. The entire room falls silent. And I just want the earth to open up and swallow me whole.

I . . . what? What have I done? Oh my goddess, I've ruined everything. He'll never want to sleep with me now. What if he doesn't even want to be friends? Oh shit, what if I've ruined the tea—

SILENCE! Nine shouts louder than I've ever heard him shout before.

Once my mind has officially stopped spiraling, which takes another few seconds, if I'm honest, he grabs me by the waist and yanks me to him. But rather than slap me stupid or tell me to pack my things, he gently grabs my lips with his and tells me just how much he loves me back.

It's a sweet kiss, one full of promise and passion; not the kind of passion you fall into a melted puddle over, but the kind that leaves you questioning your very existence because the person who's sharing their heart with you in that moment has just changed your entire being in one simple second. In one second, you've gone from, perhaps, maybe having feelings for someone and being in denial, to knowing for utter certainty that what you share with them is indispensable—crucial to your happiness—and that you'll do anything to protect it.

It's the kind of kiss that changes your world.

I love you too, Sweetie.

I sniff and feel the not-so-familiar tingle of tears run down my cheeks. Damn it. Now I'm crying.

Nine swipes them away with a gentle brush of his thumb. "You know, you've ruined my plan slightly."

"Oh, that." The memory of Connie spilling the beans ripples across my mind, and I feel instantly guilty. "Sorry," I say through a hiccup.

Nine sighs and pulls away from me. "Never mind. At least she didn't you tell you the deets. Because I never told the team."

"Soooo," I say, trying to be suggestive, "you have it all planned out?"

He nods. "Just need some time to get everything ready." He leans down to whisper in my ears, but in true Nine fashion, he mentally says, *Don't worry. You'll love it. Promise.* He pecks me on the cheek and sits by Arrie, who is still flicking through my research notes, oblivious to my world changing before his very eyes.

"I just . . . err . . . need some air." I run out of the room like my life depends on it and race to the kitchen door—past Dea, who's sitting at the table reading the news—and into the garden.

The stars are bright tonight, and I briefly wonder if that's a coincidence. Suddenly I'm able to see, and I don't even know why I didn't notice before. I'm totally in love with them all, and fuck if I don't want to wrap them all up in a Christmas cracker and keep them to myself. Does that make me selfish? They're sharing me, why shouldn't they be allowed to be shared?

Well, I guess they are in a way—with each other. I would never stop them from being together as more than just friends; what happens in the team stays in the team.

"Hey," Dea says from behind me. "Are you okay?"

I turn around, fresh tears on my face, and he fazes right up to me and wraps me in his arms. Yup, I'm definitely in love with this one, too. But we have a lot to work out. Like why I'm weirdly addicted to his Angel form, and what he and Nine talked about when I left.

"Tell me what the matter is . . ."

"Oh." I sniff. "It's nothing. Honest."

He looks down at me with a look that says, 'yeah, right.'

"I might have just told Nine I love him, and now I'm scared, and I'm totally in love with the rest of you, too. I'm confused and concerned, and I have such bigger issues to be dealing with right now than my love life, and—"

Dea places a finger to my lips and sweeps me up, placing me gently on the grass. We gaze up at the stars in silence for a while, finding comfort in his presence in a way I don't with the others, and it gets me thinking.

"Why is it different between me and you?"

"I honestly do not know, Angel."

"Whenever I'm around your Angel form, it's like I've come home. Like I can't get enough of just touching you and knowing you're mine . . ." I gasp. "Sorry, that sounded crazy, and you're totally not mine."

"I am yours. Always." He turns to me and kisses me on the

forehead. "Just not yours alone."

"I would never get between you and Nine."

"I know. That is one of the reasons I love you, Angel."

I shiver. "You too, huh?"

"I think you will find the others feel the same way."

"But I don't get it . . . How? You've all known each other for so long, but I've barely been here a year."

Dea shrugs. "Love is . . . unpredictable. Sometimes it just happens, and you cannot do anything to stop it. My advice? Just go with it and enjoy yourself. Life gets a bit tedious if you stop to ask every question before jumping in."

Can he be not wise and all-knowing for, like, just a minute? But goddess, he's right, isn't he?

"So you're saying I should do everything that makes me happy that I can? Just in case I live a depressing immortal life?"

Dea nods. "Mortals do the same thing because they have a short lifespan, but for us, it is not about dying and not living life, but about making sure the lives we do live make us happy."

So far, I've tried to put my former life behind me, but I don't think that made me very happy. Maybe I should be trying to find a way of doing both: having my old life and my new one together.

But there's one thing I want to do first, and luckily, the man in question is lying right beside me. "Dea?"

He moves his head to the side in question, and I press my lips gently to his. His hands grip mine and yank me over him so that I'm now straddling his waist and leaning down to continue the kiss. "Yes, Angel?"

I take a deep breath, gathering all the courage I can, and say, "I love you."

A smile lights up his face, and his eyes that are usually that amazing galaxy color turn a bright gold as he gazes up at me. "I love you too, Angel."

"C'mon," I say after one last quick kiss, "maybe you can help us."

"With what?"

"Teleportation crystals that take us to Earth."

Chapter Thirty-Four

Turns out Dea knows the answer and that Arrie was on the right track all along. Rather than try to reverse the effects of the gugi plant, we can just use it in the other direction if we modify it with a Witch charm. So the theory is down, it's three am, and we're all more than a little exhausted, but I still have to figure out how to combine Witch charms into a Fae spell. I'm hoping it'll come naturally to me, given that I'm the Horseman of Magic, but so far, no luck.

I asked the house for a large bed in the library about an hour ago, and so far, Arrie is sprawled in the center looking oddly peaceful as he snores away, while Dea, Nine, and I are still brainstorming over how to manage this bullshit.

"Tell me again how you managed to rewrite the Fae spell in Ecuador?" Nine asks.

I sigh and repeat myself for the fifth time. "I found the key points of the spell circle, which were at each compass point, and reworked each section to include us into the spell."

Nine sighs. "That's not helpful."

"No, because that approach will not work here."

"Well . . ." I smile as an idea comes to me. "Maybe it will." I look at Nine and Dea, who both look at me with matching confused expressions.

"Your thoughts are running too fast to see, Sweetie. You'll have to explain."

"We've been attacking this with magical theory in mind, following rules of magic, because that's what everyone has to do." They nod. "Well, I'm the Horseman of Magic, I don't need those rules. Why can't I just write the charm into the spell?"

Nine frowns. "Because no one can do that," he grumbles. "You can't just rewrite a spell to suit your needs, you have to write it with the rules in place otherwise they won't work."

"What happens if the spell does not work?" Dea asks.

"It could just be a dud and won't activate, but at worst, a spell like this could scatter the user's existence all over the ether."

It's my turn to look confused. "What the fuck is the ether?"

Nine waves my question away with a quick answer. "It's what magical scientists theorize is between two pockets of space. What we travel between to get somewhere when teleporting."

Oh. So that's the 'wherever' I vomited into. Cool.

Nine chuckles and nods.

"I'll try it first, then."

Both Dea and Nine groan in protest, but I hold up a hand. "I'm the one most likely to be able to put myself back together if it goes wrong."

Nine responds reluctantly, "She's right. If anyone can pull their particles together again, it's a Horseman of Magic."

"I still think that idea is awful." Dea sighs. "What if you

cannot achieve that?"

I shrug. "Then we get to see just how much Fate needs me." They both frown. "Look, it's the best chance we have, and I really want this to work. It'll be so advantageous to our work that it's worth the risk."

They sit either side of me and each place a hand on my knee, looking at me in complete adoration, and the attention is too much. I have to look away.

"We are with you, Angel," Dea whispers.

Nine kisses my cheek and whispers, "Always."

I assume they've had some kind of internal chat during the last few hours and are both up to speed on . . . everything. Goddess, I can't get my mind around it.

Errrgh, I'm gonna have to spill the beans to Connie on Friday.

Yup. Don't worry. You don't need to talk to us about anything. We're all on the same page.

"Definitely," Dea adds.

"Okay then." I take a deep breath and remove myself from between them. "Time to try writing a Witch charm into a Fae spell."

"Yes." Nine looks like a kid in a candy store, and I briefly wonder if he's tried this before.

"Yup, and with no results other than a few blown-off fingers."

I look at him with fear. "Blown-off fingers?" I don't want to blow off any of my fingers, goddess damn it.

"Don't worry, they grow back pretty quickly."

"Not the point!"

Dea chuckles behind me and places his hands on my shoulder. "You will be fine, Angel. I promise."

He doesn't know that for certain, but I'm thankful for the

attempt at comfort nonetheless.

Right. Time to attempt this magical bad boy!

I can do this.

Taking a deep breath, I focus on the spellbead in front of me. At the moment, it lies there completely see-through, but as I pour my magical intent into the bead (which are specially created to hold magic for a limited amount of time), it turns a silvery-white color.

"There," I mutter, "a reversal spell with directional intent."

Stage one complete.

Fae spells are a little harder, as I have to apply all of the ingredients and runes to the crystal first and then include the incantation. So far, I just add the spellbead to the ingredients and hope that works. Yes, this looks a lot like a Witch's cauldron as I dip a glowing crystal with runes etched into the side into a pot of liquefied ingredients. (I am just as surprised by the lack of magical-looking voodoo as you.)

Incantation time.

This is the kind of magical voodoo you see in the movies, and I can't help but bounce on my feet a little. (And guess what? This you can do in any language, so I choose Japanese.) It feels right. Using my first and native language for something as powerful as this.

"With this crystal, I imbue,
the power of Fate and magic anew.
With this intent, I enspell,
a way to travel and keep us well."

"That should do it."

I open my eyes and look at the crystal. It just looks like the usual purple crystals Dea hands out at the beginning of missions. Guess we won't know until we try it.

Grabbing it out of the potion bowl (which Nine frequently

reminds me is not a potion bowl but an ingredients bowl—cue eye roll), I grab it in both hands and assess the magic. All the runes are in place, the ingredients seem to have worked, and I can tell the intention is right.

With no reason to be concerned, I smash it at my feet and think of somewhere I know on earth, somewhere I can picture easily but not get into trouble when I pop in. Unfortunately, I can't really think of anywhere good, since my experiences so far have all been in official buildings, hotels, and dangerous places. The safe-ish place I think of, however, is that party house Prince Lucien frequents.

At least I won't be arrested or stabbed. Hopefully.

Best of a bad bunch and all that jazz . . .

It takes a little longer than I experienced going the other way, but I eventually pop up in the front garden, which is empty because there's no party being had.

Strange.

I seem to be in one piece: all ten fingers and all ten toes wiggled just fine, and I have them attached to all four limbs. Reaching my hand to my face, I feel two eyes, one nose, two ears, and a mouth with all my teeth still intact. Boobs and dick are firmly in place, and I can still switch between forms just fine. Oh, and my favorite feature—my pale-pink, waist-length hair—is fine, too.

So far, so good.

Now I need to get back, but the blackness of the atmosphere here is making me curious. Why is it so quiet? Now I'll admit, I didn't really pay attention to the news over the last week after we turned the world on its head, but I had every plan to begin all that nonsense again the moment we start getting back on track tomorrow. So I haven't seen anything about New Orleans or the Vampire Royal Council having problems.

Maybe I should have been paying more attention? I mean, Dea was reading the news, so he would have said something. Right?

Well, maybe not. He could have been trying to shield me while I was taking a few days and we were all recovering. Especially Connie.

Dammit, Dea!

I expand my Vampire hearing as far as possible, but nothing other than a gentle breeze and a few rolling cans echoes back. Strange.

Cities are usually full of sounds that I have to block out as background noise, but New Orleans is . . . silent.

Should I investigate before heading back?

Ugh. I have no idea. And I didn't think to take one of those cool contact pods with me before I teleported here because I am supposed to be going right back.

The guys will worry, so I should be quick.

At a full Vampire sprint, I run through a few streets to find nothing but empty houses and rubbish strewn across the equally empty streets. What the fuck?

It's like the apocalypse or some shit.

I run toward the Vampire Royal Council building and see lights still on through the shaded windows, so they must still be up and running. But what about the city's general population?

I race through a few more streets to find a couple of back alley bars open and a few Vampires lurking around. But no humans. It's empty except for Vampires. Even the Shifters have vanished.

Okay, I should head back.

Just as I think that, a group of four Vampires walk out of the shadows I noticed them lurking in earlier and smile at me.

A slimy, greasy-haired blond man leads the group, and by

the looks of his cruel smile, I'm not going to like whatever he has to say. "What do we have here?"

"Horseman of Magic, isn't it?" one of the Vampires on the left asks.

"What do you want?" I ask, more confidence in my voice than I feel, as I try to suppress the shaking in my hands.

I'm here alone. No backup. No weapons. Only my teleportation crystal to get me back home. And I know I should use it, I do, but I am soooo curious. I need to know what happened here.

"What happened here?"

They all stop walking and look at each other. "It's been a week since you and your Horsemen friends came here and started a human-Vampire war, and you're asking how?"

"W-W-What?"

Shit. All the pieces are coming together. The fake fight. The video recordings of it going live online. Shit. Shit. Shit. I turn to run away, ignoring the calls of the other Vampires wanting to goad me into a fight, and find an empty backyard to activate the teleportation crystal in.

I land back in the library to Dea and Nine fussing over me. They both check me for injuries, but I wave them off.

"Shit, Sweetie, are you okay?"

Turning sternly to Dea, I ask, "What has been happening in New Orleans?"

He flinches. "I did not know that is where you would go." He gives me an apologetic smile. "Humans have evacuated the city."

Nine looks at him. "What the hell, bro?"

"I did not want to worry Angel until we returned to work fully."

I punch him in the arm with a little more force than

necessary, and he stumbles backward. "It could be the middle of the night and that shit should have been mentioned." I poke him in the chest. "Never try to protect my emotions again." I sigh. "Not at the expense of the war."

Dea nods. "I was just trying to help."

"I know." Rubbing my hands up and down his arms, I lay a gentle kiss to his lips. "Just don't let others suffer because of me. Please."

He nods.

Well, no one says a relationship this . . . multifaceted would be straight forward.

I can see the sun peeking over the horizon out of the nearest window and sigh. I look over to where Arrie is sleeping on the bed and decide that he looks like the perfect place to curl up and sleep. His body is so warm as I crawl up next to him and wrap an arm around his chest.

"Killer . . . ?"

"Shhh . . . It's just me. Go back to sleep."

He looks so cute, I have to suppress a giggle.

(But shh . . . don't tell him that.)

Chapter Thirty-Five

"All right," I say to Dea the next morning after breakfast. "Come on. Spill it, Angel dick."

Connie splutters a laugh, and the sound is music to my ears. Dea shoots her a 'what the fuck' look, but she just shrugs. "She's right. Sometimes you can be an Angel dick."

He sighs as he finishes shoving his plate in the dishwasher. "I just did not want to worry you, Angel." He places his hands on either side of my arms. "But New Orleans was evacuated three days ago. Humans left. Only Vampires stayed, but there might be a few other species left, too."

I shake my head. "Just Vampires. Hungry ones."

This is all my fault. Not only is this the worst possible response to us going public, but we also took out the main blood supply outside of the SC's restricted supply. "If we don't do something, they'll starve."

Nine clears his throat as he walks up to me. "We should split up. Take on different missions."

"Good plan." I look to Arrie. "Go to the Shifter Council

and ask for their aid, then pop in on the Witches and update them. Get a feel for where they're at now the world's gone to shit."

Arrie doesn't really say anything, but his face tells me he doesn't mind going alone.

"Dea," I ask, "did you manage to get the Vampire Royal Council to meet us here?"

"Yes. They will be here this afternoon. They seemed eager to speak, so I assume they will ask for some assistance."

"We'll make a plan about the blood supply and New Orleans after we've spoken to them."

Connie steps forward and grabs my hand, not meeting my eyes. "What about us?" She looks to Nine. "Am I not going with Arrie?"

"No. Because I have a special project I want you to help Nine with." She looks at me with those beautifully puzzled green eyes, and I could have kissed her there and then and never stopped. "How much experience do you have with the Hunter Society?"

She flinches. "A bit. A few contacts."

"Good."

Nine asks me what I'm thinking, which is weird in itself, but I just wave him away. "Later."

I turn to Arrie and give him the two crystals, one to take him to Earth and one to get him home. "At some point, I will work out how to teleport within Earth, but right now, that's the best I've got."

"You really managed it?" Arrie asks, surprise etching his voice.

"Yes, asshole. No need to sound so surprised." I cross my arms over my chest and have to resist the urge to pout.

Fucking dick.

Arrie just grumbles something under his breath and goes to smash the crystal at his feet, but I rush him last minute and try to wrap my puny arms around his huge body.

"Don't get injured. Be quick."

He nods and smiles at me as I let go, and he's off in a plume of red smoke.

Damn those things really are cliché.

"Okay, Nine, Connie?" They both look at me with a gentle smile. "Meet me in the library."

They nod and walk off to the library, probably both curious as hell about my secret plan. I'm trying not to think about it too much, lest Nine overhear, so I instead turn to Dea.

"When is the meeting scheduled for?"

"Three pm in the conference room in the east wing."

"East wing? Conference room?"

Dea smiles and chuckles at me, but he eventually offers me his hand. I take it, enjoying the sense of mystery this house provides. "Let me show you."

I prepare myself for a nice, small adventure as Dea carries me bridal style through the kitchen doors and down the servant's hallway. We pass many rooms I haven't seen before, and soon I'm lost and dizzy from all the twists and turns we've taken, but eventually we come to a more professional-looking section of the house that's clearly designed for formal meetings with important people.

"This is . . . what exactly?"

Dea puts me on my feet. "This is the meeting wing. We hold important meetings with important people here."

The whole place feels like an office, from the clinical smell to the pristine white-washed walls. Ugh. Not to my taste.

"You do not seem impressed, Angel?"

"It's just very . . . office-like. You've seen one office, you've seen them all." I shrug and turn to go back the way we came.

But Dea grabs my arm and spins me back, wrapping his arms around my waist. "Then maybe I should find a better way to entertain you." He lifts me off the ground and pulls me toward him, where I wrap my legs around his waist and sit there staring into his amazing galaxy eyes.

"Your eyes are beautiful."

"Thank you." He walks us over to the couch in a small lounge area of the waiting room and lays me down. "But you're definitely the most beautiful thing in this house."

Goddess, damn him. I'm a molten puddle of feelings all over again, and this time I can't escape them because he knows I love him.

"It wouldn't be a mistake this time . . ."

Dea leans over me on the couch and rests on his forearms. "No, with you it would not. But with Nine, it would."

Right. I forgot about that. He wants to be my first, and the others all agreed. Doesn't mean I can't enjoy the moment.

Having allowed myself to relax around the team more of late, especially Nine and Dea, I relax into the moment and grab his lips in a crushing kiss that I hope portrays everything I'm feeling in this moment—from the love and happiness of being accepted, to the ease of sharing them all and seeing them smile. It's all perfect.

Dea pulls away and looks at me with tears in his eyes. "I love you too, Angel."

I brush the tear that threatens to escape away and give him what I hope is a questioning look.

He sits up, pulling me with him and into his lap. "It is nothing of importance, but I will tell you anyway."

"Story time?"

He smiles weakly. "Story time, Angel." He clears his throat.

"About five hundred years into our lives, we met this group of lion Shifters who were being hunted for their manes in what is now the plains of Africa."

"Wow. Lions?"

He chuckles. "Yes. They were . . . impressive, to say the least. But they were struggling against a local Witch Coven who used their manes as an ingredient in some potion that made them stay young. It became popular all over the continent and provided many riches for the Witch Coven."

I know exactly where this is going.

"Their Shifter pack was being decimated, but no one knew what to do about it. We passed them in the area while on another mission and decided to stay and help. We tracked down the Witches and scared them into stopping their cruel hunts. Instead, Nine encouraged them to pay the lion Shifters for wads of their manes."

"Clever Famine."

"It is his job, after all." Dea leans back, and I can see him shutting himself off from the world.

I don't want that. So I turn in his lap to face him and grab his face between my two hands. "It's okay. It's just us right now."

He takes a deep breath. "The plan worked, of course, but it started a war between Shifters and Witches, and we felt semi-responsible, so we tried to help."

"Did it work?"

He shakes his head, no. "We tried, but . . . nothing worked. Eventually, they fought themselves to extinction. Both sides."

"The Witches and the Shifters?"

"We do not always win, Angel." He coughs. "But anyway, while the others left when they saw no point in helping a defeated cause, I stayed."

His eyes avoid mine, and his cheeks are a slight red color, but I just sit there and smile at him, encouraging him to continue.

"There was this Shifter. Haji." His hand traces the tattoo underneath his black t-shirt, and I realize this must be *the* Shifter. "He was . . ."

Dea doesn't have the words, so I help. "Perfect?"

He looks at me and nods. "Perfect."

"How long were you together?"

Dea looks at me with surprise etched all over his face. "Six years, until he died in the final battle between his people and the Witch Coven."

Tears flow down his face freely now, and I don't make a move to catch them. Sometimes, crying frees the soul. This feels like one of those moments.

"I—"

"Please, do not pity me. It was a wonderful six years." He wraps his arms around me. "But that was not the point of this story. Ever since then, I have never . . . ."

Wait a minute. "You haven't been in a relationship in 1500 years?"

He shakes his head. "We are immortal, Angel. Loving a mortal can only end one way."

"What about Nine?"

Dea chuckles. "I knew you would ask that. But Nine and I have only been a relatively recent . . . thing. Two hundred years, at most."

I smile. "It can be scary to love without knowing what the future holds." I lace his fingers through mine. "But how about we try together?"

"I would like that."

Chapter Thirty-Six

I walk into the library an hour later, trying my best not to cry at Dea's pain and be a blubbering mess, but these guys make me feel so many emotions, it's crazy. (I swear I'm not a crazy mess all the time. Pinkie promise.)

"Sweetie?" Nine wanders around the corner of the bookcase and frowns at my tears before rifling through my mind. He instantly sobers any facial expression and opens his arms for a hug. "Come here."

"Hon?" Connie walks around the same corner and runs to me the moment she sees me crying. "What's wrong?"

Nine chuckles. "Nothing's wrong. But Dea told her the story of Haji, and now she can't stop crying, and she hates that it's making her cry in the first place."

Connie giggles and pulls me into her arms, and I just let her, absorbing every modicum of comfort I can get.

Goddess, why can't I stop crying? I have a really cool idea, plan, and stuff to put in place.

"You have a plan?" Nine asks. "A secret plan that you're

not letting me see?" The curious look on his face is enough to stop the hiccupping tears.

"It's . . . a . . . surprise."

"And I'm supposed to help with this? You realize how un-nerdy I am, don't you?"

I laugh. "Relax. There's two parts to the plan, and I need someone to do the non-nerdy bit."

Connie cracks her knuckles. "Let's do this!"

I lead them both to the pile of paperwork in the study area and yank out the giant A1 sheet of paper I was doing planning on before Arrie woke up the other morning.

"Meet Operation Anti-Hunter Society."

The schematics before me are pretty basic, and mostly consist of a mindmap with several main branches for the initial stages of development, and then of smaller things to consider.

"I want to develop a quest society. You know, like in all the fantasy games?"

Nine laughs, clearly not taking me seriously, so I frown at him, and he shuts up. "You're serious?"

"Yes." I cough to clear my throat. "The issue with the Hunter Society is that it was formed with only one purpose in mind. But what if anyone could ask for help? What if a family of Vampires needed some new complicated Fae spell to help build them better daylight control for their new house? What if the Witches needed some help guarding the change for their new coven location?"

"You want to create a digital help board? Where anyone can apply their skills, no matter their species?" Nine looks at me in awe for a moment, and I go a little shy. "That's . . ."

"Brilliant," Connie finishes for him. "That's brilliant."

"I just thought that it would help bring communities

together: magical and non-magical, higher supes and lower supes . . ." I pause, taking in what Connie just said. "Wait, you think it's a good idea?"

Nine grabs me by the waist. "I knew there was a reason you were the new Horseman, Sweetie. And this"—he gestures to the basic schematics of my plan—"is why."

Connie joins us with a smile. "So where do we start?"

"Well, we need a data-app that people can download to their personal chips and access whenever. That way, they can look for and/or post new jobs on the go."

"It should match to a website, too."

I nod as Nine's mental cogs turn; he has that faraway look on his face matched with that curious smile that's a dead giveaway.

"And we'll need backing," Connie says. "That's where I come in, right?"

"Right." I sigh. "Leave the Vampires and Fae for a minute and just focus on preparing a pitch for the SC, Shifter council, and the Witches. We probably won't get the Witches on board, but it will be good to include them anyway."

She nods. "I'll help Nine plan the data-app so I know what it's going to look like, and then I'll get to work."

"Sweetie," Nine says, "the Vampire Royal Council are starting to arrive."

I groan. "Right. Gotta go. I'll be back later." I wave as I run out of the library and to the office wing of the house Dea showed me earlier.

"Ah, Angel, there you are," Dea says from behind me.

The foyer is starting to fill with the members of the Vampire Royal Council, and having this many Vampires around after we just spent a whole week trying not to be seriously injured by many of their kind is more than a little unnerving. But I spot Prince Lucien in the background, trying his best to blend in and not stick out.

He smiles and waves at us before sprinting over. "How is my little Horseman?"

"Ugh. I hate that nickname." I sigh but laugh, brushing it off. "Things are not good, Lucien. Not good at all." I turn to Dea and ask, "Did you invite . . . you know, him?"

Dea shakes his head. "I told the king we would like an audience with the Council without him present. He was none too happy but obliged."

"Ohhh, and the drama unfolds. Who are we talking about?" Prince Lucien's white hair ruffles as he laughs at our seriousness.

"You'll find out, little Vampire Prince." I smirk at him and watch as the doors open and the king walks in. "Here he is."

"Indeed," Dea mumbles before turning to the nearest member of staff we hired last minute for this event and says, "Please open the meeting room doors and start ushering people in."

The small, mousy-haired man bows his head and hurries to do as asked.

"Time to yell at bunch of Vampires," Dea whispers in my ear as we watch everyone filter into the room beyond the foyer.

The room is a pretty standard meeting room, but the chairs are loungers and the seating is arranged to mimic the Vampire Royal Council's hierarchy, with a couch at the front for the king. Prince Lucien, I notice, sits at the far back, away from everyone. He must not be favored among his kind.

Wonder why? Sarcasm laces my thoughts.

I walk to the front of the room and decide that I want to do this in my male form so I can avoid all the Vampire-ness of the situation. I stand at the front, a snarl on my face as I try to look as menacing as possible, and face the king.

"This is not a pleasant visit. I have bad news, and quite frankly, I couldn't care less if you believe me or not."

The king sighs and goes to stand, but I hold out my hand to keep him sat.

"I'll take questions and debates later. You need to listen first. I'm done playing politics. I'm tired."

He nods, allowing me to continue.

"The Rogue Vampire Faction have teamed up with the Fae Court and Bandio Bontanos. They're being led by Prince Phillipe of the Vampire Royal Council." I hold out a hand to silence everyone's gasps and rising fury at the accusations. "You're going to ask for proof, and I have nothing concrete, but we're pretty sure they're working against the Supernatural Council and are wanting to start a war."

I wait for the gasps and rising tide of whispers to die down before continuing.

"Now I know Your Majesty has a telepathic ability, so I will allow you to read my mind, but only of the facts of our last mission. Nothing more."

That earns a stunned silence. I don't think anyone expected that, but I want to be honest with them.

"I want to always be honest with you. I'm not someone who likes lying or playing games of deceit, but the world's peace rests on our shoulders, and your time as ruler is nearly up."

The king rises at this and looks at me with a smile. "Very well, Horseman of Magic. Please allow me to examine your mind and see where your claims are coming from, then we can all discuss this rationally."

Dea steps down from his place behind me to follow me to the king's couch. I don't think the king will try anything stupid with Dea present, given his ability to persuade the soul to feel pain.

Eesh, even just the sound of it has me wincing.

"It might be a little uncomfortable," the king says as I sit next to him. "Just focus on your last mission and where it started. If there's anything you don't wish me to see, just skip ahead to the next part. Like a movie."

I nod and take a deep breath.

A shiver runs through my brain, like when you suddenly realize you're cold and a shiver runs through your body involuntarily. It's like that but inside my head, and I can do nothing to stop it.

Memories flit past my closed eyes so quickly I have a hard time stopping to process them, but eventually I find the moment we were 'attacking' the Vampires and staging a coup.

I think I hear the king chuckle at my villain attempt, but I can't be sure.

He keeps sifting through, watching us get caught and entering the derelict building that suddenly pops into full development the moment I step onto the path (I do skip past my bathroom break, though—don't want the king seeing my dick).

He watches the entire conversation we have with Prince Phillipe's wife, and I feel the king stiffen beside me at the sight of her bruises. He is none too pleased about my treatment of her, but he understands my pain; I just want answers.

I skip us ahead to the Fae Court, the announcement, and then Connie being stolen and our plight to get her back.

Finally, after what seems like forever, he leaves my mind and I open my eyes and sway a little.

"Easy," Dea whispers beside me. "You are okay, Angel."

The king grimaces at me. "I am reluctant to agree with

Magic, but agree with him I must. There is no way anyone but the future Vampire King could motivate the Fae Court that way. The queen might be a little cruel at times, but she loves her people. It would have taken some persuasion to put them in harm's way."

"What kind of persuasion?" I ask.

"The alliance kind. Marriage between firstborns, maybe. It is hard to say. But something substantial."

I bristle at the idea of forcing two people into marriage, but now really isn't the time. Standing back up to my position, the king stands and announces his thoughts to the council.

I watch the room react in horror, and then chaos ensues. Everyone is shouting, everyone is arguing, but one little voice stands out beside me. Prince Lucien has walked up to the small stage I'm stood on with a smile on his face.

"Thank you," he whispers. "Now they might believe me."

"You knew?" I ask.

"Yes. I have always wanted to work alongside the SC. It is for the benefit of everyone, after all. But he has always been against their ruling."

"He is not the only one by the looks of it." I gesture to the room's growing debate about which side they should be on. "And you are not the only council to be having this problem. Loyalties are dividing everywhere we look."

Prince Lucien places a hand on my arm and smiles. "You'll do fine, little Horseman. You've got this."

I address the room. "May I have your attention, please?"

The room gradually grows more silent as the seconds tick by, and eventually, I have the whole room's attention once more.

"My advice to your council is to pick someone else as the next king. Someone whose loyalties are not as divided, someone who is more liked, and someone who is more willing to work alongside other Courts and Councils." I clear my throat. "We need to improve our solidarity over the coming months and form a solid unit of peace. If possible, I would like to set up an embassy for each species willing to work alongside us; the embassies will come together to motivate and communicate with the outer reaches of our people. That means that anyone involved will have to get along with each other: Vampires and Witches, every Shifter species, and so on."

I'm kind of making things up as I go here, but our team can't keep up with this complex level of communication.

"I will oversee everything myself and arrange monthly meetings to hear any complaints direct from the councils. The embassies will be set up here, in *Sheruta*, and will work as a go between for us and you. Any and every species will be seen as equal, and we will set up as many embassies as needed."

That is all I have to say. I'm sure they'll argue for hours over it, so I intend to let them at it and walk off the stage and out of the room.

Dea excuses us and gives them the use of the room until sundown, then follows me.

"That was amazing in there, Angel. You really caught their attention."

"Really? Because it felt like I was trying to herd a bunch of deaf sheep."

He chuckles. "Welcome to politics. But I think you have just made things easier for us in the future."

"I damn well hope so. I don't want to keep having to video message every Council and then send one of you to chat. It should be easier than that."

Dea rubs circles into my shoulders, and I the stress leaks

out of me. "You should get ready. Nine's surprise will be waiting for you at sundown."

Chapter Thirty-Seven

Get ready. Get ready for sex with Nine. How in the hell does one 'get ready' for that? What do I need to look like? Ohmigoddess, I need a shower and to de-hair. In both forms. You know, just in case. Not that I plan on losing both immortal virginities in a single night, nor am I particularly comfortable with the thought of sex in my male form yet, but I want to be prepared for all eventualities.

Currently, I'm pacing the floor of the bedroom, trying to make a mental list of everything I need:

1. Pick out underwear and clothes
2. Have a shower
3. Wear deodorant and perfume
4. Put some makeup on

"Fuck, fuck, fuck. I'm soooo not prepared for this."

What if everything goes terribly? What if my vagina feels weird or something? What if I sound stupid? What if I don't know what I'm doing?

"Oh dear." I hear a familiar female voice in the doorway

and have never been happier to see Connie in all my fucking life.

"Thank the goddess!" I yank her inside and slam the door. "You have to help me."

Connie smiles and sits me down on the bed. "You need to stop freaking out and trust that Nine knows what he's doing." She takes both hands in hers and looks me in the eyes. "He knows you. Better than any of us. Trust me, he has this down. Just turn up as you."

"But I want to be a more confident me." I sigh. "Like you."

Connie smiles. "Thank you, but I'm not confident. I'm just old and know that being worried about every little thing in life is a pointless way to live." She leans in and plants a small kiss to the corner of my lips. "Just go have a shower and pick something nice to wear. Nothing else matters."

"Right." Okay. I can do that. "Shower and nice clothes."

"Tell you what," she starts with a grin. "You have a shower, I'll pick out something for you to wear. I know parts of his plan." She taps her nose, and I pout.

"That's so unfair," I mumble as I plod to the bathroom and get the shower running. I usually bathe, given the size of the damn bath, but I want to be quick.

By the time I've washed (twice), shampooed and conditioned my hair, and de-haired everywhere else, I have been in the bathroom for forty-five minutes and am starting to have a butt-ton of questions I need a fellow woman to answer. Unfortunately for her, Connie is the only woman around, and really, the only woman I know.

I walk out of the bathroom wrapped in a towel, letting my hair dry naturally. "Connie? If I have questions, may I ask . . . ?" I trail off at the sight of the scene in front of me.

Dea and Connie both sit on various items of furniture

around my bedroom and are mid-discussion when they suddenly stop talking to look at me.

Dea blushes at the sight of me in nothing but a towel that barely covers my ass, but Connie just smiles.

"What are you doing here?"

Connie coughs to get my attention and thumbs toward Dea. "He wanted to tell you to stop freaking out and just enjoy yourself." She gets up off the bed and grabs my hands. "And yes, you can ask me anything."

I look to her and then to Dea. "This is definitely a woman discussion."

"Right," Dea says. He walks up to me and nudges Connie out of the way before wrapping me in a hug. "Remember, you wanted it to mean something. To be important. To be a memory you can look back on. He is just doing what you asked, Angel." He places a gentle kiss to my forehead and unhooks my towel, which I let it fall to the floor, not really caring about them seeing me naked by this point. "Besides," he says as he brushes a wet strand of hair behind my ear, "you are perfect. And Nine thinks so, too." He trails a single finger down the side of my jaw and neck, going ever lower as he traces the outside of my breast and rests a single hand on my waist.

Goddess, damn it, that feels . . . surprisingly hot. He doesn't really do anything, but I feel the light, feather-like touch all throughout my body, and now it's shaking to be touched more by this man I'm slowly coming to realize I'm in love with.

I stand on my toes and wrap my arms around his neck. My lips crush his in what I hope is a forceful, heated kiss, and I grin in delight when he stumbles backward and has to steady himself on the wall.

"Angel . . ." he groans beneath our kiss. "You are making

it hard to leave."

I'm vaguely aware of Connie watching us from somewhere in my bedroom, but in that moment, I don't care. Everyone knows the score by this point. All I want is for someone to take away the nerves and fill me with heat so I don't go to Nine a mess of anxiety.

"Good," I say as I pull away, "then I'm doing my job well."

"A little too well." He grabs my legs and lifts me off the floor in one smooth motion.

I wrap them around his waist, vaguely aware that I'm butt naked but not really caring.

He pulls away from the scorching hot kiss and takes a deep breath as he smirks at me. "Feeling better?" he asks as he puts me back on my feet.

I nod, not embarrassed in the slightest. "Much. Thank you."

"Now leave." Connie pushes Dea out of the room and slams the door in his face. "Now that," she says as she turns back around, "was hot."

"Oh, I . . . err . . . just . . ." Now I'm embarrassed. Goddess damn it. I was doing so fucking well with the whole modern female confidence thing.

Connie walks up to me with an expression I only recognize from our drunken night out and heated make-out session. A sultry smirk that lights her eyes on fire and makes me squirm. She's turned on. A lot.

"You like watching?" I ask, genuinely curious.

She shrugs. "It's kinda hot." She wraps an arm around my waist and pulls me flat against her. "Promise you'll let me watch one day." She looks embarrassed by her request, but I just smile reassuringly.

"You can do more than watch, babe." I lean in and kiss

her, aiming for something hot but ending up tumbling us onto the bed in the process. "We can threesome any time you like." I wink at her, and I climb on top, straddling her thighs and leaning down.

Connie looks surprised by my outburst of confidence, but somehow it feels so . . . right. So me.

I've only become unconfident because of recent pressures, but I am a naturally confident person it seems.

"R-Really?" She seems unsure, and I can't help the feeling of the tables turning here.

"Yes," I say as confidently and full of adamant emotion as I can. "I want to see Dea come undone." I gasp in surprise at the filthy words coming out of my mouth, but I resign when I realize they're all true. I really do want to see him come undone. To lose that control.

Connie chuckles. "I've never seen him lose control. Not once." I can't hide all of my disappointment at that, and Connie notices. "But," she says, "if anyone can do so, it's you and Nine."

Fuck. Just the thought of being the one to make him lose control has me fighting the urge the bite my lip in anticipation.

"Like the idea, don't ya?" she asks.

Who the hell am I to care if she knows about my fantasies? She's in a lot of them anyway.

"Come on," she says, shoving me off her, "we need to get you dressed and ready."

I go silent, the confidence oozing out of me with every step we take to get closer to my closet.

What is it about this one time with Nine that has me so worked up? Is it just because it's my first time with any one member of the team? Or is it because it's with Nine in particular? Maybe it's because I said I loved him?

Gah! I don't know the answer.

Connie holds up an outfit I'm having trouble associating with sexy. It's nothing more than a pair of dark green jeans, a black vest tee with matching studded jacket, and a pair of worn combat boots.

"Why that?"

Connie looks at me and says, "You'll be going to *Sheruta's* western forest. So you can look great underneath the clothes, but you should definitely wear something comfortable for walking around in out there. Just in case."

Makes sense. "Okay . . ." I grab them from her and put them to one side, awaiting her choice of underwear.

She turns back around and grabs the matching set of bra and panties she laid out for me. They're simple black lace, but with enough detail to make it a little more than just plain.

Her smile falters. "You look disappointed?"

"Err . . . Not disappointed, just surprised."

She chuckles. "I was being serious when I said you should go as yourself." She puts the underwear down and walks over to me. "I don't want you worried about looking a certain way or acting a certain way; you should just be you."

I agree with her, I really do, but it's just . . . "I guess I want to be someone more . . . sexy."

"There's time for that in our immortal future, but right now, I think Nine wants you to be yourself. And yourself is already pretty fucking hot, hon."

"Okay. If you say so."

"I do." She shrugs. "Now put the outfit on!"

I salute the fashionable drill sergeant in front of me and put the underwear on first, then the outfit. Connie leaves me in peace to do so, so I get to look at the underwear in the mirror before covering it. I have to admit, it does have a certain charm. Especially with my pink hair. It all looks so . . . me. I quickly put on some casual clothes in my male form, hoping Nine doesn't have a plan quite that big.

Walking out of the closet, I watch as Connie gets a few makeup supplies ready. "I assume," she says upon seeing me, "you can manage your own hair?"

I nod and quickly whip a little wind around it, drying out the final bit of water, then flatten it in place and let it hang naturally from my shoulders. "Done."

"Damn. That's fucking efficient."

I sit on the stool she's prepared for me. She puts on some light foundation, some awesome smoky eyes that I'm jealous of not being able to achieve by myself, and then finishes it off with some clear, cherry-flavored gloss.

"Done." She pulls me up and nudges me out the door. "Now go!"

"Where?"

"To the western forest."

"Right, the blob of green to the west near the mountains on the map?"

"That's the one!" She pushes me out of my own bedroom door, and I'm off, sprinting down the hallways and out the back door of the kitchen in a flit of Vampire speed.

Chapter Thirty-Eight

I fly there—because who the hell would walk when they can fly?—and notice a small firelight in the distance straight away. I really hope that's where he is and I'm not about to interrupt someone else's night.

Yup. Come on down, Sweetie.

Oh, err . . . hi.

Stop being so nervous, he says as he filters through my memories of my evening with Connie and the brief encounter with the guys. He pauses, however, on my hot kiss with Dea and takes particular note of the confidence it seemed to give me. *That's . . . fucking hot.*

Do you all like watching? Is that a Horseman thing?

You're going to lecture me on watching? You, whose first sexual encounter with any of us was watching me suck Dea's cock?

Well, he has a point. A really damn good, sexy point. So I leave it be and fly down to the fire. As I get closer to the ground, I notice it's a bonfire, but one contained by stones and lifted off of the forest floor so as not to cause permanent damage to the area.

Once firmly on the ground, I look around and gasp. He's created a clearing in the forest (or made use of one) and set up an actual low-to-the-ground bed at the top, complete with duvets, rose petals, fallen leaves, and a small table to the side with snacks and drinks. But the rest of the clearing is just as beautiful: String lights hang from tree to tree, making use of the witchlight bulbs they use in the town square at night, and cast an enamored light around the clearing. A clear path has been made around the fire, outlined with leaves and decorated with vines that hang from the trees. It's all so . . .

"Perfect. It's perfect, Nine."

I can feel the sting of tears threatening to burst the banks, and I have to sniffle them back before I look like an idiot.

"You could never look like an idiot, Sweetie." He walks down the pathway to meet me and stops just in front of me, taking me in. "Connie did a wonderful job persuading you to just be yourself."

Really?

Yeah, you look beautiful just as you are. "Come on." He grabs my hand and guides me toward the bed. "We can have something to eat or drink if you like? Or we can just chat?"

He's fiddling with his fingers, I notice, and I wonder if he's nervous.

This is different than with anyone else. This—he gestures to the decorated forest clearing—*means something. I've never done this before.*

Oh, I see. "Well, let's make our first time special then, shall we?" I grab his hand and move us onto the bed, where I just lie there and snuggle into his side, making the most of our unlimited time together.

"So," Nine says, "I saw your concern about your male

form. I just wanted to say that we don't have to do anything you don't want to do." He goes to say something else but stops.

"Go on."

"Well, I know the others want to share some of your first times, and although that is completely up to you, it would be unfair of me to leave them out."

Goddess, he's right. And honestly, that's a load off my mind. I'm just not ready for sex in my other form, and there isn't a pressing magical need for it, either, like with my Vampire nature.

He grabs my chin and leans up to me. "You need this. I'm making it special because I love you, but this is more than that. Your Vampire side needs to feed properly, and this will help." He sighs. "Even if you still choose to take your time with the others, you'll have me to keep you stable."

I laugh at the thought of trying to persuade Arrie to go slowly.

Nine laughs alongside me. "You're right. You two are quite fired up recently." He raises his eyebrows in question, but I don't know what to say.

"His . . . err . . . roughness, I guess, speaks to my Vampire nature. It . . ."

"Turns you on?"

I nod. "Yeah."

"Don't worry," he says, "we'll go as slow as you like. Or not at all." He adds a wink to the end there. "There's something we need to chat about first, though." He rummages around his side of the bed and brings out what look like a potion bottle. "This is a contraceptive potion. It's made by Witches. The issue is that I have no idea how effective this will be on you, but they're the same ones Connie uses."

I take it from his hands.

"You just need to take it before you have sex. Connie takes one every morning, just in case." He shrugs. "They don't have any side effects or anything, so if no sex is had that day, then they're harmless."

"Good to know." I pull the cap off and down it in one. "Tastes like strawberries," I say as I lick my lips. I look to Nine and know I can just ask the question on my mind. "No diseases with us, right?"

He smiles. "Right. Diseases don't even infect us in the first place."

"Good." No need for anything else to get in our way. "I'm a little . . . nervous."

"Don't be," he says on a sigh. "We can spend the entire night here with no expectations and wait until morning if you like. There's no pressure."

And, he adds in his mind, *if you like, I can help take away those nerves?*

You can?

He smiles in that devilish way of his.

Whatever he's about to do, it's going be his usual cheekiness. Relief floods through me that we can spend the entire night just being ourselves and that there's no pressure.

He grabs my hand and lifts me onto the pathway. He must have clicked a button on some kind of sound system because music dances to life all around us.

"Dance with me?"

I nod, already liking the idea of dancing around the bonfire with Nine. It's all so . . . beautiful. I really don't have another word for it. He's put in so much effort, it's crazy. This wasn't what I was expecting.

Nine wraps his arms around my waist and guides me along the makeshift dancefloor, dipping me at all the right moments, kissing me as often as possible, and never saying a word. Eventually, the song ends, and I'm a little disappointed we can't keep dancing, but Nine puts on another tune, so we keep going.

This is a good distraction from my nerves.

This is not the distraction. This is just the warm up.

What?

This is the distraction.

He closes his eyes and lowers his mouth to mine, his lips molding perfectly against my own, and I gasp in surprise when he places a picture in my head of him and Dea, both naked, in the middle of a field. Given the lack of clothes and buildings, I have no idea of the time era, but they look perfectly content.

They're chatting away as Nine rests on Dea's bare chest and traces his golden tattoo. Dea laughs at something Nine says and then flips him onto his back and kisses him with reckless abandon in that way that makes your heart melt and your knees shake. Eventually, though, the kiss deepens and becomes more desperate, more needy, and Dea's hand lowers down Nine's body and wraps around his cock in a tight enough hold I can practically hear Nine's groan from here, despite this particular memory having no sound.

As if Nine is reading my mind (which he probably is), sound filters through, and I can hear them both moaning perfectly.

"Brother," Nine asks, "are you sure?"

Dea grips him tighter, causing Nine to groan louder. "Yes. Now lie there and take it like a good boy."

"Yes, sir," Nine says through a laugh. But that laugh is quickly cut off by Dea's lips wrapping themselves around the head of Nine's cock, and I get the pleasure of watching Nine come undone for a change.

Nine takes the memory away before Dea can finish, and I moan my disappointment before I can stop myself.

Nine laughs and whispers in my ear, "Not to worry. You'll get to see me first hand later."

I shiver with pleasure as I feel my core ache with a familiar tingle of need. "Fuck, Nine . . . Why is that so hot?"

He shrugs. "Probably the same reason why guys find it so attractive when two women have sex."

"Soooo," I start, and he giggles, "you find me and Connie . . . attractive?"

"I find you and any of the team attractive. I don't really have a preference when it comes to gender, but yes. You and Connie together is rather hot."

"When was that memory?" I ask as I pepper kisses down his neck and graze one of my fangs along his neck, making him shudder.

He clears his throat. "Year 623. It was one of our first times together. Before we were anything but friends, of course."

That's why Nine asked if Dea was sure. Makes sense.

I continue kissing Nine, having grown more than a little needy since that hot memory, and Nine roams his hands under my tank top, grazing the underside of my bra.

"I want to see that underwear first hand," he says, a little breathless from my attention. "I looked away when I was looking through your memories of this evening, so I didn't ruin anything."

I chuckle. "Lie on the bed then."

He looks at me in surprise, but he smiles and does as I say anyway.

I slowly walk over, trying to at least be semi-sexy, and shove my jacket off and let it fall to the floor.

I thought this would be nerve wracking, but it's not; Nine

doesn't care either way.

And with that final thought of confidence, I lose all of my inhibitions and worries and just go for it.

Tucking a finger underneath the hem of my tank top, I inch it up and over my breasts before throwing it to the floor.

Nine's breath hitches when he watches me go to unbuckle my jeans, and the heat in his eyes spurs me on.

I slowly shimmy out of them, having taken my boots off earlier, and stand there in nothing but a thong and bra.

Nine's eyes practically salivate at the sight of me, and although I don't see what he sees, I understand, because as he stands up to meet me, he also removes his clothes one article at a time; he matches my semi-sexy tone and goes with it, bless his soul.

You look . . . pretty fucking tasty, actually.

My face heats into a flame as I think of the right words to say, but Nine grabs the back of my neck and leans me into a kiss before I can scramble together a sentence. He kisses me as though we have all the time in the world to savor every moment of this night, and I guess, in a way, we do, but I'm eager to show him just how ready I am to be his.

Tonight isn't about the team or our group relationship; tonight is about just the two of us. Tonight, I am just his.

His hands roam up my back and trace gentle patterns up and down my spine, but I need more. Want more.

I lean into the kiss and deepen it, hoping to convey what I want, and boy does Nine deliver.

He pushes me onto the bed and climbs on top, straddling my waist. We're both still in our underwear at this point, but I do not miss his hardening cock straining to be free of those boxers. With a gentle caress, he grabs my hands and lowers his grip to my wrists, where he shoots them above my head in a fierce shove that has me whimpering.

"Not wanting to take things gently, Sweetie?"

I shake my head, no. I don't think gentle is my thing right now. Maybe later, but right now, with my Vampire nature edging further over the edge of lustful insanity, I just want this man to fuck me.

Fuck, you're hot like this. Lying here and allowing me to restrain you.

I giggle, understanding his hidden meaning. He can't ever truly restrain me because I'm stronger (much stronger), but I'm letting him do what he wants, purposefully taking the submissive role with ease.

"Don't worry," I whisper in a huskier tone than I knew I could pull off, "I'll take control later." I go to lift my head, but I find myself slightly restrained by his weight pressed into my wrists.

"Nuh-uh," he says with a shake of his head. "Don't make me tie you up, Sweetie."

I shiver at the thought, the growing heat pulsing through me only grows hotter with the idea of being tied-up with any member of the team.

Maybe another day.

I whimper as he peppers kisses down my jaw and along my collar bone, taking his time to lick, nip, and tease his way farther toward my breasts. The moment his tongue first flicks over my nipple, I arch into him, wanting more.

He flicks harder, caressing each nipple in turn with small circles of his tongue until I can feel the effect pooling in my soaked panties.

Bucking my hips, I beg for more. "Nine . . . please."

"Let me see your fangs," he commands, and I nearly moan but manage to hold it back.

My fangs descend, and the smirk on Nine's face could not

have been more devilish. What is the nerdy fucker up to?

He releases my wrists, so he has two free hands, and uses one to palm my breast as the other runs fingers up and down the sensitive peaks of my fangs.

"Fuck," I whisper, not holding back the moan that leaks at alongside it.

My hips move of their own accord this time, and I can't help the needy whine that escapes at the sight of Nine's cock now poking out of the top of his underwear.

Nine doesn't say anything, mentally or physically, and I revel in the teasing perfection he's managing to do to my incredibly needy body.

Connie's right, he's good at this, I think to myself as the hand palming my breasts shifts lower, stroking the skin of my abdomen before delving deeper. Low enough that I squirm underneath him and move my own hands down his chest and along the gentle ridges of his abs.

I want. Now.

"Nine, can we—?"

"No," he says in a more commanding tone than I've ever heard him use before. "I'm not done with your body yet."

His tone sends a pleasant shiver down my body, and I can't help shifting my thighs to create some kind of friction.

Nine frowns and rips my legs apart with a knee, clearly wanting to be the one to bring me pleasure.

His fingers finally reach the apex of my thighs and tease my opening.

"Come on, Nine . . ." I beg as he refuses to give me what I want most. "Please."

"God, I love hearing you beg." He slips one finger in, and it's enough to have me writhing all over again.

Fuck, he's good at this teasing shit. But seriously, I want to fuck him. Can't a girl just get fucked?

He chuckles in my mind and whispers, *You'll get me soon, Sweetie. Just let me have my fun first.* He smiles before slipping another finger inside and lowering his head to my navel.

Trailing kisses down my body, he takes his time getting to his destination, but when he does, fuck am I glad he waited. He laps quick, forceful strokes of his tongue against my clit in time to the rhythm of his fingers, and it takes everything I have not to scream out in pleasure.

Don't hold back. There's no one out here to hear you but me.

He slides a third finger inside and curls them slightly to hit the world's best part of my body, and I convulse around him as I let out a half-stifled scream and bite my lip, accidentally drawing blood with my fang.

"Fuck," I say between gasps, coming down from the amazing high. "You're good at that."

Nine chuckles but says a simple, "Thank you."

I sigh a breath of relief as a peaceful calm washes over me; the type of calm I haven't felt since before drinking blood. "Wow. I didn't realize how on edge I was."

Nine's hands travel up my body and graze my nipples on the way to trace the outline of my lips as he leans over me. "Yeah?"

I nod but stay otherwise silent.

"Don't worry, we're not done."

My breath hitches. I never considered multiple orgasms before, but more of this man? I'll take it.

Got any preferences on how you want your first time to be, Sweetie?

Ummm . . . I haven't really considered it, if I'm honest. I shake my head, a little shy at having to make any choices.

Nine settles himself between my legs. He rubs slow, lazy circles over my clit until I'm writhing beneath him and begging him to fuck me properly, and finally, after more pleas than my dignity cares to admit, he lines his cock up and slowly enters.

He goes slowly, allowing me to get used to the feeling of being stretched and filled. It's so different to using my own fingers, or to Nine's fingers, for that matter, but fuck, it feels so good.

"You doing okay?" he asks.

"Yeah," I reply on a breathy moan. "So good."

He slowly goes deeper, burying himself to the hilt, then stops and looks at me.

I try to shift my hips to encourage him to move, but he stays steadfast. "Nine . . . ?"

Yes?

My hips buck and shift as much as possible, but he refuses to help. Instead, he rests on his elbows and smirks at me like the cruel fucker he is.

"Please, I want . . ."

What do you want?

"Fuck me. Please, for the love of the goddess, fuck me."

He chuckles and begins moving. Slowly at first, and I can feel the familiar pleasurable tension building already, but soon he picks up the pace and is thrusting higher toward release.

Fuck. Shit.

It's only been less than a minute, and I can feel my release there, just over the edge of the cliff. Is this too soon? If he continues, I'm going to—

Nine thrusts harder and presses a thumb to my clit and begins rubbing small circles. "Let go, Sweetie."

My head falls back onto the mattress as I arch into him.

He takes one nipple into his mouth and sucks and nips while he rolls the other between his fingers.

I can't hold on any longer, and another toe-curling orgasm

overtakes me. I cry out, louder than I thought I would, and hear Nine groan.

"Fuck," he whispers. "You're so . . ." He's watching me with rapt attention and looks to be struggling to hold back his own release.

Grabbing him by both arms, I flip us over and pin his arms to the bed above his head, just like he did to me. At first, I shift my hips in a slow, circular motion, getting used to the feeling, but the moment I feel his cock hit the right spot, I lift myself up and down and watch his expression go from wonder to scrunched up in pleasure.

Nine's moans get louder as I move faster, finding a rhythm that makes his hips buck beneath mine and his eyes go wide in surprise.

Fuck, Sweetie. I can't keep holding back if you . . .

I crash my hips into him harder, trying not to hurt him, but my concern was ill-founded, as his eyes glow a bright orange and his lips snarl with a hiss.

He likes being dominated, it seems.

It that what Dea's like with him?

Yes. Even Nine's thoughts sound breathless. *Dea likes to tie me up, spank me, and make me do whatever he wants. He's a control freak, but it's fucking great in the bedroom.*

Fuck, I want him to do that to us both.

"Fuck, yes." He grabs my hips and lifts me a few inches above him, giving himself enough room to fuck me. And boy does he fuck me. *I want him to tie us both up and watch him spank you with your ass in the air.*

His control snaps, and I watch him buck, writhe, and thrust beneath me with reckless abandon, all the while hearing his delicious moans getting louder. "Yes, yes!" His cock stiffens further inside me, and he screams his release into the night air.

His body quickly goes slack, as though all the energy leaked out of him.

I roll off him and curl into his side.

We lie for a few minutes after the waves of tension subside (hell, it could have been a few hours and I wouldn't have noticed), me lying on top of his sculpted chest as I run gentle circles over his collar bone in a haze of sexual high.

Nine? I ask mentally.

Yeah?

Thank you.

He chuckles beneath me. *No need to thank me. That was amazing.*

That it was, but I mean thank you for everything else. For being you. This night has been amazing. I love you.

I love you too, Sweetie. How about we get some sleep?

"Mmmhmmm . . ." My eyes are beginning to close as sleep takes hold.

The last thing I remember is Nine lifting me off of him and placing us both under a duvet as he holds me tightly in his arms.

Chapter Thirty-Nine

Morning comes far too quickly for us both, and I wake with a groan at the amount of sunlight piercing my peaceful sleep. "Why is it so light?"

A deep chuckle resonates from beneath me and vibrates my head. "Morning, Sweetie."

"Morning, Nine."

Flashes of the previous night enter my mind, and I smile. I did it. I actually slept with a member of the team. And it was fucking amazing.

More laughter sounds from beneath me. "You are welcome."

"How much longer do we have?" I mutter, enjoying one of the only peaceful nights sleep I've had since waking up immortal.

"Only until lunchtime I'm afraid. I need to get back to that data-app design for your big plan."

I groan. "Right." I flop off of him and lay on my back under the duvet. "And I need to start making plans for the embassies."

"Huh?"

Right, I didn't tell anyone how mine and Dea's meeting with the Vamps went or my on-the-spot decision.

I quickly fill him in, showing the entire afternoon in flashes of memories.

He whistles. "Wow. Big plans, hey?"

"I guess. You think it'll help?"

"I think it's a big political move, Sweetie." He rubs a hand over my shoulders and leans in to kiss me.

I take the kiss and go with it, wondering how much more fun we can have before we have to leave.

Knew you'd be a handful, he groans. *It'll take more than just me to keep both your forms satisfied.*

"Lucky I have four of you then."

Speaking of . . . They're going to be all over you now you've popped your immortal cherry. They've been holding back.

"That was them holding back?" Eesh. But really, I like the idea of having three—four—people wanting to sleep with me. (Color me basic, but it feels good. Remember? No judging. I have a world to save. I'm allowed to indulge.) "So, err . . ." I cough to clear my throat. You and Dea?

What about us?

What did you talk about when I left you both alone in the library?

Ah, that. He climbs on top of me and rubs a thumb down my cheek. "We talked about you, actually."

"Me?"

"Yeah." He rubs a hand across the back of his neck, and I can see the twitch in his smile falter and can tell he's nervous about whatever this was. "We agreed to try to make us all work together. Like, all three of us."

I look at him confused.

"You make us complete, Horseman of Magic. We know you're going to pursue something with Con and Arrie, and that's okay, but between us three, we want it to be . . . together. Like, all three of us, rather than a weird, unbalanced triangle."

I just smile at him like an idiot. "Oh . . ."

"It's totally okay if you'd rather be with us separately. We don't mind, it's just—"

I shut his rambling up with a kiss I hope conveys everything I'm feeling. The heat, the love, the all-encompassing feeling of rightness. Eventually, I pull away. "Yes, I'll be your girlfriend. Both of yours."

He smiles. *I love you.*

"I love you too."

Unfortunately, we have to head back. So there's no morning fun after all, but hey, the night was amazing. I couldn't have asked for a more understanding partner, and by the time I walk into the kitchen at eleven am, I'm practically glowing. Much to the delight of all three members of the team waiting for us at the kitchen table.

They look at me with those smug smiles, and Connie puts down the magical newspaper to look at me with raised eyebrows.

I just nod and look away, too embarrassed to actually talk about it in front of everyone.

"Hey," Nine says as he turns me around, "don't do that. None of us care. You could sleep with all of us separately every single day, and we wouldn't judge. Not ever."

Okay.

You okay?

Yeah, actually. I'm doing great.

And I really am. For once, I feel good about the prospect

of my future. I'm surrounded by people I love. What's there to be worried about?

Chapter Forty

The fate of the world. Right. Forgot about that.

While Arrie is due back this evening with news from the Shifter Council and Witch Coven (of which, he's been updated regarding the embassy idea), Nine and Connie are still busy creating my wonderful stamp on the new world.

That leaves just me and Dea, and I'm hoping he can help me with something. We're sat at the tail end of lunch together after Nine and Connie disappeared twenty minutes ago, and I'm dying to ask for his help, but I don't really have a plan, so have kept quiet for now.

"Is there something you wish to say, Angel?"

"Errrm . . . maybe. Actually," I say, thinking back to Nine's comment about us three being together, "there are lots of things I have to say, but maybe now isn't the best time to address them all."

I shuffle around on my chair, trying to see if any part of my body actually feels different; it doesn't. And that fact makes me feel somewhat disappointed. I'm not sure what I thought

I would feel like after finally sleeping with a member of the team, but I certainly expected to feel something. But oddly, it feels just like before: like I have friends, boyfriends, a family, a home, and I'm still exploring what that means.

"Perhaps you should start with the important things first, then."

"Right." Clearing my throat, I begin. "I want to try to work on some Fae spells, see about playing in water to unlock my water Witch magic, and then do some research about our Angel magics connecting."

There. The important stuff.

"I guess we also need to make plans with the *Sheruta* Council about building embassies and see if they will allow more free passage between here and Earth, too."

Dea nods. "I will send a message to the *Sheruta* Council with an update of our plans and see if they can do anything to assist." He gets up after putting the newspaper down and walks up to me, offering me his hand. "In the meantime, maybe we should go for a swim in the lake. It is certainly warm enough for it, and you can see about your water abilities and perhaps try out some water-related Fae spells." He gently pulls me to my feet and wraps his arms around my waist. "But right now, I want to remind you that I exist."

"Huh? What does that mea—?"

He cuts my question off with a searing kiss that would have melted any woman's panties clean off. Including mine. It sends my knees buckling and my breath hitching, but luckily, Dea catches me and lifts me onto the kitchen countertop.

"It means I want you to remember that you have more boyfriends—and one girlfriend—than just Nine to juggle."

His fingers trail themselves down the side of my neck and dip underneath the edge of my tank top, slinking close to my nipples but not close enough.

My heart flutters a million miles a minute, and I swear I'm ready to drag this man back to my bed. His lips are still pressed firmly to mine, with enough pressure to know exactly what he thinks about the idea of me and Nine fucking in the woods, but he delves deeper when he slides his tongue past my defenses and tangles it with mine.

He slides me to the edge of the countertop and places himself between my open legs, and fuck, he's hard as steel beneath those jeans.

Gasping for breath, I break away and whisper, "Had a hard night?"

He does not miss my innuendo and groans. "Yes, very." He doesn't give me time to respond and, instead, returns to kissing the life right out of me. But this time he thrusts his hips against my center, and I groan against him, my fangs descending in the process.

Fuck, I forgot to feed this morning. I can feel the pulsing of my arteries like a suffocating cloth around all my senses.

Dea, not missing a beat, turns his head to expose his neck. "Help yourself."

I don't hesitate. I snap my head toward his neck and slam my teeth into his artery, and shit, fuck, shit . . . that feels so good. I thought sleeping with Nine would help balance me, and it absolutely did (I'm no longer crazy), but it's just made me want more . . .

And right now, Dea is offering himself up on a sexy silver platter. My hand slides below his waist and to the buckle of his jeans, which I make quick work of undoing, and then delves below his underwear to grip his cock.

He groans against me, and I can't help but take one final mouthful of that smoky lavender nectar before unlatching and looking up at him. His eyes are swirling a bright gold, brighter than I've ever seen, and I'm curious . . .

I grip him harder and stroke a couple of lengths from base to tip, then watch as his knees buckle and his breath gasps and those beautiful, golden galaxy eyes of his glow so bright I look away.

"What's gotten into my Angel of Death this morning?" I smirk at him. "I've never seen you this worked up before?"

Dea looks straight at me. "I have just spent the entire night imagining my two lovers in all kinds of compromising positions and not being able to join in. It has been one torturous twenty-four hours, Angel."

I chuckle to myself as I think of the effect just the thought of Nine and I have on this man. "Well then, next time, you'll just have to join us." My hand speeds up as I test his reactions, and I can't help but swirl my thumb over the tip.

The moan he lets out is music to my ears.

I grip harder and speed up once more, hoping I'm doing a good enough job, but one more look at Dea's face screwed up in pleasure tells me I'm managing all right.

The bite marks on his neck haven't quite healed yet, so I lick a teasing tongue over them, putting as much pressure on them as I can.

Dea's hips jerk forward as he gets himself off using my hand, and I watch as the moment he loses control overcomes him. He buries his head in my neck and bites down in a sensitive spot between my neck and shoulder, causing me to squirm and moan, but Dea doesn't notice because he's too busy muffling his own moans of pleasure as he speeds up and explodes into my grip.

And fuck, I would pay to see that control snap. Even when coming he's controlled and polite. One of these days, I'll shatter that control into a million pieces.

"Now can we get on with magic for the day?" I ask as I pull my hand free and go to clean up at the kitchen sink with a satisfied smirk.

Dea walks up behind me and places a hand on my waist as he whispers in my ear, "Thank you, Angel. I am more than happy to return the favor." His hand skirts the waistband of my jeans, and I shudder.

At the sound of those words, my body betrays just how much it wants that cock all to itself, and I involuntarily arch backward. "I would, but I really want to get something done today."

He pulls away and grabs my now-dry hand. "Another time, then."

"It's a date."

Chapter Forty-One

The lake, it turns out, is a beautiful, serene piece of the garden I've yet to explore, or it could be a new feature. Who knows? It's tucked away in a copse of trees that allows the perfect amount of smattering light to filter through and sparkle off the water. The lake itself is large enough to fit a small swimming pool in but intimate enough to be a great outdoor area. The large rock and mini-waterfall on the right side of the lake creates a picture of tranquility as it perfectly matches the pond lilies and various flowers scattered around the water's edge and the lake bank.

"This place . . . It's beautiful."

"I am glad you like it, Angel." Dea leads me by the hand toward the lake. He removes his jeans and socks, but remains in his underwear and t-shirt, and wades into the water. Turning back around, he smiles. "Are you joining me?"

Right. Water. Need to be in the water for it to work. Most likely. Why didn't I think to grab some swimwear before we left? Oh well. Might as well join him.

Removing my own jeans and socks, I wade in after him. Luckily, my tank top falls past the top of my ass, so I'm not showing much.

"How did you intend to try this out, Angel?"

"Ermm . . . I really was just hoping I could splash about a bit and it all just come to me."

Dea chuckles. "I doubt it will be that easy, Angel. Air was the first, and fire came to you when you were angry." He swims up to where I'm sitting just off the bank up to my waist in water. "Maybe we need to incite a great need for your water abilities first."

Hmmm. "You know, that's not a bad idea." I punch him gently on the arm and swim out to where I have to swim to stay afloat. "Now what?" I mutter to myself.

What kind of emotion does water make me feel? Is it calm like the gentle, tranquil placidity of this lake? Or is it angry like the lashing of ocean waves against an unforgiving cliff of dirt and stone?

Eugh. This is starting to feel a lot less science-y and lot more hocus-pocus-y. How is water supposed to elicit emotion?

"What is going through your mind, Angel?" Dea's behind me quicker than I thought possible, making me jump and choke on water. "Sorry," he says through a laugh.

I get the feeling he isn't sorry at all.

Rolling my eyes, I say, "It's hard to think of magic in this way. In a non-scientific way. How can water cause emotion?"

"Well, that depends on how it is used."

I turn and look him in the eye with a questioning gaze.

"If one were drowning, then the water would cause fear, no? If one were thirsty, then relief."

"I see. So there is logic there."

Dea grabs my waist and spins me around, pinning my

back to his chest. "There is logic underpinning everything we do, if only you look hard enough to see beneath the human surface." He cups water in his palm and lets it trickle out of his hands.

See beneath the human surface? Maybe if I think about it from a new angle?

I take a deep breath and dive underneath the surface of the water, peeling my eyes open and looking around. My Vampire sight allows me to see even the darkest of crags in the lake's bed; every creature, plant, and stone can be zoomed in on and examined. And for a while, that's all I do, examine the underneath of the lake beyond what most people can see, but it doesn't really help me gain any new perspective. So I break the calm surface of the water and inhale sweet oxygen.

I don't really need to breathe, but it's sweet heaven when I can. I take lungfuls of the candy the world offers so freely and promise to never take its honeyed goodness for granted again.

"Any insight?" Dea is still lounging in the water where I left him.

I swim up to him and shake my head. "None."

"Okay. Well, for now, let us work on some Fae spells involving water."

I nod. "Good idea. If I get any clever ideas, I can always change back and try them out."

I get out of the water and change into my male form, taking off my trousers in the process, and wade back in. Our clothes lie on the crest of the lake bank, and I can't help but smile at our clothes mixing on the floor.

Swimming back up to Dea, he grabs my hands and floats me in front of him. "I know a few water-based Fae spells, so we can start there if you like?"

"Sounds good."

"First off, moving water should be easy. You should be able to do whatever you like with the water pool here, for example." He gestures to the entire lake, and I smile.

I can feel the power rippling underneath my skin, and it itches to be let free and utilized. I can't help the maniacal smile that lights my face as I gently push the water around me like a kid splashing about in the local swimming pool.

"That is good." Dea lies on the bank near our clothes, sunbathing in nothing but his underwear.

It's more than a little distracting.

Nine, are you seeing what I have to work with?

Nine groans in my mind. *That's just mean, bro.*

Dea chuckles. "I could always make it worse, you two." He moves his hand lower and grabs the hem of his underwear.

Since I had hold of the cock beneath that material earlier, I know exactly what he's hiding underneath, and I'd be lying if I say I don't want to see what I could only feel before.

I have things to concentrate on here, and so do you two. Behave!

"Easy for the man who actually got some last night," Dea mumbles under his breath.

I know you got some earlier, bro. Quit complaining.

"You do?"

I was watching.

He would have winked if he were actually with us.

Con's yelling at me to focus, and I don't want to have my feet chopped off like last time. Gotta go.

"Feet chopped off?"

Dea laughs from where he lies, his hands firmly on the ground beside him. "She got stabbed in the chest by three swords like fifty years ago because Nine was too busy mentally flirting with me, and she cut off his foot as penance."

I struggle to contain my laughter but fail miserably.

"Goddess, that woman," I groan.

Dea just nods in agreement and goes back to explaining different techniques of how the Fae use water in some of their spells. Some are just used as an ingredient in a larger spell while others are full-on attack spells. But one is pretty fucking cool: a water weather spell.

"It is only supposed to be used by multiple Fae at once, and controlling it can be tough, but I do not see why you should not be able to at least accomplish it."

"Controlling it?"

Dea looks at me with slight concern but shrugs his shoulders. "Might take some practice."

"So what does it do?"

"It raises the water from a particular source into the sky and forces the clouds to become heavier, therefore making it rain. On its own, that is not particularly useful, but it can be the smallest detail that turns the tide of battle. Plus, it could be useful to cast the spell with a time limit and then change into your female form and use the rain as a weapon via your Witch powers."

I stare at him dumbfounded. "My powers really are limitless, aren't they?"

"That is probably the point, yes."

The thought kinda scares me, if I'm honest. But I don't have the time to waste on such pointless thoughts, so I turn around and try to lift the water into raindrops.

"So how do I do this?"

"You need to lift drops of water into the sky, and as the temperature increases, it'll take less energy to bring those water drops to boiling point, therefore creating water vapor to increase cloud capacity."

"Cloud capacity? That's a thing?"

"Yes." Dea takes a breath. "It will require you to hold the rising water spell while you perform a heating spell. It will also require you to practice how much water you will need to raise on any given day based on the initial cloud coverage available."

"Okay, so today, for example, I will need lots because it's a clear day." The sun beats down in rays of heat, and I'm thankful for the refreshing cool of the water I'm treading.

"Right."

Okay, I can do this. I raise as much water as I think it'll take to create some kind of heavy cloud (though truthfully, I have no fucking idea how much water that'll take) and mutter the spell under my breath in Japanese.

"Water rise,
beyond this earth,
and beyond my sight,
to the heavens
and in to the night."

I repeat that spell over and over again until I have a giant ball of water in the sky I'm struggling to hold.

"Okay. Time for some heat." I look to Dea expectantly, but he's looking at the sky in a look of wonder. "Dea!"

"Oh, right." He looks to me and tells me the incantation and circle for the heating part of the spell.

The circle I create with pure magic power pretty easily, but I'm struggling with the wording of the spell. As I tumble over the words in Japanese, I manage to finally get it right.

But it's too late. My hold on the giant ball of water thirty thousand feet in the air cracks, and I watch in awe as it crashes to the ground.

"Angel!"

I vaguely hear Dea's scream as an entire ton of water

dumps back into the lake with such force it throws me out and into the air.

"Angel!"

The sound of the water meeting its brethren back in the lake is like a crash of thunder against my ears, and they go deaf as the water encompasses me.

Shit, shit, shit.

"Transform!"

Right. Female me can handle this better.

I am about a hundred feet in the air, the water having splashed back into the lake already—though splash is downplaying the tidal wave that soaked Dea and would have put a human in real danger—as I change into my female form in an instant and fly myself to the mud-soaked ground.

I look up at Dea and smile. "Sorry."

He scoops me into a hug and squeezes tight before putting me back on my feet. "You okay?"

"Yeah." I take a deep breath and laugh at his reaction. "You remember I'm immortal just like you, right? I couldn't have really been seriously injured . . ."

"But, but . . ." He trails off, not really knowing what to say by the looks of things.

The adorable moron. He really is cute.

Bro, that was such an overreaction.

I laugh out loud so hard I cough up what I think is more water, but it turns out I'm choking on air. (Me, an air Witch, choking on air. Yeah, I know, right?)

"Shut up, asshole," Dea mumbles as he sulks where he stands.

I wrap my arms around his waist and place a sweet kiss to his cheek. "Thank you for worrying."

He smiles down at me and kisses me back. "You are

welcome."

"Right, time to try again!" I shift back into my male form and run into the lake once again.

But one look around tells me I'll need to raise the water level. Oops. May have made too big of a splash. I use intention and a basic water rune circle to pull all of the leftover water from around the lake back into its intended hole.

"There."

I spend all afternoon repeating that spell and eventually manage it, but it does take some insane levels of concentration and more tidal waves than I care to admit to creating.

"Fuck, I'm starving," I groan as I lie by the side of the lake panting for breath after finally having managed to do the spell correctly. "Food time?"

Dea chuckles. "Yup. Arrie's not back yet, so we should get dinner ready."

At the thought of Arrie not being back yet, I flinch. I hope he's okay.

"He will be fine, Angel," Dea says, as if reading my mind.

Chapter Forty-Two

We make an extra helping for Arrie and have to put it in the fridge because he doesn't get back in time, much to my disappointment. Nine sends him a message using the video-screening technology, but I don't hold out hope.

I have a bad feeling. Something is very wrong.

"Where would Arrie be at this point in time?"

Dea is the one who answers after swallowing his mouthful of spaghetti. "Most likely at the Witch Coven."

Nine rubs my knee in his usually comforting manner, but it goes in vain because I'm constantly reminded of the lack of Arrie every time I lift my head, given his empty place at the dinner table is right in front of me.

"We did not leave the Witches in a very humble fashion on our last visit, Angel, so I am sure things are . . . . tense. But he will be home and well soon, I promise."

Dea's right. He's the Horseman of War, for fuck's sake. Who in their right mind would go head-to-head with that tank?

"You're right." I rub the back of my neck, trying to get rid of some of the tension. "Just got a bad feeling, that's all."

It's okay. You're allowed to worry about him.

Just feels strange worrying about someone who two weeks ago made a career out of hating me.

Nine laughs. *He's a big softy really.*

Clearing the table (using some fancy air magic rather than doing things the boring way), I don't really know what to do with myself.

"Update?" I turn and ask Nine.

"In the middle of creating the data-app, and Con has a plan for getting backers and people to use it."

Connie puts a hand on my shoulder. "I'll start putting that plan into place tomorrow. Have any more of those teleporting crystals?"

I nod. "I'll make some more of both, and I might try and see if I can make some Earth-to-Earth ones, too. Should be useful."

Connie smiles and whispers, "You're always useful."

Nine yanks a piece of paper out of his pocket and hands it to me with a kiss on the cheek. "The list you asked for." He walks out of the kitchen and, I assume, to my library, where he's creating my masterpiece.

I don't think I asked for a list, but I unfold it anyway and smile at the contents.

1. Anti-sickness charm
2. ~~Teleportation crystals~~
3. More throwing knives
4. Unlocking beads

I fold it into my pocket for later. For now, I need a distraction from my strange worry over Arrie. Why has he been gone so long? It's supposed to be quick. If it were anything minor, like a flight delay, he would have noticed Nine's message.

Goddess damn it, Arrie, you're such an ass for making me worry.

"Hey," Dea whispers in my ear, making me jump, "let's watch a movie."

"Okay."

There's a butt-ton of stuff I should be doing, like mastering the bo staff, working on unlocking my water or earth Witch powers, practicing more Fae spells, quickening my shifts, creating more charms—

"Stop." Dea places both hands on my shoulders as he guides me down the corridor to the underground cinema room. "Arrie is going to be fine, and you have worked hard all afternoon. Do not overdo yourself. You need to rest regularly."

I just nod, not trusting my voice to work.

"What would you like to watch, Angel?" he asks once we've gotten through the doors at the end.

"Not fussed. You pick."

He picks something or other (I'm not really paying attention) and lowers the couch. "Come here." He pats the space in the very corner and grabs a blanket from the stack behind the couch. Tucking me in like a burrito, he kisses my forehead and wraps an arm around my back and starts the movie.

Romcom. He picked a romcom for me. N'awwww . . .

Fucking softy.

Dea groans beside me. "Shut up. Just trying to make her smile, and romance seems to distract her."

Nine laughs inside our heads and goes back to whatever he's doing.

"Thank you," I whisper.

The movie is good, honestly it is, but it isn't distracting

enough. Where is that Horseman of War? And why isn't he back yet? Why hasn't he responded to Nine's message?

"This is not helping, is it?"

I shake my head. "Sorry."

"Do not apologize. If it were you or Nine not responding to my messages and being gone longer than logically expected, I would be as worried as you."

His admission takes me aback. "Really?"

He clears his throat and looks at me with a light blush coloring his features. "Yes." His eyes avoid mine after that, and I can't help but smile at his embarrassment.

It's cute as hell.

"Hey," I say, turning his chin back toward me, "don't be embarrassed. You are allowed to feel and have emotions. Please don't hide them. Not from me."

He wraps an arm around my shoulder. "Then in that case, you should know I would like to sleep next to you tonight. If that is okay?"

"You are all always allowed. No need to ask permission."

He smiles, and we watch the rest of the movie in relative peace, his admission easing the concern for Arrie.

Arrie is on his way back, Sweetie.

"Really?" I jump off of the sofa and nearly fall off the floating platform, or I would have, if not for Dea catching me. "Thanks," I mumble.

Yup. He just messaged me back. He's just flying back to Colorado and is only a few hours out.

Relief floods my system, and I have to sit down. "Thank fuck for that." Now that I'm not worried, a new feeling overtakes me: anger. "What the fuck took him so long?"

He said he lost the teleportation crystal. You can grill him when he gets in.

Tell him to come find me straight away.

Will do.

"Now what would you like to do?" Dea says from beside me, his hand resting on the small of my back, inching just below the waist line of my skirt.

I do not miss the suggestion in his tone, I just choose to ignore it. Instead suggesting, "Let's hit the gym? You can help with my bo practice?"

Dea groans but grabs my hand. "Fine. Come on then." He smiles, though, to make sure I know he isn't being serious. He'll wait for me to be ready—without being butt-hurt, I hope.

The gym is a peaceful place by this point; a place I can vent all my frustrations without hurting myself or the others. It allows me to just be me. And tonight is no exception. Concern for Arrie has left me edgy, and that didn't vanish when I learned he is indeed okay. The fucking asshole. If he is injury free, he will not remain so when he fucking gets home.

"How far have you gotten with bo practice?" Dea asks as he grabs a practice sword from the rack and changes into more comfortable attire: sweatpants and a loose-fitting tee.

"I can pull off a few maneuvers without falling over, and I can handle the basics pretty well." I also change, and then grab the bo I left beside the sword rack.

"Well then, Horseman of Magic, show me what you have got." His adorable Victorian English accent makes that phrase all the more hilarious, and I have to stifle a laugh before mirroring his ready stance.

I make the first move, swiping left with a whoosh of air, knocking him back a step before he regains his balance.

"Nicely done." He looks impressed, and damn if that doesn't make me giddy.

Death is impressed with me.

Score one for me!

Dea lunges at me, trying to aim low, but I sidestep and speed around him, going for a gentle tap to his back. He quickly spins, however, and rolls out of the way.

Damn. So fucking close.

Try again, Magic. Try again.

This time I use my Vampire speed to outmaneuver his spin attack, and he smiles with a wicked sort of glee, one of the corners of his lips higher than the other. I know that smile. He's about to up his game.

With one foot to the left, he dodges right and fazes circles around me, too fast for even my Vampire eyes to catch. But he isn't too fast to sense.

One circle.

Two circle.

Three circle.

Four—

I hold my bo out, and he smacks right into it, flipping over and falling on his ass. "Bet that's the last time you'll be trying to out-speed me, asshole."

He jumps to his feet with a grimace and probably a sore ass with the momentum he hit that floor with. "That is what you think, Angel."

The wooden sword drops to the floor with a thud, and before I know it, he yanks the bo staff out of my hand and wraps me in an embrace so tight I'm worried I might actually feel it, but he lets me go pretty quickly. He smirks at me, and I'm about to ask what the cheeky smile is for, until he sweeps his leg out and sends me flying to my ass.

"Payback is sweet."

He smiles down at me and offers his hand, but I ignore it

and get to my own feet. The chuckle that escapes his lips has me smiling.

"Come here." I hold out my arms. He looks at me with dubious concern for a moment, so I say, "I'm being serious. No tricks. I'm not the asshole here."

More laughter fills my ears as he walks toward me and wraps both arms around my waist.

I place a lingering kiss to those delicious lips, playing with his lip piercing as I ease my tongue into his mouth with sweet and tender strokes.

"Angel?" he asks as he pulls away.

"Yeah?"

"Can I tell you a secret?"

I nod, tension suddenly filling the room.

"I prefer your male form in terms of sexual attraction." He looks to the floor with a sheepish layer of sweet-red embarrassment heating his cheeks. "I know that might not be okay, but—"

I grab his lips with my own and try to convey everything with that simple kiss. It isn't deep or hot or anything more than a tender peck, but he smiles once I pull back.

Changing to my male form, I smile at him. "You mean you prefer me like this?"

"In terms of sexual attraction, yes. But everything else does not really rely on sex. I love you. And you are you no matter your form."

I don't know what to say to that. Am I? Do I really not differ form to form? Am I still me like this? All these pesky questions I never have an answer to pervade my mind, and the spiral it sends me into makes me dizzy beyond my ability to stand.

Dea steadies me with a questioning look, but I just wave

his concern away. "Talk to me," he whispers as he leans closer to my ear.

"I just . . . It's hard, you know. Never just being one solid person, never knowing what to expect from those around you. But you all make it so much easier. Thank you." Tears creep into the rims of my eyes, and I swear I'm so fed up of crying that once this whole war thing is over with, I'll never fucking cry again.

The door behind us slams open, forcing me to quickly wipe my eyes, and in walks a face so familiar it hurts.

"Arrie!" I run to him and wrap my arms around his neck. "Arrie," I whisper, snuggling my face into his neck. "Where. The fuck. Have you been?" I say through gritted teeth. Yanking my head away and putting my feet to the floor, I take a step back and glower at him. "Huh?"

He sighs and runs a shaky hand through his hair. Mumbling something in his native language under his breath, he finally takes a breath and explains, "The Witches. They were challenging. Tried to lock me up for your crimes. Then I lost the crystal." He sighs. "But the Shifters are helping the Vampires as much as they can. Taking in strays, offering up empty homes in the Shifter Underground, and feeding them."

I flinch. "That does not excuse the lack of messaging! Do you know how worried we were?"

Arrie exchanges a glance with Dea, who I hear chuckle behind me. "You were worried about me?"

Damn. Fuck. Shit.

"Really?" He tries to grab my hand, but I yank it away.

"Still mad at you."

He chuckles, the pleasant kind of laugh one makes when they're happily surprised by something, and fuck damn it, I'm lost. All the anger floods out of me as I run and jump on him, forgetting all about that control I'm supposed to be showing or the angry frustration I was feeling not a minute ago. This man makes me crazy, and that laugh weakens my defenses every damn time.

I smother him with the longest kiss I've ever been a part of, and I revel in the feeling of completeness I feel now that I finally have my entire team here. Home. Safe. And I'm going to remind him exactly why that is such a good idea.

Shifting my body down slightly, I press myself against every inch of him, and the groan that escapes his lips has his hands clenching my ass tighter.

Your team, 'ey?

Groaning, I mutter, "Way to kill the mood, Nine."

Arrie grumbles beneath me but tightens his hold on my ass even further, where he helps keep my legs wrapped around his waist. "I'm gonna kill that *fjandinn*."

Dea's in stitches of laughter behind us, content to watch our reunion from the side lines, it seems. "Come on, you two. Let us go to bed. It is late."

I climb down from Arrie's hold and drag them to bed but when I get there, there are dozens of boxes, wrappers, and other gifts on the bed. "What's all this?"

Arrie runs a hand behind his neck. "I thought, since you didn't have much, I'd pick some more clothes up for you." His eyes dart away from mine.

But I force his face back to mine with a smile. "Thank you, Arrie." I place a gentle kiss to his cheek.

Dea blows out a breath behind us, and I scowl at him.

They help me put it all away, and the moment my head hits that pillow, I'm a goner. Asleep in the land of nod, snuggled between two amazing men, and sometime in the night, Nine and Connie join us, creating a familiar snuggle pile that always keeps the nightmares away and makes me smile uncontrollably.

Chapter Forty-Three

The next morning, Connie leaves for Earth, where she's arranged a meeting with all four pillar communities (I know, I'm shocked too) in the heart of Colorado, meaning she doesn't have to travel too far. Apparently, the Fae are holocalling in, as they don't trust the other communities. Plus, Arrie managed to persuade the Witches to at least hear us out. So, all in all, it's a win-win, if slightly compromised. Connie made me prepare a speech, which I had Dea's help in creating, and she's to read that on my behalf.

The rest of us are in the library, researching various things to help tick items off my list; also, creating Witch charms and Fae spells helps harness my powers, so I'm doing two things at once.

Horseman of Magic for the win!

"Dea?" I ask, suddenly remembering something else we should be doing, "have you managed to get hold of the SC?"

He groans from a couple of book stacks back. "No. They are ignoring my calls." He peeks around the corner of the shelf and grimaces at me. "I am sorry, Angel."

I sigh. "That's okay." How can I get them and the magical communities to communicate if they aren't even talking to us? "Why aren't they talking to us?" I mumble. "They came to the ball." Goddess, all these politics are so confusing.

"Ah!" I hear Arrie gasp from beside me. "Medical charms." He throws a book at me, which I catch, and continues looking. Arrie's helping me create anti-sickness charms, which I'm still surprised haven't been created yet.

"Maybe I could open up a magic shop after the war is over. Unique charms and spells . . ."

I'm just muttering to myself, but Dea looks over and smiles. "That sounds wonderful, Angel."

Arrie grunts but smiles and returns his eyes to the stack in front of him.

Awesome plan. Should totally do it.

"I was just joking." Goddess, could you imagine it? Me, owning a magic shop? Hahahahahaha. Hilarious. I'm nearly giggling at the ludicrous idea.

"Why not?" Dea asks.

"Because that requires responsibility, and thought, and customer services, and . . . Just no way."

"Right," Arrie says, "because saving the world is just a lazy person's job."

I huff at him and search through another shelf, content to mull in my own thoughts for a while. Me, a magic store owner? As if anyone would buy anything from someone the world hates.

Shaking those pesky self-doubting thoughts from my mind, I focus on the task at hand: referencing sections, chapters and pages from all the books the guys are handing me. We can then read them and make notes later.

"Found it!" Nine yells from several stacks back. He hasn't handed me a single book the entire time we've been here and instead has been off looking at something on his own. He runs over with a massive volume that looks a thousand years old and is bound in black leather with faded gold lettering on the front.

The lettering is in some ancient language I can't read, so I pull the translational bookscreen from my pocket and grab it from Nine's hands.

ANGELS: MYTHS AND FACTS.

"What is it?" I ask, curious as to why this is what he's been looking for.

"Well," he says, scratching his head, "I said I'd do some research into the whole Angel magical connection thing, and I have. I was searching for a book I'd read a long time ago. Sorry, it took me a while to find a copy." He hops on the spot, clearly nervous about something.

I raise a questioning eyebrow, and he sighs.

"Look, it's complicated. Can you just read the section on Angel mating toward the end, please?" He sighs at my sound of surprise. "It'll help. Promise."

"Fine." I huff and go over to my desk. Dea follows, eager for an answer as much as I am. "Let's see."

I place the bookscreen over the old-fashioned contents page and the flicked to the right page: ANGEL MATING AND MAGICAL BONDS.

"Fucking Christ, this is gonna piss me off, isn't it?"

Dea chuckles. "Probably. But know that I do not care what it says, it does not change anything."

Sure. As if.

I skim the page and can already feel my blood boiling beneath the surface. This can't be the answer, surely?

"One of the common myths of Angel lore is the concept of bonds between different Angel magics," Dea begins reading out loud. "It has only been seen in full-blooded Angels, and the effects are mostly seen only in Angel form . . ." Dea's voice trails off, coming to the same realization I did two minutes earlier.

I sit there, staring at the page, well aware of all three guys staring at me. I don't know how to feel. On the one hand, I'm already in love with Dea, so it doesn't really matter, but on the other, I am sick of magic controlling my life. What gives it the right to decide who I'm attracted to? And does this mean I'm only attracted to him because our magics bonded? Does he not really love me?

An arm yanks me back from the book. "Watch the book!"

Looking down at my arms, I notice they're on fire. "Shit." Quickly changing forms, the flames puff out of existence as quickly as I grow a dick. "I'm going for a walk," I whisper.

Dea calls after me and Nine tells him to give me some space, but I can't deal with them right now. There's a part of me that knows talking to them will help, but right now, the thought of talking to the very person I'm magically bonded to scares the shit out of me.

"Why didn't it happen the moment I first saw him change?" I mutter to myself. I'd seen his Angel form a few times before that moment in the Vampire Royal Council room. It doesn't make sense.

I wander the corridors of the house, walking past empty rooms, used rooms, the servants' quarters, and doors I have no idea of the contents, if any. "This place is like a maze," I mumble for the thousandth time since I woke up in this house.

It's been months since then, and I'm practically a whole different person; it seems like it was just yesterday when

I was worried about who I was and who I'll become. I'm still worried, but it's different now. I have a home, a family, friends, boyfriends, a girlfriend, and most of my memories are coming back.

Sighing, I come to the decision that it's time. I need to speak to Mr. Compton and learn everything there is to know about the old me. Plus, he's with the SC, so he can take a message back to them.

Nine? Where I am? I look around a strange-looking corridor made of wood and stone.

Wow. You're in the original layer of corridors. We haven't been there in some time. Hang tight. I'm sending Dea.

The brick, stone, and wood are layered to create compact walls that've stood the test of time for nearly two thousand years, it would seem. This must have been the original house, before it got upgraded over the years. There are rooms with no doors littered down the hallways, but every single one is bare of life. Empty. Cold.

"Angel?"

"Dea," I say under my breath as I turn around from peering into another vacant room. Standing in front of me is the man in question.

"Angel, I . . . I am sorry." He looks to the floor, his cheeks redder than a tomato, and the tension in the corridor could not be thicker.

"It's nothing to apologize for," I say. "It's not any more your fault than it is mine."

"I did not know Angels mated. I thought mating was just a myth."

"I know."

He runs gentle fingers up my bare arms and finally looks me in the eyes; his piercing gaze never fails to take my breath away with those sparkling galaxy-like eyes unlike any other I've gazed into. "It does not change anything."

"I know."

He frowns, confused at my acceptance, no doubt.

"I'm not concerned about us, Dea." I grab his hands and step into his arms, which he wraps around me. "I'm concerned that magic rules my life, and I'm just supposed to go along with it like it's nothing. As though I control it. But I don't." Tears creep along the edges of my eyes before they finally fall. "*Chikushou*," I grumble.

Swiping away the tears with a fury usually only reserved for Arrie, Dea laughs at my silly antics. "You are allowed to be upset."

"Just feels like I'm always upset these days."

"If you count the number of laughs as well as the tears, you will likely find they even out. We just tend to only see the tears."

There he goes again, his never-ending, well-spoken wisdom that makes him sound like a poet.

"C'mon." I grab his hand and drag us down a corridor.

"It is this way." He pulls us in the other direction.

"I knew that."

Chapter Forty-Four

Back in the library, we all fall into a rhythm as the guys search for books and online information that might help, and I tag, highlight, and reference them for later. By the time we have a pile taller than male-me, we stop for dinner and return.

"Ugh. Reading," Arrie grumbles.

"Get used to it!" I punch him in the arm and watch him smile as he goes to rub it better. "Baby."

Arrie grumbles something in what I can only assume is Norse, and I sigh.

"C'mon, we need to start going through this information and putting my magic to good use." I run to the desk, my pink hair flying behind me, and pick up the first book on creating Fae-spelled objects.

"Still reckon it would last longer if you put the Fae spell into a Witch charm." Nine wraps an arm around my shoulders.

"I concur," Dea says. "It would be a more solid spell, too."

"Okay, let's try it."

After creating a charm bead, I change form and imbue a

basic Fae spell to make someone forget the last five minutes for an hour.

"That was easy." And it was. It's similar to the Witch charm I put into the Fae-spelled teleporting crystals the other day, but the other way around.

We spend the rest of the evening playing around with my powers, learning that joining my Fae and Witch abilities is pretty simple, but I can't use them at the same time (obviously), so it has to be planned; I can't, for example, create an attack spell using both unless it's imbued into an object first.

Earth-to-Earth teleporting crystals are also pretty simple, as are anti-sickness charms (turns out medical spells aren't doable for the Fae—something about the Fae magic not reacting well with the internal body of any Animalia).

"What next?" I ask, right before the doors to the library, which have remained open these past few days, slam closed, right behind a walking blonde beauty who smiles at me in a way that has my insides melting and my eyelids fluttering.

"Connie!"

I sprint and leap at her, throwing all of my female weight at her body, but she catches me with ease and wraps my legs around her waist as she holds me up with a firm two hands on my ass.

"Hey, hon. You doin' okay?"

"Much better now."

She laughs and leans up for a kiss, which I happily answer with my own slightly steamy kiss that lasts longer than I think she anticipated. When we finally break for air, she smiles and places me back to the floor. "C'mon." She grabs my hand and takes me back to the guys and our heaping piles of books.

"Hey Con," everyone greets at once, not even looking up from their books.

"You soooo have them whipped, hon." She motions a whip crack and laughs at her own joke.

Goddess, it's good to have her back.

Nine looks up from his book. "Have much luck?"

Connie nods and shakes her head at the same time. "Kinda."

I wince. "Explain."

"Well . . ." She takes a seat on the floor and sifts through the volumes in one of the piles. "The Vampires and Shifters are on board, the Witches don't really care either way, and the Fae are against it."

"Well, that was about the outcome I was expecting," Nine says. "It doesn't really effect the Witches either way. If they wanted to ask for help or post jobs, they can do so without having to reveal their species, but they probably won't be taking jobs until they finally comes out of the closet."

"Right. That makes sense." I nod.

"And the Fae don't want to make peace with the humans. They want turmoil so their less-than-savory practices can continue." He sighs. "But they probably won't stop their people from using it. But don't expect many Fae users."

I sigh too. "And the rogue Vampires are probably going to cause mayhem too." How do we stop people from misusing it? "It's a great opportunity for communities to work together in all kinds of ways. Why can't everyone just see that?" I groan.

"Hey," Connie soothes, "they will. It'll take time."

"Yup," Nine adds. "We're going to have to show them ourselves."

"What does that mean?"

"We'll have to take the jobs and make them public, film some of them, get promo going, and make people see the use of it."

"Filming? Us?"

Dea coughs. "We are being hounded by media mongrels for interviews as it is. The world wants to know who we are. We are going to need to do some media control at some point." He puts his head back into TALES OF ANCIENT WITCH CHARMS.

Ugh. Great.

Hey! This was your fault to begin with. You made us go public. Remember?

Ugh. Stop being so right all the fucking time.

Nine laughs, and the others just look at us with weird adoring smiles and giggle under their breaths.

"What?"

"You are both adorable, Angel," Dea says.

Adorable? "I. Am. Not. Adorable. I'm a fucking lioness. Don't make me shift into one to prove my point!"

Arrie bursts into a fit of laughter, dragging Connie down with him, and soon we're all just laughing in the library so hard I have to hold my sides and dry my tears.

Goddess, it's good to laugh.

I spend the rest of the evening practicing various Fae spells and Witch charms until I'm exhausted with all the back-and-forth switching of my forms. I mean, seriously, could my Fae and Witch abilities not be in the same fucking form? Ugh.

I'm running out of energy.

"Okay," Nine says as he stands up. "It's past midnight and you're exhausted. Let's go to bed." He grabs my hand and looks to the others. "You lot coming?"

Dea looks away, Arrie awkwardly coughs, and Connie just looks to the ground.

"What's going on?" I let go of Nine's hand and walk up to them.

"Well," Connie begins . . .

"Just spit it out." I hunch my shoulders and sigh. I'm tired, hungry, and magically exhausted; give me a fucking break. "Please?"

She nods. "You sure you two want company? We could sleep separately if you like?"

"Oh. Ohhhhh." I look at their awkward faces and sigh. Again. Sitting on the floor, I make them all face me while I prepare my speech. "No. We're not doing that. Just because I've had sex with Nine does not make our relationship any more valuable than the ones I share with all of you. I know we haven't really figured out the details . . ." Goddess, damn it, this is hard. "But I still"—I look away from their piercing stares and to the floor—"like all of you. We're still, you know, like a thing, right?"

Goddess, I haven't ruined everything, have I?

I can handle the silence that ensues. What I can not handle is the snickering Connie is trying to hide and the awkward cufuffling laugh Arrie is trying to swallow.

"All right! I get it. I'm shit with words. Just stop making it harder." I get up in a huff and go to take my magically exhausted ass to bed.

But Connie runs to me and grabs my hand. "No, wait. We're sorry." She spins me around and wraps her arms around my waist. "I'm sorry. That was mean of me." A small smile creeps onto her face and makes her eyes sparkle. "But you were just sooooo cute." She pecks my cheek and whispers, "Yes, I'll be your girlfriend." She unwraps herself from me and walks away. "But I'm not tired." She shrugs. "Need less sleep than all of you weirdos."

Right. Of course.

"I'll keep working on some advertising plans for the app

and see if I can't get ahold of the SC for you. You wimps go to sleep."

"C'mon, Sweetie." Nine grabs my hand. "Let's go."

Arrie and Dea follow us into my bedroom in silence, and I worry my lip until Nine tells me to stop.

They're both fine. They were just a little worried about interrupting us.

"Oh . . ."

Dea looks at me in confusion, but I wave him off.

I'm too tired to deal with my relationship drama. It can wait until tomorrow.

Stripping down to my pants and vest tee, I crawl into bed. I could have sworn this bed was smaller earlier. Hmm. Never mind.

The guys join me, with Dea and Arrie either side of me, and Nine on the opposite side of Dea.

"Night guys."

Arrie plants a gentle kiss to my temple while Dea grabs my hand and whispers, "Goodnight."

Goodnight, Sweetie.

"Come on you lot! Time to get up. You've all slept enough."

Whaaa? Sunlight pours through my bedroom window, and heat from either side of me trickles sweat down my front and back. But when I remember whose heat it belongs to, I smile. Totally worth it.

"Come on!" Connie jumps on the bed, and all four of us groan.

"Fuck off, Con!" Arrie grumbles from my right.

I could have just air-lifted her off the bed, but I'm enjoying the havoc in a weird, my-version-of-perfect kind of way.

"What's up?" I sit up and rub the sleep from my eyes.

She crawls up from the bottom of the bed and places a leg either side of me as she straddles my waist. "I finalized the advertisement plan, organized some safe, low-key media control, and have worked out twice. I'm bored!" She pouts and grabs my hand. "Come on! Wake up and cause more fun."

I giggle and lean into her.

"I could get used to waking up like this," Nine whispers just loud enough for us all hear as he watches Connie and I embrace in a less-than-innocent kiss that takes my breath away.

Like usual.

"Mmm," Arrie moans from beside me, struggling to keep his eyes open. "Definitely."

"Okay, okay." I push Connie off and hop over Arrie to get out of bed. "Let's hear these plans of yours."

We all get showered, dressed, and ready while Connie rattles off a schedule of advertisement that could run without any input and media meetings, interviews, and goddess knows what else to keep us in a positive public light.

"So," Nine says as he steps out of the shower in nothing but a towel wrapped around his waist. "I was thinking we should hire an agent to deal with all of our press appearances?"

He strips down to his birthday suit while Dea and I openly ogle his lean form and gets dressed into sweatpants and one of his geek-shirts; this one has a picture of a t-rex drinking tea, with a caption saying TEA-REX.

I can't help but laugh when Nine smiles at the pun in the mirror.

"Sure. Seems helpful." I turn back to Connie. "So, we have a group interview this afternoon, right?"

Connie nods. "And we need to make our profiles on the

app to actually get it started before we go live this evening."

"You know," I start as I pull a fresh pair of bat tights on, "you're better at this lifestyle management than I thought you'd be. Remind me to have you organize my training schedule in the future."

Connie pecks me on the cheek and winks. "You don't want that," she whispers, "I'd just organize an orgy every time you got stressed. That would make the stress drop right off."

I laugh as I blush.

Nine just looks at me with a knowing smirk. *Could totally be arranged.*

Stop distracting me. Lots of training to do today.

Nine laughs and directs me to breakfast, where we basically all eat toast while we try our hardest to keep up with Connie's energy levels. Seriously, she's like a bunny on dusted steroids.

Does she ever calm down?

Not when she's happy. And you're her first partner in a long, long time, so she's pretty happy.

Looking at her radiant smile as she bites into another peanut-butter and marshmallow-fluff toast sandwich, I can't help but be happy for her. For us. Things aren't perfect, but maybe this weird relationship could work.

It's about time something went my way for a change.

Now I just have to figure out how to save the world before there actually ends up being a war.

Chapter Forty-Five

We all sit in an office in the official meeting foyer of the house as Jeremy Bouler sits in front of us with a scowl that matches his defensive posture and stupid floor-length cloak.

He doesn't want to be here.

"Drew the short straw, Mr. Bouler?"

Dea shoots me an irritated glance, and Connie groans. "Behave," Connie warns. "He's probably anxious about meeting five supernaturals he didn't know existed until a week ago."

"That assessment would be correct."

"Well," Dea starts, offering him a hand to shake, "I can personally guarantee your safety during your stay here in *Sheruta*, Mr. Bouler."

"Thank you." He shakes Dea's hand. "That is most appreciated."

"I'm sorry," I interrupt, "but who do you work for?"

He smiles at me—or he tries to. Bless him. He isn't very good at dealing with my randomness. "Of course. I'm one of the head reporters for the Supernatural Council. It's nice to meet you . . . ?"

I bristle at him being with the SC, but I force a smile nonetheless. "Magic."

He raises an eyebrow in question.

I sigh. "This is Death, War, Conquest, and Famine." I point to each in turn. "And I'm Magic. Dea, Arrie, Connie, and Nine have all nicknamed themselves, but I haven't had the brain space to think about it recently."

"Right." He writes some basic notes down. "So," he starts, "the four—five—Horsemen of the Apocalypse?"

Dea takes point—thank the goddess—and explains their backstory. Leaving out the details, of course, but he gets the main point across. A small recording device hovers around us, flying to each of us as we fill in some of the gaps in Dea's story. Well, the others do. I don't come in yet. Obviously.

I'm not that old.

Yet.

I grimace.

"So, it's been you guys all along? Like some kind of behind-the-scenes kings—and queen?"

Dea grimaces. "That is not how I would describe it. While we help and have the power to do what we wish, we usually just advise. The magical community tends to do what it wants either way."

I remember the Fae being a pain in our fucking asses. "He's right," I say. "We can advise all day long, but keeping the peace is challenging. Being separate from all of the magical communities and not being human allows us a unique vantage point."

Nine chimes in with, "Plus, we have respect in the magical community. We've helped solved many issues, and even smoothed the coming out process a hundred years ago."

The interviewer, who's gained some degree of confidence over the last hour, nods and asks, "So, you just advise and step in when things get out of control?"

We all nod.

"Okay. So, where do you come into all this?" He looks at me as he asks his question.

I don't know what to say. What am I supposed to say? I don't want to worry the human community.

Dea says to explain that your seal was broken by an unknown party and you've been training here ever since. Don't bring up the war. It'll cause panic.

Right.

So that's what I do. I tell my story, minus the war part.

"Have you ever left *Sheruta*?"

I nod. "I've visited each pillar court and council."

Mr. Bouler looks to Dea. "And the SC were already aware of your existence?" He looks doubtful.

"We helped form the SC, so yes, they know of us."

Mr. Bouler's mouth hangs open in shock. "This is not going to go down well."

"How can we help?" I ask.

He looks at me with a soft smile. "The public aren't going to like the governing factions keeping things from them. Especially humans. They're going to ask what else is out there." He sighs. "Heck, they already are."

"I see." I rack my brain to think of a way out, but I can't. "It might help for them to know that the magical community didn't know about our existence either. Just the leading councils and covens."

He nods and writes it down. "It might help do some damage control." He worries his lower lip and picks at his fingernails, eager to ask a question he isn't sure he should ask.

"You can ask us anything, Mr. Bouler." Dea looks at him with a reassuring smile. "Though I will not guarantee an answer."

Mr. Bouler smiles and sighs in defeat. "Why now? Why come out of the closet now? After two thousand years in hiding?"

We all fidget slightly, shifting in our seats. I really don't want to lie to this man; he seems sweet. But reporting on the real reason isn't an option.

"Mr. Bouler," I start, "I don't want to lie to you. But public knowledge of everything we're doing isn't an option right now."

Mr. Bouler nods.

"It became necessary for a recent problem we are trying to solve."

"Is this problem something we humans should be concerned about?"

I look to Dea, who nods at me, before I turn back and say, "Yes. But rest assured, we will do everything in our power to help."

A small Fae serving girl in a casual dress enters the room after knocking, air lifting a dozen trays of tea, cakes, and pastries. "Dinner, as requested." She curtsies and places all the trays on the tables in the far-left corner.

Food! Finally. All this talking and worrying is sending my stomach on edge. Looking over Dea's shoulder, I zoom in and see my favorite cake from the café and airlift one my way.

Mr. Bouler gasps, surprised. "You . . . just lifted it to you . . ." he sputters as I bite into the cakey goodness.

"Yeah, air Witch magic."

"Right." He still looks confused, bless him. "Witch magic.

Something I'm not allowed to put into my report."

I snort. "Right. Witch closet."

Mr Bouler laughs, and I can't help but feel happy that this guy was sent to us and not some snotty woman determined to cross every fucking line in the sand.

"So," Connie says, "you're coming back every day this week, right?"

Mr. Bouler nods over a cup of jasmine tea. "Yes. Each day has a different agenda. Today was an introduction. Tomorrow is about your powers."

"I hate being a show monkey," I complain.

"Stop complaining!" Connie yells. "This is all your fault in the first place."

I poke my tongue out at her and return to our interviewer, who looks at us with a thoughtful smile.

"You all must be really close?"

Dea coughs and looks to me in question.

Do I want the world to know about our relationship? Well, I certainly don't want to hide it. I'm not ashamed. I just . . . maybe now isn't the right time?

Before I can make up my mind, however, Arrie stands and walks to the food table. "We're just friends. But yes, we're like family."

My face pales and my heart goes a mile a minute.

Just friends? But . . . I thought . . .

Looking to Mr. Bouler with my best attempt at a neutral expression, I nod my agreement amidst holding back tears. "Like family," I choke out. I change form and take a calming breath.

Don't burn the human. Don't burn the human.

Mr. Bouler looks stunned again, and I get the feeling I'm going to continue surprising him all week.

"Thank you for being so patient with us, Mr. Bouler," Connie says. "I think we're about done for the day."

He nods and gets up to shake all our hands. "It was nice to meet you all."

After he leaves, everyone looks at Arrie with an accusatory scowl.

"What were you thinking!?" Connie yells. "Just a friend?" She walks up to him and swings a left hook to his face, but he blocks with ease. "Did you not sound that out in your head first!"

Nine steps up to them with his palms out flat in surrender, clearly not wanting to get involved in the fight. "Yeah, dude. That wasn't cool. It was her call to make."

Arrie looks at him in confusion. "It was our call to make, not hers. You act as though her opinions are the only ones that matter. That her feelings are all that counts." He clenches his fists and storms out of the room.

He didn't even look at me.

Why didn't he look at me?

I stand in the wake of his exit, dumbfounded and confused. The others all turn to me with gentle, comforting looks, but I don't want their pity. I don't know what I want.

"I'm going to, err . . . go somewhere else." My legs take me out of there as quickly as they can, my male form not being as fast as my female form.

I can hear Nine and Connie talking about it if I strain my ears hard enough. They're all on my side, it seems. But in this instance, there isn't a side to take.

Chapter Forty-Six

We all spend the following week showing Mr. Bouler our lives, powers, and what we do; starting some ad campaigns on my sparkly new app and gaining as many profiles as possible from allies and friends; and we're all dodging around Arrie's bad mood and my current drama. Before I know it, it's Friday and the first job request comes through.

"Guys, guys, guys, guys . . . Look, look, look, look!" I shout as I run through the house at top Vampire speed to collect everyone.

"Huh?" Nine asks as he steps out from his bedroom with tired eyes and a yawn on his face. "What's up?"

"We got our first job request!" I jump up and down and cause Nine to smile with pride at me.

Connie and Dea stand behind me, both looking happy my plan is starting to work.

"Well," Connie asks, "what's the job?"

"Oh, right." Need to actually look at the job posting. "Japan, $4,000, removing a spell from an old magic book.

Posted by the Magical History Museum of Tokyo."

I go silent for a moment while the others patiently wait for me. "Tokyo?" But I'm avoiding going back there. If I go there, I'm sure I'll get a million flashbacks and visions of my time living there. "Fuck."

It has to be me. No one else can disable a spell without dragging a Fae along. And that's un-damn-likely.

"I can go with you, Angel. If you would like?" Dea places a hand on my shoulder. "We all can."

I shake my head. "Too much to do here. I want someone managing the political nightmare of creating the embassies, and I need you to contact Mr. Compton for my return."

Nine nods, but Connie looks at me in shock. "Mr. Compton? Really?"

"It's time. I have questions I need answers to. Before another reporter arrives and starts asking questions about my mortal life."

"If you're sure, hon." Connie yanks me into a hug. "But you can do it at your own pace."

"Con's right," Nine says. "We spent a long time exploring our pasts. You don't need to do it all at once."

"But yes, Dea," I add, "you can come along."

He smiles behind me. I don't need to turn around to know that because I can tell by the hazy look of love on Nine's face. That man is an open book.

I am not.

Whatever you say.

"What's going on?" Arrie's familiar grumble echoes down the hallway. "Meeting?"

Dea shakes his head. "Got our first job posting on the new app. Angel and I are going together."

I accept the job request as myself and attach Dea's profile

to the listing, so they know it'll be both of us.

Arrie grumbles something in Norse under his breath and walks away. Again, without even looking at me. Has he changed his mind? Maybe he doesn't like the idea of sharing? Or maybe he thinks I'm taking away his family? Goddess, there are so many options for things I could have done wrong. Maybe—

Stop. Stop giving him exactly what he doesn't deserve. Enjoy your trip with Dea all alone, and come back and deal with him then.

Right. First day on the job. Eeeeek!

"Gossip night before you go?" Connie looks at me all excited. "Your turn to pick something for us to do!"

"Sure."

Shit, shit, shit. I totally forgot. I have to do something, but what? Fuck, fuck, fuck.

How about going to a bar in Sheruta town? You've not been, Con loves going out . . .

Great idea!

Mwuhahaha! Conquest and Magic are going out drinking. Goddess, I hope she doesn't get me too drunk.

An hour later, I'm in my closet stressing about what to wear. This is becoming a regular occurrence. What the fuck do I wear to a bar? Maybe some jeans and a low-cut tee? Maybe something with sparkles? Ohhh, what about that sparkly dress with the low-cut back—that'll show off my back tattoo. Nah, that's too slutty.

"How about you just wear some jeans and a nice top, hon?"

"Ah!" I jump around with my fists raised and notice Connie's shock of blonde hair dazzling in the setting sun seeping through the open closet door. "It's just you," I say, relief washing through me.

Her laugh echoes through the small room, and I feel my cheeks blush crimson. "Relax. Just me." She raises her hands in mock defeat. "And jeans and a slightly slutty top would be great for the bar I've chosen."

Even though tonight's date is my choice, I left the details up to someone who's actually been to the bars in *Sheruta*; lest I take us to come crummy shithole.

"Err, right." I grab my trusty pair of black skinnies and shimmy into them. "What top?" I whisper to myself as I search through the rack of them.

I've gained quite the collection over the last few months, with every member of the team helping me fill it.

"Oh!" I yank a shimmery purple crop top off the rack that I've yet to wear. "Let's give this one a go."

"Isn't that the one Arrie got you when he went to see the Shifters last week?"

Ugh. Just the reminder that this top is only here because of that dickhead is enough to make me put it back on the fucking hanger.

"Hey, no. Don't let him do that. You can look fabulous without him." She throws it back at me. "I think it'll go great."

Connie herself is sporting a fabulous miniskirt in a dark, grungy green color paired with a long-sleeved orange top with a relatively modest neckline for her. And she finishes it all off with a pair of bright orange heels that make her look even taller than usual.

After finalizing my outfit, we're off. "Want me to fly us there? Or do you want to retain your hairstyle?"

She giggles, and I can't help but thread my arm through hers. "Don't mind," she finally answered, "but I'd rather drag our date out as long as possible."

She has a point. If I fly us there, we'll lose an hour between traveling there and back. Walking in the setting sun it is. Not a bad start to a great night.

"I know this is a sore subject, but I'm sorry Arrie's being such an idiot."

I wince as she says his name. "It's . . . fine. Not your fault."

"Still . . ." She avoids looking at me.

"Hey!" I stop us halfway down the main road from our house. "You are not his keeper. He's capable of making his own choices. And certainly capable of making his own mistakes." I roll my eyes. "So he can make his own apologies."

"I know," she says through a sigh. "I just wish he would open up to you more. Maybe there was a reason, you know."

A reason? Yeah, like he doesn't want to be tied to me while I make a fucking mess of this entire relationship. Not to mention while I destroy the damn world.

"Stop spiraling." She gets us walking once more and holds my hand. "It should be a fun night. And if you need to unload any of your drama on me, I'm all ears." She gives me knowing eyes.

I know what she wants: the dirty deets of my night with Nine. "Sorry, but I'm not talking about that." Not yet, at least. Who knows what I'll say if she gets me too drunk.

Her evil smirk tells me she's come to the same conclusion. The fucking bitch.

An hour into our date, and we've downed enough shots to have us fully dancing without a care in the world in a bar that had some cool air darts I rocked at. It's a small, rustic place with good company, smiles, and familiar faces. Seems *Sheruta* is finally getting used to me. Or I'm getting used to them. Either one.

"Soooo . . ." Connie begins as she grabs my waist and

presses her body flat against mine. "Your first time with Nine . . . How was it?" she whispers in my ear just loud enough for my Vampire hearing to pick up on.

"It was . . . perfect." And it was.

"He can't hear us out here. So don't hold back on me now!" She runs her hands under the hem of my crop top, and every touch sends a sizzling fire under my skin, spreading to every crevice of my body. "C'mon, help a girl out, hon."

I let my hands roam over her waist and ass, and I eventually give into her pleading eyes. "It was . . . as romantic as it was hot. He'd created a witchlighted clearing in the forest and had a bed, rose petals, and a bonfire set up so we could enjoy ourselves no matter what we chose to do."

Connie pulls back to look at my face and smiles. "Really?" She swears under her breath. "Damn. That fucker makes it really hard to be romantic."

"Well, we had sex, and then we cuddled all night and came back the next morning." She looks upset at my lack of details, but I go on to say, "Oh, and then I got Dea off in the kitchen. I told them both I loved them a few days previous. And I'm somehow mated to Dea's Angel form."

Connie coughs and splutters. "Hold up. That's a lot to unpack." She takes a deep breath. "Let's start with getting Dea off. In the kitchen? That's where we all eat!"

"We cleaned up! You wouldn't be complaining if it were you."

She shrugs. "Probably not." She takes another deep breath and moves to behind me as she wraps her arms around my waist. "Now, about the whole saying you love them. Really?"

"It just sort of slipped out when I told Nine. I panicked and then told Dea when we were chatting about it."

She chuckles behind me as she peppers kisses down my

neck. "I can just imagine your internal panic."

I spin and throw my lips against hers so hard she stumbles back and has to catch us both. Her hands roam to the hem of my crop top, and I let her slip them underneath and roam wherever she wants.

We have great fun dancing on the barrier of inappropriate behavior all evening. Eventually, when we can barely walk anymore, much less dance, we decide to head home. I don't trust our ability to walk so elect to fly us there.

Turns out, flying drunk is just as dangerous as walking drunk, if not more so. At least when walking, the only directions you have are forwards, backwards, sidewards, or downwards. When in the air, you have every direction imaginable, and the potential of me flying us into a wall or the ocean is pretty high.

"Weeeeeee!" Connie spreads her arms out on either side of her body and is pretending to be some kind of a superhero. "Hero of Conquest to the ressscue!"

I concentrate on trying to get us home in one piece, and eventually, after losing the way multiple times and nearly smacking us into the ground more times than I have fingers to count them on, the house comes into view.

Connie laughs and points out the garden.

Now to land without beheading us. Hmmm. Concentrating on the ground rapidly rising before us in all its spinning glory, I try to slow down when noticing the porch but only serve to speed us up.

The porch, made of some kind of glass, smashes as we crash through it and land in a bloody heap on the floor. We're both bleeding, I can smell it, and when three pairs of feet rush to us, we can't stop giggling.

"What the fuck?" Arrie groans.

"Did you fly drunk?" Dea scolds.

"What were you thinking?" Nine asks behind an obvious laugh.

I try to stand up, but I can't. Something is keeping me trapped to the floor.

"Shit, your leg is pierced to the floor with glass." Nine runs over and yanks the glass out while Dea heals me up in no time.

"See, all good!" I spring up like a bunny rabbit and go to walk to my room, but I stumble and fall into Arrie instead. "Oops, sorry."

Arrie sighs and picks me up, then goes to grab Connie, and deposits us both in my room before walking away. Still, he doesn't look at me once.

"One day, I'm going to punch that f-f-fucker so hard in the balls, he'll forget his own gorgeous ref-f-flection."

"Yas, girl! You go for it. Heeee . . ." Her face pales as she hiccups. "Shit." She runs for the bathroom and slams the door behind her.

Well, it was fun while it lasted. I focus hard and change into my male form so I can take care of Connie. It's my choice of date, after all. But when she doesn't come out of the bathroom for over fifteen minutes, I go in to investigate and find her passed out on the floor by the toilet.

Scooping her up, I tuck her into bed and ask the house for a bucket (just in case).

CHAPTER FORTY-SEVEN

"You are the one that got so drunk you crashed through the porch ceiling, Angel," Dea says as we rock up to the museum that hired us. "Deactivating a Fae spell may require your female form's Witch powers."

Ugh. Even the thought of being in my female form sends a wave of nausea through me. "Let's just hope that's not the case, or I might vomit all over the ancient book." So far, I've stayed in my male form to avoid the hangover.

Dea chuckles but quickly hides it behind a frown. "You should be more responsib—"

"Bite me, Angel of Death."

Dea stops us at the front of the museum steps and yanks me to his lips. He devours me in front of at least twenty people coming and going through the front door, and I do nothing to stop him. Just when I think he'll pull back, he nips my bottom lip and smirks. "Do not make threats you do not intend to keep, Angel."

A shiver runs through me from the small tingle of pain he

caused, and the need to bite him back echoes around every inch of me. "Shouldn't start something you don't intend to finish." I push him away and turn back to the front doors.

Dea grabs my wrist and flips me back around, however, as he presses a lingering kiss to my lips. "Who says I do not intend to finish what I started?"

Damn this man. He's so . . . candy-like. Like I could eat a shit-ton of what he's dishing out and still need more. An addiction. That's what this man is. A gothic addiction.

I smirk at him and press a kiss to his cheek before turning back around.

Get your head in the game, Magic. C'mon, you need this.

We have small cameras attached to our shirts to record real-time footage for promo purposes, and I click mine on and signal Dea to do the same. It's time to get this show started.

The museum is huge. So huge, in fact, that I have a hard time navigating us, even with the Japanese signage. "This way?"

We've been instructed to meet our employer at the gift shop, but I have no damn clue where that is. Goddess help me, this is ridiculous.

"Maybe we should stop and ask for help?"

I scowl at Dea. "I am more than capable of navigating, Dea." So help me goddess, I am going to strangle this man.

"Hmm? Then maybe a map might be of use?" He points to a display of maps on one of the many information desks littered throughout the displays; this one focuses on navigating tourists through the Hall of Shifter Fame.

Every type is represented here, and I find myself smiling at the equality shown; from war-winning tiger Shifters to an HIV cure-finding pelican Shifter, no one is exempt from recognition here. It's . . . nice.

"Shifters are some of the most balanced magical species in the world. You would like them."

"Maybe we should meet them before we leave?"

"I could introduce you. They are, after all, the only pillar community you have yet to meet."

I nod with dwindling enthusiasm as we walk past the next statue, and I stop to read the plaque. "Defeater of Invaders?"

Dea bristles. "Not all of their history fits with the modern worldview of peace. There have been numerous wars and fallings out over the centuries. This one celebrates the day Theobrim slayed the leader of a human pirate fleet that continuously wreaked havoc on his local fishing town."

"Hmmm, I see."

I don't see. Not really. Why would they celebrate senseless violence that does nothing to connect to the modern world? It's not even important anymore.

A voice interrupts my musings. "Horseman of Magic?"

I turn to meet the face of a handsome young man with piercing blue eyes and dark hair. His badge catches my eye— he works for the museum. "Yes. I'm here to complete a job your company requested." I gesture to an invisible Dea beside me. "And this is the Horseman of Death."

He nods toward Dea.

"I hope you do not mind, but we are recording the job today so we can create a real-time promotional video."

The man hesitates before pressing a hand to his ear and nodding. "Of course not. We're not dealing with anything sensitive today."

Someone else is pulling the strings. Strange.

I shrug and walk past him, gesturing forward. "Shall we?"

"Of course." He turns and walks ahead of us. "Please, follow me."

He leads us through a set of staff doors and down winding corridors to a room that has my eyes widening in amazement.

"Where are we?"

The man turns around and says in a gentle voice, "The back room. It's where we keep our stock before putting it on display, and it's where experts do their studying."

"Cool." I've never seen the inside of a museum before. It's . . . more corporate than I expected.

Eventually he leads us through a door at the back and into a plain-looking office, where a squalid man sits in a grand desk chair and pours over an old tome's front cover that has dust and dirt still imbedded in its leather.

"Ah," he says, looking up, "Magic. Death." He looks to each of us in turn. "It's so lovely to meet you. Please, do take a seat." He gestures to the two seats in front of the desk. "Thank you for taking our request."

I nod. "It's our pleasure, sir." We both sit, and I move to touch the book. "May I?"

The man nods and scoots it my way.

The moment I touch the leather-bound tome, I can feel the magic seeping around it, suffocating its knowledge. Preventing me from opening its pages. But why?

"Excuse me, sir, but do you know why this book is sealed?"

The man sitting behind the desk frowns. "It's rumored to contain dark magic. Magic forbidden by the Fae."

Forbidden by the Fae? What on earth could be insi——?

"Death magic," Dea whispers, somewhat taken aback. "This book contains death magic spells."

The Shifter behind the desk bobs his head side to side. "Supposedly. But death magic? Really? I doubt it." He scoffs, not believing.

"Sir?" I grab his attention and wave the book in front of

me. "Whatever is in this book is contained by a powerful Fae spell. It will take a few hours to break it."

The man considers for a minute before he looks at me with a smile and says, "Well, then get on with it." I sigh as he continues. "It's what I'm paying you for, after all."

"Very well."

Dea places a hand on my shoulder. "Angel, I do not think this is the best use of your magic."

I turn to look Dea right in his galaxy eyes, imploring him to trust me with a small smile and reassuring nod that I know what I'm doing.

Roaming my hands over every crevice of the book, I quickly disarm the spell, but what I'm attempting to do next will take me quite some time. "May I get a glass of water, sir?"

"Of course." He motions to some guard behind us by the door, and a glass of water appears in less than a minute.

Good staff.

After a couple hours of sweat-inducing spellwork, I finally lay the spell I want over the book and hand it back. "It's done." Everyone's waited and watched with apprehension as I worked—which was a little unnerving, if I'm honest—but the look on the director's face is worth the extra effort.

"It's able to be opened. No side effects?"

I smile. "None whatsoever." I gesture for him to go ahead.

He opens the first page and pours over the inscriptions in some ancient language I don't recognize and has the look of a child with a brand new toy to put together on Christmas day.

"Come on, Dea. I want to meet the Shifters of Tokyo!" I yank him out of the room.

Turning both our cameras off, Dea turns me on the spot as we get on the subway and pins me to the side of train. "Are you insane?"

I laugh. "Maybe a little, but trust me. No one is performing spells from that book without some serious consequences."

He looks at me in befuddlement before smiling. "You spelled it?"

"I did." My smug smile says it all. "Removing the spell was easy, but it took time to create a spell that would nullify the effects of any spell attempted from that book."

"Nullification?"

Nodding, I say, "Yup!"

He runs his hands over my shoulders and gently rubs the tension out of them. "Knew there was a reason I love you, Angel."

The words still take my breath away, and for a moment, I stand stunned, before I turn around and kiss the ever-loving-fuck out of my boyfriend.

He chuckles before turning visible ('cos that would look weird to everyone looking on) and returns the kiss with equal need.

Feeling my cock harden beneath my jeans is still a surreal experience, and if I can help it, I try to sleep in my female form so I don't get that particular problem in the morning. Groaning, I lean into Dea, who presses me flush against him with a single hand flat on the small of my back.

"Dea . . ." I gasp between kisses.

"Shhh, Angel. Do not worry, you will have to wait until later." He pulls away and winks. "Much later, because you wanted to meet the Shifter Council."

I groan under my breath and mumble a few choice words in Japanese before turning back around and putting some distance between me and the Angel of Death.

"As if that is going to help," Dea whispers from behind as he wraps two hands around my waist and grinds into me from behind.

Peeking over my shoulder, I notice he isn't visible anymore. That fucking asshole!

He trails breathy kisses down my neck and across my bare shoulders until we come to our stop and I can finally run away and breathe again. Damn that man.

Dea runs after me with a few hearty laughs before dragging me down a few streets and into a local park.

"The Shifters live in a park?"

Laughing at my curiosity—like the fucker he is—he yanks me into the nearest copse of trees and pins me to a tree. "No, but I needed some privacy for this." He pins my hips to the tree as he undoes my belt buckle and reaches for the waistband of my boxers.

He hesitates. "If you would rather do this in your female form, I understand."

Letting out a breath I didn't realize I was holding, I hesitate. What do I want? Right now, my cock strains my jeans and I want anything to release the pressure, but I don't think I want to have sex in my male form yet.

But . . . does it really matter?

What's the difference, really?

Dea smiles and pulls his hand away. "I know you want it. What is holding you back?" He does up the button of my jeans and frees me from the tree.

I shrug, not knowing how to answer his question. "I dunno." Thinking about it for a moment, I add, "It just feels a little . . . uncomfortable to think about."

He frowns at me, and I can tell I've hurt his feelings.

"Not being with you," I rush, trying to defend my previous feelings, "just sex in a body I'm not used to. Like, it's somehow not really me."

"I see." He frowns still, but he's lost the insulted expression and grabs my hand, running soft circles over my thumb. "Maybe you should spend more time in your male form, so you can become more comfortable with it still being you."

"I guess."

"You know"—Dea stops our walk to look at us—"you never have to use this form this way. If you would rather stick to sex in your female form, that is okay with all of us."

I shudder at the thought of spending eternity uncomfortable being half of who I am. "No." I'm more stern than I intended, and it seems to take Dea by surprise, too. "That's not what I want. I want to feel comfortable being me. It just might take some time." I turn to face him and ask, "Go slow with me?"

I can feel the embarrassment heating my cheeks as I ask something so unfair of my boyfriend.

He just smiles and pulls me into a hug. "Always."

Chapter Forty-Eight

Turns out, the Shifter Council is under the park, and it expands to underneath the city, too. It's . . . weirdly breathtaking; as beautiful as it is rugged. Moss grows up stone walls in beautiful murals while wooden benches litter the underground alley we walk down, escorted by two tiger Shifters in their animal form.

"So," I whisper to Dea, "are they going to hate me too?"

Dea chuckles and whispers, "No. They are a lot more flexible and open minded. We have always liked them, even before all of"—he gestures around us—"this."

Nodding, I continue following our escorts down twisted paths and across stepping-stone ponds (this place makes the house look like a simple two-story) until we reach a room with an earthy table and chairs set up in the center that's bigger than most rooms in the house back home.

"Damn, what goes on in here?"

"They hold their tribal meetings here. It is a place where any and every species can be represented. Though, they tend to stick to the main mixed packs and a few older pack lines."

Packs? That sounds so . . . old school.

"Yes, we do," a deep rumbling voice booms through the chamber, echoing all around us. "It's also where we convene to meet important people, like the new Horseman." A man steps out of the shadows, taller than anyone I've ever seen, and beaten in muscle mass only by Arrie (that isn't really a competition, though). His eyes glow a silent silver that pierces the dark room with an echo of moonlight I feel the need to shift beneath.

It's like an itch under my skin that has me wanting to claw it off and run under the moon.

"Nice to see you have some Shifter instinct, Horseman." He relaxes as he lets out a breath and his eyes turn to a dark brown that I can only see because I can see so well in the dark with my Shifter eyes.

Dea laughs beside me in that gentle Victorian manner of his, and I could have punched him square in the face if I wasn't so worried about making a good first impression. Instead, I step forward and hold out my forearm. "Magic. It's nice to meet you."

The man grasps my forearm and shakes. "Cal, head of the Shifter Council here in Tokyo."

Whoa. This guy is like the guy. *The* guy. Equal to the Vampire King, Fae Queen, and the Witch Coven. But he's so . . . relaxed. Normal.

The man sighs. "I get that a lot. People look surprised to see us Shifters being so regular."

"In my defense, I met the Vampire Council first, then the Witch Coven, then the Fae Court. I had stick-in-the-mud expectations."

His laughter booms throughout the room, and he clasps

my shoulder. "I saw you demonstrate your powers at the ball. I have to admit, I'm impressed, young one."

"Thank you."

Shyness clearly outlines my features because he removes his hand and says, "We know how to chill and party like the best of them. It's part of our charm. Isn't that right, Death?"

Dea nods. "That it is, Cal. That it is."

"The Shifter Council will convene in two hours, but in the meantime, why don't you let us show you around?" Cal offers me his arm.

I look to Dea in question, who smiles and nods for me to go ahead. Taking a deep breath, I wrap my arm through Cal's offered one and step up beside him. "Well then, Cal, looks like you're my escort for today."

I figure since I'm in Shifter territory, I should remain in my male form; plus, Dea's right, I should spend more time male so I can get more comfortable with just being me.

"So, err . . . I hope you don't mind, but I have a question." Cal avoids my eyes, and I find myself curious what he's worried about.

Nodding for him to go ahead, I pull my arm out of his and walk by myself.

"You have both a female and male form, right?"

I nod.

"Isn't that a little . . . tricky?" He coughs to clear his throat and looks awkward as fuck. "Sorry."

I wave away his concern. "It's okay. It is hard. It's not easy having the downsides to both sexes, but it's also helpful." He looks confused for a moment before he goes to ask how, but I cut him off. "I understand the plights of many being in this non-conforming form. I understand how important shifting is to you Shifters, how important a sex-positive lifestyle and the blood supply are to the Vampires, how important being surrounded by a natural environment is to the Witches, and how important respect is for Fae spellwork considering their culture."

He looks surprised for a moment before smiling. "I guess that makes sense. You were brought to keep the peace."

I scoff and look straight ahead—anywhere to avoid his eyes. "Yeah, somehow."

Cal laughs but takes my arm again. "You have a tough road ahead of you, young one. But you'll do great. You have the Horsemen behind you, after all."

I look back at Dea and smile.

Cal shows me the entire underground area within a five-mile radius, and I have to admit, I'm impressed. They have a fucking brilliant system. Shifters are welcome above and below ground; they can live happily among humans but will always be welcome and have a safe space here in the Shifter Underground.

The Shifter Underground is as large as Tokyo itself, and far too large for us to explore it all in a single day; they even have forests and spaces for pack runs for species that need the space, hiding spots for smaller Shifters that need hibernation spaces and hidey-holes, etc. It's impressive. They're so inclusive.

This is what the rest of the world should be like. Making some small adjustment or addition to their lifestyle and environment to help others feel more included and considered.

But eventually, our tour comes to an end as we're expected back in the Council Chamber for me to officially meet the Shifter Council.

Nervous. Excited. Apprehensive. Terrified.

I'm a ball of emotions I can't untangle for the life of me, but Dea rests a hand on my shoulder and whispers, "You will do fine." Making my nerves calm somewhat.

I can do this.

I think.

Taking a deep breath, I step into the room with the giant table from earlier; only this time, those seats are filled and others spew out across the room, looking for any place to stand where they can see.

Cal pulls me to his side and announces me on some kind of stone stage I swear wasn't there before. "The Horseman of Magic has come to meet the Shifter Council."

Everyone cheers, hollers and hoots, and I find myself smiling. This is the warmest welcome I've had so far. And it is indeed welcome.

"All right, all right. Settle down. Settle down."

Quiet hushes over the room in a wave of eager silence as I step forward to say hello. "Hey!" People smile at my lack of formality, but I just continue. "I just popped in to say hi, since I haven't formally met you yet. Thank you for welcoming us." I bow low and step back, allowing Cal to take over once more.

"Okay, all non-council members, please leave."

The standing crowd ushers out in moans of disappointment and disapproval.

"I am sorry," Cal whispers, "I couldn't keep them away now you've gone public."

"It's okay. It was nice. Made a change."

Cal laughs with some gusto while the stragglers exit the chamber, and we're left with the filled seats, a mixture of smiles, laughs, and a few frowns.

Seems even the Shifters are divided somewhat. Never mind, I can't be liked by everyone.

"Horsemen," an elderly man says from the closest council seat, "it's good to see you once more and meet your newest member."

I bow my head and cough to speak. "I have to ask, and I'm sorry for doing so, but why isn't everyone Japanese if you're based in Tokyo?"

Cal smiles but hands the question off to a weedy-looking man halfway down the table. When he opens his mouth, he speaks in fluent Japanese, which takes me by surprise considering his Chinese features. "Once, the Shifter Council was solely Japanese, but as globalization took place, more and more Shifters came here looking for sanctuary, to be a part of our new open world. Now we have a massive mixture, with not a single race taking dominance in terms of figures."

"It sounds like you are a very loving species," I reply in Japanese. "Thank you for answering my question, and sorry if asking was rude."

He waves off my concern. "You were curious. There's nothing wrong with curiosity."

The council seem pleasantly surprised with me, and I can't figure out why. I'm just having a conversation with a fellow nerd.

"While you're here, Death, Magic," Cal starts as he takes his seat at the head of the table, "we would like to officially pledge our support to your cause."

I falter in my stance, and if it wasn't for Dea holding me steady, I may have fainted. "Wha—?"

Cal laughs and asks, "You're surprised? That does not bode well for our fellow supernaturals then."

I look to Dea, asking permission to give them an update, and he nods. "It's been difficult. Everyone has their own issues, problems, and things that make our job harder. The Vampire Royal Council are with us, too, but the rogue Vampire faction have been causing mayhem at every turn. Now the Fae have joined them, we don't know what to do. And the Witches are still staying out of things, as usual."

My disgust doesn't go unnoticed, because a few of the council members grimace.

Cal looks concerned. "Well, that's half of the pillar communities' official governments helping you. If you can get the Witches on board, it'll be the world against one."

He's right. All isn't lost just yet. Since they're so willing to help, I might as well inform them of my plan to create embassies for their representation on *Sheruta*. And boy doesn't that go down well. A few are a little apprehensive, but mostly, it's met with warm applause.

"We want a triad running every embassy so representation is equal. One member chosen by yourselves, one member chosen by us, and one chosen by *Sheruta*."

Everyone looks at us in confusion for a moment, but Dea steps in. "*Sheruta* would like to have their own representation, given that their Shifters are run outside of your council."

Cal looks to the men and women around him and nods. "Very well. When you're ready for us, we'll send over the two members chosen."

Chapter Forty-Nine

"Well?" Dea asks as we walk back to our hotel. "What do you think?"

I jump forward and yank him to me. "They're amazing. I'm so glad I could meet them." I take a breath and whisper, "They're so . . . peaceful."

"We get along with them, and they actually like us. Though, they get a little antsy around Connie and Arrie."

I laugh. "They're Shifters. They're used to being the physically strongest in the room, which is okay if the strongest is one of them."

"Right. They aren't too fond of Vampires, either, but they get along well enough."

"Makes senses. Vampires are pretty strong too."

"Ready to call it a night and go back to the hotel? Or we can go back home?"

Right, with the new crystals, we can return whenever we want. Ha! Knew they were a good idea. Woo, go me!

"Can we stay the night and return in the morning?" I

ask, trying desperately to avoid anyone—Dea, specifically—noticing the blush burning my cheeks. "It would be nice to spend some time together."

"Of course. I would love that, Angel." He hesitates. "Just promise me something?"

"Hmm?"

"That if you would prefer to spend the night in your female form, then you will do it?"

Damn this man for being so fucking considerate. "Okay," I whisper.

Dea grabs my hand and pulls me to the side of the street out of people's way. He wraps his arms around my waist and smiles. "I love you for you, and that does not change based on your gender. I have a preference for your male form, since I prefer men to women, but I also like your female form." He sighs. "I am sorry if I am confusing you further. Con mentioned I do that a lot." He mumbles something under his breath and looks away, flustered.

"Don't you fucking start with the whole mumbling thing too. I get enough of that shit from Arrie." Ugh. Just saying his name frustrates me. Don't think about him right now, Magic. "And I understand. You wouldn't be disappointed if our first time was in my female form?"

"So long as it is you, Angel, I will never be disappointed."

The hotel is a luxury hotel Dea splurged on, but it's not, unlike Connie's choice, sex-related. Nice, simple, fancy hotel.

We order room service, I have a shower in both forms, and we have a few drinks over a dinner of steak ramen. And fuck don't I love ramen. How can anyone not like this stuff? I thought I'd be too scared to enjoy the evening, too nervous, but so far, we've spent it joking, messing around, talking, and chilling together. It's almost perfect.

"Angel?" Dea asks from his spot on the bed beside me.

"Yeah?"

"Would you prefer our first time to be with Nine?"

He looks a little concerned about my answer, but I'm not. "No. I don't want to have my first time with Nine mean more than anyone else's, you know. So I want to conquer the Horsemen of the Apocalypse one a time." I wink, and that serves to make him laugh.

"Okay. Well, I am going for a shower." He gets up off the bed and turns back around to me. "Would you like to join me?" He holds out his hand in offer.

And I take it.

I thought I would be scared, like I was with Nine, but I'm not. This man, this sexy-as-sin Angel of Death, is mine. I might share him with Nine, but he's mine. And tonight, I will show him what that means.

As Dea suggested, I'm in my female form, and I'm trying not to feel guilty about it. Like, really trying. But in my male form, I'd be hard as steel right now, and the fact that is my comparison shocks me a little. And then makes me smile.

Maybe I'm more comfortable with my dick after all.

We walk into the bathroom, and as Dea turns on the shower, I slip my clothes off and strip down to my underwear. It's not like I've never been naked in front of this man before, but it means so much more now.

When he turns back around, his eyes smolder under the soft lighting, and I shrink under his intense gaze. But he doesn't let me. He grabs my chin and whispers, "You are not allowed to avoid my gaze tonight."

I smile and try to nod, but his harsh finger forces my head to stay in place.

He smirks and brushes his lips against mine, never letting

his finger slip. "This should be fun, Angel." He kisses me again, deep and sensual, until we're both out of breath and have to come up for air. "Nine told me a bit about your time together. I hope that's okay."

I try to nod again, but I can't.

"And you sound . . . perfect." He says that last word on an exhale, as though he's been dreaming about this moment for forever.

Dea unclips my bra and removes it, folds it, and places it neatly on the pile I'd thrown my clothes into earlier, then he goes to remove my panties, sliding them off my legs with gentle fingers and small caresses over my smooth skin. He hums satisfaction against my thighs, his breath tickling pleasure across my skin, causing goosebumps and shivers to break out.

"May I please undress you?" I ask, breathier than I'd intended.

He looks up at me with a smile, his eyes a gentle gold. "Yes, of course, Angel." My name shivers off his skin as I run my hand through his hair.

I help him up, kiss his lips, skimming over his piercings, and breathe a sigh of relief that I can finally let go of this building pressure to be with this man. This need boiling inside me . . . It hurts.

I need him.

I brush his t-shirt off, undo his jeans and slide them off his legs, until he's standing in front of me in nothing but his underwear. His tattoo glows under the soft lighting, and it shimmers beneath my touch, as though alive and responding to my unanswered question: May I?

I know it's been 1500 years since Dea's last lover, other than Nine, but it's important that I understand their history, their roots. They've lived such a long life, had so many memories and deaths on their doorsteps, made so many friends, and I want to understand all of that. I want them to know that I'm okay with that.

Dea smiles down at me, tears in his usually stoic eyes, and slams his mouth to mine, slamming me against the cold bathroom wall. He doesn't stop, lashing his emotions at me with every forceful swipe of his tongue, breathing me in with every gasping breath, before diving right back in, like I'm some pool of life he can't escape.

"Dea," I whisper, "are you okay?"

"I am more than okay, Angel." He gives me a small kiss to my cheek and checks on the shower. "It is warm enough for us."

I walk up behind him and wrap my arms around his waist, reveling in the muscle, the skin, and the overall feeling of touching him without restraint.

Dea slides his underwear off and gets in, offering me a hand to follow.

The water beats down on his body, his hair falling in elegant waves down his face, and I trace the mini waterfalls outlining his chest and abs with my eyes, not able to look anywhere else.

"You're beautiful," I whisper.

Dea chuckles. "Thank you, but you are exquisite, Angel. Like an ocean I cannot help but jump into on a scorching hot day in the middle of the desert." He runs his hands up my sides, trailing a finger around the edges of my curves and down my thighs. "I will never get enough of you."

Hands trace patterns all over my skin while his mouth meets mine under the shower stream, and we bathe in one another's presence, sinking into each other's scent and memorizing every ridge, curve, and dip on our bodies as we wash each other, kissing trails of love down thighs, washing care and caresses into hair, and staring meaning into eyes where there wasn't any before.

This is different than with Nine. Connecting to Dea is more physical, more shown, because we don't have that mental connection to rely on. So I need to show him how much he matters.

With the intention of doing just that, I kneel and run my hands up his thighs.

"Angel, what are you—?"

My hand wraps around his gorgeous length, wet from the shower, as my tongue licks the head, and he bucks.

"You do not have to do that, Angel . . ."

I wrap my lips around his cock, easing a moan from his lips before he can protest any longer. I want this. I want to taste every inch of him, every gorgeous, chiseled inch, and I'm going to start right here. I want to make him look how he did that night with Nine, with his head thrown back, his hand in Nine's hair, and moaning his release down Nine's throat.

Fuck, that was a good night.

I take more of his cock until I can't any longer, and I wrap my hand around the rest, squeezing and twisting, moving up and down.

And Dea's knees buckle as he groans. His hand twitches toward me, but he pulls it back. Restraining himself.

I know what he wants. So I stop and look up at him. "You can do whatever you like, Death. I'm not fragile."

He looks down at me with those golden galaxy eyes and pins me there, a scowl ripping across he features. "You want that?"

I nod. Fuck yes, I do. I want this man's control. To feel those hands on me that usually work so well on Nine. "Yes, please."

"Shit." He grips a firm hand on my head and guides me back to his throbbing cock. "Then sit there and suck my cock, Angel. Kneel and please me."

I want nothing more.

So I wrap my lips around his cock again, and this time I suck harder, hollowing out my cheeks and squeezing a little tighter as I move my hand faster.

"Angel," Dea moans.

Is he going to beg? Is his control finally slipping?

"Fuck this," he growls. His hand rips me from his cock and yanks me up by the hair, before he slams my body against the tiled wall face-first. "No way are you making me come first."

No. No he's not going to beg.

How did I ever think otherwise?

He smooths gentle hands down my back, kneading tension from shoulders, and trails tender fingers down my stomach and lower, until he reaches the apex of my thighs and the source of my uncontrollable need. "You are going to come first, Angel," he whispers in my ear as gently as he declares his love. "You will always come first with me."

The inside of my thighs are ticklish, and as he starts tracing patterns upwards, I giggle and squirm.

"Ticklish?"

I nod.

"How about here?" He traces a line up my entrance, dipping his fingers inside an inch before removing them.

I shake my head.

The cold of the bathroom tiles on my breasts has my nipples pebbling, begging for attention. But I don't know how to ask for that.

More ticklish patterns trace as he breathes deep breaths

into my ear, and then he presses one finger gently inside, refusing to move.

But I want it to move. Need it to. "Dea . . ."

I shift my hips, trying to build friction. Anything.

But he pins me in place with his body. "Do not even try. You will moan and scream when I let you, Angel. And no sooner. Is that clear?" He punctuates his question with a thrust of his finger, curling it to graze just the right spot.

"Yes," I moan.

He moans into my neck, tickling soft breaths into the crook between my neck and shoulders. "God, you sound delicious."

He adds another finger, moving them faster, growing the pace with my moans. "Dea, I . . ." I want him to move faster, to make me feel good. "Faster, please." I shift my ass backwards, into his cock, and feel him thrust involuntarily forward.

For once, he does as asked, and moves his fingers faster, grinding his palm against my clit in the perfect combination of pleasure, like he's done this to my body a thousand times before and knows exactly how to get me off.

"Yes," I breathe. I shift my hips against his hand, riding the rhythm he's set. And I'm so close. So nearly there already.

But Dea screams in pain, echoing across the tiled room.

What the . . . ?

I spin, trying to see what's wrong, and gasp.

Dea's Angel form. He turned into an Angel while fucking me. Christ almighty, we have some seriously unique problems.

But the concern and confusion wash away as I look into those eyes, those gorgeous eyes that have captured me from day one, like a fish in a net, and I'm helplessly drawn in. He's reeling me in, and I can't stop. I don't want to stop.

"Dea," I whisper as my hands trace his skin.

"Magic." His hands grab my hips and slam my body

against his.

I wrap my legs around his waist as he wraps his wings, damp from the shower, around my body, the feathers like silk against my skin. His cock is inches below me, and I want it. I want him inside me. Now. "Fuck me."

I watch the moment his control in this form snaps, and it's beautiful. His eyes pierce me with gold light as he steals my breath with a hard kiss, one that makes me gasp and hiss as he shifts his hips against mine, desperate. Pleading.

"Yes, Angel," he moans when I throw my tongue into his mouth. "Yes."

He slams the shower door open and fazes us to the bed, where he throws me onto the sheets and flies on top of me, wings spread out across the room, his gaze drawn to mine like a moth to a flame.

"I want you, Dea." My voice is a dreamy, hazy and off-kilter. But I mean every word. "I want you inside of me."

His hands grab mine and pin them above my head, while his knees hook beneath my thighs and push them up.

I want to run my hands down that beautiful golden skin, up the ridges of his abs, and around the hardness of his cock. I want to touch him.

But he doesn't let me. Instead, he lines his cock up with my entrance slams home with a grunt, forcing a scream out of my throat that quickly turns into a series of unintelligible moans and words that I'm pretty sure should have been a sentence.

"Angel . . ." He seems to be struggling for words, too. And he hasn't even moved yet. "You feel so good." He catches my response in a kiss before the words can form, and fuck if it isn't the best kiss of my life. "You are perfect, my love."

My hips beg for him to move, to create some kind of

friction, to give me what I've wanted since I woke up in a magical house and had to deal with this out-of-reach man and his insistence on torturing me with his beauty. Eventually, I can't take it, and I scream, "Move!" at him. "Do something. Anything. Please."

Dea chuckles.

Great, even his Angel form is a dick. What a surprise.

"You want me to move?"

I nod, my face scrunched up in some kind of tortured form of pleasure.

"How much?"

How much? Is he kidding right now? I bend my head and nip at his nipple, causing him to groan and shift his hips ever so slightly. I nip at the other one, and his control slips with a growl and a snarl.

His hips pound against mine. He doesn't start off gently like Nine did, he takes me body and soul, his eyes never leaving mine as he slams into me with enough force to have my head hitting the headboard. "Fine." His hands squeeze mine, still pinned above my head. "You want to be fucked. Then I will fuck you."

He pushes my knees higher, and the angle deepens his thrusts, hitting new places and stealing new moans. "But you are still coming first, Angel. I will not stop until you are screaming my name and begging for release."

I'm already begging, I want to say. But just as the first word reaches my tongue, he slams harder against my hips, causing a lance of pain to spin through me, spurring the pleasure on, higher, until my clit is bursting with need and my body's demand to orgasm is too much.

"Dea, for fuck's sake, please . . ." He's pleasing me, but it isn't enough, and he knows it. His smirk says it all. He's keeping me on the precipice. Never quite hitting the right places. Never quite letting me come. "I just want to come."

The smile that graces his features is beautiful and menacing, and I'm both enthralled and nervous about what's going on in his mind. What's he planning?

"You want to come, do you?"

I nod.

"Then," he says with another harsh thrust of his hips, "beg me for it." He kisses me, long and hard. "Lie there with my dick inside of you and beg me to let you come."

I have zero dignity, it would seem, because his words please me, like the gentle caress of a tidal wave against my ears, and I have no issues with begging. Not from him.

"Please, sir," I try out, watching for his reaction. Nine once mentioned Dea might like it.

His face lights up, his eyes glowing brighter. "Yes?"

"Please, sir. May you please make me come?"

"Hmmm . . ." he says, "since you asked so nicely." He releases my hands and shifts my knees into a better position, higher, more comfortable, and then tweaks and pinches my nipples.

"Dea, yes!" My moans turn into screams, my hips slamming upward as much as possible as I run my hands down his chest, grazing his nipples along the way.

"You like that, huh?" He pinches them harder, my breasts thrusting out toward him, and then he reaches down and pinches my clit with the same harsh fingers.

Pleasure shoots through me like lightning, lighting me up from the inside out. And I'm so close to tumbling over the edge, my fangs slip and my eyes burn bright, causing Dea to gasp.

"You can feed if you'd like," Dea whispers, a slight pause

in his dominating ministrations from earlier. "I do not mind."

I shake my head. "I'll feed later. Just fuck me, goddess dammit."

That makes him laugh, and he pinches my clit in small, harsh circles as he thrusts harder, his hips bruising mine with every pleasure-damning kiss of his cock.

"Shit, yes," I scream. My orgasm rips through me, and I thrash, my strength slipping free as I yank Dea into me. "Dea . . . Fuck." I can't hold back any more, and I flip us over, straddle his waist, and ride it out. Wild and free.

My hair spills out around me, and Dea's wings fan beneath him, a gorgeous pattern of black and pink and both mix together.

"Angel . . ." he moans as he meets my hips with damning thrusts, bucking into my clenching pussy. His face scrunches as his eyes glow bright gold beneath the lids. "Angel!" He grabs my hips and slams me down on his cock, hitting the back of me with both pain and pleasure. His wings lift us off the bed slightly as he fills me, his release slamming into me as he screams my name, his control a distant memory.

As we both come down from our high, my muscles relaxing and my mind coming back to me, Dea lowers us back to the bed.

"I am so sorry, Angel," Dea says when his wings vanish and his regular forms pops back into existence beneath me. His breath hiccups. "I am so sorry."

"Huh?" Why is he sorry?

"I did not want to have sex with you in that form so that you can always have free will. I am sorry I took that away from you."

"Oh." I lean over his body and place a delicate kiss to his lips. "No, Dea. I wanted that. More than anything."

He breathes in my kiss, hanging onto it like a lifeline, before he breaks away with a chuckle. "Fuck, Nine was right."

"Huh?"

Dea swears under his breath, and I get the feeling he wasn't supposed to have said that out loud. "Err . . . Sorry, it is just that Nine mentioned you were hot to watch when you come." He rushes out that last part, as though he's worried he might offend me.

I reach up and run a thumb over his cheek. "I'm not offended. If anything, it's hot as fuck that you guys talk about sleeping with me."

Dea breathes a sigh of relief, his usual, non-dirty-talking persona resting back in place.

"Thank you," I whisper just before falling to sleep.

"What for?" He wraps an arm around my waist and pulls me close to him.

"For letting me be myself."

"Ah, that. You are most welcome."

Chapter Fifty

Back at the house, things are wild. No one is anywhere to be seen when we get there, so I change into my female form and use my Vampire hearing to discover they're all in my library; I left it open for them, given that it's the best place for research.

"Library."

Dea walks up with me, his fingers laced through mine. When we get there, however, papers fly everywhere, Nine is cursing in Chinese, Connie is yelling at Arrie in Danish, and Arrie is avoiding the book she's throwing at him.

"Hey!" I shout, using air magic to carry my voice to each of them. "What the fuck's going on?"

Nine sees us and relaxes, his eyes flicking to our hands and smiles; Connie runs up to me and squeezes me hard enough to hurt; and Arrie huffs and sits down among a pile of books.

"Thank fuck. These two are driving me insane," Connie says. "Please take back control. I'm dying here without you."

"How did you lot get anything done before me?" I giggle.

"Dea was in control."

Right. So with both of us gone, they return to being a band of squabbling children.

"Right, so someone give me an update so I can order you about like a badass."

Nine steps forward and wraps us both in a hug with a deep breath. "App marketing is going well, jobs are flowing in, and we already have a few profiles from our friends and allies around the world. Connie is mad at Arrie still over the interview week, which has been published by the way, and Arrie and I have been trying to organize the *Sheruta* Council to dedicate buildings for the embassies, but they're being difficult." He looks to Dea and pleads, "Please handle them. I might just drain all their accounts if I have to step foot in that building again."

Dea gathers Nine in a loving kiss before letting him go. "I will go down there this afternoon."

"Oh, and hon?" I look to Connie. "Mr. Compton is in a random guest room I asked the house to create. It's in the east wing."

Blowing out a breath through a tensed jaw, I head to the east wing, with a few helpful directions from Nine. It's above the cinema room on the same floor as our bedrooms, but it's opposite Dea's wing of the house. You know what, one day I'm going to draw a motherfucking map.

The door in front of me is so ordinary, so normal, so unlike the truths that lay beyond it. Am I scared? Hell yes. But will I let it defeat me? No fucking way.

Knock. Knock.

A gruff voice echoes from within, telling me to enter.

One deep breath at a time, I ease the door open and step into a pretty ordinary room. I'm not sure what I was expecting, but considering this moment feels like a milestone in my immortal life, the environmental expectation was set pretty high.

Seems not everything is like you read in books. Go figure.

"Taylor," Mr. Compton gasps when he notices me enter. "It's good to see you." His rugged frame looks exactly like it did before—regal, slightly graying, but still handsome in a weird, old uncle kind of way.

"Please," I say, "call me Magic." I smile and ask if I can take a seat in the lounge area.

"Please." He gestures to the two armchairs untouched by the window. "I hear you have questions and are ready to know the answers?"

I nod. "I was trying to avoid my past and carve a new future, but it's become impossible." I take a deep breath. "I want to more about who I was. Who my parents were. How come I can't access my Angel powers now, despite having accessed them in this immortal form once before? Who were my friends? I just want to know—"

Mr. Compton holds up a hand to stop me. "I get it, Tay—Magic. I really do. But I won't be able to tell you every aspect of your life. No one will. You'll have to be patient."

I huff. "Okay, well then let's start with my relationship to you and why I'm fluent in both Japanese and English."

"Ah, that I can answer."

I order some tea from the house, and we get started.

"You were born in Japan, and you lived there until your parents passed. But I brought you to the US with me when you needed protecting, which is why I placed you in a local Witch Coven. You used to visit Japan frequently as a teenager, though I was never sure why. Eventually, you enrolled in a Japanese high school that offered a boarding option when you were fifteen, and you never came back to the US unless it was on a job or seeing me."

"So I basically lived bilingually, linguistically and culturally, hence the language thing."

He nods. "What would you like to know next?"

"Who killed my parents?"

He flinches. Everything in him tenses up and he avoids my eyes. "It's not a nice answer, Magic." Looking into my determined eyes, he sighs. "The SC. They put the original hit out on your parents. I tried to stop them. I did everything I could."

He works for the people who killed my parents? That's . . . "They trusted you, didn't they?"

He nods. "I spearhead the supernatural-human relations department, so I have access to sensitive information about difficult supes and humans. I use that info to broker peace. But not everyone in the SC wants that. Some of them, mostly humans, think it's about time the supernatural community backed off and left humanity alone."

It's my turn to flinch. "Get me a meeting with the Supernatural Council."

He looks at me and laughs. Like, actually laughs. "They don't meet like that. Not all at once anyway. What would you have me do?"

"They're ignoring our calls; they won't agree to a meeting. I can't help if I don't know their issues."

Mr. Compton sighs. "You're right about that. The issue is they don't want your help." He looks about, as if trying to determine if there're enemies nearby. "There are some within the SC that want to use your public outing and paint you as the figurehead of the enemy. The figurehead of supernaturals."

"They want us to be evil."

He nods.

I sink my head into my hands. "I should never have staged that coup. It was all fake." Tears rim my eyes. "I've made a tentative situation a whole lot worse."

"Hey," Mr. Compton soothes. "We'll get through this. You'll get through this."

"How?" I look at him in complete despair, my hands shaking and my voice quavering. "How am I supposed to save the world? I don't even remember your name! And when they find out what I did for a living when I was mortal, both the supes and the humans will hate me." Tears crawl from the corners of my eyes to my chin in small rivulets, and until now, I didn't realize how much this was getting to me. "I just feel so helpless."

Mr. Compton gets off his seat and yanks me to my feet, wrapping solid arms around my frame and providing me with a safe space to cry. "My name is Nigel. And I'm still your godfather. You might be immortal now, and strong enough to seriously kick my ass, but I'm still here for you."

I try my best not to get snot and spit all over my godfather's fancy blue shirt. Goddess, I'm so pathetic.

"Want me to stay for a while? I can call in for a couple weeks' holiday?"

I nod, not trying to speak or do more than I'm capable of in my diminutive form.

He pulls me off him and looks me in the eyes. "It's okay to fuck up—it's okay to fuck up so badly you think the world might end—but it's not okay to quit. We need you, Horseman of Magic. No matter how long that takes."

Chapter Fifty-One

The garden is beautiful and sunny today, and I can't help but feel refreshed and at peace with the morning sun edging the chill off the air. Arrie threw my workout clothes at me this morning and walked off, trusting that I'll meet him at our usual time and place.

Progress.

Maybe he'll actually speak to me so I can yell at him?

One could hope.

I'm just stretching my male form as I warm down from my beginner's yoga session (ugh, beginner) when I notice a movement in the trees slightly too big to be an animal.

Who's there?

Changing into my female form, I zoom my Vampire vision in, and his white-blond hair glistens in the sun speckling through the tree branches. He's too big to hide behind a copse of trees, and I can see the outline of his arms in the shadow.

Sighing, I jog to where he stands and glare at him with my arms folded over my chest in distaste.

Arrie just wipes an embarrassed hand over his face and grabs my arm and drags me to his usual clearing kicking and screaming.

Once he's deposited me onto the forest floor, I stand and place a fake smile on my face. "Hello, friend." Oh yeah, I'm in full bitch mode. With feet stood hip-width apart, I prepare to block Arrie's oncoming punch.

But it never comes.

He stands facing me, mouth slightly open, eyes downcast. Is he about to . . . apologize? His mouth closes into a grim line as he throws a left hook. Then a right hook. Then a jab.

Guess not.

Sighing, I block his simple attacks with ease. I've come far since we first started, even learning to counter his attacks with some of my own. The issue is I've become used to his fighting style and strength. When punching other people, I'm too overpowering. I need to learn how to rein it in, lest I hurt someone without intending to.

I block Arrie's oncoming series of jabs and send a flurry of my own, my rage and frustration at Arrie's recent assholeishness (totally a word) brewing over the edge of my restraint.

Fire tingles across my skin before I can stop it, and it lurches toward him, causing him to stumble back with wide eyes.

Arrie's eyes look hurt; not physically, because the idea that I could actually harm him is ridiculous, but emotionally. As though he can sense where my mind is at. Or it's written all over my face. Yeah, it's probably the latter, right?

"Killer, I . . ."

The use of my old nickname in that warm, affectionate tone has tears forming in the corners of my eyes, and goddess damn it, I'm not crying over this asshole. Nope. Never. "Save it."

I try to turn around to leave, but Arrie catches my arm and spins me back around. "No. Wait!"

My patience is truly running out, and something inside me flips. Something dark and disturbing. An anger that's more than just him—it's everything I've been pushing down, every frustration, every internal scream. "What do you want from me!" My voice is a shrill scream that surprises even me. "You hated me, then you liked me, then I thought maybe you . . . But now you just want to be friends?" I can't keep the hurt out of my voice as I throw the words at him.

"Magic, stop." His command has my words halting and my mouth hanging open.

He's never used my new name before.

"Just calm down before you do something you'll regret." His hands are out in front of him, and I don't miss the slight tremble in his knees. He's afraid of me. "Just take deep breaths."

"What are you—?"

That's when I notice it. The dark bubble of dust surrounding me like a cloud. The death magic from my mortal life . . . . It surrounds me like a cocoon. Suffocating me. And it's growing stronger.

Hands wave through it, like washing through the ocean but colder, darker, and I realize that I can touch it, connect with it. I can shape it.

Muffled voices penetrate the bubble, but Arrie's is the closest. "You need to calm down."

"Calm down? Then how about you shut the fuck up!"

Taking a deep breath, I place my mind elsewhere, somewhere calmer, brighter. Warmer. I block out all the noise, frustration, and anger in a few deep breaths and snap into my male form with the kind of efficiency I wish to have on an everyday basis.

I look to Arrie, who looks like he's just had his soul played with, and turn away. I walk past Connie, Dea, Nine, and Nigel, who are all stood on the edge of the clearing with wide eyes and shocked expressions, and go to pour myself the world's largest cup of coffee. I also may or may not have asked the house for a giant pile of candy.

I'm going to practice my magic, something I have come to associate with calm placidity, like an internal version of yoga, and I'm going to forget Arrie exists.

"Stupid fucking asshole," I mutter an hour later as I fail yet another attempt at a simple Fae spell intended to flip a single page of a book. "Would it have been so hard to apologize like a normal person?"

Yep. I'm well and truly failing at my attempt to forget Arrie's existence. "Arrgh!" He's such a . . . There isn't a word strong enough.

The plasmascreen next to me pings, and I look over to find a new job has been posted on the app. Opening it up, I read the job and recoil, a pitying sadness washing over me. HEALER NEEDED FOR THREE-YEAR-OLD DAUGHTER: $65,000.

I scan through the description, and the more I read, the more I feel for this family. Their daughter has picked up some rare magical disease while on holiday that no doctor knows what to make of. She's dying. And there's nothing her parents can do about it.

Nine?

Yeah?

Send Dea on the new job. Film it with permission.

On it. And Sweetie?

Yes?

You should really talk to him.

Ugh. I shut out Nine's mental probing for a while, ignoring his persistence. They can all go shove themselves into the nearest broom closet. I'm not being the one to go to him; he's the asshole here (right?), he can come to me.

Chapter Fifty-Two

Two days later, I send Nine and Connie to the Bahamas on some conflict resolution job between two Shifter packs, Arrie to Greece to defeat some kind of weird magical sea monster no one has ever heard of, and I'm left on my own—well, Nigel is still here. Luckily for us, all agreed to have their jobs filmed to help with promotion in exchange for the price being wavered. This whole marketing malarkey is a nightmare, but at least I have Connie spearheading it.

"So, with everyone gone, what are you going to do?"

I shrug over the breakfast table as we eat some fancy French toast thing Nigel asked the house for. "Dunno," I say around a mouthful. Swallowing, I take a breath. "More training probably. Dea and Nine have been handling the *Sheruta* Council for the embassy inclusion here in-realm, we're mid-campaign for the app, and there's been no insane, war-level threats recently."

"I got a call from the SC this morning, and they've passed the motion to section off New Orleans."

"What?" I choke for a minute before getting my bearings. "But if they helped instead, we could clear the area, increase blood supplies, and re-establish the neighborhood."

"I know." Nigel looks downcast by the entire ordeal. "But what can I do? I'm not even on the Council."

"I have to talk to them. This is getting out of hand. If they stop pressuring the magical community, everything will ease up. The Fae and rogue Vampires will likely stop being so damn stupid."

"They won't hear you out," he mumbles. "They don't want to be affiliated with you at all. They see you as a threat, would be my guess. They know you've created peace among the Vampire Council, that you're allied with the Shifters, that you've created this new fancy app to combat their Hunter Society. They see your potential."

See, that's all well and complimentary, but it does make my job harder. How can I get them to listen if I can't even see them?

Think, Magic, think.

"Don't do anything stupid, Tay—Magic."

"Me? Do something stupid? I don't what you're talking it." I plead innocent with wide eyes and play with my pink hair like I used to when I would visit him as a child.

He chuckles, then turns serious for a moment. "Don't start a war with the Supernatural Council."

Goddess, he's right, isn't he? I can't do anything brash, like go on live TV and accuse them of everything they've probably done and air it to the masses. That would cause a riot, only steering humans toward war, not away from it. No. Whatever I do, it has to be something smart and underhanded.

Just as we're washing up, I have an idea. "Nigel? Where does the SC keep their plans and records?"

His eyes go wide. "What are you thinking?"

"Well, I can't really do anything about what they've already done, but I can prevent them from doing more. If only I know what that is."

He smiles. "Breaking into the most secure server in the world? Should be a piece of cake, right?"

We both break into a fit of laughter and start planning a heist with more gusto than I thought possible from this straightlaced man.

A few hours later, we've detailed every inch, every negative possibility, and have a strategy. The plan is, in its foundations, simple: break into the Chinese SC headquarters, get to the server room, plant one of Nine's little hidden bugs he once showed me, activate it, download the data, and leave. The question is whether to leave the bug in place to gain future data or remove it and not risk getting caught. On the one hand, we'd know all their plans—past, present, and future—but on the other, we could start a more damaging war if they figure out who that bug belongs to. The last thing the world needs right now is a fight between the Supernatural Council and the Horsemen of the Apocalypse.

I don't want to sit on the opposite side to the SC, but what choice do I have? They won't even sit down and let me introduce myself. How can I work with that?

At least this way we could prevent further damage. I just hope this plan doesn't backfire like the last one.

Chapter Fifty-Three

"You should commercialize these crystals. It would be of real benefit to the world."

I scoff while we walk to the hotel we're staying in before our mission this evening. "That would require the Witches working with the Fae, unless you wanted me to make every piece of technology for the entire world?"

"Ah. Witches."

"Yup."

We walk down brightly colored streets with gray backgrounds, like a wonderful mixture of the past and present, in silence, other than the occasional question from Nigel.

I haven't bothered waiting for the others, and I instead just left them each a message saying I have a plan and am going to the Chinese Supernatural Council with Nigel. I know I should wait for them, but I don't want them talking me out of my plan; they love working with the SC. But it's time to do something about those tyrants.

Arriving at the rundown hotel, we check in and wait out

the evening while going over the plan. "Nigel, we're not going to get caught, are we?"

I have my doubts. Serious ones. But I'm not too worried about being caught myself—it's Nigel being captured that bothers me. Would they execute him? Shit. I can't risk his life. He isn't breaking into the building with me, but he is still waiting at the drop point. He's still in danger.

"You don't have to come with me. You can stay here."

Nigel places a gentle hand on my shoulder. "Can't do that, kiddo. You need me."

He's right of course, I do need him. Only he knows the layout, since maps of SC buildings are not public, so he has to guide me on the comm systems.

"But—"

"No buts." He grabs a towel before heading into the shower. "You're still my goddaughter, and I won't stand on the side lines while you risk everything for this war."

I nod, vaguely aware he believes in this all-out war that's coming. Maybe it's already here, and all of this mess is the war. Goddess knows. Can't Fate give us a hint every now and then.

We powerwalk down the street, avoiding busy sidewalks and large groups of people, mostly sticking to back alleys and underground walkways. In a couple of miles, there's an old bus station that's been cornered off for reconstruction; that's the drop point. Just one mile from the building, free of people, few cameras . . . It's perfect. We don't talk as we walk, but we occasionally give each other sideways glances of concern and confidence-inducing smiles; well, I guess his are supposed to be confidence inducing, but they come out more of a grimace.

He doesn't like this plan.

I don't care.

This is a necessary risk. And if all goes to plan, I'll be in and out before anyone notices. You know, assuming I don't accidentally burn down the building or fly into a stranger or Vamp out at the smell of blood or suddenly need to shift or a hundred other issues associated with my volatile magic.

Deep breaths, Magic. Deep breaths.

"Okay," Nigel says, "we're here."

The fence in front of us is easy enough for me to airlift us over, even with the barbed wire curling around the top. Feet on the ground, we both exhale.

"Find a good place to hide, preferably away from any cameras."

Nigel looks me in the eyes. "You got this, kiddo."

"I know."

I take off in the opposite direction, heading to the back of the construction site, where there should be a concrete wall. On the other side of that concrete wall should be an alley that leads onto the main street heading toward our target building.

A few more air-sped steps around various corners and over fallen-down walls, and bingo. A concrete wall. I leap over it and land silently on the empty other side, where garbage cans are stacked with rotting garbage and a black cat streaks through the shadows.

Between my Vampire strength and speed and my air magic, I'm as silent as Dea.

The main street is littered with people—just as we suspected. While we avoided people on the way here, from here on out, it'll be useful to blend with the crowds.

I have my hair tied back and a black cap on, hopefully hiding my identity. We aren't massively well-known yet, but I don't want to risk the chances of someone recognizing me from that viral video because of my long pink hair. (I know, it's a travesty hiding it under a damn cap.)

Goddess, I'm really doing this.

Shaking the crazy, unconfident thoughts from my head, I walk down the street with a smile and pep to my walk. I want to look like a normal tourist, so I've dressed the part. Another bonus to having two genders: the ability to work two different outfits. In my female form I'm all touristed out, magicam dangling around my neck; but, in my male form, I'm wearing all black in the hopes of blending with the shadows when I sneak through the building's upper window.

Three blocks of shops, stalls, and color, and I'm ready to gauge my eyes out. So many people, so many colors, so much noise. Ugh. With shops' closing times being midnight in most countries, late-night tourism is a real issue for inner-city dwellers, but alas, I have no issues there. *Sheruta* is perfect.

There's a tall, gray, official-looking building up ahead, and one zoomed-in look at the sign on the front revolving doors tells me it's my target. The Chinese Supernatural Council.

There are at least twenty floors to this monstrosity, but Nigel said the records are kept on floor fifteen, so I need to enter as close to that as possible. I checked online maps before leaving, and there should be an alleyway toward the back, so I head that way.

From there, I can find the nearest open window.

This alleyway, much like the last, has garbage cans strewn everywhere, garbage overflowing, and the repugnant smell brings an eye-watering sting to my nostrils.

Looking around, I notice an open window three floors up from ground level with a light off. Hopefully those windows aren't safety locked, or I'll have to break in, and that could trigger an alarm. If I try a window too high, someone might notice me, so I can't really go higher than floor five.

I airlift myself up to the open window and pull, trying to edge it open wider, and to my surprise, it isn't safety locked. I fly in and land silently on the carpeted floor. The room in question looks like a regular office, so I take a moment and relax.

Switching on my comms and camera, I bring Nigel into the picture. "Nigel? Can you hear me?"

"Loud and clear, kiddo. You got in I see?"

"Without a hitch." I pace the room and calm my nerves enough to switch forms—and then turn the second comm on. "Did the comms and camera switch okay?"

"Yep. Like a cock-a-doo."

"Like a what?"

He sighs. "Never mind."

Okay, Magic, time to go. Yanking the door knob, however, I realize I'm locked in. Shit. I didn't think about that.

First time heist and whatnot.

Err . . . quick way to unlock a door with my powers?

Aha!

Switching to my female form, I use air magic to carefully move each pin and tumbler (waaaay more tricky than it sounds, by the way) and, after fumbling and messing up a dozen times, I finally manage it with a silent fist pump.

"If you can find a way in the doors of each room, that would be great, but I wouldn't be surprised if they used electronic door locks. You got lucky whoever's office that is is old-fashioned."

"Got it."

I move through the corridor in my male form as silently as possible and find the stairs pretty quickly. Taking a deep breath, and grumbling somewhat about how I'm about to run up twelve flights of stairs, I sprint forward.

The quicker I get up there, the quicker I can fucking leave. This place is a death trap, and finding me here would start an even bigger war.

By the time I'm ten floors up, my breathing starts to labor and my muscles scream. Shit. This is harder than I thought it'd be.

"C'mon, Magic. You're a Horseman of the Apocalypse for fuck's sake. Get up those damn stairs!"

Fucking prick. "Like to . . . see . . . you . . . try."

He laughs on the other end, and I grimace at him while sticking him the middle finger over the camera.

Just five more floors to go. You can do it, Magic. And when you get back, we'll work on your male fitness, promise. I have it easy with my female form because of my Vampire strength, but Shifters are only a bit stronger than the average human; they rely on their animal strength. And the Fae are not made for physical activity outside of long-range attack physiques.

Floor thirteen . . .

Floor fourteen . . .

Floor fifteen . . .

"Phew!" I wipe sweat from my forehead and stand in front of the door whose edges glow pale blue from the digital lock system. "Shit."

"Know how to hack digital locks?"

"Not in my immortal life. Reckon I could do it as a hunter?"

I hear Nigel shuffle on the other end. "I'm not sure, kiddo. Maybe. If anyone could, it was you."

Okay, past-life memories, now's your time to shine. C'mon, c'mon, c'mon. I try to think back to the many nightmares I've had about my previous mortal job, to a few of the buildings I've broken into, but nothing specific about picking digital locks comes to mind.

Staring at the panel on the right side of the door, the one you usually scan your datachip through, I raise my hand as though to swipe a chip across, and . . .

Come on, Taylor, you can do this, I mentally chant to myself. It's just a simple digital lock. All you have to do is rewire the thing to open. And then, bingo, you're in.

I yank the bottom of the pad open and see thousands of crisscrossing wires threading throughout the system. All I have to do is determine which one opens and closes the door, and then rewire it to the connectors.

It crosses my mind that this is fucking insane; I'm breaking into a secure building to handcuff someone and drag them to the SC.

Using a nimble finger to follow various wire paths, I eventually find the right one and swap the connectors, watching as the blue sheen around the door switches to green.

So all I have to do is swap the connectors on the right wires. Sounds easy enough. Assuming no one has updated the system since that memory.

"Magic, you okay?"

"Oh, yeah. Sorry Nigel. Flashback."

"Okay."

Yanking the bottom of the panel open, I see a familiar set of wires and get to work. It takes me much longer to determine the right ones without memory of the theory behind this movie-level BS, but I manage it, and eventually the light turns green,

"Wow. Color me impressed. You're like a real-life assassin." He hisses and mumbles, "Sorry."

I wave him off, and then remember he can't see that. "It's okay. Let's just get this done."

The corridor itself is much like the others, only this one has people stationed every few hundred meters.

"Shit," I whisper. I'm gonna have to take them out. But I don't really want to kill them. They're just doing their jobs after all—that's not a moral sin or a crime.

Okay, I can do this.

I sprint down the corridor, my feet padding along the tiles in silence, and stop around the first corner. Two night guards stand ten feet from me, and by the looks of it, they're human. I sniff the air. Yup. Definitely human.

Gathering my wits, I connect to my Fae magic and whisper an air-connection spell, which essentially connects my magic to the air around me, and use it to manipulate the air around the guards' heads.

I slowly seep the air away from them, creating two small pockets of vacuous space around each of their heads, and watch them suffocate.

Just enough to knock them out . . .

They slump their shoulders as their heads fall, their necks no longer able to keep them up.

I whoosh the air back to them and run up to either side, whacking my hands against their necks, eager to ensure they're still alive.

A faint pulse meets my fingers, and I sigh in relief. "They're alive." I just hope they stay down long enough to not pull the alarm while I'm here.

They'd organize a sweep of the entire building the moment the alarm activates, so I have to make sure my little bug and I are out of there before then.

Two more corridors, two more sets of night guards.

Damn, this floor is heavily guarded for some simple records. It makes me wonder what else is here. But I don't have time to check every locked room.

"The door to the server should be around the next corner."

I put a thumbs up in front of the camera attached to my chest and move on. Rounding the next corner with ease, two more guards meet my eyes, but I snuff out their oxygen and watch them faint.

"That is damn effective, kid."

"Are you going to call me kid even when I'm sixty?"

"Yup."

Sighing, I unlock the door—finding my digital hacking skills speed up the more I practice—and step inside.

It's a room filled with many banks of computers, all glowing that familiar blue of magical tech light that permeates every technological invention in the last century (been doing a lot of reading, don't judge my inner nerd).

Where the fuck am I supposed to stick the bug?

"Does it matter where you stick it?" Nigel asks in my ear.

I hesitate and mumble, "No idea."

"Great," he whispers.

"Don't be a dick. I didn't think the server would look like this."

"All right, all right, don't get your panties in a twist. I'm looking up server blueprints now."

In the meantime, I switch to my female form, who has the bug in her back pocket, and wander around, getting the layout of the room. I don't have to exit the room because I'm going to use a crystal to get back home straight from here, but it'll be good in the event security is alerted and I have to fight.

The room itself is filled with black and glowing-blue machinery—row upon row of plasma-filled metal banks that I assume make up the computer—that has my head spinning as I try to navigate the maze of technology. Walls of plasma-filled metal tower above me, and I quickly find myself lost the more I try to navigate.

"Okay, you need to find a good, accessible point and place the cyberbug into the system, attach it to the wire, and go."

"It's that simple?"

"It's that simple with Nine's cybermagic tech."

Goddess bless that sexy nerd of mine. I'll thank him later, but right now, I'm sure I'm running out of time.

I open a few panels and try to find some kind of wiring, any; so long as we get in, it should be fine. Well, according to Nine and Nigel. But I'm running out of luck for the evening it seems, because the universe is giving me nothing.

"C'mon, Fate, work with me here," I whisper to myself. And just as the last syllable comes out of my mouth, I open up the nearest section and find some wiring. "Okay . . ."

I attach the wires just like Nine explained back when I was merely curious—never thinking it would come in useful—and open the app on my plasmascreen that it connects to.

"Yes!" I shout, but a little too loudly because the door to the server room opens in the exact moment. "Shit."

Chapter Fifty-Four

The bug is still doing its thing, so I can't leave now. I still have data to trawl through. I want everything: plans, names, money trails, communications. Anything and everything I can get my hands on.

"Change into your male form, kiddo."

Right. The only form the general public know is my female one—I haven't publicly shown my male form yet.

I switch with effortless ease and continue watching the download progress. It's 54% complete, but I'm not sure there's enough time to get to 100%.

"Stop! Put down the bug and put your hands in the air!"

I sigh, hoping this guy is just some dumb human, and turn. The more time I can give the bug, the better off we'll be. I have to keep this man busy.

The man in front of me has mousy-brown hair, a small stature, and holds a magigun in his shaking hands. Taking a whiff of the air, I note he isn't human.

Looks like I'm shit out of luck.

But what he is exactly is a mystery. He smells kind of like a Witch, but this is a strange place to bump into one of their kind. Why would any Witch work for the SC? Moreover, why would the Witch Coven allow it?

They know more than they're letting on when I last visited, clearly, but that's a problem for later.

"What do you want?" I ask. "Money, power, a fight?"

His eyes flicker to mine for a moment as surprise etches onto his face and his hands lower. But only for a moment. He's quick to raise it again and make me lose my opportunity. "You ain't gonna buy me off, hacker. I'll drag you in just like everyone else."

His weedy voice grates my Shifter ears, and I can't help but wince at the timbre.

Seems he wants to do this the hard way. Without wanting to give away my dual nature in this form, I blast him back around the corner with a quick Fae spell I mastered for basic defense.

"A Fae. Bloody typical," I hear him moan as he crawls back around the corner and comes straight for me. "Your kind are always causing problems, you sick fuck!"

Nigel has gone quiet in my ear, and I don't want to give him away by asking if he's okay, so I keep his cover.

I don't bother responding to the strange man in front of me; I agree, the Fae are a bunch of sickos. Instead, I hurl more basic defense spells at him, hoping one will stick enough to check my bug's progress.

Eventually, after a few failed attempts, I manage to knock the magigun out of his hands and use it to knock him out with. (I know, it's a little clichéd, but what's a gir—guy to do?)

Yanking the plasmascreen from my pocket, I watch the download tick to 87%. Damn. It still isn't done. I really don't want to wait for this guy to wake up, but it looks like I have no choice.

I sit on the floor for a bit, watching the man's chest in front of me rise and fall with his even breaths; like this, he's more peaceful, less harsh, and I wonder if I can just knock him out a bit longer with that Fae spell I used on the night guards. But I decide against it—I don't want to kill him.

That isn't who I am anymore.

91%

93%

94%

Time ticks on as I watch the download complete itself.

A sigh and a groan comes from the direction my new weird friend is lying, and I curse my eternal bad luck.

"Can you just stay down for another five damn minutes?"

He smirks. "Nope. Sorry." He aims his magigun at me and fires.

But being the quick-thinking bitch I am, I duck and move out of the way just in time.

The look on his face is priceless. Yes, asshole, I just dodged a magical bullet. (Cue audience round of applause.) Thank you. Thank you very much.

"How did you—?"

I cut him off with a hand in the air, informing him to stop. "You're not very good at this, are you, kid? Let me give you a pro tip: train harder."

100%

I rip the bug from the wires, slam the container closed, and grip my Earth-to-*Sheruta* crystal hard in my back pocket.

It lays in the palm of my hand as I smile at my would-be murderer (you know, if he was any good at his job and if I could actually die) and say, "Bye bye." Waving, I smash the crystal on the ground and think of home.

But just as the swirling vortex of ether sweeps into nothingness, I feel a sweaty palm on my arm. Opening my eyes, I witness, in horror, the sight of the young man's hand gripping my arm as we travel home together.

Chapter Fifty-Five

"You little fucking shit!" I scream the moment I land in a heap in the middle of my library. "What the fuck do you think you're doing, asshole?" I whirl on the young man from earlier with a clenched fist and a spell at the ready.

"Stop!" he screams. "Who are you? What are you?" He stammers most of the words out before pleading, "Please don't kill me."

Sighing, I unclench my fist. "I'm not going to kill you, idiot. But you have caused me a significant number of problems. You can't be here."

Nigel pops out of the air with a look of abject horror on his face, and for a moment, I forget about the weedy little nobody who hijacked a ride on my teleporting crystal—which I didn't know was possible—and wrap my arms around Nigel's neck.

Thank the goddess he's okay.

"Nigel?" the young man asks. "Is that you?"

Nigel unwraps my arms and tears an exhausted hand

through his hair and down his face. "Hey, kid."

Kid? He's practically a man. One, I hasten to point out, who tried to kill me not two minutes earlier. How the fuck do they know each other?

Before I can ask that very question, thundering footsteps echo across my bedroom and library before the rest of the team sprint into our tense space with different questions.

"Where have you been?" Dea shouts.

"What mess did you make this time, hon?" Connie winks and smiles, but it falls off her face when she notices our latest intruder.

"Sweetie, do you want to explain what the fuck you think you were doing!" Nine shouts both mentally and physically. Nine's rage explodes beside me in a ball of red-haired fury I haven't seen before. "You could have caused a massive problem for us! You could have been seriously injured! You could have messed everything up!"

"Silence!" Dea roars. "Now is not the time for this." He looks to the young man and asks, "Who is that?"

The question is aimed at me, but since I don't have an answer, Nigel answers for me. "That is Aki Angelis." He turns to me and grimaces. "Your brother."

"W-What?"

The End for Now . . .

Author Ramblings

Thank you so much for getting this far and not cursing my name to the four winds. It's too late, you say? Oops. I'd apologise for the cliffhanger, but it honestly felt good to write. Maybe I'm a little evil? And if this hurt, then be prepared for book three. Just saying.

This book was all about Magic struggling with their gender and sex identity, so they spend most of their time only using their male form for magical purposes. This denial, while annoying, is important to their growth. And the team, especially Nine and Connie, will be instrumental in helping Magic break through this identity barrier. It is also something I'm trying to handle with as much grace and tact as possible, which is why you always read about me separating the concept of sex and gender. Just because Magic has the ability to switch between a male and female form does not make them inherently gender fluid. And while this might confuse Magic, resulting in some less-than-healthy thoughts, the team will inevitably bring Magic back down to Earth and help them understand that their form-changing abilities does not define who they are. But the effect this ability has on their identity is something I will continue to explore.

The romance in this book was relieving to write. It felt good to give Magic some happiness and progress things past the angst stage. And yes, I'm getting just as pissed off with Arrie as you are. I swear, I'm going to lasso his plot outline-wandering ass and tame it into submission. I've never had such an unruly character before. He's such a fucking dickhead. But I love him as much as I love the others, and thank you for also loving him while he figures his shit out.

About The Author

Freida Kilmari, an author, writer, and editor from south-west England, has a passion for unique fantasy, one that started with the likes of Philip Pullman, Derek Landy, and JK Rowling. With their fantastical words, she spent her childhood and young adult life vying to create her own world of words one day. Eventually, after finishing her degree and settling into being a business owner, she started writing fantasy romance with LGBT+ twists, and from there, she's kept twisting tropes, retelling fairy tales and legends and myths, and seeing just how far you can push the boundaries of sexuality and gender.

Living in south-west England, she owns and runs Penmanship Editing, a fiction editing business that strives to make the most out of each author's unique story, words, and heart. "Every writer is different, and it's those differences that make our work a part of who we are." She's worked on over 100 books in the last two years and has received praise from authors and other editors alike for her encouraging and togetherness approach in a field that is lacking uniqueness and empathy.

www.ingramcontent.com/pod-product-compliance
Lightning Source LLC
Chambersburg PA
CBHW011922190726
48283CB00009BA/2848